THE HIGHLAND DEAD

MORAG PRINGLE

Storm

Ebook ISBN: 978-1-80508-360-3
Paperback ISBN: 978-1-80508-362-7

Cover design: Sara Simpson
Cover images: Shutterstock

Published by Storm Publishing.
For further information, visit:
www.stormpublishing.co

ALSO BY MORAG PRINGLE

A Rachel McKenzie Mystery

The Liar's Bones

For Stewart

PROLOGUE

The dimly lit alley was perfect for their purpose.

Caroline rested her hands against the cool, dank wall. Behind her the man's breath quickened, drowning out voices from the nearby street. Power surged in a heady mixture of shame and arousal. *Christ, she was actually doing it. Ordinary, boring Caroline, primary school teacher. And it felt so bloody good.* She thrust the image of six-year-old Jack and four-year-old Lexi, who were tucked up in bed at home, from her mind. She wasn't hurting anyone. Not as long as no one found out, and that wasn't going to happen. She swallowed the giggle that bubbled to her throat.

His breath came faster now and her hands moved against the wall, steadying herself against him. Suddenly he moved away from her, leaving a chill on her skin. *No, he mustn't stop now. Not when she was so close.* She moaned with frustration. Then she felt his weight once more. This time the hands that held her hips had moved, one across the back of her neck and the other to cover her mouth, making it difficult to breathe. She felt the first stirring of fear. *What was he playing at? This wasn't the way it was supposed to go.*

She tried to wriggle out of his grasp, but he was too strong. She pushed against the wall, but the weight of his legs pinned hers on either side and left her no room to manoeuvre. Anger surged. He couldn't change the rules of the game. Not without her agreement.

She shook her head from side to side, trying to dislodge his hand.

'Isn't this what you wanted?' he whispered in her ear.

She struggled again in his grip but he held her fast. She thought of calling for help. But then all this would come out. The school might find out. Worse, Richard and the kids would learn how she liked to get her kicks. She couldn't let that happen.

She bit his hand, hard, tasting blood.

He pulled away with a sharp intake of breath. She spun around. 'What the fuck do you think you're doing?' she gasped.

He looked at her with pale, emotionless eyes. A small smile tugged at the corners of his mouth as he reached into his trouser pocket. 'Well now,' he said. 'You're not going to make it easy after all.' His smile broadened. 'I think I like that better.'

She looked at his hand. Was that a syringe he was holding?

Caroline's heart kicked against her ribs, in real fear now.

Her mind flashed to her children again. What had she been thinking? They needed her. Why couldn't she be happy with what she had? In most people's eyes she had the perfect life. Fuck it! She wasn't going to go down without a fight. She raised her knee and kneed him in the groin. He grunted with surprise. The blow that followed stunned her as her head smashed against the wall. Then she felt a sharp, stinging pain in her neck, and a strange, not unpleasant sensation flooded her veins. Her legs buckled and she fell onto her hands and knees, only vaguely aware of the gravel on the ground digging into her flesh. Her lungs wheezed as she struggled for air. *What was happening?*

She looked up at him.

'Help me,' she whispered through numbing lips. Something terrible was happening to her. Couldn't he see?

The scent of aftershave drifted on the still night air. It was the same one Richard always used. Proraso.

In the nearby street cars passed, high heels clicked and, in a pause, a giggle, followed by a low masculine laugh. *Help me!* She put all her fading energy into forming the words, but she couldn't force sound from her frozen throat. Her legs and arms became heavier and she slid onto her face. Stones scraped her cheeks. *Was she dying? Why wasn't he doing something to help her?*

He looked at her as if she puzzled him, but still he made no move to help her. 'Did you really think you could do this? And not have to pay some sort of price?' he asked, as if he actually wanted to know.

He squatted next to her. 'Let go,' he said. 'Just let go. It will be easier.' His voice was reassuring, almost tender. And then like the light, it faded into nothing.

ONE

EIGHTEEN MONTHS LATER

Rachel McKenzie took a deep breath before entering the office she shared with her colleagues in the Death Unit.

Mainwaring was behind his desk, his chair leaning back precariously as he contemplated the ceiling. Her boss had put on weight in the short time she'd been away, the hair on his stomach sprouting through a gap where his shirt buttons strained to meet. How the hell would they get him up if he ever fell? Possibly better to pretend they'd not noticed and leave him there.

She resisted the impulse to scuttle past his door, head averted. She'd spoken to him on the phone on her return from Uist and received the expected bollocking. It had been blistering: phrases like 'off your rocker', 'unprofessional', 'out of control' had been bandied about, but eventually he'd asked after her health and for a moment she'd thought she'd heard a sliver of concern. She'd been mistaken. His next words were to get her backside back to the office, did she think she was on holiday? Didn't she know there were cases piling up? It was as if she hadn't been begging to return as soon as she'd landed back in Inverness, as if it hadn't been him who'd insisted she took time off. In response she'd insisted on coming in on a Friday, rather than waiting until Tuesday. Monday was a public holiday and she couldn't face more time on her own going over the events on Uist. He'd finished with a warning. 'Stay in your lane, Rachel.' As if she were a car! 'Any more shenanigans like Uist and your job will be on the line. I had to intervene with the Crown Agent, who was not best pleased. He doesn't like to see his fiscals on the witness stand. He felt the need to remind me there's a queue of lawyers ready to take your job.'

No one need worry. She'd no intention of coming face to face with a murderer again.

Now, *back in her lane*, her gaze swept the open-plan office.

Alastair, his feet propped on his desk, was chatting on the phone while admiring his reflection in his highly polished shoes. Suruthi's dark head was bent over a pile of papers while Clive risked Mainwaring's wrath by doing pull-ups on the door frame just out of their boss's line of sight. He dropped lightly to his feet and grinned his welcome.

It was good to be back. Mainwaring and Alastair Turnbull notwithstanding.

Calling out a greeting, Rachel slipped out of her cycling jacket, sat down at her desk and switched on her computer.

Clive and Suruthi hurried over.

'Good to see you back, but are you sure you're up for this?' Suruthi asked.

'To be brutal, you're looking a bit peaky,' Clive added, crouching down and scrutinising Rachel.

The day after her return home, Clive and Suruthi had appeared on Rachel's doorstep, laden with homemade curries (Suruthi) and a bottle of vodka (Clive), desperate for the lowdown on what had happened on Uist.

They'd left disappointed. Rachel had given them the briefest details. She couldn't bear to go over the night she'd witnessed two men being murdered and thought she was going to die herself. She still had flashbacks, horrible nightmares, from which she'd wake up with the sensation her heart was racing out of control, that it was moments away from stopping forever.

'Leave her be, you two,' Linda said, joining Clive and Suruthi. She'd turned up on Rachel's doorstep too. Instead of food or drink though, she'd brought a hot-water bottle and a sleeping tablet. She'd filled the bottle, bundled Rachel off to bed, forcing her to swallow the tablet before tucking her in. Rachel had been mortified – and embarrassingly close to tears. The last time anyone had done that had been her mum. They meant well but Rachel wished they'd just leave her alone. She loathed being the centre of attention, however well intentioned.

Finally, after a 'yes of course', 'never better', her colleagues melted away and Rachel turned to the morning's reports. It was the Death Unit's – or the Scottish Fatalities Investigation Unit to give it its Sunday name – responsibility to investigate any sudden or unexpected deaths across the Highlands and Islands and decide whether action was required. This morning Police Scotland had reported six: a fatality on the A9 – police had a drink driver in custody; two deaths in nursing homes – a woman in her nineties and a man in his seventies – different homes and different doctors; both had been ill, and the nursing homes weren't required to notify the Unit but, since Harold Shipman, people were overly rigorous when it came to letting them know. In addition, there were the usual dispiriting number of drug overdoses, three over the last few days. All had been homeless. Last year 244 homeless human beings had died in the streets of Scotland and even at this time of year it wasn't uncommon to find at least one poor soul apparently fast asleep in a doorway or slumped on the pavement, but who would keel over when prodded, well beyond saving with naloxone.

Rachel sighed, leaned back in her chair and stretched. The landline on her desk rang and she picked it up. Although Linda and Clive were notionally in charge of answering the phones, they were both on other calls.

'Rachel McKenzie. Scottish Fatalities Investigation Unit North.' It was a very long-winded way of identifying their office and didn't really describe what they did: decide whether sudden deaths needed further investigation and instruct the police accordingly. In some ways Rachel would have preferred to answer calls as her boss did, with a long, drawn-out D-e-a-th.

'Could I speak to Alastair Turnbull,' an exasperated voice asked. 'And don't even think of telling me he's out of the office again!' Rachel had no need to glance around. She'd seen him slink out a couple of minutes ago. Probably to place a bet on the one thirty.

'I'm afraid Mr Turnbull *is* out of the office at the moment. Can I help?'

'This is the fourth time I've phoned and he still hasn't returned my calls. This simply isn't good enough.'

Rachel wasn't surprised. She and Suruthi often had to cover for Fuckwit Turnbull, as they thought of him privately.

'Why don't you tell me your name and why you wanted to speak to him?' Rachel asked.

'I'm sorry.' The woman on the other end of the line let out a sigh. 'This is Dr Burns. I'm calling from Inverness General.'

'How can I help, Dr Burns?'

'It's about the death of my friend, Gillian Robertson. No one seems to be looking into it and I want to know why not. The police won't tell me anything – say they haven't been instructed yet by your office.'

'When did this happen?' Rachel asked.

'Almost two weeks ago.'

Not very long ago then. It took far longer to look into sudden deaths than people imagined. There were around a hundred sudden deaths in Scotland every day. Most in the central belt but a good number across the Highlands and Islands.

'The pathologist wouldn't tell me anything either,' Dr Burns continued, 'So I called your office and got through to the fiscal dealing with Gillian's case. He said he'd get back to me. But he's blanked me – not returned my calls –or taken them...'

'Whoa, slow down. I haven't been in the office for a while so I'm not up to speed. Let's go back to the beginning. What happened to your friend?'

Dr Burns gave an exasperated sigh. 'I told all this to your colleague the one time I managed to speak to him. And I'm sure it's all in the police report.'

'Which I will read as soon as we finish speaking.' Rachel entered the name Gillian Robertson into the database on her computer. 'In the meantime, how can I help?'

'I want to know what happened to Gillian, why she died and what the police are doing to investigate her death.' The doctor's voice cracked. 'God, I can't get used to saying that out loud.' She took a moment before continuing. 'It doesn't make sense. Gilly was young and fit. She shouldn't be dead! Unless I missed something! But what? And if she realised she was miscarrying, why didn't she call me? Her mobile was right there next to her bed. That's what I told the police, but I think they thought I was being hysterical. But then last week when Steve, her ex, mentioned that she thought she was being watched...'

Now she had Rachel's full attention.

'She thought she was being watched?'

'That's what she told Steve.'

'Did he tell the police?'

'I'm not sure. I told him he should.'

Rachel made a note on her pad.

'What did the police say when they interviewed you at the scene?'

'To be honest, they didn't seem overly concerned. They said they'd send a report to your office and that Gillian would have a PM and it would be up to the procurator fiscal to decide whether her death needs further investigation. When Mr Turnbull wouldn't return my calls, I called police headquarters. But I can't get anyone there to speak to me either.' In the background Rachel heard the wail of an ambulance.

'Why do you think your friend's death might be suspicious?' Rachel asked.

'Apart from the stalking – or watching, whatever it was – a number of reasons. Oh God, I'm being paged. I need to go. I'm telling you, though, something is not right and nobody seems to be doing anything about it!'

'Give me time to have a look at the police report. What number is best to get you?'

'Oh, thank you.' Dr Burns's tone softened. 'You have no idea how relieved I am someone is finally taking me seriously.' She rattled off a mobile number. 'If I don't answer it's because I'm in theatre. I'll call you back when I'm free.' And before Rachel could reply, the doctor ended the call.

Rachel turned back to her computer. Her search had brought up only one file in the name of Gillian Robertson. The report had come into the Unit just over two weeks ago.

Rachel read the report quickly.

Gillian Robertson (twenty-eight), a senior nurse in Inverness General A&E had been found deceased by a friend, a Dr Kirsty Burns, who had called the police.

Rachel leaned back in her chair, jolted. Could Gillian Robertson be the Gillian *Boucher* Rachel had been at school with? Who'd become a nurse. And Dr Burns – Kirsty Burns? It made sense. That's why the doctor's voice had sounded familiar. Gillian Boucher and Kirsty Burns had been best friends and prefects at the high school Rachel had attended.

Gillian had been the one everyone had wanted to be friends with – bubbly, pretty, confident, popular. Kirsty was quieter, more serious, with a sharp wit. They'd been bright, Gillian the school valedictorian, if Rachel remembered correctly.

Rachel's chest tightened. The last time she and Gillian had met was at one of the lowest points of Rachel's life. To say she might not be here now had it not been for the nurse was no understatement. She owed her big time.

Rachel pushed painful memories away and returned her attention to the police report.

She skimmed through it. Gillian had been found dead at home by her friend and doctor, Dr Kirsty Burns. There had been no evidence of foul play; the body had been lying on the bed, undisturbed, with no sign of a struggle or defensive wounds – the heavy blood loss was due to the miscarriage she'd suffered. There had been no indication of a forced entry and nothing missing, despite jewellery, a laptop, and expensive speakers being in clear view. After the police arrived and been satisfied there were no suspicious circumstances, Mrs Robertson's body had been removed to the hospital mortuary for a PM.

Alastair hadn't yet returned so Rachel searched the records to see if a post-mortem had been carried out and a report sent to the office. Failing to find one, she called the mortuary and was put on hold before eventually being connected to the pathologist.

The pathologist, while polite, charming even, promised she would get around to Mrs Robertson as soon as she could but that as Rachel was probably aware there was a substantial backlog of cases she and her colleagues were currently working their way through. They were all important to someone, she noted tersely.

'Do you have a time of death?'

'I'm afraid not.'

'Initial thoughts?'

'Nothing on the face of it to suggest foul play, but I'll only be able to confirm that once I've done a PM.'

Rachel thanked her and ended the call. With a quick glance her boss's way, Rachel picked up the phone and dialled Kirsty's number. The other woman picked up after a couple of rings.

'Hello?' she sounded distracted.

'Dr Burns? This is Rachel McKenzie. From the Fiscal's office. We spoke earlier.'

'Oh, thanks for getting back to me. Do you have an update?' Kirsty asked. 'Are you going to tell the police to have a closer look?'

'No. Not yet. In the absence of a post-mortem, which hasn't been scheduled yet, I need more information before I can refer it back to my police colleagues.'

She should speak to Mainwaring before she went any further – particularly as it was Alastair's case. However, she wasn't going to. Not until she knew more.

Rachel glanced at her boss again, caught his eye, and when he frowned turned her chair so she was looking away from him. How did he manage to make her feel three years old when she was a fully grown, intelligent woman?

'In the interim,' Rachel continued, 'I think it would be useful for us to meet.' She'd learned that stuff – the important stuff – usually came out when people were face to face. Although meeting with Dr Burns could not be called 'staying in her lane', Gillian – and by association Kirsty – deserved an hour of her time.

'When?' Kirsty asked.

'After work today. Around five thirty?' Everything urgent in her current in tray could be dealt with before then.

There was a pause on the other end of the line. 'Could we meet at the hospital? I'd come to you but I have an outpatient clinic that doesn't usually finish until after five and I have to pick my daughter up before six thirty.'

'I can do that,' Rachel replied.

'Great. Thank you. Go to the gynae ward and ask them to page me. I'll be with you as soon as I can.'

'I'll be there,' Rachel said, and disconnected.

TWO

Rachel left the office just after five, only escaping Mainwaring's disapproval by dint of it being her first day back.

She cycled to the hospital, weaving through rush hour traffic, skirting around parked cars, found the block where the gyn ward was situated and asked the nurse at the workstation to page Dr Burns. Rachel was informed the doctor was on the way. She took a seat in the corridor outside one of the four-bedded wards. The smell of antiseptic and overcooked food brought her back to her own, thankfully short, hospital stay a couple of weeks earlier. Nurses in pink scrubs hurried past. A woman in an overall pushed a trolley with a gigantic teapot and a stash of cups and saucers. A patient pushing a drip on a stand made laborious progress along the corridor.

Dr Burns appeared a few moments later. Kirsty hadn't changed much since school. She was as tall and willowy as Rachel recalled, although even thinner. Her once hip-length hair was cropped to above her ears, accentuating her high cheekbones. Despite the new lines bracketing her mouth and the furrow between her brows, she was still drop-dead gorgeous, even in crumpled blue scrubs. The Kirsty Rachel remembered had always been immaculately groomed. But life as a doctor – and grief at the loss of a friend – was bound to take its toll.

'Good God, Rachel McKenzie! I didn't realise it was you I was speaking to. I had no idea you worked with the Fiscal's office.'

She gave Rachel an appraising look. If she was recalling Rachel's history, she gave no sign. 'It's good to see you again, despite the circumstances.' When she held out her hand, Rachel noticed Kirsty's nails were bitten down to the nailbed. 'You look just the same,' Kirsty added.

No, she didn't. The years had taken their toll on Rachel too.

'I didn't recognise Gillian's name, or yours, at first either,' Rachel admitted. 'I knew Gillian by her maiden name. I'm so very sorry about her death. I remember her from school – you too. You gave me a break when I really needed it.'

Kirsty ran fingers through her cropped hair. 'You mean when we didn't report you when we caught you bunking off?' She smiled. 'God knows everyone needs a break. I'm glad every-thing turned out well for you.'

Not exactly, Rachel thought but didn't say. Overlooking her playing truant was the least of what Gillian had done for Rachel.

'Shall we go along to the doctors' on-call room? It's just outside the ward. I'm sorry I had to ask you to come to me,' Kirsty continued as she led the way, 'but life is pretty frantic. If I'm late picking up my daughter again, the nursery manager will go ballistic.'

She opened a door and waved Rachel through. 'After you.'

The doctor's on-call room was a clutter of half-finished drinks, empty crisp packets and discarded chocolate wrappers. Along a wall were kitchen units atop which were a kettle, a plastic bottle of milk and several used mugs. A number of hospital faux leather armchairs were arranged in groups, except for two which had been placed together as if to form a makeshift bed.

'Sorry about the mess,' Kirsty said, removing an empty family-sized kettle crisp bag from a chair, scrunching it into a ball and shooting it into wastepaper basket as if it were a mini basketball. 'Doctors aren't the tidiest. You'd think it would be the opposite.'

She indicated the chair she'd removed the crisp packet from. 'Please, sit down. Can I get you a coffee?'

'No thanks. I know you're in a hurry.'

Kirsty flopped into a chair beside her. She took a deep breath. 'OK. Let's talk.'

'Tell me about Gillian,' Rachel said. 'I remember how close you were in school.'

A smile crossed Kirsty's face, erasing some of the lines.

'I've known her forever – we started primary school the same day – were pals until we finished school – went to uni together, she to do nursing, me to do medicine – were bridesmaids at each other's weddings. She was there for me when my husband died, and I was there for her throughout her divorce.'

'I'm sorry about your husband.'

Pain flashed in Kirsty's eyes. 'Thank you. It was a shock.' She picked at a nail bed. 'We'd only been in Zambia for eleven months when it happened. It had been a dream of Tembo's for so long – to go back to where he'd been born – a dream for both of us – to work where we could make a real difference. We thought we'd be there a couple of years at least. I never dreamt he'd be killed in a car accident.' Kirsty's nails were digging into the palm of her hands as she quietly started to cry. Rachel waited in silence. She knew too well how grief could creep up unexpectedly. In some ways she envied Kirsty's ability to show her grief, to embrace it as a normal part of life. Eventually Kirsty blew her nose. 'Sorry, it keeps catching me by surprise. Sometimes it feels as if Tembo only died yesterday and the shock hits me like a punch to the guts. I'm only able to function on a daily basis because I don't usually allow myself to think of him until Beth is asleep' – she gave Rachel a wry smile – 'then I indulge myself. I thought I had my share of grief, and then Gilly dies. I still can't believe it.'

'You said Gillian was divorced,' Rachel said. 'Was she pregnant with her ex-husband's child?'

'No. Her desire for a child was part of the reason they got divorced. Steve has two children from a previous marriage and always made it clear he didn't want any more. I suspect Gilly thought she would change his mind in time. But in my experience that rarely happens.'

That didn't mean the baby wasn't Gillian's ex's. It wasn't unheard of for women to 'accidentally' get pregnant, particularly when they were desperate for a child.

'When she got pregnant she wanted to be under my care, wanted me to be godmother,' Kirsty continued with a smile. 'A typical best friend relationship. You know how strong female friendships can be.'

Rachel didn't, as it happened.

'Take me through the day you found her.'

'You mean the whole day? From when I got up?'

'Maybe later. For the time being, start from the time you were supposed to meet.'

The anguished cries of a labouring woman came from somewhere beyond the corridor and Kirsty closed the door, cutting off the unnerving sound.

'It was a week last Saturday. We'd arranged to meet for lunch. I'd bumped into her in A&E the day before and she said there was something she wanted to talk to me about. I asked if it was urgent – if she was feeling OK, but she waved my anxiety off. Said it was something to do with my boss. Naturally I was curious.'

'Your boss?'

'Dr Ballantyne. He's the clinical director for obstetrics and gynaecology. Of course, I asked Gilly if it was pregnancy related and she just laughed and said that she'd never felt better. She'd been very nauseous in her first trimester.'

'Did Gillian give any hint of what she wanted to tell you?'

'No. A&E was going like a fair. A three-car pile-up was on its way in and I had patients waiting to see me. She said it could wait until we met.' She paused and blinked away tears. 'I never imagined that would be the last time I'd see her alive.'

'Go on,' Rachel prompted gently, after giving Kirsty a few moments to compose herself.

'My mother was visiting and was happy to babysit Beth.' Kirsty's lips twisted into a wry smile. 'She's not always keen as she already gives up two afternoons a week to look after my daughter. I don't blame her; she has a busy life. Anyway, you don't need to hear all that. I don't even know why I'm telling you this stuff. Where was I? We'd agreed on one o'clock, but when Gillian still hadn't arrived by quarter past I began to get worried. Gilly was never late. And if she'd been held up it was totally unlike her not to let me know she was running late. I kept trying her mobile, but she didn't pick up.'

'It was definitely ringing?' Rachel asked.

'Yes.'

'So it wasn't out of charge.'

Kirsty nodded. 'I kept trying, but when it got to two, I realised Gilly wasn't coming. I was worried – it was so unlike her – but I tried to tell myself, unlike her or not, she must have forgotten. People say pregnancy hormones can wreak havoc with your memory. I think it's an old wives' tale but it was one I chose to believe that day.' Her eyes filled. She blinked the tears away before they could fall.

'I decided to go to her flat. See if she was there. It's near the hospital, so wasn't much of a walk.'

'Talk me through what you did. Step by step.'

Kirsty took a gulp of coffee, sucked in a shaky breath and closed her eyes. 'I'll never forget a moment of that day.'

McGregor's had been mobbed when Kirsty had arrived, packed with the usual Saturday lunch crowd, and she'd been lucky to bag a table. It was their favourite place to have lunch, being near the hospital and halfway between their flats. Kirsty kept looking at the door, ignoring the frustrated glances of the waiting staff, certain Gilly would appear at any moment. But when it had got to two o'clock and there was no sign of her, she'd accepted that Gilly was a no-show. She'd got worried then and decided to go to the flat.

Before leaving she picked up a cake from the bakery counter – a lemon meringue, Gillian's favourite – left a sizeable tip and walked the short distance to Gillian's flat.

Getting no answer when she rang the buzzer of the communal door of the Victorian sandstone tenement where Gillian lived, she stepped back and studied Gilly's ground-floor flat for signs of activity. The anxiety that had been building deepened when she saw the sitting-room curtains were closed. Could Gilly have hooked up with someone the night before and not returned yet? She hadn't mentioned that she was meeting anyone, but it could have been a spur-of-the-moment thing. Surely she'd have phoned to beg off, though. Or could Gilly be ill? Too sick to answer her phone? Needing help?

Too impatient to search for Gillian's spare key in her over-sized handbag, she pressed one or two of the other flats' bells at random until she heard a responding buzz indicating the front door had been unlocked. Balancing the cake she'd bought for Gilly in one hand, she shoved the door open with her shoulder. She knocked – then banged – on Gillian's front door. Still no answer. And calling through the letterbox proved equally fruit-less. She kept thinking of the closed curtains. Anxiety was turning to dread. She rummaged in her bag for the key her friend had given her.

Pushing the door open, she called out, 'Gilly, it's me, Kirsty. Are you OK? What the hell happened to you?'

When there was no reply, her anxiety went into overdrive. Normally when Gillian was at home there would be music blaring. She tried to tell herself she was overreacting. Gillian was probably waiting for her at McGregor's. It was possible she had taken a different route to Kirsty and they could have just missed each other. But then why hadn't she phoned?

Kirsty peered into the sitting room, switching on the light against the curtained darkness. That in itself was strange and set alarm bells ringing again. The room was empty. Kirsty opened the curtains, letting light flood in. Despite Gillian's countless knickknacks, the room was tidy apart from a used mug on the coffee table. Kirsty placed the cardboard cake box on the table and picked up the photograph of her and Gilly from the mantelpiece. It had been taken outside Òran Mór six years earlier, when Gillian had been an A&E nurse in Glasgow. They had their arms around each other, more for support than anything else, and Gillian's gold curls had been a chaotic beacon against the white of Kirsty's T-shirt. Kirsty had been hungover for days after. It had been worth it. It had been a great night.

Recalled to the present, Kirsty whirled around as Flash jumped onto the floor beside her, the soft thud of paws audible in the silence. He meowed and wound his body around her legs, obviously in search of food.

Something was definitely wrong. Gilly was besotted with Flash, delighting in seeking out the choicest titbits to supplement the best cat food available for her pampered pet. Picking up the squirming cat, Kirsty went back into the hall; she'd check the bedroom before trying Gillian's mobile again. An odd but strangely familiar odour in the hall made the fine hairs on

Kirsty's skin stand up and her heart race. The door to Gillian's bedroom was open a crack and Kirsty nudged it wider with her foot, staying in the doorway, inexplicably reluctant to enter, dreading what she might find. As in the sitting room, the curtains were closed and the room was in darkness. The metallic smell was stronger here, underlaid with the pungent odour of urine. Kirsty's heart banged against her ribs, sending little blips of fear to her throat. She could hardly bear to acknowledge the message her brain was sending. However she knew the smell of blood too well.

From the doorway, she could make out the shape of her friend's sleeping body on the bed. There was something about the unnatural stillness. 'Wake up, Gilly. It's me. Are you OK?' She could hardly force the words past her constricted throat.

She flipped the light switch but the light wasn't working. Galvanised, she crossed the room and flicked on the bedside lamp, screwing up her eyes against the sudden brightness. Her heart stopped. Her friend was lying on her back, her head facing away from the door. She was in a T-shirt and Lululemon leggings, her favourite at-home gear, her knees drawn up, her hands by her side, her face hidden by her red-gold hair that fanned around her like a halo. It looked as if she'd simply gone to sleep on top of the bed.

Kirsty touched Gillian's shoulder. The coolness made her flinch. Kirsty brushed aside the springy curls to search for her carotid pulse even while she knew in her gut it was no use. Gillian was dead. She crouched beside the bed and placing a palm on either side of Gilly's face turned it towards her.

The pale, blue-tinged expressionless features were recognisably Gillian, but without the animation, Kirsty could almost make herself believe it wasn't her friend. Gilly's pupils were fixed and dilated, her eyes half open and already clouded over with the milky opacity of death. Flash jumped on the bed with a plaintive cry. Only then did Kirsty notice the rust-coloured pawprints on the duvet and pillowcase.

Horror-struck, Kirsty ran her eyes down the length of her friend's body. Blood pooled under her hips, soaking her leggings, saturating the duvet on which Gillian lay.

Kirsty retched. She had seen death before, but this was different. This was Gilly. Her dearest friend.

Shivering, Kirsty stepped away from the body. Reaching for her mobile, she dialled the emergency services with fumbling fingers, although there was little point in an ambulance coming with its lights and sirens. Gilly had clearly been dead for a while.

'I am so sorry to have put you through it again,' Rachel said when Kirsty faltered to a close. A trolley rattled in the corridor outside. Someone called out a cheery greeting. The anguished cries of the woman in labour had eased to sporadic groans.

'I still can't believe it,' Kirsty said. She started to sob quietly.

A woman in scrubs came into the on-call room and, noting the distressed Kirsty, quickly retreated, leaving the door open. Rachel turned her gaze towards the corridor, giving Kirsty a few moments. A constant stream of staff and relatives scurried past, patients shuffled along holding on to drip stands, while others in wheelchairs or on trolleys were pushed along by porters. The cry of a newborn baby cut through the air followed by delighted laughter. The wail of an ambulance got increasingly loud before being cut off as it arrived at the hospital door.

Hospitals were a microcosm of the world, Rachel thought, where some of the highest and lowest moments in people's lives took place.

'Tell me about the stalker,' Rachel asked, when Kirsty was composed again.

Kirsty dabbed her eyes and blew her nose. 'I don't really

know much. Only that she told her ex she thought she'd been followed – twice. Even asked if it was him. He said he just laughed and she joined in. Gilly never said anything about it to me. I think if she were truly worried she would have. But now I'm not so certain. Surely it should be checked out?'

'Did he tell the police?'

'He said he did. Last week. He'd forgotten about it until something reminded him.'

Rachel made a mental note to check it out. 'So the day in A&E was the last time you saw or spoke to Gillian?'

'Yes.'

'How did she seem?'

'Happy, excited, tired.' She paused. 'Normal.'

'You said she was recently divorced. Why are you sure the baby wasn't her ex's?'

'Because, according to Gillian, he was so certain he didn't want more kids that he had a vasectomy.'

'How did he feel about her pregnancy? Even if he didn't want Gillian to have his child it doesn't necessarily mean he was happy that she was expecting someone else's.'

Kirsty dismissed Rachel's question with a shake of her head. 'He was devastated when he heard she'd died. Although they were no longer married, Gillian and Steve still saw each other regularly.'

'Do you know if she was planning to meet someone, before or after she'd met you?'

'If she was, she never mentioned it to me.'

'Do you know who the father of her baby was?'

'She wouldn't say. Said since she had no intention of involving him in the life of her baby it was immaterial. If I had to guess, I'd go for Dr Jamie De Banzie. I'm pretty sure I saw them emerging from one of the houseboats on the canal late last year. Gilly laughed when I asked her, but she didn't deny it either. I think she was embarrassed. De Banzie's a bit of a player. Some of the female staff refer to him as Dr De Babe. The gossip is that his wife heard about his affairs and chucked him out. Gilly said she was looking for good genes for her baby, and the best way to get the right sperm donor was ...' she paused and flushed.

'Was...?' Rachel prompted.

'A "zipless fuck",' she said reluctantly. Rachel recognised the phrase from a book by Erica Jong, *Fear of Flying*. It was a reference to the joys of no strings sex. For women.

'That makes Gillian sound a bit... you know,' Kirsty continued. 'All it means is that she wanted a baby with someone who wouldn't want to be involved, or even know they had a child. De Banzie fits that description perfectly.'

A loud beeping noise sounded. Kirsty took a mobile from the pocket of her scrubs, checked her watch and grimaced. 'It's my boss. Do you mind if I see what he wants?'

'Sure.'

Kirsty dialled a number and put her mobile to her ear. She listened for a while. 'Can it wait, Dr Ballantyne? I was about to leave.'

She listened for a few seconds longer.

'OK, I'll be with you in five.' She slipped the phone back in her trouser pocket.

'I'm sorry, I need to go. Nick wants a word. Doesn't seem to appreciate I have a child to collect.'

Rachel stood and Kirsty did the same.

'I'll talk to the police,' Rachel said. 'Find out where they are with Gillian's case. I'll also try and push Gillian's PM to the top of the list. At least then we will know if there's anything to worry about.'

Kirsty gave a relieved smile. 'I feel so much better having spoken to you. Maybe I'm wrong and there's nothing suspicious about Gilly's death, but I really appreciate you taking the time to look into it.'

'That's OK. As I said, I owed Gillian a favour.'

Kirsty looked at her watch again. 'I really have to go. You'll keep me informed? If there was anything – an underlying heart condition, pre-eclampsia – and I missed it, I'd feel awful, but at least I'd know.'

Rachel nodded. She'd promised she'd look into it and she never broke her promises.

When she and Kirsty parted ways, Rachel took out her phone, pulled up a number and thumbed out a text. A moment later it pinged a reply. DI Du Toit would meet her in fifteen minutes.

From his bird's-eye view, he watched the woman he'd seen talking to Dr Burns leave the hospital. Who was she? Not a patient, otherwise Kirsty Burns wouldn't have invited her into the doctors' on-call room.

She was smartly dressed in a tailored white blouse tucked into dark trousers. A police officer then? A detective, maybe. Didn't they usually travel in pairs?

She put on a cycle helmet over her curly hair and pedalled away as if trying to break a speed record.

He'd find out who she was. And what she wanted with Kirsty Burns.

But first he had something else he wanted to do.

THREE

At six thirty-five, Kirsty was jogging along the pavement, weaving impatiently through the pedestrians blocking her way. Her gut clenched. She was supposed to collect her daughter before half past six, and she'd been late once this week already.

Beth attended the nursery five days a week, two of them until lunchtime, the other three for the whole day. Life would be much simpler if Kirsty could persuade the nursery manager to take Beth full-time, but places were highly sought after and the current arrangement was the best the nursery could offer. As it was, the nursery had been making noises that Beth might be better placed somewhere else. Somewhere that could keep her late and accept her early. Kirsty didn't want another nursery and neither did her daughter.

But everything was about to change. For the better. The reason Nick had asked to see her was to tell her that he'd spoken to the Dean who'd agreed to re-instate her onto the training scheme. It meant she could continue her training, and apply for a consultant post at Inverness General in time.

It was a piece of good news in what had been a horrendous couple of weeks, a horrendous couple of years. She'd be able to put down roots without having to wonder if she and Beth would have to move to a different part of the country. She could put Beth's name down for the local primary school, hire someone lovely to take her to school and pick her up after, stay with her until Kirsty got home. They could have a normal, stress-free life.

It was almost quarter to seven when Kirsty came to a panting halt in front of the nursery. She found a dejected Beth and an annoyed Mrs Campbell waiting for her at the door.

'Where were you, Mummy?' Beth asked plaintively. 'I been waiting ages. I want to go home.'

'Dr Burns,' said Mrs Campbell, a severe-looking woman in her late fifties. 'I think I've explained before that the nursery day ends at six thirty, and not a minute later.' She held up her hand as Kirsty began to speak. 'I know, let me guess. Another emergency at the hospital. That's all very well, but I believe I've explained before that if you can't make it in time, you must arrange for someone else – your mother, perhaps – to collect Beth.'

Kirsty stooped to pick up her daughter's sullen frame.

'I'm sorry, sweetheart, I'll make it up to you, I promise.'

Kirsty smiled at Mrs Campbell, doing her best to sound suitably chastised when she really wanted to swear. 'I'm so sorry. There was a meeting I couldn't get out of. I got here as soon as I could.'

The expression on Mrs Campbell's face made it plain she wasn't interested in Kirsty's excuses.

'I'm afraid this is the last time we are going to keep Beth for you. Can I suggest that there are other nurseries more suited to your domestic arrangements?'

The snooty cow was referring to her single status. Places at Happy Faces nursery were hard to come by. Its reputation meant that demand far exceeded supply and it would be easy for Mrs Campbell to fill Beth's spot with the child of a more reliable parent.

'I promise it won't happen again,' Kirsty said meekly. She would do whatever she had to, to protect Beth's place. Her daughter was happy here, and it was convenient, situated halfway between the hospital and home. She couldn't bear to move Beth again. God knew, her child had had enough disruption in her short life already.

Beth wriggled out of her mother's arms. 'Mummy, let's go. Now!' she demanded.

'Come on then,' Kirsty said, taking her small hand. 'Thank you, Mrs Campbell. Sorry again. We'll see you on Monday, won't we, Beth?'

As Kirsty strapped Beth into her pushchair something moved in the shadows. Her skin prickled. Was someone hiding in the trees watching her? She stared into the thicket of trees to the left of the nursery but could see no one. It was probably a cat or a fox. She'd been spooked by Gilly's death, and her thinking she'd been followed, that was all. But it wasn't the first time she'd felt herself watched.

She bent to kiss the top of her daughter's head. 'Let's get you home, sweetie.'

FOUR

The headquarters for the Police Scotland's Highlands and Islands division and the Inverness Justice Centre – or Injustice Centre as some of the more cynical cops called it – were next to each other on Longman Road. It was the first warm evening of the year so DI Du Toit had suggested they meet outside the imposing modern building of steel and glass. He gestured towards an empty bench in the forecourt.

'It's a lovely evening, so I thought we could talk out here,' he said in his accented gravelly voice, giving her one of his quick smiles. 'I miss the sun.'

Although she barely knew him and hadn't seen him since Uist, the sight of his stocky figure, kind eyes and quiet smile immediately warmed her. They sat side by side, slightly facing each other. Traffic barrelled past in a constant stream.

'How are you?' Kirk asked. Not a casual, polite enquiry, but as if he really wanted to know. 'I didn't think you'd be back at work so soon. Are you sure you're ready?'

'It's much better for me to be back at work, to keep busy.' She didn't mention the awful nightmares that woke her in the night, her heart racing. The sweats, the terror, being chased and going nowhere, the endless circular visions of exploding blood and death.

Instead they briefly discussed the case Rachel had been involved in recently. She'd been interviewed at length by the police and her colleague in Homicide was preparing the case to take to court. It would continue to haunt her until it was over.

'Constable MacDonald is being transferred to Serious Crime,' Du Toit said. 'She'll be working with me and my team.'

'She'll be thrilled,' Rachel said. Selena, the police officer Rachel had worked with on Uist, had passed her CID exams a few weeks earlier and had told Rachel how much she wanted to work with CID. Now, it seemed she'd got what she wanted. No doubt at least partly due to the role she'd played in solving the case in Uist.

'But don't get any ideas about making her your personal conduit to Police Scotland,' Du Toit warned Rachel.

'Wouldn't dream of it,' Rachel replied. But Selena's appointment to Du Toit's team could be useful. Selena was clever, brave, ambitious and, Rachel had to admit, slightly in thrall to her.

'Why did you want to see me?' Du Toit asked, glancing at his watch.

Rachel took him through the talk she'd had with Kirsty, including that she'd known both the dead woman and the doctor from school. 'Kirsty is worried Mrs Robertson's – Gillian's – death isn't being investigated properly. She's certain her friend – and patient, as it happens – couldn't have bled out following a spontaneous miscarriage, which is Police Scotland's working hypothesis. To be fair, according to the police report there was no evidence of a break-in, nothing to indicate Mrs Robertson had been attacked or hurt in any way, and nothing appeared to have been taken. However, Dr Burns mentioned that after Gillian separated from her husband she'd had a series of hookups – likely in the hope of falling pregnant as she desperately wanted a child of her own. Although it appears she stopped dating when she discovered she was pregnant, I wonder if one of the one-night stands could be the stalker she mentioned to her husband? Maybe one of them wasn't happy to be ditched once she got pregnant?

'Kirsty Burns doesn't strike me as the kind of woman to fret that something isn't right without good reason,' Rachel continued. 'She's too level-headed. If there's any truth in Gillian's feeling she was being watched, isn't that enough to warrant further investigation?'

Du Toit frowned. 'I don't know anything about this case. Leave it with me and I'll make sure both the ex-husband and father of the baby have been interviewed. But, on the surface, it seems straightforward. In which case I'm not altogether surprised no one has been chasing it up. The force is under considerable pressure at the moment. Police officers are leaving and not being replaced. My team has been cut to the bone and the divisional commander is determined to keep the force on a short leash. We've been instructed by him to focus on major crime, and cases where we know murders have been committed.' He gave her a keen look. 'What does Douglas have to say?'

Rachel shifted uneasily. 'I haven't spoken to him about it yet.' Her boss would not be pleased she was taking matters into her own hands without consulting him.

Du Toit's eyebrows shot up. 'Don't you think you should?'

Of course she should have. In particular she should have talked to Alastair. For all she knew, Alastair was on top of it and she was making an almighty idiot of herself. She shouldn't let her dislike of him colour her judgement. But she had skin in the game, so to speak. And, of course, she'd discuss it with him when she knew more.

'I wanted to speak to Dr Burns and you first,' she said. 'Find out if we should be pushing things along.'

Du Toit stood. 'I'll speak to my colleagues. In the meantime,

I'd better get back to work. I said I'd do a double shift tonight. There's no one else to cover.'

Rachel hesitated. While she'd been on Uist, she'd learned from her grandfather that, in the period leading up to her death, her mother had been convinced that her life was in danger; not from her husband, Rachel's father – who'd been convicted of her murder – but from someone she'd come across at work. Even though Rachel had no doubt her father was guilty, it had been on the tip of her tongue to mention this development to Du Toit, but, given what he'd just said about being over-stretched, she decided to keep it to herself for the time being. He was clearly overworked and it wasn't as if she had anything more to go on than a conversation her grandfather had over-heard sixteen years ago, something he may well have misremem-bered. In any case, she didn't want to use up too many favours. Not until she'd done a little investigating herself.

FIVE

Rachel gritted her teeth against the cold breeze blowing inland from the sea. It was almost May, for God's sake. Spring in the rest of the UK. Although not in Scotland, apparently. Yesterday's evening sunshine already felt like a mirage. She thought longingly of her bed. Perhaps it was a mistake to arrange to go fishing when her body hadn't completely healed. But she was keen to speak to Peter about her mother. She needed to know more about Mary Ann's last days and months. At five in the morning, daylight was at least half an hour away and the street, illuminated only by a single streetlamp, was deserted except for two drunks staggering along the road towards the towpath. They had their arms around each other's shoulders and were chanting an incomprehensible version of some football song as they waved their cans of lager like conductors' batons.

Rachel groaned inwardly when the shorter one noticed her. 'Hey, gorgeous,' he said, weaving towards her, dragging his friend with him. 'Fancy a wee drink?'

Rachel smiled tightly and shook her head. She opened her car boot and checked she had everything: two rods, her waders, waterproofs, and some sandwiches in case they didn't catch anything.

As she straightened, she realised that while she'd been distracted the men had moved closer. They were now almost directly behind her, so close she could smell cigarette smoke and stale booze on their clothes. Suppressing a sigh, she turned to face them.

'Ma pal asked you if you'd like a drink?' Big Drunk, enunciating his words with aggressive care, thrust the can under her nose. She'd been right about it being lager. Grolsch. He was wearing a black T-shirt that said *I'm with Stupid* with an arrow pointing to the right. His mate was on the left. Before she could help herself, Rachel's lips twitched.

'Something funny, hen?' Small Drunk demanded. His eyes were glazed, the pupils the size of the head of a pin.

Rachel lost the smile. 'Not at all. But no thanks to the drink. It's a bit early for me.'

She looked over Small Drunk's shoulders. The street was still empty. No convenient walker taking their dog out for a pre-dawn walk, no even more convenient police car patrolling the streets.

With a bit of luck, they'd be on their way soon. Most of the time Inverness drunks and crackheads were harmless. Most of the time. She tried not to think of the report she'd read recently in the newspaper. The one about the woman who had been found in an alley in Glasgow, only yards away from the main road. The proximity hadn't stopped someone from slicing her abdomen open. But this wasn't Glasgow, it was Inverness.

'Bit of a stuck-up bitch, are you?' Big Drunk said.

'Or a dyke,' his friend sniggered.

Fuck's sake. Why did men like these think women considered it an insult to be thought gay?

In the distance she heard a car – a taxi, by the rumble of the engine – pass by. There were no lights in any of the nearby cottages and she'd flung her phone on the passenger seat earlier, where it remained.

She sized the men up. The big one moved slowly, like a lumbering bear, while the smaller one looked like a gust of wind would knock him over. Since she'd returned from Uist she'd sworn to herself that she'd get back to the peak fitness she'd had before work had absorbed most of her waking hours. Unfortunately the new regime had yet to fully kick in. However, if the worst came to the worst, she'd easily outrun these goons.

On the other hand, why the hell should she?

'Sorry, guys, I need to go.' Rachel turned back to close her boot.

Hands gripped her hips, pinning her to the car bumper. A pelvis ground into her buttocks.

Really? He was going there? Anger turned her body hot. No one, absolutely no one, was allowed to touch her without her permission.

Suddenly, without her knowing how it got there, the gutting knife from her fishing bag was in her hand. Since Uist, the knife had become her talisman, her stake for the heart of monsters. She whirled around and pressed the tip of the blade against the flesh spilling over the top of his jeans. 'Get the fuck away from me,' she hissed.

After her mother's body had been found, Rachel had taken self-defence classes, worked out, lifting weights, and running 10k, but when she felt threatened what did she do? Pull a knife! Well, too late to back off now.

A headline flashed before her eyes: *Lawyer involved in stabbing*. As if she hadn't been in the press too often already.

Small Drunk had moved away and was leaning against the lamp post. He was too busy trying to drain his can of lager by tipping it almost vertical while keeping an eye on the street to observe what was happening a few feet away from him.

Her glance swivelled from Small Drunk back to the man in

front of her. He looked up from the blade pressed against his stomach and she saw surprise and fear flicker in his eyes. She could only imagine what he saw in hers. The knife might be small, but it was sharp. He attempted a laugh.

'Calm it, darling. Just having some fun.' He stepped backwards. 'C'mon, Chris. Let's leave the crazy bitch alone. Ma mate lives down the road a bit. You want to see if we can get some mair drink aff him?' He slung his arm over Small Drunk's shoulder and together they weaved their way back down the street, towards the canal. As she watched them disappear, memories of the last time she'd held her gutting knife in her hand flooded back. She'd used it then. And had nightmares ever since. Suddenly she couldn't breathe. She bent over, resting her hands on her knees and gasping for air. Her heart felt as if it were going to jump out of her throat, seize up. It felt as if she was going into cardiac arrest here, in the street.

She stayed like that, taking deep slow breaths until the dizziness and the tightness in her chest passed. Heart still banging against her ribs, Rachel straightened. She wasn't having a heart attack, although it felt like it. She glanced up, thinking she'd seen a swish of a curtain from the corner of her eye. Bile rushed to her throat. If anyone had seen her pull the knife and snapped a photo, she was screwed, her career well and truly screwed. Her boss's words rang in her ears. If the Crown Agent wasn't thrilled about one of his lawyers ending up in the witness box, she could only imagine how he'd feel about one of them getting charged with aggravated assault. She slipped the knife back into her pocket and shivered, huddling deeper into her fishing jacket. She'd realised in Uist that she was capable of violence, maybe even capable of killing someone. Was she more her father's daughter than she wanted to believe?

SIX

Forty minutes later with the early-morning mist curling across the river, Rachel flicked her fishing line over her shoulder. The line landed in the water with a gentle tap in the soundless air. Standing in water over her knees she waited for the fish to bite. Only the distant, irregular thrum of lorries heading along the A9 disturbed the silence. In an hour or two the sound of passing cars would be constant, but by then, they'd have packed away their gear and would be heading back to the city.

Over the time the drive had taken, her heart rate had dropped, her breathing returned to its normal rhythm and the tightness in her chest dissipated. Nevertheless, the sickening thought she'd inherited her father's violent streak continued to play through her head. Had she been suppressing it all along? Had recent events brought it to the fore? What if it was something she couldn't control?

Ten metres to her left, Angus was also thigh-deep in the river, while back on the bank, more comfortable on his camping stool as he boiled a pan of water, was Peter, her father's best friend and Rachel's godfather.

It was the first time she'd been fishing with Peter and his

son, Angus, in years, although Peter had invited her often. On this occasion the invitation had come from her. The knowledge she was using her godfather was something else that didn't make her feel great.

It had surprised her that Angus had decided to join them. She'd heard his life as a KC was frenetic, his social life too. She slid a glance in his direction. He looked tired, the sharp planes of his face drawn tight over prominent cheekbones, his eyes hollowed out. No wonder. Rumour had it that Scotland's most promising defence counsel was in increasing demand with criminals and that he turned no one away.

A tug on her line told her a fish had bitten. She reeled in her first catch of the day – a flipping, squirming rainbow trout. Rachel caught it in her hands, feeling its sticky scales under her fingertips. She slipped a finger into its mouth, deftly unhooked the barb, and considered the fish for a moment. It was a decent size, big enough to provide breakfast for the three of them, and there was a good chance she wouldn't catch anything else.

Rachel glanced around. Neither Angus nor Peter was paying any attention. Overhead, seagulls circled waiting for scraps. She dropped the arm holding the fish to her side and let the trout wriggle from her grasp back into the water where, with a flick of its tail, it disappeared. It deserved another chance. And maybe she did have a heart.

'Tea's up,' Peter called over.

Rachel reeled in her line and waded back to the bank of the river. Peter held out an enamel cup for her and she wrapped her hands around it, savouring the warmth. Despite her waterproofs and waders, she was frozen from standing in water up to her thighs for the last hour.

'How are you doing?' Peter asked. His familiar presence, the burr of his voice, was like being folded in a duvet on a cold day.

Rachel knew he wasn't talking about the fishing.

'I'm OK.'

'Have you been to see your father?'

Rachel shook her head. She hadn't visited her father in prison since he'd been found guilty. What was there to say to the man she'd adored as a child – until he murdered her mother and let his only child think she'd been to blame for her disappearance?

Rachel and her godfather stood in silence for a moment, looking out over the water. Angus had caught something too. She doubted he'd be throwing it back.

'You must be proud of him.' She flicked her eyes towards the Porsche parked under the tree behind them. 'I see his name in the papers all the time. Scotland's criminals' favourite brief.' That wasn't the only reason his name was in the media. Usually, it had to do with the glamorous minor celebs and Scottish media stars who accompanied him to the events he attended. The days when Rachel had known him as a skinny youth with fuzz on his chin were long gone.

She'd been fishing with her father, Peter and Angus since she was four years old, Angus seven. It was time her father had carved out from his busy practice to spend with her and she'd loved spending time with him – with them all. Plucked from her warm bed, warmly wrapped up in waterproofs, wearing her own little waders. The four of them had gone climbing too. Living where they did, in such close proximity to the mountains, it would have been unthinkable not to. She'd been ten when she and Angus had started climbing on their own. After school, during holidays, on summer evenings.

She'd stopped going fishing when he left for Edinburgh uni – it just didn't seem cool anymore, nor did it fit with the nights she slipped out of her bedroom window to spend time with her friends down by the river smoking joints and swigging alcohol. Climbing was different. She couldn't give that up. She'd always craved the adrenaline rush too much. She slid another glance in Angus's direction. Perhaps the true reason she'd stopped going fishing was that Angus stopped coming.

He'd come back from uni looking pretty much as he did now. Hot as hell. Her cheeks grew pink as she remembered the night they'd spent in the bothy on top of Braeriach when she was nineteen. The night had been freezing, the sex anything but.

'Aye,' Peter sucked in a breath. 'I suppose. But I worry too. He never stops working. His mother and I hardly ever see him. I'm surprised he agreed to come today, but he was adamant.' He tipped the dregs of his tea on the ground. 'This is the most time we've spent together since he became a KC.' There was no bitterness in his words, only regret. Like Rachel, Angus was an only child.

Rachel touched Peter on the arm. 'He's always been driven. It's probably what makes him so successful.'

Angus was wading back to shore, a trout the size of a salmon in his right hand, his third catch this morning. She gestured with the teapot in his direction. Angus nodded and Rachel refilled her cup and another one for him.

'Aye, maybe.' Peter didn't look convinced either and they watched in silence as Angus dropped his catch into the bucket. Despite the exhaustion hollowing out his features, he was still hot. He was tall, over six three, lean, always beautifully and fashionably dressed. Just as he'd done for years, he wore his dark hair longer at the front than at the back. He had brilliantly blue, some might say icy, eyes, sharp cheekbones and full lips that rarely curled in a smile. But when they did. Oh boy.

'I heard what happened when you were on the Western Isles,' he said, taking the mug of tea from her. 'It's the talk of Edinburgh.' His lips twitched. 'It's rumoured you took down a cabal of drug runners single-handedly and came out without a scratch. I thought I'd better see if there was any truth in it, check on you myself.'

'It wasn't single-handed, and I spent a couple of nights in hospital with hypothermia, so it wasn't altogether without consequences.' She didn't mention the mental scars the experience had left. 'In case you haven't noticed, I'm an adult. All grown up and perfectly able to make my own decisions.'

He gave her one of his quick smiles. 'I think we can both safely assume I did notice.'

Rachel felt the heat rise up her neck. He clearly remembered the night on top of Braeriach too.

His expression grew serious. 'Are you telling me there's actually truth in the rumours?'

'Some. But most of it has been hugely exaggerated.' Which wasn't exactly true. She *had* exposed a murderer, solved another killing, and helped bring down a drug ring.

Angus gave her a searching look before taking out his gutting knife and quickly and efficiently preparing the fish he'd caught for the pan.

'How's life for you these days?' Rachel asked her godfather. Peter had been a consultant pathologist until he'd taken early retirement.

Peter grinned. 'Six months in and it's great. I don't know why I didn't do it years ago.'

Crouching down, Angus relit the camping stove and set a frying pan on top. He added a dob of butter.

Rachel turned her attention back to her godfather. 'Talking about work: is it possible for a woman who is thirteen weeks pregnant to miscarry and bleed to death? For it to happen so suddenly she hadn't time to call for help?'

She'd been turning the conversation with Kirsty over in her mind all night and done some reading. Maybe Kirsty had been mistaken when she thought Gillian would have known what was happening to her and had time to summon help?

Peter took a swig of his tea. 'Not necessarily. She could have had some unexplained pain and bleeding earlier in the pregnancy. Miscarriage could follow on hours, days or weeks later.'

Kirsty had said the pregnancy had been uneventful.

'What if she'd had a scan two days before she died and it confirmed the pregnancy was ongoing?'

'Sadly, the fetal heart can disappear at any time without warning. Although it's less common for everything to be OK right before a miscarriage, there's still a lot we don't know.'

It was increasingly looking like Kirsty had been mistaken. Neither Deputy Dawg – the irreverent nickname his team had given Mainwaring due to his hangdog expression and remorseless pessimistic attitude – nor Alastair were going to be happy if Rachel stirred up a hornet's nest for nothing. Nevertheless, she would wait until the PM results were in and she'd heard what Du Toit had to say before calling the dogs off.

'There's something else I wanted to speak to you about.'

The scent of cooking fish drifted on the air.

Peter lifted a questioning eyebrow.

'As Angus mentioned, I was in Uist recently. It's where my mother was born and brought up.'

'Yes, I know. I gather she and her parents were estranged?'

'Yes. While I was there though, I went to see my grandfather.' She grimaced. 'I was going to give him a piece of my mind, but it turns out we might be at the very beginning, or perhaps the very end – he's very frail – of some kind of relationship. He didn't treat my mother well, but he's the only family I have left.' The last came out more defensively than she wanted it to. Her grandparents had let her mother down when she'd needed them most and Rachel would never fully forgive them for it; nevertheless, the partial reconciliation with her grandfather was one of the good things that had come out of her time in Uist.

'You still have your father.'

She shot him a look. 'No, I don't. As far as I'm concerned,

he died the day he was found guilty of my murdering my mother.'

Peter regarded her steadily.

'But,' she couldn't believe she was saying this, 'what if there's a chance, even a very, very small one — that he didn't kill her?'

Peter paused, his cup halfway to his lips. 'I thought you were convinced of his guilt.'

'I was. I am. At the very least, I want to return to one hundred per cent sure. What if there's any truth that someone else had it in for Mum?'

'Why the doubt now? We were both in court when the prosecution made their case.'

She addressed Angus, who had come to stand next to them: 'Do you believe my father is guilty?' When her father's trial had taken place, Angus had been devilling with the firm of advocates representing her father.

'The jury found him guilty. Despite my firm trying its damnedest to get him off.' He gave a rueful smile. 'It stings they couldn't.'

'It stings he was guilty,' Rachel snapped.

A smile ghosted across his lips. 'Prickly as ever, I see. I thought you'd perfected the cool, calm facade our profession likes to adopt.'

'Like you?' she fired back. To be fair, Angus had always been a man of few words. Many of their climbs had been undertaken in near silence. Ironic then that he made his living by using language to persuade not guilty verdicts from juries.

'It works for me.' He loaded three plates with fish and handed one, along with a fork, to his father and then Rachel.

She'd seen him on and off through university. He'd appear out of the blue, ropes and backpack in hand, and insist they climb a Munro. There had been a gap of a couple of years when she hadn't seen him at all. They'd met again when her father had been charged with murder and hired the firm Angus worked for to represent him. There had been no talk of climbing Munros then, or anything else for that matter. She'd been so focused on the trial, constantly going on at Angus to make sure his firm left no stone unturned to prove her father's innocence. Back then, she'd still believed her father to be innocent. Eventually, Angus had barred her from his chambers and then, when she'd pitched up one night, drunk and distraught, from his flat. The memory made her wince. She'd hardly seen him since.

'What's brought this on, Rachel?' Pete asked around a mouthful of fish. It was fully light now, the glen on either side of the river suddenly painted in golden light. 'Why the doubt now?'

Father and son studied her intently.

'Apparently before Mum went missing, she told my grandmother in a phone conversation – because unbeknownst to my grandfather they'd kept in touch – that she'd learned something unbelievable and horrible and thought her life was in danger because of it.'

'I never heard any of this,' Peter said with a frown. 'What about you, Angus?' His son shook his head. Peter turned back to Rachel. 'What do you think she was referring to?'

'Gran said it was connected with Mum's job.'

Angus frowned. 'The police spoke to her colleagues when your mother first went missing. It was an obvious line of enquiry, given the nature of your mother's work. That's how they found the colleague who testified that your mother planned to leave your father.'

'But later? When they found her body. Did no one have anything else to say? Mention threats? People who might have wished Mum harm.'

'Not as far as I know. My firm would have been keen to find anything to help your father's defence.'

Why was she going down this rabbit hole anyway?

'That's just it. He didn't really have a defence, did he? He tried to blame everyone else – my mother's fictional lover, ex-clients of his.' *Even me*, she added silently.

Before the trial, she'd believed her father's claim that someone else was responsible for her mother's murder. Over the six weeks the trial took, she'd changed her mind. Everything had pointed to her father's guilt.

Thinking back to that time still made her nauseous. She left her fish half-finished and put her plate on the ground.

For some reason, sitting through the trial, watching the sparring between the advocate defending her father and the prosecutor determined to convict him, had fascinated her. It was then she'd decided to go back to university to study law and hopefully, one day, if she played her cards right, find herself in court as a prosecutor.

'Don't you think you've been through enough?' Peter said gently. 'If there was any chance your father didn't do it – and God knows I couldn't believe he was capable of murdering Mary Ann either – Angus's firm would have found a way of proving it.'

She knew that. She was grasping at straws because a tiny kernel of her still wanted him to be innocent.

But *something* had been troubling her mother in the days leading up to her disappearance. And Rachel was going to find out what it was. Why hadn't she asked about her mother before? Tried to get to know her?

Because thinking about her had been too painful. Was still painful.

'How well did you know my mother?' she asked Peter.

Angus was clearing their plates and re-packing his cool bag.

'Not that well. Mary Ann was happy to stay at home or do other things while your father and I took you and Angus fishing and climbing. She and your father invited me around for dinner a few times after my Lou died, but never said very much. She struck me as a very private person. Shy anyway.'

'But you knew Dad well. Did you never suspect what was going on in their marriage? The abuse? The coercive control.'

Peter looked pained. 'I promise you, if I'd ever had a sniff it was happening, I'd have called your father out. As it was, we rarely spoke of anything except fishing and climbing. Typical men's talk. Some of the time we talked about our jobs – he liked to hear about my more interesting cases' – he smiled as if recalling their conversations – 'and I liked to hear about his. Your father knew some pretty serious criminals. He used to shake his head at some of the stuff they got up to. But I think part of him enjoyed hobnobbing with crooks. He particularly liked defending them in court and getting them off.'

Rachel's father had been a solicitor advocate, which meant he was able to defend his clients in court.

Had her mother known about her father's dark side? That he was drawn to the people he represented. If so, it should have been a red flag. A clue to the man he was.

'Although,' Peter continued, looking at his son, 'I think money played a part. He was well paid for the work his firm did. Most of the clients they represented were well-off. He wasn't interested in legal aid cases.'

A thought struck Rachel. If her father had been earning good money, where had it gone? A chunk on his defence for sure, but the rest? Her father hadn't spent a penny on the family home after her mother had left. Was that lack of funds or disinterest?

'Going back to Mum, what did you guys talk about over dinner?' She felt the familiar stab of pain that she'd never got the chance to know her mother as an adult. That all she knew about her – little as it was – had been innuendo her father's advocate had brought to the trial and the memories she had of her mother as a child. Her heart hardened against her father again. Not only had he robbed her mother of life, he'd taken away the possibility of a future where she and her mother would have become close again, friends even.

Angus passed Rachel on the way to his car and gave her shoulder a sympathetic squeeze, taking her by surprise.

Peter got to his feet. 'I think you should let it go, Rachel. I understand you have regrets, guilt even, but in my experience those feelings rarely help when it comes to getting on in life. You're doing well, carving out a life for yourself. A good life.'

But she wasn't Peter.

And she wasn't good at letting go.

SEVEN

SUNDAY

Soft rain fell, greasing the road as Ashley Carmichael huddled in the doorway of an office long since abandoned for the day. The streets, lit by the faint yellow glow of the streetlamps were quiet apart from the occasional hiss of tyres on wet tarmac. It had been a rubbish night for punters so far. She gave a sigh of frustration and laid her hand on her stomach. If she and her baby were to have any kind of decent future, Ashley needed to save as much money as possible as quickly as she could. Once her baby was born she wasn't going to work the streets ever again. Her life was going to change.

The last year had been tough. Working the streets was hard. And scary. Maybe if she'd got a proper job, when she'd arrived in Inverness, she wouldn't have got into the H. But no one had wanted to give a fourteen-year-old a job. That's how old she'd been when Mum kicked her out. A lump lodged in her throat. Everyone thought her mum was the best thing ever, so prim and proper, with her neatly kept garden with tubs of flowers on the doorstep. And maybe she had been, up until she'd let Tim move in. Everything had changed then. Mum had thought the sun shone out of him. But Ashley had taken an immediate dislike to his snake-like eyes and later, his wandering hands. She'd been twelve when he started abusing her. She'd told her mum, like the school said you should, but Mum hadn't believed her. To be fair, she had challenged Tim but he'd claimed it was Ashley who had come on to him. And it was him she'd believed, Ashley who'd been told to leave. It still hurt. Would never stop hurting. What kind of mother could do that? It wasn't as if Ashley had anywhere to go. Her real dad had died when she was eight, and his parents were dead too. She'd been disbelieving, until her mother had dragged her upstairs to the bedroom, yanked a trolley bag from the cupboard and given Ashley five minutes to grab what she could. Mum had watched her, arms folded, a look of distaste distorting her pretty face. Ashley had begged through snot and tears for Mum to let her stay. She'd nowhere to go. For a split second, Mum had looked as if she might change her mind, then Tim had walked in and that had been the end of it.

She'd gone to her uncle Robert, her mother's brother. He'd let her stay for a week before telling her she needed to leave. Ashley guessed he'd spoken to her mum and she'd repeated the version she'd chosen to believe.

'That will never happen to us, baby,' she whispered now. 'Mummy is going to take good care of you.' She leaned against the wall, closed her eyes and allowed herself to dream. She was going to love this baby so much. She already loved it. Maybe the council would give them a wee flat and, now she was clean, maybe she would get a proper job. Might even go to evening classes. Sit her Highers. She'd been good at school once. Mags had offered to help. Maybe she'd even take the baby sometimes. She was more a mum to Ashley these days than her own mother had been.

Voices drifted over, a car door slammed and deposited a woman on the street.

There were only three of them still working this patch

tonight. They all had their specific spots. Most of them had their favourite clients; the clean ones, the ones who didn't argue about wearing rubbers, who did it, paid up and left. The clients had their favourites too. The two didn't always match.

Another woman spilled out of a car and she and the other one left for home. Now it was just Ashley left. Hopefully Jody would be along soon.

She felt twitchy. It wasn't easy coming off the H. She'd tried before – three times – and failed. The methadone she'd taken at the pharmacy earlier that day was wearing off and she was getting twitchy. The stuff they gave you to wean you off the H was nothing like the real thing. She supposed it was better than nothing. A man wearing a long coat emerged from the shadows, taking her mind off her jitters. She didn't recognise him as one of the regulars. He had a baseball cap pulled low on his face, so she couldn't be sure.

When he beckoned, she hitched up her skirt another inch and tottered towards him on four-inch heels. He nodded towards one of the vacant buildings. Ashley hesitated. It was dark there and out of the reach of the CCTV cameras the council were always trying to repair. But it was nearly three. There were unlikely to be many more punters. Making up her mind, she followed him. At least it would be quick. No need for a car journey.

He was waiting for her at the back of the building. Her heels crunched as she walked towards him. The clouds parted and for a moment the moon cast a watery glow on the cobbles, illuminating rubbish and discarded syringes.

Once more she hesitated, a sixth sense making the fine hairs on her skin stand to attention.

'It's all right,' he said softly. 'Your man told me where to find you.' The mention of her boyfriend reassured her and Ashley walked right up to the punter.

'I have something for you,' the man said, holding out a

loaded syringe. She looked at it, then at him. Something wasn't right. Taffy would have told him she wasn't using any longer.

But seeing the syringe had fed the worm of desire in her. She ran a tongue over her lips.

Car tyres squealed in the distance. The man glanced over her shoulder to the mouth of the alley. 'Go on. It's good stuff, I promise. The very best.'

She swallowed. 'It's cash or nothing.'

'You can have both. Your man said it would be OK to give you some instead of some of the cash, as long as I gave him some too.'

The sense of unease got worse.

'Taffy knows I don't use anymore. Why would he tell you I did?'

'He told me about the baby. About you wanting to keep it. He said you didn't want to hurt it but I told him this stuff was good. It won't harm your baby. It's better than the shit you get on the street. This is pure.'

She ran a tongue across her lips. One wee hit couldn't do any harm. And it would definitely be the last. She held out her hand.

He snatched his hand away, hiding it behind his back.

'No,' he said firmly. 'You can have twenty quid now, the H afterwards.'

The hunger for oblivion was impossible to resist now. She took the money he held out to her and shoved it into her bra. 'OK then. What do you want?'

'Take off your panties and then turn around.'

Ashley slipped out of her thong and turned her back to him, planting her hands on the wall in front of her. She just wanted it to be over so she could feel the drug working its magic. If only he'd get a move on. He was doing something behind her, hopefully putting on a rubber. She felt hands on her shoulders and he turned her to face him. He'd taken off his coat and put it in a black bin liner and had put on a pair of blue latex gloves. Ashley suppressed a sigh. Whatever fetish he had, it probably wasn't anything she hadn't come across before.

'Here,' he said quickly, holding out the syringe. 'Take it. You can have it now if you like.'

She hesitated. What was she doing? Hadn't she made a promise to her baby? Maybe she should just tell him to fuck off.

Her fingers reached for the syringe, almost as if they had a life of their own. She found a vein in the back of her hand, inserted the needle and pressed the plunger.

Almost immediately she knew something was wrong. This wasn't the high she recognised. A weird sensation was spreading through her body, making her limbs numb. She slumped against the wall. The punter's face swam in and out of focus.

Her legs buckled and she slid to the ground. He crouched beside her. She tried to scramble to her feet but her paralysed legs wouldn't obey her commands. What the fuck? Had he given her bad stuff?

'Help,' she cried. At least she tried to. Only a soft moan came out of her mouth.

'You keep still now,' he said. 'It will be over soon.'

What would soon be over? What the fuck was he talking about?

He crouched by her side and smiled. Hope surged. Maybe he didn't intend to kill her? Perhaps he liked to have sex with unconscious women? Maybe Jody, Taffy even, would come into the alley and chase him off?

Something sharp stabbed the side of her neck. Almost immediately she couldn't breathe, couldn't drag air into her lungs. She was suffocating. She clawed at her throat. Everything was beginning to fade around her. She could not die. Her baby would die with her. That could not happen.

Ashley made one last effort to beg for her life, her baby's

life. It was no use. She couldn't even form the words in her head.

'Let go,' he said. 'It will be easier.'

She focused on her baby, begged her for forgiveness and allowed the darkness to take her.

EIGHT

On Sunday morning Rachel drove to the village of Moy. The weather had changed again and today it felt as if the summer was very close – the sun bathing the fields in gold. Spring was Rachel's favourite time of year. A time filled with promise, tractors spraying crops that would soon be ready for harvesting, fields of yellow rape like blankets of sunshine. It was too early yet for the swarm of summer tourists, the serpentine of cars and convoys of motor homes spreading along the Highlands and Islands like dye in water.

Normally driving anywhere in the Highlands lifted her spirits, especially when the sun was out. But not today.

Her stomach had churned throughout the twenty-minute drive. The last time she'd visited her childhood home was six years ago. She'd come a couple of weeks after her mother's body had been found, in an awkward attempt to reconnect with her father.

They'd gone fishing, walked in the Cairngorm mountains, talked about everything apart from her mother and her murder. Back then she couldn't even have imagined he'd been the perpetrator.

The large Victorian sandstone house was in a wide tree-lined avenue and set back from the road, shielded by a brick wall. Her father always fancied himself as a bit of country squire, even though the size of the land their property stood on was only a couple of acres.

It was a house meant for a large family. Had probably sheltered one when it was first built a century ago. Presumably that had been her parents' intention when they'd bought it. Was it her mother's choice to have only one child? Or had she been unable to conceive another? Or had the marriage already broken down by then? These were just some of the questions that adult Rachel would never be able to ask her mother now.

Her parents must have been in love once, otherwise why get married? Especially if the marriage had been so distasteful to her maternal grandparents that, to all intents and purposes, they'd essentially disowned their only child.

What had changed over the course of her parents' marriage? When had love turned to hate?

She got out of the car and peered at the house through the black iron gates, one of which was listing slightly on its hinges. It looked forlorn.

A house this size could hide many secrets, some of which Rachel had learned as her father's trial progressed. Were there others? If so, it was time to discover what they were.

She pushed and the rusty gates scraped open, just far enough for her to squeeze through.

She let herself into the house, the instantly recognisable smell of home engulfing her. Her father had put it in her name in a pathetic attempt to curry favour. Maybe she should have sold it – she could have afforded to buy something in Inverness, maybe in Clachnaharry, which had begun to feel like home. It wasn't as if she didn't have a moral right to it. Her father would never return and her mother would never need it. But for some reason she couldn't articulate, even to herself, she hadn't been able to bring herself to put it on the market. Perhaps because it was the last link to her mother.

She walked along the flagstoned hallway, pausing for a moment in the doorway of the kitchen. That was weird. Someone had left it tidy. Immaculately tidy. Her father had considered housework beneath him. There were no dishes in the sink, or food in the fridge – and only a couple of tins in the larder. Even the pine kitchen table where she'd done her homework had been scrubbed. Had her father predicted his arrest and cleared up? Maybe he'd called in a cleaning company? The sitting room was the same: sofa cushions perfectly plumped, carpet vacuumed. However the walls needed to be repainted, the carpets replaced. She hadn't really noticed the general air of neglect the last time she was here, but then she'd had a lot on her mind.

She ran her finger along the mantelpiece – no dust. Same with the grand piano with the family photographs still neatly displayed on top.

Her mother and father, arms wrapped around each other, smiling into the camera. Her father posing next to his beloved Land Rover. Rachel and him in waders, holding rods, her mother and Rachel at the top of Ben Nevis, ski poles tucked under armpits.

Rachel was transported back in time: the fishing trips with her father, hill walks in the Cairngorms, the family skiing trips, Christmas carols around the grand piano, board games in front of the open fire. There had been laughter, she was certain. She had been happy here once. They'd *all* been happy here, once. Unless her parents had been pretending even then? It was time to separate the truth of her life from the fiction.

She picked up a photo hidden behind the rest. It was of her and Angus – her grinning ear to ear, rope over her shoulder, Angus gawky and self-conscious next to her. It was one of the last truly happy days she remembered. She climbed the stairs to her bedroom. The bed was made the way she always made it, tidy enough but would never pass muster in a hospital. The teddy someone had given her when she was a baby was on the windowsill, as if waiting for her to return. She picked it up and hugged it to her chest, instantly comforted, and just as quickly, although there was no one to see, embarrassed.

Finally, she made her way to the top floor and her parents' bedroom. She pushed the door open tentatively, her heart pounding in her ears, feeling sick.

Even as a self-absorbed teenager how could she have remained ignorant of what was happening behind the closed door of her parents' bedroom.

Was this where her father had killed her mother?

She visualised her mother's head slamming against the wall, her father's hands around her neck, squeezing the breath out of her body; her mother clawing at his hands, her legs kicking, flailing, getting weaker, the light getting dimmer, until there was no light at all.

Rachel slumped against the wall and slid down to the floor. She thought her chest was going to explode.

They'd never discovered where her mother had been murdered. Her body had been stripped and bathed with bleach. If she had been killed in the house the SOCOs hadn't found any evidence. However, there had been four years between her mother disappearing and her body being found. Plenty of time for her father to make certain no evidence remained. All they knew for sure was that she hadn't been killed where she'd been buried, wrapped in a black bin liner, in a shallow grave deep in a forest.

Rachel's heart continued to race. It felt as if it were lodged in her throat, making it difficult to breathe. She fought the panic by taking slow, deep breaths until her pulse slowed.

She went back through the house taking her time, looking in

cupboards, under the beds, rifling through shoeboxes finding nothing of interest. Apart from old bills. She pulled down the ladder and climbed into the attic. She rifled through suitcases of clothes, finding a remembered dress of her mother's, burying her face in its silky folds. Her old toys, reading books, school reports were there too, neatly stored in cardboard boxes. Another box held dozens of vinyl records and as she thumbed through them she recognised her mother's favourite groups. Finding a turntable next to the box, she set them aside to take home with her.

Disappointingly, she didn't find diaries, or letters. Had her father disposed of them? Had any even existed? If so, they weren't here. Whatever secrets the house had, it was keeping to itself. Perhaps it *was* time to sell. Let another family give the house back its soul.

She carried the record player and box of LPs down and out to her car, placing them in her car boot.

She was locking the front door, checking to make sure it was secure, when she felt a hand land on her shoulder. She whirled around to find Mrs Ferguson, their nearest neighbour, standing behind her. She'd been too engrossed in her thoughts to hear anyone approach.

'Oh, it is you, Rachel. I was about to phone the police when I saw the gates were open. We've been keeping an eye on the house. Decided I'd better scoot over to make sure it wasn't being burgled.'

'Mrs Ferguson – I didn't hear you.'

'I think you're old enough to call me Lorna,' she said with an amused lift of an eyebrow. 'I came along the burn,' she continued, referring to the stream that ran through the bottom of their gardens. It had always been used as a shortcut by the two families. 'I thought we might have seen you before now.'

A gust of wind whipped Rachel's hair across her face and she shivered.

'Look, it's chilly out here. Why don't you come over for a cup of tea? I'd love to hear how you're getting on.'

Lorna had always been nosy, dropping in at their house for one reason or another. And Rachel's father had been close to the Fergusons, had been Bill Ferguson's solicitor, and he and Mum had socialised with the Fergusons regularly. Perhaps Lorna Ferguson could tell her more about her mother's last weeks. If Mum had been worried about something, maybe she'd confided in her?

'Thank you, that would be lovely.'

The Fergusons' home was similar to Rachel's parental home – but more substantial and much better cared for. Accessed through a grand gilded gate, the driveway was lined with trees all the way up to a circular turning point large enough for the several cars parked in the driveway: Rachel spotted a Tesla and two Porsches, one a sports car, the other a large SUV.

'I don't want to intrude if you have visitors.'

Lorna laughed. 'Oh, they're all ours.'

The business must be going well. Rachel couldn't remember exactly what Bill Ferguson did, except it involved imports and exports. Lorna worked part-time as an admin officer, although Rachel couldn't remember where.

Storm doors opened onto a marble-floored hall large enough to host a five-a-side football match, if it hadn't been for the enormous plant pots planted with mini palm trees taking up most of the space. A sweeping staircase that wouldn't have been out of place in a stately home was at the far end.

'As you can see, we've done some work since you were last here. When was that? Several years anyway.'

Rachel remembered exactly when it had been. At a BBQ shortly before Rachel's mother had left. The Fergusons loved hosting social events.

She hadn't thought about that day in years. Now memories rushed back. At first the atmosphere had been relaxed, everyone talking and laughing, glasses in hand. But watching from a deckchair on the periphery of the garden, a sneaked vodka masquerading as a tonic, Rachel had become aware of a weird tension in the air. Voices had been raised, someone had shouted, people had stood stiffly to the side, or made their excuses and left. Rachel had used the distraction to slip off to meet her friends. Now she wondered who had been shouting at whom? Dad at Mum? But there had been several raised voices, a sense of menace.

Had her father been planning his wife's murder even then?

She swallowed the nausea that had risen to her throat and focused on Lorna's obvious pride in her renovated home instead.

The remainder of the Ferguson interior was as flamboyant as the McKenzie home was old and battered. The interior had been scooped out, walls removed, rooms enlarged, ceilings raised.

Lorna led Rachel into a kitchen with a marble-topped island almost the size of Rachel's kitchen at its centre. All the built-in appliances were stainless steel and top of the range. A pale mauve sofa large enough to seat a family faced a TV the size of a small cinema screen, flanked by Bang & Olufsen speakers. The room had been extended at the back with patio doors looking out to a deck and down the hill to the burn that lay at its foot.

'Your home is lovely,' Rachel said when Lorna gave her an expectant look.

'I'm so glad you like what we've done. We've recently dug into the ground to create a media room. We're in the process of deciding if we want a swimming pool.'

Rachel was waved towards the over-stuffed sofa.

'Coffee?' Lorna asked.

'Please. Black. No sugar.'

Lorna spooned coffee grounds into a cafetière, poured

boiling water from the kettle that sat on an industrial-sized cooker, and poured it on top.

As she waited for the coffee to brew, she turned back to face Rachel. 'What are you up to now? Last I heard, you had qualified as a lawyer. Taking a leaf out of your father's book then?' Lorna put the cafetière and two cups with matching saucers on a tray.

Rachel felt a flash of irritation. She *had* gone into law because of her father, but for the opposite reason most people followed in their parents' footsteps. At the very least, it was a tactless thing to say.

Lorna pressed the plunger down on the cafetière, poured the coffee and passed one of the cups across to Rachel.

'Thank you for keeping an eye on the house,' Rachel said.

'That's no problem. I hope you don't mind, but when your father was sent down I got cleaners in. We imagined you'd be back at some point and wanted to leave it clean and tidy for you.'

Rachel hadn't thought the Fergusons were close enough friends to clean up the McKenzie home on their behalf. She cringed internally, uncomfortable at the thought. She supposed she should be grateful. It hadn't occurred to Rachel to do anything of the sort. After her father was found guilty she couldn't bear to even step over the threshold.

'We thought you'd sell it,' Lorna continued. 'Your father certainly seems to think it's the best thing to do.'

Rachel frowned. 'How do you know what my father thinks?' Then realisation dawned. 'Does Mr F— Bill – visit him in prison?'

Lorna wrinkled her nose. 'They were good friends, Rachel.' She considered Rachel over the rim of her cup before continuing. 'I've been once or twice too.' She swallowed noisily. 'I know most people around here would think that was wrong, but I felt'

– she paused as if searching for the right word – 'sorry for him, I guess.'

'I think a murder victim trumps a murderer, no matter how friendly you were.' The cool and collected facade Angus had mentioned was still a work in progress.

'Yes. I know.' A band of red rose up Lorna's throat. 'But it's complicated. I still find it hard to accept your father was responsible for her death. He's so charming.'

Rachel turned away from Lorna, looked out of the window towards the burn as if something down there had caught her attention, and used the few moments to suppress her annoyance.

Apart from the nosiness, she remembered a mild, quiet woman, with nothing very interesting to say for herself. Even back then Lorna had struck Rachel as a people pleaser, happy to look after everyone's needs before her own. She deserved Rachel's sympathy rather than her approbation. 'I'm sorry,' she said. 'That was rude. But you do know my father is guilty?'

'I guess,' Lorna said, sounding not entirely sure. She placed her cup and saucer on the table. 'It must have been tough for you. You and Mary Ann had such a close bond.'

Maybe once. Before Rachel entered her teens.

'What did you think when Mum went missing?'

'Don't know, love. Didn't know what to think, to be honest. People go missing all the time, don't they?' Lorna Ferguson was turning out to be even more of a wet rag than Rachel remembered.

'Did Mum ever confide in you?'

'About what?' Lorna looked startled.

'About anything – wanting to leave my father, how things were between them. The four of you were friends and most friends talk.'

Lorna lifted the empty coffee cups from the table and put them down next to the sink.

'I knew she wasn't happy with your father,' she said, almost reluctantly.

'Did she tell you that?'

'Not in so many words. Your mother was too private to share her personal life – at least with me. It was your father and Bill who were the friends, your mum and I the hangers on, so to speak. But she dropped hints, I saw things. The odd bruise, the look in her eyes. I wondered sometimes if she was scared of your father.'

'Didn't you ask?' Rachel snapped. Had her mother's last years been filled with missed opportunities to get the help that might have saved her life? Anger vied with sadness in Rachel's chest.

Lorna's knuckles as she gripped the edge of the sink were white. She kept her back turned to Rachel.

'No one likes to poke their nose in other people's marriages. I did ask her about the bruises once but she fobbed me off. Gave me some spiel about tripping over and banging her face on the coffee table. She was obviously embarrassed.' She turned to face Rachel and sighed. 'Most women find it difficult to admit they're being abused.'

'Did you share your suspicions with your husband?'

'As a matter of fact, I did. He rejected the idea out of hand. Said your father wasn't the kind of man to put a hand on a woman.'

But the world was filled with men who put their hands on women, men who watched child porn, who abused children. And most of them were someone's husband, brother, father, son; perfectly normal-looking men on the outside. Lorna must know that. On the other hand, some women – women like Lorna – were cocooned in such a bubble perhaps real life never touched them. Unlike Rachel's mother, who must have come face to face with life's ugly reality both at work and at home.

Given their different worlds, maybe it wasn't surprising that

Lorna and Rachel's mother hadn't been close. But they had spent time together. They would have had to talk about something.

'Did Mum ever speak to you about her job?'

'Sometimes.' She filled a small watering can from the tap and watered some houseplants on the windowsill.

'Did she ever mention a client who frightened her?'

Lorna frowned. 'Not that I can recall. Probably due to issues of confidentiality – your mother wasn't the kind of person to break the rules. Probably never ran a red light in her life.' Was that a touch of contempt Rachel heard in her voice?

Rachel leaned forward in her chair. 'What was she like? What did you think of her?'

'As I said, I didn't know her that well. But what I did know of her, I liked. She was very clever, perhaps even more so than your father. She had a sense of humour, loved fashion. But she was quiet, reserved – you know what I mean. Your father was the party animal. Surely you remember her? She doted on *you*.'

'I was fifteen when my father killed her and, to be honest, I was such a brat when I became a teenager all I can remember is how often we clashed.'

But Rachel the child remembered love. The teen Rachel had chosen to deny it.

'Oh, sweetheart. Mothers and daughters, particularly teenage daughters, clash all the time. It's part of becoming an adult.' She gave Rachel a rueful smile. 'But I gather you were a bit of a handful. Unlike your mother, you had no respect for rules – bunking off school, smoking at the bottom of the garden, sneaking out of your bedroom window when you thought no one was looking. Makes it hard to believe you became a lawyer. Just like your dad.'

Rachel suppressed a shiver of distaste. 'I am nothing like my father.' The very thought revolted her. Perhaps because she was beginning to realise there might be some truth in it. The thought propelled her to her feet.

'Thank you for the coffee. But I should go.' There was nothing more to be learned here.

'It was very nice seeing you,' Lorna said, accompanying her to the door.

Rachel drove out of Moy, the familiar mountains in the distance, usually a balm to her soul, unable to loosen the tight band in her chest. Only then did she realise that Lorna hadn't asked her to come again. But it wasn't only that. Something nagged at her memory. Something important she'd known once but had forgotten. She tried unsuccessfully to dislodge it. Hopefully it would come back when she stopped thinking about it.

NINE

By the time Rachel got home from Moy, the light was draining from the sky.

The village of Clachnaharry had been a fishing village but was now part of Inverness, the town centre only three miles away, less if you took the towpath. There were only a few dozen houses in the village and until a couple of decades ago most of them had been abandoned and falling into disrepair, but their location, combined with their proximity to Inverness, had secured the village a second lease of life. Most were second homes but a handful were still owned by locals – something Rachel should have thought about before she'd agreed the let. The locals had no fear or embarrassment when it came to quizzing her about her life. She'd become adept at fending off their questions. Turning the conversations back to them usually helped. The only exception to this was Rachel's neighbour on the other side of the semi-detached cottage, an older woman with inexpertly dyed red hair and a questionable taste in clothes. Whatever she'd done in the past – and Rachel had a fair idea – Rachel found Mags's reticence about herself perfectly agreeable, content with the few words they exchanged when they found themselves on either side of the low garden wall as they pegged their washing on the line, the odd foray into each other's house when either needed something; Mags usually something from Tesco's, Rachel to look for Honey, the stray cat who took blatant advantage of them both.

The cottage suited her too. It had been renovated after the millennium with the basic structure staying the same – a sitting room on one end, a kitchen diner at the other with two bedrooms in between. It had everything Rachel needed in terms of furniture, a dishwasher, washing machine and a position the envy of her fellow villagers.

The kitchen and sitting room looked towards the sea, a natural barometer of the weather. Rolling white-crested waves meant wind, a flat sea, a calm, windless day.

Running into the sea and also visible from her window was the Caledonian Canal connected to the Beauly Firth via a sea lock. Beyond the sea and the canal was the Black Isle, and beyond it, appearing tantalisingly close on a clear day, was Ben Wyvis.

Thick walls dampened the sound but not the charm of the railway line that ran within touching distance of Rachel's back garden. On the other side of the railway line and over a bridge was the inn that offered decent food, cold wine and beer, and a game of darts, or a choice of board games and books. Perfect for whiling away an hour or two in front of the woodburning stove, if that was your thing.

As Rachel emerged from her car, the appetising smell of curry drifted on the air, making her stomach rumble. However, she wanted to work out before eating – if she had anything in her fridge or cupboards, that was. There was always the inn, but she tried to keep eating there to a maximum of twice a week.

Her front door opened onto a hall that ran the length of her house. As she entered she stepped on a folded sheet of paper that had been slipped under her door. She shoved it in her pocket as Honey strutted over, tail in the air, and wound around her feet with a plaintive meow. Rachel bent to tickle her behind the ear. She hadn't meant to become a pet owner, but she'd found Honey in one of the abandoned buildings close to the canal, foraging for scraps, emaciated and flea-ridden. She'd taken her to the vet, and unsurprisingly there had been no identifying chip. Rachel couldn't bear to have her put down, so adopted her instead. Six months later, Honey's coat was sleek and shiny and she was here to stay. In return for Rachel's help, Honey was fast and loose with her affections, sometimes preferring her neighbour's house to Rachel's. Over time she and Mags appeared to have become joint owners of the cat.

Rachel fed Honey, worked out with weights for forty minutes and then fed herself: a cheese toastie with some limp lettuce on the side, followed, after a brief internal struggle, by a slab of stale shop-bought chocolate cake. She poured herself a glass of wine and was about to carry it through to the sitting room when she remembered the note.

There were three sentences scrawled in a large, looping hand on the piece of paper, once part of an envelope. It was from Mags. Between the commanding Glaswegian tone and fondness for vibrant red hair dye, Rachel couldn't help but think of her as Red Mags and sometimes barely managed to stop herself addressing her as such.

I need your help. Can you come see me? As soon as you get home?

What sort of help could Mags need? If the rumour mill was to be believed, Mags was bound to have plenty of experience getting herself out of tricky situations. Unless she'd been arrested and wanted advice. Or Rachel to intervene in the mistaken belief Rachel could sort it?

Rachel glanced at her watch. She longed for a bath followed

by Netflix in bed, but if the tough-as-nails woman next door was in urgent need of her help, then Rachel had best find out why. She cast a longing look at her glass of wine. It would have to wait.

Rachel tapped on her neighbour's door, hearing the slip-slap of feet as Mags made her way to answer. Mags always wore her husband's slippers, although they were three sizes too big for her and he'd been dead for over a decade. Rachel waited patiently as the locks and chains rattled. As far as Rachel knew, she and Mags were the only residents in the village who had chains as well as locks on their doors. Eventually the door opened on its safety chain. Through the crack in the doorway, a faded blue eye peered out at Rachel.

'Oh, it's you, hen. Haud on a minute.' The door closed and there was more rattling before it opened again. 'Come in. Come in.'

Something was definitely up. Mags's hair was awry, the crease between her brows more pronounced than usual.

Rachel stepped inside, trying to ignore the smell of stale grease and cigarettes. Mags's cottage was the mirror image of hers but that's where the similarities ended. Rachel's wasn't modern by any means but as far as she could tell, Mags's had barely been touched in terms of decor or home improvements since Mags and her husband had inherited it from his parents.

Rachel's shoes stuck to the linoleum as she followed Mags along the hall and into the front lounge.

Mags bent and poked a dying coal fire. Sparks shot up and one landed on the bubblegum-pink shagpile carpet. Mags stepped on it with her too-large slippers. As always, when she was indoors she was wearing her nylon overall, almost exactly the same as the one Rachel's grandmother had worn. If a spark from the fire landed on her, she'd go up like a rocket.

'Tea?' Mags asked.

Rachel shook her head. The last time she'd accepted a cup

of tea, she'd found something that looked suspiciously like a toenail clipping at the bottom of the mug.

'If you're sure.' Mags lit a cigarette and popped it in the side of her mouth. Her lips were ringed with bright red lipstick, most of which had missed its mark.

She fluttered her hand at Rachel. 'Sit down.'

'What can I do for you, Mags?' Rachel resisted the temptation to glance at her watch. 'Is something wrong?'

Mags took a deep draw of her cigarette before answering. 'It's Ashley. One of my girls.' She narrowed her eyes at Rachel, waiting for her to react. When she didn't, she continued.

'She's a working girl, if you know what I mean. And ahm sure you do because you're a lawyer so you can't be that naive.'

Rachel nodded. In a village this size, people talked. One of the downsides of living here. It was ironic life had deposited Rachel next door to a prostitute or a madam, or whatever Red Mags was.

'As long as none of them are on the streets against their will, or trafficked, I don't have an issue.'

Mags leaned forward. 'Used to be a working girl myself. Still go out now and again. Some of the punters have a fancy for an older woman. 'Sides, I like to keep my eye on the younger lassies, you know. Some of them can be a bit daft, particularly when they're using.'

She glared at Rachel as if she were to blame.

'Go on,' Rachel said. This was the most info Mags had shared to date. She had to be worried.

'Ashely didn't go back to her bit last night.

'And that's unusual?'

'Yes. She never stays oot all night. Taffy would go looking for her if she did. As it happened Taffy was in the cells down at Burnett Road. Ashley's very young. She thinks of me as her mammy. She likes to check in with me. And I like to check in with her,' she added with a self-conscious grimace, pinking up.

'Maybe she's gone to visit someone? A friend perhaps?' Rachel asked, hoping Ashley wasn't lying in an alley or a dosshouse, shooting up. She decided to put it to Mags. The possibility must have occurred to the older woman.

'Aye, maybe in the past, that's where I would have found her but not the noo.' Emotion thickened her Glaswegian accent. In one of their over-the-fence chats, Mags had told her she'd lived in Glasgow until she'd married.

'How can you be so sure?' Rachel asked. Unfortunately it was where most prostitutes spent a chunk of their free time.

'Because she's pregnant, and aff the drugs, that's why.'

Sadness washed over Rachel. She knew the statistics. Many drug-abusing women wanted to give up using when they were pregnant. Too few succeeded.

'I know what you're thinking,' Mags said. 'But Ashley really wants that baby.'

'Maybe she's gone to stay with her parents?'

Mags shot Rachel an incredulous look. 'The lassie's mam is a waste of space. Took Ashley's stepda's word over her own daughter's when Ashley tried to tell her what the sick bastard was doing to her. Threw her out.' Mags's voice caught. 'Her own child! So naw, Ashley would never go there.'

It was a familiar story. Too many women on the streets were there because of abuse.

'Maybe she wanted some time on her own. If she wants to stay clean, perhaps she thought it best to distance herself from friends that still use?'

Mags gave an exasperated click of her tongue. 'No, I keep telling you. She wouldn't go far from me. Especially not now, when she has the baby to think of. She's scared of being on her own.'

'When did you last see her?'

'A couple of days ago. I've looked everywhere. All the usual places – asked about. No one has seen her. Not even Taffy, her boyfriend, tho as I said he was in the cells all Saturday night. He's worried too. She's not been near the centre either.'

'The centre?'

'Aye, the women's centre, No. 79. It's a place for working women, down near the hospital. Where we can get a cup of tea, or a shower, advice – methadone. See a doctor or a nurse. Pretty much anything.'

'Maybe she changed her mind about having the baby? Or had a miscarriage?'

'I've tried the hospital, but the fuckers wouldn't tell me nowt. Said I had to be next of kin. Should have effing lied.'

'Did you report her disappearance to the police?'

'Aye – not that they could give a flying fuck.' She pursed her lips and gave a disgusted shake of her head.

Rachel wasn't surprised the police hadn't been overly interested in a missing prostitute. Around a hundred people a week were reported missing across the Highlands and Islands, but the great majority resurfaced within twenty-four hours. The police tended to concentrate on tourists or walkers who went missing, assuming rightly or wrongly that *they* hadn't gone missing voluntarily and definitely wanted to be found.

'I'm telling you, there's nowhere else she'd go,' Mags continued. 'She'd come to me if she were in trouble. Summat's no right. I feel it in ma water!'

Living as she did, Mags's instincts were probably pretty reliable.

'How can I help?' Rachel asked.

'People will listen to you. You're not a nobody like me. You can phone the hospital – and the police, get them to look for her.'

Straight away Rachel thought of Du Toit. He might be able to help. It was worth a shot. But before she did that, she'd check with the office in the morning that no deaths of young females had been reported in the last two days.

She stood. 'I'll do what I can. Ask around. I'll let you know what I find out.'

Relief swept away some of the deep lines on Mags's face. 'I'm worried about her, you know.'

The concern in her voice was raw.

Mags walked Rachel to the door. 'What was going on yesterday morning?' she asked suddenly.

Rachel's stomach lurched. 'What do you mean?'

'That ruckus. With the drunks.' Mags paused to belch. 'I saw you pull a knife. I would have come to help, but you looked as if you was managing fine.' She jabbed another cigarette into her mouth, lit it and frowned. 'Would you have used it? Because – bit of advice, pet – never pull a knife unless you're prepared to use it.' She squinted at Rachel through a haze of smoke.

Rachel looked Mags directly in the eye. 'I don't know what you're talking about. There was no knife. I told the man I was a plainclothes police officer and that was enough to make him scarper.'

Mags frowned, then gave a bark of laughter. 'Oh, there was a knife all right, hen. And I think you would have used it.' She looked at Rachel with undisguised respect. 'You're like nae lawyer I've ever met. Pretending to be the polis, then pulling a knife. But let's say no more about it.' She opened the door for Rachel. 'Let me know as soon as you find anything out.'

TEN

TUESDAY

Mags still hadn't heard from Ashley by Tuesday morning, so as soon as Rachel arrived in the office she asked her colleagues whether there had been any reports of the death of a young woman over the weekend.

Everyone shook their heads. Apart from three deaths in a two car RTA, it had been a quiet few days for unexpected deaths, especially given it had been a holiday weekend.

'Why are you asking?' Alastair asked. He was spinning his iPhone with his finger.

'Because she's been reported missing.'

He chuckled. 'I'm surprised you're not out looking for her yourself; thought you were Inverness's answer to Wonder Woman.'

She ignored him, but jeez the guy did her head in. 'If anything comes in, could you let me know?'

She picked up the phone, dialled the number of the Inverness General Hospital switchboard and asked to be put through to medical records.

When the call was answered she gave her name and position with the Fiscal's office before asking the man on the other end whether they had an Ashley Carmichael as an inpatient on one of the wards. She listened to the tapping of a keyboard for a few moments. 'No. Not as an inpatient anyway.'

Rachel gripped the phone more tightly. 'In A&E then?'

'No. All I can see is an outpatient appointment a couple of weeks ago.'

'In maternity?'

'That's right. But that's all I'm allowed to tell you.'

Rachel thanked him and hung up.

Her next call was to Du Toit.

He picked up straight away. 'You couldn't even give it to lunchtime, could you,' he said tersely.

'Before we talk about Mrs Robertson, I've something else I want to ask you.' She explained about her next-door neighbour, what she did for a living, and that she was worried about one of the girls she'd taken under her wing. 'Ashley Carmichael, if that is her real name. I gather she's sixteen or seventeen – Mags wasn't sure. Slim, shoulder-length hair. Pregnant, although she might not be showing yet. You don't have her in the cells by any chance? Or' – and she really hoped not – 'found a body matching that description.'

'No bodies of young women in the last few days, as far as I'm aware. I'll find out about the cells. I'll ask patrol cars to keep a lookout, but don't hold your breath. Like it or not, a missing prostitute isn't going to be a priority with the constables.' His tone was clipped. Rachel was aware she was testing his patience. 'Remember the Highlands and Islands division is not your office's private force – or to be more accurate, *your* private force.'

'That's not fair,' Rachel retorted, stung. 'A missing, vulnerable, pregnant young woman is Police Scotland's business. Should be everyone's business.'

'I hear what you're saying, but she can't be a priority. If she doesn't turn up soon, that will be different.' Before Rachel could protest, Kirk continued. It sounded as if he were tapping the end of his pen on his desk. 'As far as Mrs Robertson is concerned, you were correct. It hasn't been treated as a suspicious death. The only reason it was referred to the PF was because it is mandatory when it comes to deaths involving pregnancies. The senior officer who attended the scene saw nothing to make her think the apartment needed to be secured. Mrs Robertson's parents have already been and cleaned the flat, I'm afraid. Let's hope for everyone's sake the officer's judgement was correct. They did, however, follow up with the ex-husband. He was babysitting his two daughters all evening – and his new girlfriend stayed over. I gather the pathologist put the time of death between 7 p.m. and 10 p.m. No way he could have popped out during that time without them noticing. The comment Mrs Robertson made to her husband about someone watching her, wasn't followed up. It should have been. I'll put Selena on it. In the meantime, the best thing you and I can do now is wait for the results of the PM.'

'What about the father of her baby?'

'I've put someone on it, but at this point Mrs Robertson is not a priority. Look, I've got to go.'

'Before you do, one last thing. Would you have followed this up?' Rachel had to ask.

A good thirty seconds passed before Du Toit replied: 'I would have asked a few more questions.'

ELEVEN

Annie Colston pulled her dressing gown tighter as she walked into the sitting room. Hearing the words *tired all the time* from a show on the TV, her attention was drawn to the image of a doctor with slicked-back hair discussing 'women's problems' with an overweight presenter. Annie plonked herself on the sofa, noting but uncaring that a flurry of dust almost obscured the TV.

'It's called TATT for short,' the doctor was saying smugly as he crossed one perfectly ironed trouser leg across the other. 'We GPs see it often, especially in middle-aged women.'

Tired all the time. Tatty. Yes, that's exactly how she felt. Too tired to clean the house, do the shopping, cook a meal, or any of the hundred and one things she knew she should be doing.

Heaving herself off the sofa, Annie padded into the kitchen where Radio 4 was blaring to the empty room. She rarely listened to what was being said: the constant noise made her feel less alone.

Reaching up to the top of the fridge, she felt past unopened cookery books and bowls containing buttons and discarded hair clips, until her fingers found what they were looking for. She eased the bottle of vodka down and studied it, tipping her head to the side. One more little drink couldn't hurt.

Splashing an inch into the tumbler, she hesitated and added one more. Then she carefully returned the bottle to its hiding place.

Swallowing a mouthful, she welcomed the heat as it hit her belly, savouring the spreading numbness. Taking her glass, she returned to her bedroom upstairs, trying to ignore the unmade bed and pile of unwashed clothes strewn around the floor.

She sat on the edge of the too-big double bed and dragged a brush through her hair. The children would be home from school any minute and she needed to put some clothes on before they did. She let her dressing gown fall to the floor. She should have waited to hear what the cure for TATT was. Maybe she should see her GP? Maybe he could give her something to take away this terrible lethargy that had been creeping into her bones since Caroline had died? God, was it already a year and a half ago? It seemed like yesterday. And was it really six months since David had left her?

'I don't recognise you any longer,' he had said the day he'd moved out. 'You make me feel old – old and trapped. I've tried to make things better between us but you've given up. Well, I'm too young to give up on life, Annie. I want— no,' he said, correcting himself, 'I *need* more than this.'

Perhaps if he had held her, coaxed her, she could have found the words to share her despair. She could have made him realise that it wasn't his fault, that in time things would get better. But he, baffled by her rejection, spent more time at work, and she couldn't blame him. She hadn't complained, glad that he had something that made him happy, knowing she was a millstone around his neck. When he told her he was leaving, she hadn't put up a fight, but with head bowed had simply acquiesced and watched silently, tears streaking her cheeks as he'd packed his bags. She didn't ask if there was someone else because she knew he would tell her and she couldn't bear to hear it.

As he left he had turned to her. 'I've said goodbye to the children but if you can't pull yourself together then you will leave me no choice but to sue for custody. If you can't do it for us, do it for them. They need their mother.' His tone softened. 'Please, Annie – try.'

She couldn't lose the children. Without them she might as well be dead. If David carried out his threat, Annie knew she'd simply curl herself into a ball and never get up again.

She was dragged from her endless ruminations by the sound of the children opening the front door. They bounded in carrying the sounds of their laughter and bickering with them. Once she would walk the short distance to meet them every day, but recently she had found excuses to avoid doing even that.

'Mum, get ready. Remember you promised to take us shopping today. To get Sophie's birthday present,' her daughter Susan called, divesting herself of bags and jacket on the hall floor, where they would lie until either Annie nagged her to pick them up or did it herself. Annie's heart sank. She had promised. It was a small thing to do for them, but they might as well have been asking her to climb K2.

Forcing herself to sound keen she replied, 'OK, give me a sec while I change.' Put a bra on and shuffle into last week's jeans was what she really meant.

She finished dressing and surveyed herself in the mirror. She looked awful but she would have to do. Giving herself a mental shake, she picked up her car keys and called to the children. 'OK. Into the car, guys. Let's go.' She started to go down the stairs but, without warning, she was overwhelmed by a feeling of nausea and a wave of dizziness. She grabbed at the banister and almost managed to grasp it but her fingers slid off the polished wood. She fell, banging her knees on the stairs and tumbling forward until finally she came to a stop at the foot of the stairs.

'Mum, Mum, are you all right?'

Annie looked up through a haze of pain into her children's anxious faces. Jack stepped away from his sister, frightened speechless.

'I'm OK,' Annie said, pushing herself into a sitting position. 'Help me up, would you.'

Her children came around to either side of her and, each grabbing an arm, strained to lift her.

'I'm fine,' Annie tried to reassure them when she was on her feet. 'My ankle's a bit sore, but I don't think anything's broken.'

Susan looked shocked and upset, but Annie, even through her fuddled state, recognised something else. Anger – and hurt.

'Oh, Mum can't you look after yourself? You've been drinking, haven't you? You're slurring your words. Well, I've had it. I don't want to live with you any longer. You don't care about us anymore. You don't even care about yourself. You were going to take us in the car. When you'd been drinking. You could have killed us.' With a look of contempt only a fifteen-year-old could perfect, Susan turned and ran up the stairs and into her room, slamming the door behind her.

Annie cast pleading eyes towards her son, who remained fixed to the spot. She held open her arms, wanting to offer comfort and, if she were honest with herself, to be given comfort in return.

He came into her arms but didn't return her hug. He stood stiffly, arms by his side. Annie let him go. He stepped back and with a last sad look he turned away and followed Susan upstairs.

What am I doing to these children? Annie swallowed the nauseating taste of her guilt and fear. If Susan told David what had happened, he would take them away, and she wouldn't have a hope in hell of winning them back. God, she needed another drink. But she couldn't. She and the children couldn't go on like this. Things needed to change and they would. She picked up her phone. Luckily, she knew exactly the person to call.

TWELVE

Rachel pulled up outside the main office of the social work department. It had taken a while to locate the place where her mother had last worked; who knew there were so many different departments and offices. The grey cement-rendered building was an ugly reminder of the building boom of the sixties.

She'd phoned earlier, explained to the woman on the other end of the phone that she was the daughter of Mary Ann McKenzie who had once worked there. Almost twenty minutes passed as she was transferred from department to department before she was transferred to the head of social work, who agreed to see her – if she could make it before six.

She was told to take the lift to the fourth floor where Mrs Winstaple would meet her.

Margaret Winstaple, the only staff member who had both worked with Rachel's mother and was available to speak to her, was waiting when the lift doors opened. She was in her early forties, Rachel guessed, with dark hair cut in a sleek bob. She was wearing a brocaded top over loose trousers. Beads hung around her neck. Her brown eyes were kind, her smile warm.

After they'd shaken hands, Rachel was ushered into a large, cluttered office.

'What can I do for you, Ms McKenzie?' Margaret asked after Rachel had refused a cup of tea and taken the proffered seat. 'You mentioned it was in connection with your mother?'

'Yes.' Rachel had thought about what she was going to say on the way over but had decided just to wing it. 'Do you remember her?'

'Yes, I do.' Margaret smiled. 'She was my manager's manager, the year before she left. I hadn't long started.'

'You didn't know her well then?' Rachel asked, her heart sinking.

'No. I'm afraid not. She wasn't *my* line manager, you understand. I only really saw her at departmental meetings. I liked her approach. Some heads of department in the public service can be very pedantic, frightened to make a decision, but your mother wasn't like that. Not at all. I've tried to take the same approach in my own practice, although to be honest it isn't always easy. Especially these days when social workers, particularly those in child protection, are damned if they do, damned if they don't.'

'Is that where my mother worked?'

'Almost certainly at some point during her career. But as I said, when I knew her, she'd not long been promoted to a senior manager and had the heads of different departments reporting to her.'

'What sort of departments?'

'Oh, the whole gamut – departments linked to housing, social security, older folk. We have a broad remit within social work. Our role is to offer support, practically and emotionally, to people when they are at their most vulnerable.'

'Were you ever aware of something in particular that worried her?'

Surprise flickered in brown eyes before Margaret grimaced.

'I'm certain she would have been worried about all sorts of things. In our field it's difficult to leave the job at the door. Her role would have been to supervise department heads who in turn would have had social workers reporting to them. It's unlikely your mother would have shared particular concerns she had with me – not unless they were directly related to a case I was involved with. Far more likely to have been the other way round: me reporting to her. If something *was* worrying her, she'd speak to her line manager.'

'Can you remember who that was?'

'Yes. As a matter of fact, I can. Mrs Goodall was her name. Your phone call brought a lot back about those days. She was quite a character. We were all terrified of her.' She smiled again. 'Goodall! Appropriate name for a social worker, I always thought. But as I remember, she had a reputation for being as tough with her clients as she was with the junior staff.'

'You don't happen to have an address for her?'

Margaret Winstaple narrowed her eyes at Rachel. 'Could I ask why you're asking me all about this? I heard' – she paused – 'we all heard what happened to your mother. It must have been absolutely dreadful for you. I can't imagine the shock.' She gave Rachel another sharp, inquisitive look. 'I didn't know her family situation, but it never made sense to me that she'd chuck her job without giving notice, or even a word to anyone. She simply wasn't like that. Too dedicated, for a start.' She looked into the middle distance. 'Then again this job gets to people. Some find they've had enough and leave.' Her gaze returned to Rachel. 'Why *are* you here after all this time?'

Rachel took a moment before answering. She'd always hated to open up to people, particularly about things that really mattered. But unless she did, she suspected Margaret wouldn't be as forthcoming as Rachel needed her to be.

'For years – probably right up until her body was found – I didn't want to think about Mum, let alone try to understand the woman I believed had walked out on me. I was so angry with her, and I believed Dad was too. We never spoke about her.' She took a steadying breath. 'Now, I guess I want to know as much about her as I can.' Rachel's chest tightened. She didn't tell the woman opposite her that was only part of the truth. 'I'm proud of the job she did. I want to know more about her – particularly her last days. Were they happy? Troubled?' She wound her fingers together so Margaret wouldn't notice them trembling.

Margaret gave a sympathetic smile. 'I understand. I'd feel the same if I were in your shoes. I know Nora – Mrs Goodall – was very fond of your mother. She's retired now. Living in Beauly, I believe.' She named a village not far from Clachnaharry. She scribbled something in a notebook, tore the page out and handed it to Rachel. 'I'm not going to give you her address. That needs to be up to her. But this is her number. She's one of the few people I know that still has a landline. I really shouldn't give it to you but I know Nora well enough to be sure she won't mind.'

Rachel took the paper from her and stood. 'Thank you. And thank you for seeing me.'

'It was good to meet you. I - hope you find whatever you are looking for.'

With Margaret's final words ringing in her ears, Rachel took the lift back down to the ground floor. She wasn't at all sure what she was looking for – or what the hell she was going to do when she found whatever it was.

THIRTEEN

Rachel had just stepped out of the shower and was towelling her hair when there was a knock on her door. She opened it to find Selena rocking back on her heels, hands shoved in the pockets of her padded jacket, an enormous grin on her face. 'Selena!' She stepped aside to let Selena come in.

'It's good to see you,' Rachel continued. 'But how did you find me?'

'Easy-peasy. I'm a detective now, so I am.'

'I'd heard. Du Toit told me. Congratulations.'

'Yeah. I was lucky to get a post so soon after passing the exam. I suspect I have DI Du Toit to thank.'

'Sitting room is this way,' Rachel said. 'I think your promotion has more to do with the fact you're a bloody good police officer.'

'Gee thanks, Rachel Luach, *Rachel the Warrior,'* Selena said, translating from Gaelic into English with a smile.

Although it was usual on the islands to give people Gaelic nicknames, this was too much, even in fun.

'God no! Don't call me that! More like Rachel who almost

wet her pants, or Rachel who needs to learn to run faster and take refresher lessons in self-defence.'

Selena grinned again. 'You're a warrior in my book. Let's set up a mutual fan club. We could meet up once a week, toast each other, and tell ourselves how bloody brilliant we are.'

It was unlikely to happen. A knot of regret lodged behind Rachel's ribs. They'd forged a bond in Uist but Rachel had never imagined they'd meet again so soon, if at all. She liked and respected Selena. But she didn't do friends.

'Make yourself at home while I dry my hair,' Rachel said.

Rachel emerged from her bedroom five minutes later to find Selena in the kitchen, Honey nestling in the crook of her arm, a cup of coffee in her hand.

'Cute house,' she said. 'Reminds me of my mam's. Do you know Clachnaharry – Clach na-h-Aithrigh in Gaelic – means stone of repentance?'

How fitting, Rachel thought, giving her guilty conscious another jab.

Selena put Honey down and rinsed her cup under the tap. 'Let's go for a walk and you can show me the area. At some point I'm going to have to find somewhere to live. I'm in an Airbnb at the moment while I look.'

As much as she liked Selena, Rachel didn't want her as a close neighbour. Some people might think her life lonely, but Rachel liked it just the way it was. Company when she wanted it, privacy when she didn't.

'OK.' Rachel grabbed a set of keys, ushered Selena out of the door and locked it behind them. 'It won't take long. The village is fairly compact. A couple of dozen houses and a pub.'

'Pub is good,' Selena said.

They walked along the canal until they came to the point where the canal flowed into the sea.

'How well do you know Inverness?' Rachel asked.

'I know the town a bit – came here shopping with Mam once or twice. But not nearly as well as I know Glasgow.'

Rachel pointed across the way. 'See that bridge?' she said. 'North Kessock and the Black Isle is on the other side of it.' She gestured to the right. 'The town centre and the Department of Justice is over there. But you'll know that, of course.'

'Aye, because I'm a detective,' Selena said, her eyes sparkling.

'Is that where you'll be based?'

'Apparently.'

'Then my office is in the same building.'

'I know that too.'

They walked through the village, which took less than five minutes, until they came to the path along the canal. They turned towards the sea mouth.

'With you gone, Fergus dead and MacVicar suspended, the force in Uist must be severely depleted,' Rachel said, referring to the case she and Selena had been involved in Uist that had ended in the death of the constable, who had, as it turned out, been one of the bad guys.

'It's been mayhem. It's a brand-new force. I thought they might prevent me from taking up the post with CID until things settled down. Luckily they didn't. I think they reckoned a clean slate was best.'

They crossed over a bridge and strode along the other side of the canal.

'One of the new recruits comes from Harris, another from Fort William, and the new sergeant is on secondment from Glasgow,' Selena continued, her hands thrust deep in her pockets. 'The highlanders will have a feeling for the customs and history but won't have the personal connections me and MacSticker had. That's both a good and bad thing, I guess.' Selena's mood grew sombre. 'How have you been? You look OK, but I guess it's not always on the outside where we hurt.'

Selena was bang on. 'I'm OK,' Rachel said. 'You?'

'I'll miss Uist, of course, but I can't wait to get stuck in. I'll be working with DI Du Toit in Serious Crime.' She flicked a glance Rachel's way. 'The inspector said you asked him to look into a case. A missing girl? He's also asked me to find out if there is evidence to support Mrs Robertson's belief she was being stalked.'

Du Toit had come through. Rachel shouldn't have doubted him.

Selena stopped to pick up a stone. She threw it into the canal where it skipped across the water three times before sinking. 'On the other hand,' she continued, 'he also warned me about becoming your personal link to Police Scotland. Or ever acting for you on an unofficial basis.'

Did he now? That was quick off the mark of him. And not very grateful, given what she'd done for Police Scotland.

They crossed to the other side of the canal, passing through the gate and over railway tracks.

'He said you told him that Mrs Robertson had a preference for no strings sex. Well, where does a woman go for that? To dating sites. So I thought I'd check if she was on any. Thighearna's a Dhia! Have you any idea how many sites there are? Over a thousand! And it's all profiles with names like Hot Babe, or Big Boy, or fun-loving gal.'

Rachel was annoyed with herself. She should have thought of asking Kirsty if Gillian was a member of any sites and if so, which ones. She was also impressed. Selena had got on it straight away.

'The pub is on the other side of the railway bridge,' Rachel said.

'In which case,' Selena said, a smile returning to her face, 'what are we waiting for? You can bring me up to speed over a glass of wine.'

FOURTEEN

'Hey,' Suruthi said. 'Fancy a snack?'

Rachel looked up from the PM results on her desk to find her colleague standing over her with a plate of homemade samosas. Suruthi often brought food from home to share with the office. Even Deputy Dawg found a reason to hang about the office kitchen when a raft of delicious smells wafted in Suruthi's wake.

As Rachel helped herself from the plate, Suruthi pulled up a seat next to her and slumped into it. Suruthi was immaculately groomed as usual, her thick, dark hair was twisted into a bun at the nape of her neck. She was lightly but expertly made up and impeccably dressed in a well-cut navy suit, but Rachel noted the pallor evident under her dark gold skin.

'Were you clubbing last night?'

'I wish.' Suruthi sighed.

'You OK?' Rachel asked.

'Not really,' Suruthi replied. 'Sometimes this job really gets to me.'

Dealing with death on a daily basis was bound to get to them all, but Suruthi had worked in the Death Unit longer than

any of them. Rachel would have thought she'd become accus-
tomed to it. As much as an empathetic human being could,
that was.

'Want to tell me about it?' she asked.

Suruthi sighed again. 'Alfred Daniels, ninety, with early
dementia was found dead in his home in Fort William last
month,' she began. 'It was only reported to us because there
were some concerns from social work. Tommy O'Brien, a carer
who came in once a week to help Alfred shower, noticed some
bruises on Alfred's torso. The first time he asked Alfred he was
fobbed off with a story about a fall, but three weeks later there
were fresh bruises. Alfred couldn't come up with a story on the
second occasion, only mumbled something about being
unsteady on his feet. Tommy knew in that case there would be
more bruises on his legs, his head even, but these looked as if
they'd been inflicted where they couldn't be seen. Tommy had
been there once or twice when the daughter had visited and did
not like her attitude towards her father. At first he put her
annoyance with her father down to Alfred's dementia – some
family members do find it difficult to accept, particularly at
first – but still it didn't sit right with Tommy. He thought
Alfred was afraid of his daughter. He reported his suspicions to
the social work department, but before they had time to visit –
the poor sods are as snowed under as the rest of us – the son
found his father dead in his chair. I got the report from the
pathologist last night. She found evidence of suffocation.
Anyway, I've asked the police to look into it. So far they've
come back with a significant balance in Alfred's bank account
and a daughter in financial difficulty. I'm waiting to hear what
else they come back with, but I'm pretty sure we have a case of
murder.'

'That's horrible,' Rachel sympathised, her mind immediately going to her mother. All these terrible things going on
behind closed doors. How could a daughter kill a father, a

husband, his wife, children their parents. Yet it happened. Time and time again.

'I can't imagine an Indian family treating their elderly parents like that. Although I guess it must happen,' Suruthi said.

'Yet horrific murders happen in India too. Think of that couple who got on the wrong bus…'

Clive looked up from his computer, a frown on his face.

'Hey, Rachel.'

The tone of his voice warned Rachel she wasn't going to like what he had to say.

'You were asking about a missing woman yesterday.'

Rachel's heart stalled. 'She's been found?' If the Death Unit knew about it, it had to mean she was no longer alive.

'Ashley Carmichael. Around seventeen years old?'

'Shit!' Rachel went to stand behind him and scanned the report on screen.

The body of a woman thought to be in her late teens had been found slumped behind a disused warehouse down at the harbour. A needle had been found still lodged in the deceased's arm and it appeared that she had overdosed. Her body had been removed to the mortuary for a PM and toxicology.

Whenever that might be, Rachel thought grimly. The pathologist had made it clear they were snowed under with work and the death of a prostitute from a drug overdose was unlikely to be a priority. But somebody should care. And she knew someone who did. Mags. Rachel's heart gave a tug, Did she know yet? She'd be devastated.

Rachel narrowed her eyes as she noted the day on the report. 'But this says her death was reported to us yesterday.' She peered closer to look at who had dealt with the report. She shouldn't have been surprised. Alastair Fuckwit Turnbull. The shit. He had been in the room when she'd asked everyone to look out for a report of a female death.

She rounded on Alastair, who was tapping something into his phone. 'Why didn't you tell me Ashley Carmichael had been found?'

He looked up and frowned. 'I was going to. But then you were off who knew where, and it must have slipped my mind.'

'Slipped your mind.' Rachel struggled to keep her voice even. 'If the death of a young woman in her teens makes no impact on you, maybe you're in the wrong job.'

Alastair's expression darkened. 'Where do you get off preaching to me? Have you ever considered that it's you that's in the wrong job? You get too involved.' He leaned back in his chair and regarded her calmly. 'As lawyers we need to keep our distance. Maybe you sympathise too much with those who operate on the wrong side of the law. Perfectly understandable, given your history.'

Rachel bit down on her rising fury. Even Fuckwit wasn't going to make her lose control.

'Steady on, old chap,' Clive said, as the others looked on in uncomfortable silence.

Alastair tossed his phone with one hand and caught it deftly in the other. 'And for your information, I'm not going to be working in this shithole for much longer. I'm off to Homicide.'

Taken by surprise, Rachel glanced Suruthi's way. It should have been Suruthi going to Homicide. She was next in line for promotion.

Rachel would have given anything to wipe the smug expression from Alastair's face.

It was where most fiscals – including Rachel – worked towards –the holy grail for fiscals: preparing and prosecuting people accused of murder in front of a judge and jury. It wasn't an easy career path, demanding a forensic eye for detail, the drive and conviction to see a case through, as well as an ability to stand in front of a judge and jury with confidence and conviction. It took years to climb up that particular pole but

Alastair, despite his lacklustre performance to date, was transferring to Homicide in half the usual time. Maybe because his father, Lord Turnbull, was a senior judge.

She became aware that Clive and Linda were focusing on their desks as if they held the secrets of the universe while Suruthi stared bug-eyed in the direction of Mainwaring's office. Rachel followed her gaze. Oh, Christ. Their boss was slumped against the doorframe as if his legs didn't have the strength to hold his corpulent frame upright, glowering at the room.

'I didn't realise I was in charge of a playground,' he said. 'On the contrary, I thought I was responsible for a team of professional men and women. Can anybody enlighten me as to what is going on here?' He punctuated his question with a hearty belch.

'I was letting everyone know that I'm moving to Homicide,' Alastair said with a smirk.

Douglas made no attempt to hide his distaste. 'And I am sure we all wish you luck – and the victims on whose behalf you will be prosecuting.' The last phrase was muttered under his breath but audible to everyone in the room. 'But I have something to say about that. As you probably realise, budgets are being cut.' He held up his hand as if to ward off their protests. 'I know there's hardly a budget left to cut, but there it is. The departments across the Crown Office and Procurator Fiscal Service are to be streamlined. Everyone will be working across all the different departments' – he glanced in Alastair's direction – 'with the exception of Homicide where, as Mr Turnbull has informed you, he will be working there full-time reporting to the advocate depute.' Douglas couldn't have sounded more depressed if he'd been told the world was about to end.

There was a stunned silence.

Their boss rubbed his sternum with a podgy hand and grimaced. His notorious indigestion was clearly bothering him. 'In the meantime,' he continued, 'will the lot of you get back to your desks? The last time I looked, we had a backlog to clear. And given we are going to be a man short soon, I expect you all' – he stared pointedly at Alastair – 'to put your noses to the grindstone – close enough to rub them raw.'

As soon as she could, Rachel left the office for home. Selena had phoned Rachel to apologise for not letting her know about Ashley in person. 'The officers who had been called to the scene had pegged Ashley's death as a simple overdose – still do – so didn't think we needed to know, otherwise I would have called you immediately.' Her voice softened. 'Sorry, Rachel. I know you hoped for a different outcome.'

They agreed to meet down at the harbour where Ashley's body had been found. The area, known locally as the Ferry, was one of the most deprived in Inverness, although only a short walk through a park and along the canal to where Rachel lived.

Rachel arrived before Selena. The harbour was dreich enough during the day, but at night, when the workers had left for the day, the sex workers not yet taken to the streets, it was a godforsaken place, had the air of a part of Inverness that had been left behind following an apocalyptic event. A place no one would come to at night unless they were operating on the wrong side of the law.

As a cold wind whistled off the sea, a loud throttle cut through the silence and Selena drew up on a motorbike. She took off her helmet and climbed off her bike.

'Thighearna's a Dhia! What a dump.' Selena kicked an empty can into a ditch.

It was a thoroughly depressing place to work and die. Discarded syringes and condom wrappers, fast food packaging, cigarette ends and disposable vapes lay in the roads and gutters; a pair of men's underpants hung from the branch of a tree.

'Her body was found down here,' Selena said, leading the

way down a path behind an empty building. It was dark and stank of urine. At one time there must have been occupied houses in the field behind, but now they were deserted, the windows, like those of the other disused buildings, boarded up.

'Who found her?' Rachel asked.

'A worker, nipping into the lane for a quick pee on his way to work.'

Another wasted life, another pointless death. A lonely place to die. There was nothing more to see.

'Have the family been informed?' Rachel asked as they left the alley.

'Yeah. Apparently they weren't surprised. Or upset. They're coming to identify her in a few days. When the mother can get time off work.'

'A thought occurred to me on the way here,' Rachel said. 'Sparked by you. I wonder if Ashley had an online presence. Mags might know.'

'Mags?'

'My next-door neighbour. Also a sex worker. It was her who reported Ashley missing.'

Selena's eyebrows shot up. 'You live next door to a sex worker? Cool.'

Rachel smiled. 'She's quite a character.'

Selena put her helmet on and climbed on her motorbike.

'Someone should speak to her. Find out if she had a boyfriend or a minder. If she had any regulars. Who gave her the smack, even,' Rachel suggested.

Selena kicked the starter. 'I'll get on it first thing tomorrow.' She grinned. 'I think I'm going to be good at this detecting stuff.'

A short while later, Rachel knocked on Mags's door, dreading having to give the older woman the news about Ashley.

Mags opened the door, her eyes bloodshot, the signature red

lipstick absent. She reminded Rachel of a deflated balloon. 'Oh, it's you,' she grunted. 'I suppose you're here to tell me about Ashley. You'd better come in then.'

Rachel followed her into the sitting room and sat on the sofa while Mags took her favourite chair next to the fireplace. She prodded the dying coals with the poker as if stabbing someone she hated. The heat in the room was suffocating.

'I am so sorry, Mags.'

'Aye, well. Probably nothing you could have done about it. But she was found yesterday morning. I'd have thought you'd have heard before the rest of us and let me know.'

She gave Rachel an accusatory look.

'I only found out this morning.'

Mags hauled herself to her feet and the ornaments on the mantelpiece. She rearranged a china shepherdess, slippered foot peeping from her long dress, moving it to the front of a fluted vase and placing it next to a photo of a young woman Rachel hadn't noticed before.

'Did Ashley advertise her services online?' Rachel asked.

'Naw. We all prefer the old ways. We can keep an eye on each other that way.'

That hadn't worked out very well.

'What was the stupid bint doing, taking drugs?' Mags turned to face Rachel, her eyes moist. 'She promised me, and the doctor, she was giving up the drugs for the sake of the baby – and I believed her – even if the doctor didnae. I told her I'd help her stay aff the drugs. I even told her she could move in here with me. Stay until after the baby was born and she was back on her feet. That way I could have kept an eye on her – on them both. I've a bit of money saved. We would have managed.'

'She probably meant it when she said she was going to give up,' Rachel said gently, 'but staying clean isn't easy.'

'She managed more than a month! The Centre promised

that they would support her any way they could – and with me helping too, she had a real chance.'

Recalling what the hospital had said about Ashley having had a recent outpatient appointment, Rachel was struck by a thought. 'The doctor you mentioned. Was this her GP? Or someone she saw at the hospital?'

'No, the one at the hospital. She had one of these appointments with the doctor they give women like her – vulnerable, disadvantaged, whatever term is in fashion. I went in with her to give her support. I wasnae going to let anyone bully her into getting rid of it when she didnae want to. The doctor was nice enough but didnae have a clue about what life is really like for us. I could see she didn't believe Ashley would manage to give up the H.' Mags took a deep, shuddering breath. 'And she was right, as it happens.'

'What was the name of the doctor? Do you remember?'

'Don't see what it matters, but of course I remember. It's an easy enough name. Burns it was.'

Rachel's mind raced. Two pregnant women had died recently and they were both patients of Dr Burns. It had to be a coincidence. Kirsty Burns probably saw hundreds of pregnant women in the course of her work. Nevertheless, it might be worth another chat with Kirsty. It was certainly worth mentioning to Du Toit. And definitely time to chase up Gillian Robertson's PM.

FIFTEEN

Almost a week after her last ever drink – or so she hoped – Annie found herself in the waiting room of the gynae department in the Inverness General Hospital.

Eventually her name was called and she was ushered into the doctor's room and told to take a seat. As the doctor turned away from pecking at her computer keyboard to smile at her, Annie realised with a sinking heart that she recognised her. Dr Kirsty Burns. They'd worked together briefly when Annie had been the charge nurse on acute psychiatry and Kirsty had been doing her junior doctor rotation. They'd gone for drinks a few times but when Annie had gone on maternity leave and never returned to work, they'd lost touch.

'Annie! How have you been?'

'OK. You know how it is. I didn't know it would be you I'd be seeing. I was told it would be a Dr Ballantyne.'

'He's my consultant. We share the clinic. You can see him if you'd prefer?'

'No. It's fine. A little embarrassing perhaps.' Annie smiled half-heartedly, shifting uncomfortably in her chair. 'My GP pulled strings to get me seen quickly.'

The women spent a couple of minutes bringing each other up to date. Annie learned that Kirsty had a three-year-old daughter, no mention of a husband, and that she'd been working in rural Zambia until her return six months ago. Her eyes had clouded then, and she'd bitten her lip. Clearly the memory gave her no pleasure.

Annie wondered what caused the flash of sadness, but she didn't ask. It didn't seem appropriate in the circumstances.

As Kirsty brought Annie's records up on her computer screen, Annie scrutinised her. Her ex-colleague looked terrible. There was no other way to put it. Annie remembered her as a vivacious, energetic and caring doctor who always looked the consummate professional. Although she was still striking, today she looked, well, haggard, as if she'd recently lost weight. No amount of make-up could hide the dark circles under her eyes.

Kirsty looked up from her computer. 'I see you lost your sister eighteen months ago. I am so very sorry.'

'Thank you.' Annie's GP must have felt it was relevant to have added it to her referral letter. She'd wondered what else he'd included. She'd admitted to him that she drank too much.

'So what brings you to see me?' Kirsty asked.

Annie took Rachel through her symptoms, although she was bound to get everything she needed from the referral letter from her GP. All the intimate details of her life – the stuff she'd rather keep secret – permanently entered in her medical records. As Annie talked, Kirsty tapped at her keyboard, entering Annie's answers.

'I'm sorry,' she said, 'but if I don't do this now, I might not get a chance to update your records for a couple of days. And I don't like to do that.'

She typed some more before turning her attention to Annie again.

'I'll need to take blood and order a few tests,' she said. 'It sounds to me as if you might have a cyst, probably benign, but I won't know for sure until I get the results back. Could you roll up your sleeve?'

'*Probably* benign,' Annie echoed, shocked. 'It hadn't occurred to me that it could be anything but benign. I thought I'd had all the bad luck I was going to get for the next few years at least.'

'I don't think it is cancer. I'm being ultra-cautious. Regardless, I'd like to do a laparoscopy – you know where we stick a scope down a small hole in your belly button. If you do have a cyst, we could remove it at the same time. It can be done as a day case.'

'Damn. I don't really want to take time off... I recently started a new job. Well, job might be too grand a word for it. It's a part-time receptionist position at No. 79.'

Once more, Kirsty looked surprised.

'The clinic around the corner from here?' Kirsty released the tourniquet from Annie's arm. 'I refer quite a few of my patients there and see women they refer to me. What do you think of it?'

'I've only been there once so far. My friend got me the position. They seem to do a good job with the resources available, but it's no silver bullet. The majority trying to come off drugs seem to fall by the wayside sooner or later. They've lost five women to drugs in the last twelve months, one the other day.'

Peggy had phoned her to let her know and to warn her that the other women were distraught, even though they were doing their best to pretend not to be.

Kirsty stuck a plaster on Annie's arm and indicated that she could roll down her sleeve.

'Despite all that, I think I'm going to enjoy working there,' Annie mused. 'It's interesting and it helps me take my mind off my own problems.' Annie's voice cracked and Kirsty looked at her with sympathy.

'That's you,' Kirsty said, filling the specimen bottles. 'I'll try and get you in as soon as I can. If you can come in at short notice, that would help.'

'The sooner the better,' Annie said. 'It would be one less thing to worry about.'

Kirsty stood to indicate the appointment was over. 'Take it easy in the meantime, and I'll see you back soon.'

SIXTEEN

Rachel was brewing her first coffee of the morning when Alastair came into the tiny kitchen and closed the door behind him.

Rachel turned to face him. She wasn't short but in the tiny room he still towered over her. She hated him being in her space but she stood her ground.

'I gather you've been looking into one of my cases. Again! What is the matter with you? Don't you have enough work of your own to be getting on with? Although it hasn't escaped my notice that you spend more time out of the office than in it.'

'It's none of your business how I spend my time.'

'But it is my business when you get in amongst my cases. Did you seriously think I wouldn't find out? I've got mates in the police force too.' He narrowed his eyes at her. 'Does Douglas know?' He read her silence correctly. 'He doesn't, does he?'

'Look, I knew Gillian Robertson from school. Her friend Kirsty Burns said you wouldn't answer her calls. All I did was give them the time they should have had from you!'

'I am your senior, Rachel. I have much more experience

than you, you should respect that. The reason I didn't return Dr Burns's call is that I had nothing to tell her. I was waiting for the result of the post-mortem which is the correct thing to do. We are stretched, the pathologists are stretched, the police are stretched, it makes everything worse when we set everyone off on wild goose chases. It means we have fewer resources when we really need them.'

He had a point. But he could have met with Kirsty. How much of his time would that have taken?

'Now we've got that out of the way, I will give you the courtesy of letting you know I've heard back from the pathologist. She is satisfied, in the absence of a report from toxicology which she expects any day, that Mrs Robertson died from natural causes. Sad. But not a death anyone could have prevented. I have informed the family that if toxicology comes back clean, which I fully expect, they can go ahead and bury their daughter.'

Rachel stared at him until he moved aside to let her pass. Bugger Alastair Turnbull. Rachel still had questions that needed answers.

As soon as she'd parted ways with Alastair, Rachel phoned Kirsty and asked if she could come and see her.

'You have news about Gillian?'

'Yes. The results of her PM came back. The cause of death has been recorded as inconclusive but most likely due to loss of blood following a catastrophic haemorrhage. The pathologist is waiting for the toxicology results, but unless they are significant in any way, Mr Turnbull expects to release her body to the family so they can go ahead with her funeral.'

'I guess I should be happy. At least I know for sure she didn't die because I missed something. But about the toxicology

– something else has happened that you should know. I was about to call you to ask if we could meet.'

'Tell me now.'

'I'd rather wait until we meet.'

'Today?'

'If it's to be today – and I think that's best – I'm going to have to ask you to come to the hospital again. I have ward rounds in the morning and theatre in the afternoon. I could buy you a rotten lunch in the hospital canteen if you like?'

'That's an offer I can't refuse. What time?'

'Say about one?'

'See you there.'

Kirsty met Rachel at the door of the hospital canteen. The doctor looked tired and stressed.

The canteen was buzzing; almost every table taken, the hum of conversation not quite drowning out the clink of cutlery on plates. They grabbed a couple of trays and surfed the array of offerings in deep steel trays that had been inserted into steaming water to keep them lukewarm. They'd clearly been there for some time.

Kirsty wrinkled her nose as she asked for macaroni cheese. 'Eating in the canteen is an easy way to keep the weight off. There's a great coffee shop cum deli across the road, but I almost never get enough time to go there for lunch.'

They took a table in the corner, as far away from other people as they could manage.

Rachel speared a chunk of fish with her fork. It tasted pretty much how it looked: dry and tasteless. She took a gulp of water to wash it down. 'Do you remember an Ashley Carmichael? I believe she was a patient of yours.'

'Can I ask why you want to know?'

'Her body was found a couple of days ago. It looks like she overdosed.'

'Oh, no! That's so sad. And disappointing.'

'You remember her then?'

'Oh yes. I don't even have to bring up her notes to remind myself. She was a sweet woman – barely more than a child – a sex worker. Although I see so many women like Ashley at my clinic, she stuck out. She was referred by No. 79 – it's a small centre close to the hospital that acts as a resource for vulnerable women. She came with an older woman – a rather fierce redhead – in tow. Ashley was pregnant. Desperate to keep her baby. Touchingly determined to do the best for her unborn child. Even tried to give up drugs. She had big plans to stay clean, get off the streets. Not everyone I see in my antenatal clinic cares as much.' She pushed her half-eaten plate of maca- roni and cheese to the side. 'These young women should have their whole lives in front of them. We should be doing more to help them get off drugs and off the streets. I'd allowed myself to hope that Ashley might be one of those that made it. There was something different about her. Not just that she wanted to keep the baby. It was as if she saw her pregnancy as a way out. A reason for choosing a different life, a better life. She didn't even seem keen to go on the methadone programme. Thought it would harm the baby, despite my reassurances.'

Rachel would pluck them all off the street if she could. Put them in the care of someone like Gillian. At least give them options.

'Could Gillian have met her?'

Kirsty gave Rachel a curious look. 'Yes. If she attended A&E, which is entirely possible. The same people have a habit of returning – especially addicts. They're often found semicon- scious by police and bystanders and brought in. They're also prone to abscesses and other infections and tend to pitch up in A&E when things get really bad. I could look it up on the system, if you like. If she attended A&E it will be recorded.' She looked thoughtful for a moment as if running something through her mind. 'Why do you ask?'

Rachel answered with a question of her own. 'Did Gillian use dating sites?'

Kirsty frowned. 'Yes, but she stopped when she discovered she was pregnant.'

'Did you know which ones she used?'

'It never occurred to me to ask. Why do you want to know? Do you think it might lead to the person she thought was stalking her?'

'The police are following that up.' Unless Alastair had called them off. 'The last time we met, you said you thought a Jamie De Banzie might have been the father of Gillian's baby,' Rachel continued. 'Why did you think that?'

'Apart from seeing them together down by the canal? Hospitals are terrible rumour mills. Jamie is often my anaesthetist when I operate. And theatre staff gossip. Jamie has a reputation for screwing around. According to rumour, his wife found out he was having an affair – not the first, apparently – and kicked him out. That's when he moved into the houseboat. You know the ones I mean?'

Rachel did. If she took the right side of the canal on her way home, she passed them. They were moored close to Ness Park where Ashley's body had been found. Rachel mentally filed the fact. Kirsty leaned forward as if she were about to confide in her when a man in green scrubs with thick wavy hair, broad shoulders and an overly white smile, plonked a tray on the table.

'At last! Dr Kirsty Burns,' he said. 'I've being trying to track you down for days.'

'Speak of the devil and he's sure to appear,' Kirsty muttered. 'Rachel, this is Dr James De Banzie. Dr De Banzie, Miss McKenzie. Rachel is an old friend. A lawyer with the Fiscal's office now.'

He acknowledged Rachel with a tip of his head, pulled out a chair and sat down. 'I wanted to say how sorry I was to hear about Gillian,' he said to Kirsty. 'I only heard when I got back from Rome. She was a great nurse. A wonderful person.'

Kirsty gave him a tight smile.

'Do you know the cause of death yet?' Jamie asked. 'The police have been to see me, but they won't tell me bugger all. I don't even know how they knew she and I had something going on. Gilly didn't want anyone to know.' He paused, leaned back in his chair and studied Kirsty for a long moment. His eyes slitted. 'It was you who told them, wasn't it? She told you. I guess that makes sense. You were friends.' It was as if he'd forgotten Rachel was there.

'Did you know she was pregnant?' Kirsty asked.

Jamie hesitated and a myriad of emotions crossed his face. 'The police told me. They wanted to know if I was the father.'

'And were you?'

'No. At least as far as I know.'

'Gilly didn't tell you she was pregnant?' Kirsty asked, not attempting to hide her disbelief.

'No.' Something shifted behind his eyes. 'I haven't seen her outside work for weeks. Not since she finished it.'

'Gilly finished it?' Kirsty exclaimed, her eyes widening. The revelation, if it were true, had clearly taken her by surprise.

'You didn't know? Maybe your friend didn't tell you everything after all.' His mouth twisted in an ugly sneer. 'Is that why you dislike me? You think that I'm some kind of serial one-nighter who is only interested in women for sex?'

'It's true, isn't it?' Kirsty fired back.

'What's true? That I like sex or that I have a preference for one-night stands?'

'Actually, I don't give a damn about your personal life. It's your professional one that bothers me.'

'Specifics, please.'

'Take yesterday, for example. That baby could have died because of the time it took to get the section done. If your boss hadn't shown up, that's probably what would have happened. Where were you? In some sluice groping a medical student?'

'For the record,' Jamie said, all hint of amusement leaving his eyes, 'the reason I was late getting to the call yesterday was because I was too busy in ITU trying to save a young motorcyclist's life. Like most registrars I find it difficult to be in two places at once. A problem we all share, I'm sure you'll agree. And as for Gillian, if she didn't tell you she was the one who blew me off, maybe you weren't as close as you thought?'

Kirsty flinched as the barb struck home. 'What did you tell the police about the possibility you were the father?' she asked.

Rachel stayed quiet, content to let Kirsty ask the questions while she observed Jamie's reactions.

'I told them it was possible. The dates worked.' Sadness washed across his face. 'I wish she had told me herself.'

'Really?'

'Yes. Really. I would have wanted to be part of his life. I realise you think I'm a piece of shit, but I would never abandon my child. I've always wanted kids.' He smiled tightly. 'I would have taken him to football matches, taught him to throw a ball. I would have done everything I could to be a decent father.' Anger flashed in his blue eyes as he picked up his tray. 'She had no right to keep all that from me.'

SEVENTEEN

You don't like him much, do you?' Rachel said to Kirsty when Jamie left.

'I don't like men who think they're God's gift to women. But I was a bit unfair on him there, if I'm honest. The baby I goaded him about is doing fine. And I do know what it's like when you're expected to be in two places at once. I can't bear the thought of anything going wrong with any of my patients, and that makes me a bit OCD-ish. That's why what happened yesterday...' she tailed off. 'To be honest, I can't see him having anything to do with Gillian's death.'

Rachel was less sure. He gave the impression of a man who didn't like being ditched. It was also clear he did not like Gillian making decisions about her pregnancy without including him. Gillian might well have let him into her flat. Furthermore, he lived close to the park where Ashley's body had been found. However, none of that meant anything without evidence. She'd pin the thought in the meantime.

'You said you had something to tell me,' Rachel said to Kirsty.

'Yes. I probably should have called you last night, but I wanted to think it over.'

Since Jamie's departure, Kirsty had been steadily and methodically ripping up her paper serviette, rolling up each shredded piece and plonking them in her now empty coffee cup.

Rachel gave her an encouraging smile. 'Why don't you tell me what it is and let me decide if it's important.'

Kirsty rammed the last piece of serviette into the cup and sighed. 'This morning one of the A&E nurses took me aside. She knows Gilly and I were good pals.' She took a juddering breath. 'There's a rumour going around that someone's been pilfering morphine from the controlled drug cupboard.'

'That doesn't sound good.'

'People are blaming Gillian.'

'What on earth would make them think that?'

'Because people are idiots. And hospital staff love a bit of drama.' She chewed on her bottom lip. 'To be fair, two vials did go missing, but accusing Gilly of having taken them when she's not around to defend herself is not only ridiculous but unfair.'

'What do you think happened?'

'What do you know about how drugs in hospitals are administered?'

'Zilch.'

'Drugs like morphine are heavily controlled. In the past they went missing regularly, usually taken by staff with a habit. These days there are procedures in place to prevent this happening. In every ward and department, the nurse in charge holds the keys to the controlled drug cupboard. When a drug is needed, two nurses check the dose, witness it being given to the patient, and sign the drug register, accordingly. Gillian was a keyholder as was Suzi. Or, if they were both off duty, whoever was in charge of the ward that day. The keys have to be kept on that person at all times.'

'And Gillian was in charge the day they went missing?'

'Exactly.'

'What day was that?'

'The Wednesday before she died.'

'Have you spoken to the police about this?'

'No. Because I don't believe it. Gillian would never steal drugs, let alone take them. Especially when she was pregnant. The very idea is ridiculous!'

'Do you think this was what Gillian wanted to tell you?'

'I don't think so.' She shook her head. 'But I don't know. She didn't strike me as being annoyed the day we agreed to meet. If she thought anyone suspected her of stealing controlled drugs she would have been furious. Anyway she said she wanted to speak to me about Dr Ballantyne.'

'All the same, you must tell the police about the morphine. As well as what people are saying.'

Kirsty sighed. 'I know. But I wish I didn't have to. I don't want to tarnish Gilly's reputation. Imagine the gossip if the police get involved. Especially when Gilly isn't here to defend herself.' Tears welled in her eyes. 'God, I miss her! I thought my life was on the up, now it's disappearing down the plughole faster than the Corryvreckan whirlpool.' She sniffed and thumbed the tears from her cheeks. 'You must think me a bit of a headcase.' She gave a weak smile. 'I'm not usually so emotional.'

Rachel thought of the work piling up on her desk. The reports she had to write. The prep required for cases coming to court. She couldn't imagine the ex-prefect, the kind but profes-sional nurse, stealing morphine; and, as she'd pointed out to Kirsty, the toxicology report would exonerate her. However, by that time the damage to Gillian's reputation would be done. Rachel still had a debt to pay. 'Do you have to rush off anywhere?' she asked Kirsty.

'I have theatre in' – Kirsty glanced at her phone – 'forty minutes.'

'Is the nurse you mentioned on duty now?

'Suzi? Yes. I saw her earlier.'

'In that case, why don't we speak to her and find out if there's any truth in the rumour.'

EIGHTEEN

The nurse in charge of A&E, Suzi Matthews, greeted Kirsty with genuine warmth and Rachel with curiosity. The department was quiet with only about a dozen patients occupying the waiting area.

Kirsty introduced Rachel as a lawyer from the Fiscal's office.

Suzi blanched. 'Is there a problem? No one's reported a mistake or anything like that?'

Hospitals were required to report potentially criminal medical mishaps to Rachel's department, as well as unexpected deaths.

'Not as far as I'm aware.' Rachel came straight to the point. 'Yesterday, you told Dr Burns the rumours about Mrs Robertson and some missing morphine. What can you tell me about it?'

'None of that stuff came from me,' Suzi protested. Her indignation was either real or a very good act. 'I didn't believe it for a second. Gillian was an amazing nurse – a real credit to the department.'

'But...' Rachel prompted, getting the impression there was something Suzi wasn't saying.

Suzi sighed. 'But morphine did go missing a few days before Gillian died. And, as nurse in charge that shift, she held the keys.'

'When did you realise it was missing?' Rachel asked.

'Gillian and I went to count the drugs at the end of the shift, as we always do, and there were two vials missing. We're often so busy here, it's possible that it was used and never signed for – although that shouldn't happen. But that day we had a multiple RTA – a road traffic accident – and it was chaos in here with doctors and nurses all over the shop. The morphine could easily have been used in the mayhem and the member of staff – most likely one of the doctors – forgot to record it. Management seemed to accept that this was the most likely explanation. No one in the department considered even for a moment that Gillian might have taken it. God, she's worked here for over six years. She'd never do a bloody stupid thing that could so easily be found out. But then the rumours started circulating that she'd died from an overdose.'

'That's not true!' Kirsty snapped. 'Whatever gave people that idea? Gilly would never have killed herself! The very idea is absurd! Who started the rumour?'

Suzi glared back at Kirsty. 'I don't know where it started. You know what the hospital grapevine is like! There's all sorts of talk going around. That Gillian miscarried and was so upset she overdosed on the morphine.' She gave Kirsty a look filled with pity and her tone softened. 'You found her, didn't you? That must have been awful. A terrible shock. You were very close, I know.'

'It was one of the worst days of my life,' Kirsty said quietly. 'And that includes the day my husband died. But Gillian did not take her own life, deliberately or accidentally.'

'Was it you who reported the missing morphine?' Rachel asked Suzi.

'Yes. I didn't want to tell them, honestly, Dr Burns, but I

knew management would need to know and it would look strange for me if I didn't say anything. I was the only other person to have the keys to the controlled drugs cupboard that day.'

'Who else had access to the drugs?' Rachel asked. 'You said it might have been administered during the road traffic accident. You mentioned doctors.'

'Apart from the doctors, the nurses and pharmacy who replenish the trolley for us?' She addressed Kirsty again: 'You know what it's like when we have multiple patients in with life-threatening injuries. The resus trolley was probably lying open for a time. It's possible someone could have slipped it into their pocket without being noticed.'

'Do you remember who was working that day? Besides you and Gillian?' Rachel asked Suzi.

'I can't. Not exactly. The rota will tell us which nurses were working, if you want to have a look. But it won't necessarily tell us which doctors, apart from the A&E consultants, were down here. I could ask around and see if any of the nurses remember, if you like? Come to think of it, there would also have been plaster room technicians, porters, paramedics, phlebotomists, clerical staff. Tons of people.'

'What about patients?'

'That should be easier.' She frowned. 'Or maybe not. We register all the patients who are seen, of course, but not the people who came in with them. I guess any one of them could have taken the drug.' Suzi thought for a moment. 'The department was going like a fair. Usually Gillian thrived on the buzz when the department was busy. But that day, apart from the RTA, we had a couple of trauma patients. A young guy who had fallen – or jumped – from a bridge. He's still in a coma in the neuro ward. And a little girl came in with terrible burns.' Suzi grew animated as she remembered. 'God, yes, the wee girl – Amy – she's still in paeds. Gillian called social services. She was pretty certain, we all were, that the injuries weren't accidental – that they were caused by the mother and boyfriend. There was a scene with the boyfriend. In fact, I remember now, he threatened Gillian. That happens so often it no longer sticks out as being unusual. Perhaps he stole the morphine? He was a nasty piece of work.'

'It's possible,' Kirsty said.

Laying the theft at Gillian's door seemed pretty thin to Rachel. It sounded as if anyone could have taken it. On the other hand, although Suzi and Kirsty seemed certain Gillian hadn't taken it, they could be wrong. Nobody knew people as well as they thought. Everyone was capable of doing something out of character. Even the people you trusted the most were capable of letting you down or, even worse, deceiving you.

But the immediate question Rachel had to consider was whether the missing morphine was a factor in Gilly's death.

'Did Mrs Robertson ever mention that she was being followed, or watched?' Rachel asked Suzi.

'No!' Suzi replied. She gave Rachel a curious look. 'Why do you ask?'

'I'm following up on something her ex-husband said.'

'The last shift she worked – on the Friday? Were you on with her?' Kirsty asked, before Suzi could quiz Rachel.

'Yes. I was.'

'Gillian wanted to speak to me about something – and I don't think it was about the missing morphine. She said it was to do with Dr Ballantyne. We were due to meet up the following day and she was going to tell me then. Do you have any idea what it might have been? Did she say anything to you?'

'No, except' – she thought for a minute – 'Now you mention Dr Ballantyne, his wife came to see Gillian a day or two before she died.'

'Do you know why she wanted to see her?' Rachel asked, with a quick, sideways look at Kirsty.

'All I know is that she insisted on having a word with Gillian. She seemed a little agitated, distressed even. Said she had fallen while horse riding but didn't think she'd hurt herself. She refused to let us clerk her in. Said she simply wanted a chat with Gillian. Gillian didn't make any notes. At least as far as I know. That's what made the visit a little strange.' Suzi shrugged. 'But it could've been about anything...'

When a health care assistant arrived at the nurses' station, the three women moved away.

Suzi took a clipboard from a passing nurse with a smile of thanks. 'I've been thinking about the missing morphine. You know that we have CCTV coverage of the department? Not all of it, but it's possible whoever took the morphine is on camera. It's worth a shot. It would be an easier way of finding out who was in the department that day. It might even have a clip of someone acting suspiciously or hanging about the resus trolley.'

'How do we get a look at the footage?' Rachel asked.

'Who do we speak to?' Kirsty asked Suzi at the same time.

'I think the porters are responsible for monitoring the cameras. Why don't you go along to their office and speak to someone?'

The wail of an ambulance cut through the department. 'I'd better go and see what's coming in,' Suzi said. 'I'm sorry if I haven't been much help.'

The doors at the end of the corridor swung open and a trolley with three staff by its side was pushed through. The women stood to the side to let it rush past. The patient was being worked on by a nurse and a junior doctor. Judging by the blue-tinged lips and clammy pallor, Rachel didn't hold out much hope for the middle-aged man.

'We'll let you get on,' Kirsty said to Suzi.

Thank you. You've been a great help,' Rachel added.

Suzi was already moving alongside the trolley, and simply waved her hand in acknowledgement. 'I'll get back to you if I find out anything,' she called over her shoulder before disappearing behind a door marked RESUS.

Rachel turned to Kirsty. 'Do you think Mrs Ballantyne's visit was what Gillian wanted to speak to you about?' Rachel asked.

'I don't know – I guess so,' Kirsty said. 'I can't think of a reason why she would want to. Gilly never mentioned that they knew each other, so it is a bit strange.' She glanced at her watch. 'You still up for checking out the CCTV?'

NINETEEN

Rachel and Kirsty had to walk to a different building to find the porters' office. The small windowless room where they hung out was down a little-used corridor in a part of the hospital Kirsty confided she had never been to before. The grey-clad porters were drinking coffee and chatting.

One sprang to his feet and placed his mug on the table. He looked guilty. But these days everyone looked guilty to Rachel. His colleagues slunk away.

'What can I do for you, Doctor?' he asked, having peered at Kirsty's badge.

'I'd like to speak to whoever is in charge of the CCTV cameras,' Rachel said after showing him her ID.

'That would be Johnny, the head porter. Can I ask why?'

'There was an incident in A&E a short while back,' Kirsty said. 'I want to ask him if he saw anything on camera.'

The man sniggered. 'There's always an incident in A&E. I don't know if he'll be able to help you, love. But you can ask him yourself. No skin off my nose.' He sank into his chair again and took a swig of his drink. He pointed a grubby thumb to his left. 'He's next door.'

The room next to the porters' office was equally airless. At a desk, facing three monitors, sat a man in his fifties. He looked like a man at peace with himself, his large hands resting comfortably on a stomach that testified to the enjoyment of more than the occasional pint. The impression was strengthened by cheeks that resembled veined apples. He was watching the screens with the boredom of a man who had done the same thing for more years than he cared to remember. His desk was littered with the detritus of his lunch: a half-empty plastic sandwich box, a can of Coke and an empty packet of crisps.

'Porters' office is next door, love,' he said, barely glancing at them.

'Are you Johnny?'

'Aye. And you are...?'

'I'm Dr Burns,' Kirsty said. 'And this is Miss McKenzie from the Fiscal's office.' Rachel held out her ID. 'Could we talk to you for a minute?'

The man's eyes flickered away from the screens to her badge. He nodded before returning to stare at the monitors.

'What do you want to know? I don't think I've ever seen a doctor down here before.'

'I need to ask about something that happened on a certain day. In A&E. I don't suppose there's any chance you still have footage from then?'

Finally, Kirsty seemed to have caught his interest. Slowly he lowered his feet from the table.

'You have to be more specific, Doc.'

'First, can you explain how the CCTV system works? I know there are cameras everywhere, but I hadn't really thought about them inside the hospital before.'

Johnny pushed his bulk away from his desk and came around to stand next to the women.

'We have about twenty cameras across the hospital. That might seem like a lot, but for a hospital this size and spread over such an area, it's not much. About ten of them are in the car parks. That's where we get the most trouble. There's another three in A&E and at each of the entrances. Two cover the doors in the maternity and paediatric units. You know, in case anyone tries to steal a baby. We can't put them in any of the bays where patients are actually treated. An invasion of their privacy, you see. The remainder are spread across the corridors.'

'It's the ones in the emergency department we're most interested in,' Kirsty said.

Johnny pointed to one of the screens. 'This one's set up to monitor A&E.'

Kirsty and Rachel peered at the screen, which was split into four areas. On one of the sections, Rachel could see the reception area where a clerical officer was talking to a patient. The second image was of the outside of the department, where a number of patients or visitors were hanging about smoking cigarettes. The third showed the corridor outside resus. Every so often the doors would swing open and a nurse or doctor would rush through. Rachel watched as Suzi shouldered her way into resus carrying something which Rachel couldn't quite make out but was probably to do with the casualty who had arrived just as she and Kirsty were leaving. The last screen showed the patient waiting area. It seemed that there had been little movement since she and Kirsty had been there. Doubtless, the emergency would be slowing down the ability of the staff to see the non-urgent patients.

The second monitor was also split into screens, each showing different car parks.

Johnny picked up a mouse and clicked. 'I can't look at all the car parks at once,' he said. 'Every ten minutes or so, I change the view to different cameras. It's not brilliant, but the hospital won't spend more money. It's more to put the yobs off than anything else.'

The last monitor was divided between the corridor in the

labour suite, the nurses' station in the postnatal ward and the entrance to the paediatric ward and the special care nursery.

'What happens if you see something? I mean, if there's trouble anywhere?'

'Depends, love,' Johnny said, scratching his abdomen. 'I'm supposed to call the police, but if I did that every time some drunk got shirty in A&E, I'd never be off the phone. There was talk of having a permanent police presence, but it never happened. If I see something that could be trouble, me or one of the other porters goes and has a look-see. If it seems serious, I call the police. They know, if I call them, it usually means I need them to come running.'

'What happens to the recordings?' Rachel asked.

'They get stored on the hard drive. For a month or so. Usually. If there's anything that might go to court – an assault or some sort of trouble – it gets stored for a couple of years. In case it's needed as evidence in court.'

'Does that mean you still have the images from A&E from the twelfth?' Rachel asked. That was the day the morphine had gone missing.

'Should have, love. You'll need to give me a few minutes to try and retrieve them.' He lumbered to his feet, looking pleased to have an audience. It probably got pretty boring down here.

'Why don't you nip next door and get us a cup of coffee in the meantime?' he suggested.

Ten minutes later, their coffee only half drunk, Johnny had retrieved the images of A&E on the date Rachel had given him.

'Stop it here,' Kirsty said, as Gillian came into view on the frame.

In front of the nurses' station, a man with a shaved head and a tattooed neck was mouthing off at Gillian. Next to him, an overweight woman tugged at his arm. She looked to be in her late twenties and was wearing baggy leggings and a too-tight T-shirt. A singing duo stopped mid-song and turned to watch, ready to add their pennyworth if the opportunity arose. With the exception of a dazed couple sitting under the TV, the waiting patients listened in with interest. Apart from Gillian and the receptionist, who was determinedly ignoring the mayhem, Kirsty couldn't see any other staff.

On screen, Gillian moved towards them.

'She might have been five foot nothing but the man doesn't know what's about to hit him,' Kirsty said with a sad smile. 'It's unbearable to think she only had a few days to live.'

'Now you listen to me, Mr King,' Gillian was saying calmly to the tattooed man. 'If you can't keep your voice down, you need to leave. You're upsetting the other patients.'

'Don't you fuckin' tell me what to do, bitch.' King stepped forward.

'And don't you swear at me, or I'll have you out of here so fast your feet won't touch the ground,' Gillian said quietly but firmly, her eyes never leaving King's face.

Kirsty frowned. 'She was taking a chance. Gilly had tons of experience dealing with aggressive patients, but recently the violence has got a lot worse. She couldn't be sure he didn't have a knife, and not even Gillian could win a fight with an armed man. Where the hell was security?'

At that moment, two male staff wearing grey porters' tops hurried into the department. One was Johnny, his coat buttoned up to the bottom of his florid neck, his paunch straining at the material. The other man was the complete opposite with muscular arms and a scrawny frame. He looked as if he'd be more at home behind a desk than manhandling difficult patients out of the department. Rachel recognised him as one of the porters who'd been drinking coffee.

'Is this the man who's giving you trouble, Sister?' Johnny asked Gillian. The jut to his jaw suggested he'd like nothing better than the opportunity to remove Tattoo Man bodily from the department. At Gillian's nod he took King by the elbow. 'If you'll just come outside with me, sir?'

King shrugged off his hand and turned to Gillian. 'Don't you fuckin' think you can take the kid. Keep your fuckin' posh nose out of it.'

Johnny reached for him again, but King yanked his arm away and started towards the door, pulling the woman with him, the two porters following close behind.

Tears streamed down Kirsty's face.

'How would Gilly have chosen to spend what was left of her life had she known?' she whispered. 'I can't imagine it would have been confronting a thug accused of harming his partner's child.'

A few minutes later, there was another image of the two porters and King outside, then the porters left King, who was joined a moment later by his partner.

'I was glad of the other porter coming to help. I'm a big man, as you can see, but I'm no getting any younger. Sometimes if there's only one of you they fancy their chances. But if there's two, they dinnae bother themselves. Not that Strain would be much use in a scuffle. He's not much bigger than you are. But he was better than nothing. If you ask the male doctors to help, they run a mile. Say it's not their job. Naebody does anything anymore if it's not in their job description. It's different now tae when I first started. Then, everybody would help anybody. The unions have a lot to answer for.'

They were about to move forward in time when a flurry of activity on the screen caught Rachel's attention. Three trolleys were wheeled in from the ambulance bay. Several staff converged on them, adding to the number already surrounding them.

The camera flicked to another room: resus. Two of the newly arrived patients were wheeled in.

Kirsty pointed to an open trolley with multiple drawers.

'That's the resus trolley. The morphine is in the drawer marked D for drugs.'

Sometimes the trolley was in clear view of the camera, at others it was concealed by the bodies of staff.

'It's entirely possible a member of staff could have tossed the used vials into one of the bins,' Kirsty said. 'No one is going to root around the sharps containers to look for them.'

Rachel could see how easily it might happen, in the apparent chaos, for drugs to be used without being recorded. It might have been Gillian's responsibility to check the drugs, but as far as Rachel was concerned it was impossible to see why she should be held responsible.

The doors of resus swung open again, and Dr De Banzie hurried into the room. Kirsty and Rachel exchanged a look before turning their attention back to the screen.

A nurse handed him a curved plastic tube as he advanced towards one of the trolleys.

'That's an endotracheal tube,' Kirsty said. 'Used to get an airway to help the patent breathe.'

Dr De Banzie wasn't always in the frame but it was difficult to see when – or if – he might have taken drugs from the trolley. After a word with one of the other doctors, he left the room.

'Was this where King's daughter was treated when she was admitted to the department?'

'Yes,' Kirsty answered.

'So King might have been there when his daughter was being looked after?'

Johnny gave them a curious look but said nothing. He rewound the tape and stopped it when a little girl on a trolley was wheeled into resus, clearly in pain and distress. The woman they'd seen earlier followed the trolley. She made no attempt to comfort her daughter. There was no sign of King in any of the images.

'It's entirely possible the nurses barred him from resus,'

Kirsty said, 'especially if they thought he might have been responsible for her injuries.'

Rachel felt a pulse of rage. How could King live with himself?

'Could you run the CCTV tape for yesterday morning?' Kirsty asked, after the injured girl had been wheeled back out of resus.

Rachel looked at her and raised her eyebrows. 'While I'm here I want to check on something else,' Kirsty said, giving Rachel a small shake of her head.

'Sure,' Johnny said.

A little later, on a different screen, they watched Kirsty talking to Suzi before disappearing behind a screen. She emerged a few minutes later and dropped a couple of vials of blood into a tray on the nurses' desk. After that there was a long gap where nothing of particular interest happened, then, at the edge of the frame, an image of a nurse handing over what looked like the vials Kirsty had left in the tray. Whoever she passed them to was out of the angle of the camera.

Before Rachel had a chance to ask why Kirsty wanted to look at this particular segment of CCTV, Kirsty's pager bleeped. 'Sorry. Got to run. I was due in theatre ten minutes ago.'

Rachel stepped out of the hospital and into biting wind. She needed to let Du Toit know what she'd learned. King should be investigated. Maybe he'd been the person Gilly thought was stalking her. There was also the mystery of the missing morphine. In Rachel's opinion, it was enough to warrant a two-doctor PM and a rush on the toxicology screen.

TWENTY

Back at the office, Rachel tapped on the partition that separated her boss's room from the rest of the office. Mainwaring was staring morosely into space, lost in thought. A few minutes earlier he'd been bellowing on the phone loudly enough for Rachel to have to block her ear with a finger to hear Du Toit. She wondered idly who had been the unlucky recipient of his wrath this time.

Douglas turned to face her, his hangdog expression more pronounced than usual. It was always difficult to say if her boss was having a good day or a bad one. He always looked as if he were having a bad one. Rachel was sure she'd seen him smile once but had agreed with Suruthi she could have been mistaken.

'What sorrow doth thou bring to my door this time, Rachel?' he asked in his mournful voice.

Rachel handed Douglas the paper file she'd brought in with her. Her boss was old-fashioned so she'd printed the relevant reports out for him.

As Douglas rifled through the pages in the file, Rachel told him everything she had discovered about Gillian, including the missing morphine, Gillian's alleged stalker and her face-off with King in A&E, and finally Dr Burns's connection to Ashley Carmichael and Gillian Robertson.

'I know it's probably a coincidence but they were both her patients. That might mean something or nothing. But the sooner we rule out foul play, the better. I'd like a two-doctor PM on Gillian Robertson.'

'Why?'

'Because I have reason to think her death might be suspicious.'

Mainwaring squinted at Gillian's file and looked up with a glare. 'This has your colleague's initials on it.' The reports came to them online from the police. Whoever received the report was responsible for processing it. In this case Alastair Turnbull. It wasn't done for another fiscal to take over a case. At least not without their colleague's agreement. And Alastair had made it clear she didn't have it.

'Christ's sake, have you already forgotten about the debacle' – he glanced at the wilted, tea-stained calendar he used for a coaster on his desk – 'mere weeks ago, when you decided to trust your womanly intuition' – that sneer again – 'and second-guess the police?'

'And it turned out I was correct. Isn't it our job to make sure deaths are fully investigated?'

Douglas sat up and drummed his fingers on his desk. 'You do realise every post-mortem costs this department, eats into our budget? Requesting a second, two-doctor autopsy will be expensive.'

'Cost shouldn't get in the way of doing what's right,' Rachel said quietly.

Mainwaring stared up at the ceiling. It was so long before he spoke that Rachel wondered if he'd fallen asleep. 'Very well. I'll speak to the pathologist,' he said eventually. He gave a wolfish smile that could have signalled disdain – or glee. 'She owes me a couple of favours.'

Rachel knew next to nothing about her boss's private life. Suruthi claimed to have seen him out once, having dinner with one of the forensic pathologists. Whether it was business or pleasure wasn't evident.

'Could you ask her to check for anaesthetic drugs as well as morphine, while she's at it?' Rachel asked on impulse.

Mainwaring scratched his stomach and yawned. 'I'm going to assume you have your reasons. Very well. In the meantime, I suggest you pass this back to the police.'

'I will,' Rachel promised. 'As soon as we get the toxicology on Mrs Robertson.'

'But you also have to speak to Turnbull. Make it right with him. Or do I have to bang heads together?'

Rachel wished he'd stop speaking to her as if she were a child. She peered at him. He was pale and sweaty. He ran a finger along the inside of his collar as if it were too tight.

'You OK?' Rachel asked.

'Why are you still here?' He made a sweeping motion with his fingers. 'Shoo, I have calls to make.'

TWENTY-ONE

Annie Colston was dwelling on her forthcoming operation as she arrived at the women's centre. The hospital had called to say there had been a cancellation and Dr Burns could do it the following week.

At least Kirsty had an excuse for looking under the weather. A small child was likely to do that to you, especially if you worked full-time. It couldn't be easy for her being a single mum as well as holding down a demanding full-time job. Once again Annie felt a frisson of guilt. How easy her life must seem in comparison. Why then was she making such a tit's job of it? She parked her car a short walk from No. 79. The location wasn't the most salubrious, being close to where the women plied their trade, and Annie expected that one day soon she'd come back to her Volvo and find it missing a couple of wheels, completely trashed or even stolen. Although her new place of work wasn't far from her home, it was awkward and time consuming to reach by public transport and taking the bus was too much effort in her present state of mind. The job shouldn't be too demanding – helping the woman with forms, and any other difficulties they might have; offering a sympathetic ear if or when they wanted to talk. And generally watching out for signs they were being abused or exploited. Peggy had known Annie had worked as a psychiatric nurse for years and thought she'd handle the role easily. Annie suspected that her having a murdered sister who the police suspected was moonlighting as a sex worker might have added to the attraction of employing her.

The building that housed the centre was ugly; one of those monstrosities that had been built in the late sixties and had been admired as functional, if uninspiring. It was flanked on one side by a bookmaker's with a pawnshop conveniently right next door and, even more thoughtfully, a pub on the other. Across the road was a laundrette and just up from there an empty piece of waste ground. All in all, it wasn't the best location for a centre looking after prostitutes with a range of addictions.

Inside, it was surprisingly cosy. Peggy had told her how she had wheedled and bribed her way into some lottery funding and had used it to create a homely atmosphere for the disadvantaged women who so desperately needed its service. The front reception area always had a small bunch of flowers on the counter. Peggy brought them in every day from her own garden.

Annie was a little early for her shift. She went to the kitchen, made herself a cup of tea and brought it through to the sitting room. The fire escape door was open and, outside, three women Annie hadn't met before had arranged plastic chairs in a circle around an overflowing ashtray. Annie greeted them and was ignored, so she picked up a magazine, sat down in one of the empty chairs and lit a cigarette. Although she had given up for fifteen years, she had started again when David left. Never in front of the children, though.

The conversation ground to a halt when Annie sat down. She hadn't been there long enough for the women to get used to her.

'Got any to pass on?' an older woman asked, tilting her head in the direction of Annie's cigarette.

'Sure,' Annie said, offering her pack around. All the women accepted – the one who had asked taking several – which disappeared into her bag. Annie didn't comment on this flagrant breach of her generosity.

'Fuckin' Scottish parliament,' the cigarette thief told Annie, her bizarrely coloured red hair glinting puce in the weak sunlight. 'Making us smoke outside. Think they'd have more to worry about.'

'At least the sun is shining,' Annie said. Receiving a sour look in response, she went back to her magazine. Within a few minutes the women seemed to forget about her and started talking again. Annie, absorbed in a story about a 64-stone woman, was only half aware of snippets of their conversation, which seemed to centre on their children, the cheapest place to buy food and – she closed her ears to this – the cheapest place to come by heroin.

'Poor bitch,' the woman who had bummed the cigarettes said, stretching across Annie to extinguish her cigarette in the ashtray.

'Stupid bitch, more like,' a lanky girl with shoulder-length hair said. 'What was she doing taking the stuff after being aff it for so long?'

'Hey! Don't you talk about her like that,' the redhead remonstrated. 'She was trying her best to get by – just like the rest of us.'

Annie looked up from her magazine. 'Who are you talking about?'

'Whut's it to you?' the lanky girl said, pushing out her lower lip.

'Shut it, Chrissie,' the redhead admonished. 'I'm Mags, by the way.' She pointed at the tall, thin woman. 'Big mouth there is Chrissie, and this here is Jody.' Jody, a small girl with red-rimmed eyes, looked as if she wanted to hide. Her wrists stuck out of a too-large jumper like twigs.

'I've seen you on the desk. You're new here, aren't you?' Mags went on.

'Started last week. This is my first proper shift. I'm Annie.'

'Annie get your gun!' Chrissie sneered. 'What are you then? One of those middle-class do-gooders? Come down here to see how the other hof live? Think God will give you a place in heaven if you help save a few prossie souls?'

Annie smiled. 'I think I'm going to have to do a bit more than that if I want to get into heaven.'

Mags looked at Annie for one long minute then laughed.

'Aye.' She hesitated. 'It was wee Ashley we were speaking about. She was found deid a few days ago,' Mags said.

'What happened to her?'

'OD'd,' Chrissie sniffed.

'Oh, poor girl.'

'She was only young,' Mags said, ducking her head and trying to hide, not very successfully in Annie's opinion, that she was wiping away tears.

'What was she like?' Annie asked.

'Well she was no very big and had long blond hair,' Chrissie said.

'Lovely long hair. She dyed it tho,' Jody joined in.

'And as a person?' Annie persisted.

'A bit of a snob. Thought she was above the rest of us,' Chrissie said.

'She did not,' protested Mags. 'You only think that cos she spoke a bit posh.'

'Well she used – same as us.'

'She was trying to come aff the drugs, for the sake of the baby,' Mags insisted.

'She wasn't managing very well, seeing as she pure kilt herself with an overdose.' There was an element of satisfaction in Chrissie's voice.

'It's strange that...' Jody mused, from her corner, almost to herself.

Annie looked at her curiously. 'What do you mean?'

Jody pressed her lips together. 'Nothing.'

Mags got to her feet. 'I don't know about the rest of you, but I'm away hame. I want to catch some kip before tonight. See you later.'

Once Mags had left, the two other women seemed ill at ease in Annie's presence and made movements as if they too were about to leave.

'I must get to reception. My shift starts soon,' Annie said hurriedly. 'It was nice meeting you both.' She was aware that she sounded as if she was at some bloody tea party. She couldn't help the way she spoke. The women would have to take her as they found her.

'Sure, cheers,' the women replied, but Annie was uncomfortably aware of their laughter as she closed the door behind her.

TWENTY-TWO

After work on Tuesday, Rachel drove out to Beauly, a pretty little town about 7 kilometres out of Inverness.

It was a beautiful evening and she wound down her window, turned up the volume on her car radio and sang along with Taylor Swift. It was the best she'd felt for a while. This morning she'd run up the hill on the edge of town and she relished the feeling of getting fitter and stronger.

Nora Goodall lived in a cottage overlooking the river. As Rachel walked up the shingle path the scent of early roses and pansies enveloped her.

A short woman with steel grey hair, intelligent blue eyes and a patrician nose answered the door.

'Mrs Goodall? I'm Rachel McKenzie.'

'Of course you are! You look a lot like your mother. Same thick curly hair and beautiful mouth. Although you're a little taller than she was, I believe. Of course you've grown since I saw you last.' She took Rachel's hands in hers. I can't tell you how very sorry I was about your mother. I couldn't believe it when her body was found.'

'Thank you,' Rachel said, not knowing how else to respond.

'Don't stand there! Come away in!'

Rachel followed the older woman into an old-fashioned but delightful kitchen. 'I've got the tea things ready. I thought we could sit in the garden. Make the most of this lovely evening sunshine. If that suits you, that is?'

'It suits me very well.'

Nora beamed at her. 'If we get cold, I have a couple of throws to keep us warm.' She switched on the kettle. 'My grandson is always trying to persuade me to get a firepit, but it doesn't seem worth the bother when it's only me.'

As she made the tea, she asked Rachel about her job, where she lived now and whether she had a special someone. Rachel answered her questions as best she could, keeping her answers brief but polite.

'Now, what would you like to ask me?' Nora said when they were seated in the garden, a tray of tea and biscuits in front of them and the soothing gurgle of the river, punctuated with the song of a blackbird in the background. 'When I spoke to Margaret about meeting you, she said you specifically wanted to know about cases that might have concerned Mary Ann, her mood in the months and weeks leading up to her disappearance. Is that right?'

'Yes. In a nutshell,' Rachel said, thankful Margaret had eased the way.

Nora handed Rachel her tea and offered her a plate of home-made shortbread. Rachel took both.

'It was almost eleven years ago that I last saw your mother,' Nora said. 'I can tell you social workers are the depository of everyone's secrets. We know the worst – and occasionally – the best about people, so we tend to have a warped view of humanity. But if you are asking me if there are people who don't take kindly to the decisions social workers make, then the answer is yes. Not kindly at all. Before she was promoted, your mother would have had her share of cases like that. As we all did. But although she was quiet and reserved, she wasn't easily intimidated. She thrived on the challenges her job threw at her. And when she was promoted to a management role, she took that in her stride too. She welcomed no longer having to be on call. Said she could spend more time with you that way, particularly in the evening and the weekends.' It was another reminder Rachel had been loved. How could she ever have doubted it?

'Weren't you surprised then when she left without a word and without me?

'Yes, very much. We all were. But as a social worker we work with people who act out of character when under stress. So when the rumours that your father had been abusing her surfaced, it didn't seem so unlikely. Nevertheless,' she added after a moment, 'I would never have imagined your mother putting up with an abusive husband. Not for a moment. She struck me as the type of person who would have made him leave, or upped and left, taking you, and found somewhere else to live. She was resourceful enough. But then we don't walk in someone else's shoes. She might have been quiet on the outside, but I was sure there was a core of steel underneath.'

'She had her reasons,' Rachel said. Her daughter for a start. No access to money for another. 'She didn't talk to you about it?'

'No, sadly. I wish she had. I might have been able to help.'

'Was there anyone my mother might have confided in?' Had her mother truly been as friendless as she seemed? Then again, Rachel didn't have close friends either. Suruthi, Clive and Selena were great, good company in the office and for a night out, but friends she could see herself confiding in? Not really. There was so much she didn't want people to know – especially her colleagues in the legal world.

'I assume she discussed cases with you?'

'Yes, of course. I was her immediate supervisor. We met on

a weekly basis to talk over cases, managerial issues, that sort of thing.'

'And was she having issues, can you remember? With one of her staff, perhaps? Was something in particular worrying her?'

Nora gave Rachel a cool, appraising look.

'No one can make a career in social work without coming face to face with the worst of society, particularly in child protection but in other departments too. Most people who come into contact with us are at a low point in their lives, if not desperate. Desperate people do desperate things. I assume in your line of work you know all about that. I have no doubt your mother dealt with people who would lie and cheat if it made their lives better. She, or her junior staff, would have been involved with several families in the estates. Your mother would have stepped in when required, if she felt her help was needed.'

She bent to pluck a dying flower from a tulip.

'But it's not only the disadvantaged who come our way – we liaise with housing departments, charities, have responsibility for asylum seekers, refugees and illegal immigrants who come to the area – elderly people, child protection. Anyone who needs help and support, basically.

'But to return to your question, I can't recall any case your mother was particularly concerned about. Although,' she paused for a moment, 'I knew that didn't mean there wasn't such a case.'

'What was the last case Mum was working on, can you remember that?'

Nora smiled. 'I've kept all my work diaries. When we arranged to meet, I looked them out. I knew that if there was anything remarkable there would be a chance I made a note about it there.'

'And?'

'There were two serious cases that stuck out.'

Rachel leaned forward. 'What were they?'

'The first was a rather horrible case. We had received a report that a little boy was being abused by his stepmother. While it was being investigated, your mother decided there were sufficient grounds to place the child in foster care. Unfortunately, although the foster parents had been vetted, they'd never fostered before. They were meant to be closely supervised by us, but a series of errors and staff shortages, meant that never happened.' Nora sighed deeply. 'It turned out the stepmother was innocent. However, before the child was returned to the care of his birth parents, he was admitted to hospital with meningitis. He died three days later. The birth parents never forgave us, blamed your mother in particular. The father threatened to ruin her life if he ever got the chance.'

'How horrible. And terribly sad. Do you think he meant it?' Could this be the case her mother had been referring to when she'd spoken to Rachel's grandmother? While Nora had been speaking, Rachel's mind had flashed back to the Kings. Emotions always ran high where children were involved.

'No,' Nora said. 'A great deal gets said in the heat of the moment, and the father was a decent man. But the case ate into your mother. I'm not sure she ever forgave herself. But this happened almost four years before she got promoted, when she was working in child protection.'

Given the timing, it was unlikely the case had resulted in her mother's fear five years later. Nevertheless, Rachel would keep it in mind. Check it out. 'And the other case?'

'That was more recent. Took place around a year before your mother left. It involved people trafficking. Something what was unheard of in the Highlands and Islands until then.' Nora gave a regretful shake of her head. 'A young woman came to us asking for help. Said she'd been trafficked from Amsterdam and been kept with others in a tenement in the city. We knew about these pop-up brothels, but every time the police raided them the traffickers appear to have got wind the police were on their way and were always gone by the time they got there. When your mother heard this young woman's story, she acted swiftly. The police raided and caught the traffickers in the process of moving the women. Your mother was expected to testify in court the week after she left. Of course that never happened. Three of the gang went down anyway. Thanks to your mother. Those were the only cases I found that might have had impacted in a major way on your mother.' She looked at her watch and stood. 'Now, I really must be going. I'm meeting a friend for tea in the village and I must leave soon if I'm to be on time.'

Rachel got to her feet too. 'Of course. Thank you so much for taking the time to talk to me.'

'I hope I've been of some help,' Nora said, as she walked Rachel back through the cottage to the door. There she paused. 'I know it's as tough in your line of work as it is in ours, but try not to see the world through a prism of darkness,' she said. 'Try and find the light and the good, however difficult.' Tears welled in her eyes. 'Your mother would be so proud of you.'

Rachel swallowed hard. She hoped so.

As Rachel stepped into the cooling evening air, she shivered. Was it possible, despite the overwhelming evidence to the contrary, that her father wasn't guilty of murder, that someone hadn't wanted her mother to testify at the trial? The timing had to be more than a coincidence.

No, she was indulging in a fantasy. It didn't explain why her father had his wife's passport and debit card hidden in his safe, the lengths he'd taken to cover up her mother's disappearance. And all the other evidence that had convicted her father.

On the other hand, a fuller, more gratifying picture of her mother was emerging. Her mother had been tough, caring, stubborn, prepared to stand up for the vulnerable, even if she had made a mistake with the child. Maybe Rachel was more like her than she'd imagined. The thought gave her a warm glow.

TWENTY-THREE

Back in her cottage in Clachnaharry, Rachel went for a long run before pouring herself a glass of wine. She was too restless to watch a movie or read a book so she decided to make a pot of chilli to freeze.

As the aroma of beef, spice and tomatoes wafted through the kitchen, her mind drifted back in time to a memory of her mother – one she'd suppressed. Rachel must have been around eight or nine. She was seated at the kitchen table doing her homework, the radio playing softly in the background as her mother prepared the evening meal. Rachel vividly remembered the soporific warmth of the kitchen, the rich, meaty smells, the round mounds of dumplings on the breadboard waiting to be dropped into the stew at the right time when heat would turn them into fat, soft balls of doughiness.

Billy Joel's 'Piano Man' had come on and her mother began to sing along as she stirred. Then, when the music reached a crescendo, her mother raised her arms, closed her eyes and let her body sway in time to the music. Rachel watched open-mouthed. This was totally unlike her quiet, serious mother.

Rachel's heart felt like it was bursting. It made her so happy to see her mother happy.

Now, seventeen years later, Rachel took a gulp of wine before fetching the record player and box of albums she'd retrieved from Moy. She plugged the record player into the wall and rummaged through the box until she found the Billy Joel album she was looking for.

She dropped the record onto the turntable. There was a slight hissing sound as the needle hit the plastic rim and as the notes of the mouth harmonica filled the room Rachel turned up the volume.

Back in her childhood kitchen, her mother must have felt Rachel's eyes on her as she turned to face her. She'd smiled at a rapt Rachel and widened her eyes and beckoned her only child as if she were Baby in *Dirty Dancing*, a video they'd watched together on a number of occasions. Rachel had grinned back and slid off her chair and danced into her mother's arms. They'd held hands and spun around until they'd collapsed breathless and laughing on the floor.

Rachel closed her eyes, lifted her hands in the air and swayed her body in rhythm to the music. As the music flowed around her, it was as if she were back in the kitchen, dancing with her mother, happy and secure.

But she couldn't stop the memory of what had happened next. Her father had appeared in the doorway, his face a mask of fury as he snapped off the radio. In the sudden awful silence, her mother had scrambled to her feet and hurried to the stove, her shoulders stiff as she'd dropped the doughballs into the pan, each plop a rebuke, although Rachel was unsure to whom. Her, for not concentrating on her homework? Or Mum for dinner being late? Surely not for being happy?

Dragged back to the present, Rachel opened her eyes, crossed to the record player and lifted the needle, uncaring as it gouged the vinyl. She removed the record from the turntable and hurled it across the room. It soared like a frisbee, before smashing into the wall and shattering into pieces.

The figure watched from the shadows. Like many people in the village, Rachel didn't close the curtains when it got dark. Why bother when there was nothing between her and the sea, apart from a low wall and a chunk of tidal sand?

She should, she really should. Especially if she wanted to dance like she had an audience she wanted to titillate. Not that he was titillated. Not at all.

He was intrigued by her burst of rage at the end of the dance. *He* knew rage. He was getting to know her but clearly had more to learn. The act of throwing the record across the room was completely at odds with the cool, distant 'nothing can ruffle my feathers' facade she usually presented. Oh yes, he knew who she was now. And having found out, he'd followed her a few times, always keeping his distance, making sure she didn't see him. He knew where she worked, where she lived, who she met – and that she'd been to the hospital on at least one other occasion.

As he walked away, he considered what this glimpse into the heart of Rachel McKenzie meant. She was less predictable than he'd come to believe and that might be a good thing or a bad thing. One way or another, he was about to find out.

TWENTY-FOUR

On the other side of Inverness, Annie Colston tossed her duvet aside. Getting off to sleep without several glasses of wine was proving impossible. Giving in, she swung her feet over the side of the bed. The children were spending the weekend with David and the house felt unnervingly empty. She slipped into her dressing gown. It was a good thing she had poured the rest of the vodka down the sink, otherwise she would have been tempted to have a drink to help her sleep. Tea would have to do.

As she waited for the kettle to boil, she kept thinking about the women at the centre. Weren't they frightened out on the streets? Especially after what had happened to their friend. Taking her mug back to the bedroom, Annie looked out of the window onto the deserted streets below. How would it feel to be out there? Vulnerable, desperate and exposed.

On impulse Annie threw off her nightclothes and pulled on a pair of jeans and jumper. She wasn't quite sure where the women plied their trade, but knew it was somewhere down at the harbour. They couldn't be that difficult to find. She had no idea what she intended to do once she got there, she just knew she had to see for herself. Perhaps it was a morbid curiosity. Or thinking about Caroline. In her worst moments she imagined hearing Caroline cry out for Annie to save her. She'd had enough of doing nothing.

She drove past shuttered shops with names like 'Joe's Café' and 'Wash 'n' Go'. Many of them were boarded up. The repeated lockdowns had taken their toll. The streets were almost empty, apart from the occasional pub-goer weaving an unsteady path home. The rain had eased slightly and she turned the car heater up as high as it would go.

It didn't take long to find them once she reached the harbour. They hung about in small groups in the streets that bordered the harbour. Scared to slow down too much, she still recognised Jody and Mags stomping their feet on the ground. They looked frozen. Continuing to act on impulse, Annie drove to a nearby 24-hour Burger King and ordered several cups of coffee and burgers. It wasn't much, but perhaps it would offer the women some comfort.

By the time she returned, Jody and Mags had disappeared. Annie sat in the car, uncertain of what to do. It was a crazy idea to have come in search of the women. But she was here now. She would drop the food off and leave them to it.

The women looked at her in disbelief when she stepped out of the car with the food and drink balanced precariously on cardboard trays.

For a moment Annie stood, feeling ridiculous and uncertain of what to do next.

'Hey, you know this pitch is taken?' one of the women called across.

'I'm not a... I'm not here for that,' Annie said, horrified. Surely the women hadn't mistaken her for one of them? What had she been thinking, coming here?

'I thought you might fancy some coffee and something to eat,' she called across, humiliatingly aware of the false brightness in her voice. 'I'll leave it here then.' She bent and placed the trays of food on the pavement. Like she was feeding wild cats, she thought suddenly. Annie was about to pick the trays up again when the women turned and started walking towards her. There were three of them: a tall skinny one wearing a patent leather jacket, and two younger women, one with a nose ring, the other with her hair tied in childish bunches. Annie's heart gave a sickening thud.

'Is coffee all you've brought?' the taller woman said. 'Are you sure you've nothing more useful in that fancy handbag of yours?'

'What have you come here for?' Nose Ring joined in, her tone surly. 'Come down here so's you can feel better about yourself? Or are you one of these women who fancy giving it a try but haven't worked up the balls for it yet?'

The other women sniggered, drawing closer to Annie until she was surrounded.

'No, of course not. I mean...' Annie stumbled over the words.

'Here, let me see what you've got in that bag.' Nose Ring, who seemed to be the leader of the group, given the deferential way the others stepped back, took Annie's bag from her unresisting fingers.

'Hey, girls. Let's see what Mrs Do Good has for us.' She opened the bag and removed Annie's purse. She fingered the notes inside. 'Nearly a hundred quid. That'll do, won't it, lassies? Help us get off the street and go home to our husbands and kids. A hundred quid and a cup of coffee, oh yes and a burger, no chips. That'll mean we can all give up work and become respectable.' She almost spat the last word.

Annie realised she had made a mistake. She searched the faces, looking for a friendly one, even if she couldn't see a familiar one.

'I'm sorry. I shouldn't have come,' she said, backing away.

'You can take the money if you like. If you give me my bag back, I'll go.'

'There's credit cards here too, girls,' Blond Bunches said. 'What do you say we hang on to those for you as well?' Now that she was closer, the deep lines around her mouth were obvious. She was nearer forty than her teens. As she spoke, her parted lips revealed a row of nicotine-stained stumps.

'Take them,' Annie said.

'Don't mind if I do,' Nose Ring replied, deftly pocketing Annie's purse before thrusting Annie's handbag back to her. 'Now clear off, before Taffy gets here. He won't take too kindly to anyone trying to corrupt his girls.'

The women laughed again. Annie turned and retreated, fully expecting to feel something hit her on the back. Before she reached the safety of her car, a vehicle pulled up and Mags stepped out, clearly recognisable to Annie, even in the dim light, by her mass of scarlet hair. Jody emerged from the shadows.

'Fucking asshole,' Mags screeched in the direction of the car as it took off, leaving a smell of oil in its wake. 'Don't you fucking come back here unless you want to lose your balls.' She turned to the others, seemingly unaware of Annie's presence. 'Only gave me hof of what we agreed. Watch out for that one. If you see his car again, let me know so's I can tell Taffy.' She became aware of Annie, who was trying to slip into her car unnoticed, and stared at her in astonishment.

'What in the name of Jesus and all that's holy are you doing down here?'

'I thought you all might like some coffee.' Annie indicated the cups cooling on the pavement.

Mags laughed. 'I can see we've got some educating to do.' She picked up a coffee, took a sip and spat. 'Bloody freezing. Come on then, you can buy us some fresh. I'm due a break.'

Nose Ring looked from Annie to Mags. 'Hey, Mags, you know this daft cow?'

'Aye, I do that. She works down No. 79. Just started. Hasn't quite got the hang of it tho.'

Nose Ring thought for a moment then passed Annie her purse back. 'Here, take it. You should've said.'

It was on the tip of Annie's tongue to say she hadn't been given the chance, but she decided to let it ride. She accepted her bag with a simple thank you.

'Jeez, woman, what possessed you to come down here?' Mags muttered as she steered Annie towards her car. Jody trailed behind them. 'If Taffy had been hanging about, you would have been lucky to get away in one piece. Are you always this stupid?'

'I can see now that it wasn't one of my better ideas,' Annie said stiffly. 'I couldn't sleep. And I got to thinking. It's raining and cold. I suppose I wanted to see you were all OK.'

'For crying out loud! We're better able to look after ourselves on the street than you are. Don't think just cos you're working in the clinic that you know us. You don't. You know bugger all about our lives – and believe me, it's better that way.'

'Ashley Carmichael didn't manage to look after herself very well did she?' Annie said sharply, fed up with being lectured by Mags.

Jody tapped Annie on the shoulder. 'Why are you working at No. 79 anyway? Why are you hanging out with us? What is wrong with you? Have you no friends? Are you some kind of weirdo?'

My sister was murdered,' Annie blurted. 'In an alley off the town centre.' She took a deep breath. 'I've always thought the police believed she was hooking so didn't look into her death as closely as they should have.'

Mags and Jody stared at her, open-jawed.

'She wasn't working as a prostitute, as it happens – at least, I'm sure she wasn't – although she'd arranged to meet a man for sex. I don't think she knew him, at least not well. And I'm certain it wasn't for money.' Her words tumbled out like water in a stream. 'She worked as a teacher, was well enough paid, but I think she was bored with her marriage. Wanted to make it more exciting.' She took another shaky breath, 'Caro didn't name the person and, quite frankly, I didn't want to hear it as I was so angry with her. Perhaps if I...' She swallowed. 'They say she might have died from an accidental drug overdose. He must've forced her to take the ketamine. She craved excitement but disapproved of drugs. The police never discovered his identity. I don't think they tried very hard. No one ever came forward. I would give anything to have the person responsible caught.' Her voice hitched. 'Anything.'

And then, without the slightest warning it was going to happen, she burst into tears.

TWENTY-FIVE

Rachel was about to turn her light off when she heard banging on her front door. Her heart lurched. It was after 2 a.m. People coming to the door at this time couldn't bode well. She slipped a hoodie over her T-shirt and pyjama bottoms.

She squinted through the peephole and was surprised to see Mags accompanied by a thin young woman.

Rachel opened the door to them. Mags was dressed in a boob tube and mini skirt, the roll of flesh around her midriff protruding between the two. Her red hair had been combed into a back-teased bouffant, her lips rimmed with her signature red lipstick, her faded blue eyes lined with kohl. The young, petite woman with her was equally scantily dressed. She kept tugging in her sleeves, scratching her neck.

'Well, are you going to let us in or leave us here freezing our tits off?' Mags demanded. 'This is Jody, by the way.' She pointed her thumb over her shoulder.

Rachel stepped aside and Mags barged past, her companion following closely behind.

'You do know it's after two in the morning?' Rachel asked.

Mags's eyes stretched wide. 'I learned to tell the time when I was a sprog. Fancy that, eh?'

'I could have been asleep,' Rachel protested.

'But you weren't. Aren't. Your bedroom light was still on.'

'What do you want, Mags?' Rachel asked. She was too tired to be polite. Besides, she doubted her neighbour would notice – or care.

'Can we at least get a cup of tea?'

Rachel gave up, ushered them into the kitchen and switched on the kettle. Red Mags wouldn't have pitched up at Rachel's door if something hadn't been bothering her.

'OK, so why are you here?' Rachel asked as she waited for the kettle to boil.

Mags leaned forward, her plump breasts squeezing up against the kitchen table.

'One of the women who works at the centre – she started no that long ago – was daft enough to come down to the harbour the night. That's where we work, as ahm sure you know. Where Ashley's body was found.'

Rachel nodded. She took two mugs from the cupboard, tossed a couple of teabags inside, filled a jug with milk and placed it and a bowl of sugar along with the mugs in front of Mags and her companion. Once the kettle had boiled, she filled the mugs and passed them each a teaspoon to stir their tea.

'Her name is Annie Colston. She's posh. Not the way you're posh, but really posh. As if she could have tea with the queen, or mebbe Prince Harry since the queen's deid. I've always liked Prince Harry. He's more real, if you know what I mean?'

Rachel didn't.

Mags blew on her tea and took a noisy gulp. Rachel resisted the impulse to hurry her along.

'Anyroad, we wondered, we all did, why she came to work there. Didnae look as if she had a clue about what working wummen do and would freak out when she found out. Looked like a straight missionary-position type. We wis sure she would piss off after a day or two.'

Jody, who had yet to say a word, spooned in four teaspoons of sugar and stirred. She looked dazed. Probably high.

'She's kind, I'll say that, but lives in cloud cuckoo land. I wisnae there when she pitched up. By the time I got there, the silly cow had almost got into a fight with Annaliese and robbed at the same time. Luckily I came along before everything kicked off. Sorted things out. I gave her a right bollocking – told her she was aff her heid coming near the place . She stood there like a numpty and took it. Then she burst out crying, would you believe!'

Rachel wished she still had wine in the fridge.

'It was totally embarrassing. I didn't know what to do with meself, none of us did. Turns out her sister was kilt – Annie thinks murdered – a year and a hof ago. That's why she was howling like a banshee, scaring the punters away. When she got a hod of hersel' it came out. Her sister was having sex with a stranger in an alley, like one o' us, 'cept this woman was a teacher, with kids and a husband. But there you go! Mebbe she's right, mebbe she's wrang. There's no understanding folk. Anyroad, the polis never worked out what happened to her. Annie thought they didn't try as hard as they could cos they thought maybe she was a prossie and a drug user on the side. That's why she wanted to work at No. 79. Thinks she can make it up to her sister that way. I think she feels guilty or summat.' She paused long enough to draw breath and take another swig of her tea.

The case wasn't familiar to Rachel. But given she'd only started at the Death Unit less than a year ago, that wasn't surprising.

'Do you know her sister's name?'

'No. But it shouldn't be difficult to find. Can't be that many wummen found dead in an alley with their knickers round their ankles, could there be?'

Mags had a point. Rachel would look at the case as soon as she got into the office.

'Jody here has summat she wants to tells you. It's aboot Ashley.' She elbowed the younger woman in the ribs. 'Go on. Tell her what you told me. She's all right. You can trust her.'

Jody picked at her nails for a minute or two before seeming to make up her mind.

'Look, it might be nothing. And whatever, there is no way I'm talking to the police. Have you got that clear? But if something happened to Ashley, somebody should be looking into it.'

'Of course something happened to her, you daft cow. She's dead isn't she?' Mags snarled.

'Why don't you tell me what it is?' Rachel asked.

Jody's eyes darted between Mags and Rachel before she seemed to make up her mind. 'All right. You know how she told everyone she was giving up the H? Well, Chrissie told me she asked Ashley if she could use her stuff that night. She hadn't got hers on her. Ashley told her that she couldn't give her anything cos she wasn't using anymore.'

'Perhaps she was lying? Perhaps she didn't want to share?' Rachel suggested.

'Maybe. But she'd always shared before. She was kind like that.'

It was strange to hear that sharing needles was considered kind, but once more Rachel held her tongue. Her mind drifted back to the nights she'd spent under the bridge in Glasgow. There had been plenty of sharing then. Drugs as well as food.

'There's something else,' Jody went on, bringing Rachel's focus back to the present.

'Go on,' she encouraged.

Jody shot an anxious look at Mags again. 'How do you know you can trust her?' She jerked her head in Rachel's direction.

'Because I said so. And I never tell you wrong, do I?'

Jody sighed. 'OK. Since you think it's important. I saw someone go into that alley that night – the one where they found Ashley's body. I was hiding from Taffy – didn't know he was in the jail, did I? I was having a fix and didn't want him to see. He doesn't like us using when we're working. I was about to shoot up when I saw this man follow Ashley behind one of the empty warehouses.' She paused. 'The thing is he was dressed kind of funny.'

'What do you mean "funny"? In what way?' Rachel asked.

'He had a baseball cap pulled down low on his face. But it wasn't that. Most of the punters hide their faces in case any of the cameras are working. We put them out with stones, but the council keep repairing them. Anyway, this punter had a coat on. A long dark one. And right before he went into the alley, he stopped. Almost right in front of me. He didn't see me, I made sure of that, even though I was feeling a bit woozy at the time. Something about him gave me the creeps. A lot of them give me the creeps, but he was different.'

'For God's sake, get on with it,' Mags muttered. 'I've got a bed to get tae.'

'I think I must have made a noise, cos he turned around as if he heard something. And when he did, his coat kind of flapped open. I could see he was wearing something underneath. It looked like pyjamas.'

'Go on, Jody,' Rachel said. 'This could be important.'

'He was carrying a bag, maybe a briefcase or a small suitcase – I don't know. At the time I thought it was strange, but no stranger than most of the things we see on the street. But when Ashley turned up dead...'

'Did you see his face?'

'I only saw him for a second before he followed after Ash. And like I said, he had a cap on that hid most of his face.' Her expression grew belligerent. 'I wasn't bloody interested in how he looked. I didn't know it was going to be important, did I?'

'Did you see him come out?'

'No, I only saw him go after Ashley. I went away with a punter right after. I never saw him, or Ashley, again.'

'Why didn't you tell the police?'

'God, you are stupid,' Mags interrupted again. 'Jody's hardly going to tell the police she was working the streets while shooting up, is she? What if they charge her?'

'I don't think that's likely,' Rachel said.

'You know bugger all about us or our lives, so don't tell me what's likely.'

Actually Rachel knew more than Mags could possibly imagine.

Mags jutted her chin. 'Christ, you people! Whut kind of wummen do you think become prostitutes? Well, let me tell you, it's women like me and women like you. Even women like Annie's sister.

'Most women will do anything if they need money bad enough, and not only for drugs! You think these wee lassies who run away from home can afford hotels and such like! No they fucking cannot. And they need to eat too. Now, not everyone who becomes a prossie hates it, some like me dinnae mind it. But don't you do what the polis and the rest of them do and try and put us all together in one big lump.'

''Sides, everyone said Ash had killed herself with an over-dose,' Jody took up where Mags had left off. 'So there wasn't any point in telling the police anything. Still isn't – unless they've changed their minds about how she died – is there?'

Mags patted Jody's hand before turning back to Rachel. 'I got to thinking. Both Annie's sister and Ashley died after meeting someone for sex. What if Annie's sister was kilt? What if Ashley was kilt too? And what if the same person done them both?'

TWENTY-SIX

WEDNESDAY

A few hours later, Rachel staggered into work bleary-eyed and with a thumping headache. As soon as she'd swallowed a couple of painkillers, she sought Clive out.

'Hey,' she said, pulling up a chair next to his. 'You OK? You look a bit rough.'

Clive ran a hand over his scalp. 'Late night last night. Need to stay home more often on school nights. You don't look so great yourself. What's your excuse? Anyway, what can I do for you?'

'What makes you think I want something?'

He grinned. 'Because you only sidle up to me when you need something.'

'Harsh. But fair enough. Do you remember a report of a woman found dead in an alley about eighteen months ago? A teacher? First name Caroline.'

'Sounds familiar. Let me have a look.'

As Clive's fingers typed furiously, Rachel looked around the office. There was no sign of the boss. Alastair, for once, was at his computer, typing away. Rachel hadn't got around to telling him about her conversation with Douglas. Linda was on the phone, taking notes, as was Suruthi.

'Found it,' Clive said after a few moments. 'Caroline Telford. It was reported just before I started here. What do you want to know?'

'Can I see the police report?' Clive swapped seats so Rachel could see the screen better. The body of a thirty-six-year-old woman had been found slumped in an alley near the town centre, on Sunday 26th September 2021, by a nurse on her way to an early shift. The victim was slumped against a wall, her underwear around her ankles although there was no clear evidence of recent sex, consensual or otherwise. Neither was there evidence of a struggle.

Toxicology had found ketamine in her system and the pathologist had suggested that an unintentional overdose was the most likely cause of death.

Maybe whoever was with her panicked and left the scene?

Reading on, it seemed that's what the police thought too. But Caroline's husband had categorically ruled drugs out. He said she had never, in all the time he'd known her, shown the slightest interest in drugs. He conceded she had an interest in experimenting with sex, had suggested they tried swinging, but he'd been horrified and the suggestion had been dropped. It hadn't occurred to him she'd attempt to carry out her fantasies alone.

The police checked his alibi. It was rock solid. The four other men he'd been golfing with had vouched for him. They'd partied late into the night and two of them had even shared a room after the hotel had mistakenly allocated them one less room than they'd booked.

The police had attempted to track whoever Caroline had been with the night she died, without success. Apart from the grainy image of a man and Caroline leaving the pub together,

there had been no other images captured on CCTV. The
bartenders hadn't been able to identify him. As far as they could
remember, he hadn't ordered a drink. One recalled Caroline,
however. She'd ordered a glass of wine at the bar and took a
table on her own. The next time he looked, she'd gone. Appeals
to the public for the man to come forward had not yielded
results. Someone had tagged a note to the report. The detective
inspector in charge of the case had died six months ago from a
brain tumour. Not that it mattered, ultimately; without more to
go on the case had gone cold and after a year, the family had
been allowed to bury the body.

Rachel returned to her own desk and googled ketamine.

She discovered it was usually given by injection by vets to
anesthetise animals prior to surgery. It was also used by
medical practitioners as a short-acting anaesthetic in minor
operations, usually in developing countries where there were
no specialist anaesthetists. It was better than a local anaesthetic, not as good as a general but less dangerous. Although
ketamine didn't paralyse muscles, which would require the
patient to be intubated, it induced a state of sedation, immo-
bility and amnesia, meaning the patient would have no
memory of the operation or procedure carried out while under
its influence.

Recently it had been pedalled to students as a recreational
drug, pushed as being safer than other street drugs. Ketamine
could be injected or mixed into drinks in liquid form, or heated
and ground into powder and snorted or smoked. There had
been several deaths from accidental overdoses.

Rachel sat back in her chair. It was entirely possible Caroline had taken the drug and overdosed. But it was odd. She'd
been a schoolteacher, had no history of drug-taking, at least
according to the husband. He hadn't known about his wife

meeting men for sex in alleys either though, so he could be wrong about the drugs.

But something didn't make sense.

How had Caroline taken the ketamine? By injection? In liquid form? If so, where was the syringe? The bottle? Or whatever Caroline had used to take the drug? Unless whoever she'd been with had given it to her? That was possible. Might explain why he hadn't come forward. For all Rachel knew she'd taken it in the pub toilet.

Another thought occurred to Rachel. She studied her screen again. If ketamine was used in Third World countries, rural Zambia presumably came under this umbrella – and Kirsty had recently returned from there.

Was ketamine something Kirsty Burns would be familiar with?

One way to find out. She picked up the phone. Time to ask a friendly pathologist.

'What do you know about ketamine?' she asked Peter once they'd exchanged the usual small talk.

'Ketamine as in the animal anaesthetic?'

'I guess so. I understand it's also used on humans in Third World countries.'

'So I believe. It's thought to be safe as it doesn't prevent patients breathing on their own and doesn't lower blood pressure. But it could be unpleasant for the patient if you don't get the dose right. Why do you ask?'

'I'm looking into another case. Unpleasant in what way?'

'Imagine being operated on when essentially you're awake. There's a chance you'd be able to feel everything but be unable to react in any way.'

'That sounds horrific!'

'It's not ideal. But in developing countries it's often the best choice. Let me explain. Without a trained anaesthetist it's dangerous to put people under. You have to paralyse their muscles, and that includes their breathing. If someone doesn't know how to intubate them properly, they could die. If a patient requires lifesaving surgery, for example an emergency section, it's often the only option.'

'Given what you've told me, why would anyone take it for fun?'

'Why does anyone take any drug?'

Rachel could almost hear him shrug over the phone.

She couldn't think of anything else to ask. 'Thanks for the info. I'll be in touch.'

After she'd hung up, Rachel sat back in her chair.

How had Caroline arranged to meet the man in the alley? Had her phone records and internet searches been scrutinised? A quick check of the police report attached to Caroline's file confirmed they had. The police had found nothing there, no texts, WhatsApps, or emails that were unusual: no activity on any dating site that they could find. She made a mental note to ask Selena if they'd checked Gillian's phone for the same stuff.

There wasn't much to go on.

Except that they had three dead women; and Rachel had that weird feeling in her gut again.

It was mid-morning when Linda clapped her hands to get everyone's attention. Her usually unflappable demeanour was missing, her face pale.

'I'm very sorry to have to tell you that Douglas was admitted to hospital with a heart attack last night.' The team exchanged startled looks. 'Luckily it was mild,' Linda hurried to reassure everyone. 'He's had a couple of stents inserted but it will be a few weeks at least before he's back at work. He has let me know in no uncertain terms that he is not to be visited, either at the hospital or at home.'

Rachel wasn't surprised by the order. It was so like their irascible boss.

'In the meantime,' Linda continued. 'Staff reorganisation has been put on hold. Alastair will not be transferring to homicide. Instead he'll be stepping into Douglas's role until he returns.'

TWENTY-SEVEN

Rachel tracked down Caroline's sister, Annie Colston, to a corner villa in the Crown district of Inverness, one of the Highland capital's more affluent areas.

A woman in her mid-forties answered Rachel's knock. She was casually but expensively dressed, in a blouse and skirt, a string of pearls around her neck, although her roots were showing and there was a small stain on her blouse.

'Can I help you?'

'Are you Annie Colston?'

'Yes.' She gave Rachel an enquiring smile.

Rachel introduced herself and showed Mrs Colston her ID. 'Could we chat? It's about your sister.'

Mrs Colston paled. 'Please, come in. Let's go through to the kitchen.'

Her kitchen was large but cosy. The cabinets were painted pine, the stove a six-ring range cooker. The worktops were cluttered with the same jars and paperwork that cluttered Rachel's.

They sat across from one another at an oak kitchen table.

'Why are you here? Is there news about Caro?' Her eyes were bright with hope. 'Have they discovered anything new?'

'I'm afraid not.'

'Then why are you here?'

'I'm taking a fresh look at her case. I don't want to get your hopes up, 'Rachel added quickly, 'there's nothing new to add to the police investigation that took place when your sister died.'

'If you could call it an investigation,' Annie sighed.

'Why do you say that?' Rachel asked.

'They never found the man she was with. They said she died from an overdose of ketamine. Now Caroline could be reckless, but she was no drug-taker.'

'Tell me about her,' Rachel said.

Annie smiled to herself and was silent for a few minutes before she spoke. 'Caroline – Caro we all called her – was good, kind, a fab teacher, sister, mother, friend. She was also a risk-taker. She'd be the first to sign up for a bungy jump, take the lead skiing down a black run. I'd be the one following behind begging her to be careful. She was so much braver than me, determined to wring every last drop from life.'

'Would that risk-taking include having sex with men she didn't know?'

'Yes, if I'm honest. She said she was bored. She loved being a teacher, loved being a mum, loved Richard, her husband but I think she wanted to leave that life behind her sometimes, if only for an evening.'

'What happened the day she died?'

Annie closed her eyes. 'I met her for a drink after she finished work. She had a look on her face I recognised: the one from our childhood when she was about to get up to something and knew the adults in the room – my parents when we were children, then me as we got older – would not approve of. A mixture of excitement and nervousness. I asked her what she was up to. At first she wouldn't tell me – but I pushed her and she admitted she was hooking up with someone that night.

'I was aghast of course – she had children – and she was

married to a man she loved and who loved her. Richard gave her anything she wanted. Even another baby. They'd been trying to have another for a couple of years without luck. Caro had been told she was low on eggs and needed IVF. That's why I couldn't understand why she wanted to have sex with someone else. She said love and sex didn't always go hand in hand. Not for her anyway. Said she'd always fancied experimenting. Playing out some of her sex fantasies.' A flush stole up Annie's cheeks. 'She even attempted to persuade Richard to try swinging but he'd have none of it. She said she was going to give her own version a go. I tried to talk her out of it. Things got pretty heated...' Annie swallowed. A tear rolled down her cheek. 'I hate that we argued the last time we spoke.'

'Did she say anything about who she was planning to meet? How they'd connected?'

Annie took a hanky from her bag and blew her nose. She took a moment to compose herself. 'No. She was very secretive about it. And him. I assume she met him on the internet. She said he was married. And that suited her fine.'

'Do you know what sites she used?'

'No, I don't even know for sure that she did.'

'And you told all his to the police?'

'I didn't want to. But what choice did I have? They found CCTV footage of her leaving a pub with a man. The footage was grainy and the man was wearing a baseball cap so they couldn't identify him. It rained that night and if there was any DNA or any other evidence left at the scene it had been washed away.'

'Is there anything else you think I should know?' Rachel asked. Everything Annie had told her was pretty much what she knew already.

'I've racked my brains since she died, trying to think of something that might make the police look again.' She looked at

Rachel with bright, inquisitive eyes. 'Why are you looking at Caroline's death after all this time?'

'Mags is my neighbour. She told me about Caroline. I looked her case up when I got to the office and saw her case wasn't closed. Sometimes a fresh look helps.' Rachel stood.

Annie gave a tiny hiccup, dabbed her eyes dry and gave a brave smile. 'When she died, I was furious with her for leaving me. Leaving us all. And sometimes I'm still so angry I could wring her neck, but you know that was Caro and I'd give my right arm to have her back.'

TWENTY-EIGHT

Yet another day in paradise, Rachel thought, surveying the piles of paperwork requiring her attention. She was almost relieved when her phone rang. It was Dr Halliday, the pathologist.

'Good morning. Douglas said I should get back to you with the results of Mrs Robertson's PM. How is he, by the way?'

'I gather he's doing well,' Rachel replied.

'I'm very glad to hear it. When he asked for a two-doctor PM it sounded important. So my colleague and I stayed late last night to do it. It was the least we could do.'

'Thank you for that,' Rachel said.

'Now I know you're keen to hear what I've found,' Dr Halliday continued, 'so I'll get straight to the point. When my colleague and I re-examined Mrs Robertson's body, there was evidence – very faint evidence but definitely there – of petechial haemorrhage in her eyes.'

'What does that mean?' Rachel asked.

'It's evidence of strangulation. In my opinion, this was very likely murder.'

Rachel felt a surge of adrenaline. So Kirsty's suspicions that her friend hadn't died from natural causes had been correct. It had slipped everyone by. Someone had very nearly got away with murder.

She glanced over at Alastair, who had taken over Mainwaring's office. He caught her looking at him and pointed with eyes with his forefinger and pinkie and then at Rachel in the universal sign that he was watching her. Oh please. He wasn't a gang boss any more than she was a child. She was tempted to give him the finger in return but managed to resist. When she told him she'd been right about Gillian Robertson and that there was no way he could release her body to her parents, it was going to ruin his day.

Rachel felt a wash of shame. It was going to be way tougher on everyone who'd loved Gillian.

'One other thing,' Dr Halliday continued. 'You asked me to check Mrs Robertson's toxicology for morphine. I didn't find any traces, but you also asked me to look for other anaesthetic agents. I found ketamine. There might have been others but they tend to leave the system after a few days so the fact nothing was found doesn't mean they weren't there at the time of death. I also found a puncture wound in her thigh.'

It didn't make sense. Why would Gillian be injecting ketamine when she was happily pregnant? Rachel's thoughts spun to Caroline. She hadn't used drugs either, yet the night she died there had been ketamine in her system. OK, so ketamine was currently one of the drugs of choice, but even so. If either woman had been using recreational drugs, Rachel would have plumped for cocaine – the preferred choice of the better off.

And if Gillian had injected herself, what had happened to the syringe? There was no mention of one anywhere in the police report. Rachel would have to check with the police that they'd thoroughly searched her flat. It was unfortunate it had already been released back to the family.

In the absence of a syringe, the obvious conclusion was that someone had injected the ketamine into Gillian. Was that what had happened to Caroline? Had both women been murdered? By the same person? It was quite a leap.

'Thank you, Dr Halliday,' Rachel said. 'Have you spoken to DI Du Toit?'

'Not yet. I will send him my report shortly – as soon as I write it up. Douglas was adamant I was to let you know first.'

Rachel was touched. It appeared her boss had her back after all. She would never refer to him as Deputy Dawg behind his back again.

'Any chance you could push Ashley Carmichael's post-mortem up your list? Make it a two-doctor one too?'

Douglas was not going to be pleased she was blowing his budget. In which case neither would Alastair. 'And ask toxicology to check her blood for other anaesthetic agents too.'

'Sounds like you think we might have a problem, so I'll get on with it straight away.'

TWENTY-NINE

After disconnecting, Rachel phoned Du Toit and asked if she could buy him lunch at the Innes Bar – a favourite haunt of police officers.

'Come on. It's important,' she said when he hesitated. 'I promise you. Anyway, everyone has to eat.'

'Half an hour. That's all I can give you.'

'That's all I need.'

Rachel was about to pick up her jacket when she was aware of Alastair's eyes on her. She hesitated. She had to keep him in the loop. Whether she liked it or not, he was her boss now.

She tapped on the temporary MDF wall Douglas had erected to separate his office from the rest of the open-plan space.

'Can I have a word?' she asked.

She took him through the conversation she'd had with the pathologist. 'I'm going to bring DI Du Toit up to speed over lunch, if you'd care to join us?'

Alastair's frown had deepened the longer she'd spoke.

'What the hell are you talking about? Why is what is possibly – clearly – a murder investigation flowing through you?

If it is murder, you know as well as I do, the case has to be handed off to the homicide guys! You have been told, several times now, that you are overreaching. You haven't the experience or the seniority to be running murder investigations.'

'One,' Rachel said, 'I imagine you'd like to keep this in house when you move to Homicide when Douglas returns. Two, it wouldn't have looked good for you, when it turned out that Gillian Robertson had been murdered, and there might be at least one other, and you'd been dragging your feet, giving the killer time to cover his tracks – or worse still go out and kill more women? I can't imagine that the advocate depute will be thrilled with the latest recruit to his department when he finds out, can you?'

Alastair's mouth was opening and closing like a goldfish.

'Supposing I'm right and these women have been murdered, and it gets to court, the defence would take you and – him apart.'

Alastair looked as if he'd gone a couple of rounds with Mike Tyson – at least mentally. He must know she was right. She actually felt a wee bit sorry for him.

'Look, Alastair, can't we put the past behind us?'

He contemplated her for a long minute. She could almost hear his brain whirring as he weighed up what she said. The pros and cons, advantages and disadvantages to him.

'Very well. Carry on. Keep on top of the police investigation. But if these cases are homicide, I want every bit of evidence signed and sealed. And I promise you, if you fuck up I will personally make sure your career here is finished.'

If it wasn't for the fact that she needed to know what happened to these women, she'd have left him to it. Allowed him to make a rat's arse of it.

'I won't screw up,' she said, knowing it better be true.

. . .

Fifteen minutes later, Du Toit strode into the bar. Having arrived before him and knowing he was short of time, Rachel had ordered him a burger and chips and a Caesar salad for herself. Both dishes arrived moments after Du Toit took his seat.

Du Toit picked up his burger and bit into it. 'Thanks. I needed this,' he said, after he swallowed. He smiled. 'It buys you another twenty-four minutes.'

'I spoke to the pathologist a short while ago. At our behest she repeated Gillian's PM with a colleague.' She repeated what Dr Halliday had told her. 'So we have at least one murder,' she finished.

Du Toit raised an eyebrow. 'At least? Explain.'

She quickly brought him up to speed, starting with what she learned about Caroline Telford. 'I gather Police Scotland put the case on hold but I think they should re-open it.'

'Your reasoning?'

'Not only is there evidence Gillian was strangled, but she had ketamine in her system, as did Caroline. Neither woman had a history of drug abuse. Caroline Telford was thinking of undergoing IVF, Gillian was pregnant with a much-wanted baby. Furthermore, if Gillian injected herself where is the syringe? As far as I know none were found in her flat?' She gave him a questioning look.

When he replied in the negative, she filled him in on the missing morphine, promising she'd come back to it.

'My theory is that someone known to Gillian – that's why there's no evidence of a struggle or a break-in – immobilised her by injecting her with ketamine and, when she was powerless, strangled her.'

'And do you also know who the perpetrator was?' It was difficult to know if Du Toit was being sarcastic or teasing her. He was a difficult man to read.

'No, not yet. However, the day before she died, Sister Robertson had an altercation with a man called King in A&E.

There was evidence he was physically abusing his step-daughter and Gillian refused to let the mother take the child home. King was furious. He threatened Gillian. Furthermore, he was in the department the same day the morphine went missing. Maybe he took it, followed her home, came back later and attacked her? Although,' she had to admit, 'there is no evidence the missing morphine and Gillian's murder are linked. There was no morphine in her toxicology. Some drugs disappear very quickly from the blood but morphine isn't one of them.'

Du Toit's expression was becoming steadily grimmer. 'I'll have King checked out.'

'What about Ashley Carmichael. Was her gear found with the body?' Rachel continued.

'I'll have to check that too. Anything else?' Rachel still couldn't work out if he were annoyed or amused.

'The pathologist is going to prioritise Ashley's PM and tox screen. I've asked her to screen for ketamine and other anaesthetic agents. I assume a syringe was found where *she* died?'

Du Toit nodded.

'I think we should get it checked. I'm beginning to wonder if it even contained heroin. I know Selena is looking into dating sites Gillian might have used. Could she do the same with Caroline Telford and Ashley Carmichael?'

'I'll see to it. I'll make sure King is checked out too.'

'Something else. Jody, one of the sex workers who knew Ashley, saw someone follow her behind the warehouse the night she died. I don't suppose there are any working CCTV cameras in the area?'

'I'll find out,' he said through gritted teeth. Definitely annoyed. Du Toit hated being on the back foot.

'One more thing,' Rachel continued, 'both Gillian and Ashley were patients of Dr Burns. Dr Burns has recently returned from working in rural Zambia where ketamine is regularly used as an anaesthetic agent. I think that drugs, sex and the hospital are tied up in some weird way I can't see.'

Du Toit's burger was half gone. Rachel hadn't eaten more than a couple of forkfuls of her salad. She stabbed a chunk of chicken with her fork.

'At the very least you have one murder to follow up,' she told him. 'And in my opinion, we very likely have three.'

That evening Rachel got a call from Selena, asking if they could meet at the Clachnaharry Inn.

'The walk will do me good,' she said, when Rachel offered to come into town.

Rachel was sipping on a vodka and tonic and had a red wine waiting for the police officer when she arrived. A wall-hung TV playing quietly in the background, meaning they wouldn't be overheard.

'DI Du Toit thought you'd appreciate an update,' Selena said. 'And I thought I'd deliver it in person.' She grinned. 'Have you buy me a drink at the same time.' She took a glug of wine while Rachel waited in expectant silence. 'God, that's good,' she said with an appreciative smack of her lips.

'A syringe definitely wasn't found in Mrs Robertson's flat,' Selena continued. 'It's possible one had been found by the family and discarded unintentionally. We are checking with them.'

Selena took another sip of her drink and scanned the room. Rachel followed her gaze. Two men sat separately at tables, another propped up the bar. An older couple were tucking into a bar supper while another, younger, couple played Scrabble. It was a scene of contentment. 'When I look for a place I'm going to make sure my local is like this,' Selena said, before continuing: 'No syringe was found at the scene of Mrs Telford's death either. A syringe *was* found with Ashley's body, but none of the other gear normally used by heroin addicts. The syringe has been sent to the lab to be processed.

'My sergeant and I interviewed King under caution,' she continued. 'He blustered and cursed and denied any involvement in Mrs Robertson's death. As you'd expect. We are checking his alibi and keeping tags on him.

'Finally, DI Du Toit has arranged to see Dr Ballantyne at the hospital tomorrow afternoon. He wants to know if Caroline Telford saw one of the doctors there. He says you are welcome to come along if you're free. I suspect he thinks you'll go yourself if he doesn't invite you and would rather keep an eye on you. Now,' Selena said, lifting her empty glass in the direction of the bartender, 'my round. What are you having?'

THIRTY

The next morning, after kicking their heels down in gynae reception, Du Toit, Selena and Rachel were shown up to Dr Ballantyne's office.

A man dressed in a dark blue suit, wearing a long-sleeved shirt with incongruous teddy bear cuff links, introduced himself as Dr Ballantyne. He was clean-shaven. Expensively dressed. Authoritative.

Dr Ballantyne's office looked as if it had been recently refurbished with a new desk and matching filing cabinets; the walls freshly painted in a cheerful buttercup yellow instead of the NHS green. The office was a corner one with a far-reaching view of hills on one side and the hospital entrance and car park on the other.

The only personal item in his office was a silver-framed photograph perched on his over-large desk. Rachel leaned across and edged the photograph around and studied it while Nick finished whatever he was doing on his computer. His wife – at least she assumed the woman in the photo was his wife – looked to be in her mid-thirties with mousy brown hair and a shy smile. Her head was dipped slightly, as if she were trying to hide from the photographer.

'Sorry, to keep you waiting. I was finishing off some notes,' he said. 'Now, what can I do for you?'

'Do the names Ashley Carmichael and Caroline Telford mean anything to you?' Du Toit asked, clearly irritated they'd been kept waiting.

Dr Ballantyne shook his head. 'No. Should they?'

'What about Gillian Robertson?'

'Yes, of course I knew her. She worked in the hospital. We came across each other often when I was asked to see patients in A&E. Her death is an enormous loss to the whole hospital.'

'Did you know her socially?'

'Sort of.'

'What do you mean by that?'

'Only that in a hospital this size it would be odd if we didn't bump into each other at social events.'

'What about your wife?' Rachel asked. 'Did she know her?'

'They'd met once or twice at said social occasions.'

'And Dr Burns? Do you see her outside work?' Du Toit asked.

'No. We've only ever met as colleagues.'

'And how is she as a colleague?' Du Toit asked.

Dr Ballantyne took his time answering. 'I assume this is between us. That it won't go any further.'

'As long as it has no bearing in a criminal court, then of course,' Du Toit said smoothly.

'If you'd asked me this a week or two ago, I would have said exceptional. One of my colleagues is due to retire in the next couple of years and I'd hopes of appointing Dr Burns into his post once she's completed her training. I told her as much. She was pleased and relieved.'

'You're clearly having second thoughts,' Rachel said. 'Can I ask why?'

'I don't see how this is relevant but she's not been on her game recently. Of course that is understandable. She's bound to be grieving. Gillian was a good friend of hers, I believe.'

No one said anything as they waited for him to continue. 'I did suggest she take some time off, but she wasn't keen. I suspect she thought it might damage her chances of getting back on the training scheme.'

'And would it?'

'Not as much as making mistakes,' the doctor replied.

'Have there been mistakes?' Selena asked.

'It's not something I'm willing to elaborate on until I've heard what Dr Burns has to say. But I can promise you it has nothing do with Mrs Robertson's death.'

Rachel suspected he was talking about the mix-up with patients Kirsty had told her about. Poor Kirsty, she really was having a crap time. Her mind flashed to the porters' office. Was that what Kirsty had been looking for? She mental note to ask her.

'Let's get back to Ashley Carmichael,' Du Toit said. 'Apparently she attended Dr Burns' antenatal clinic about a week before she died.'

Ballantyne raised his eyebrows in a silent question but said nothing.

'Might she have seen Caroline Telford too?' Du Toit continued.

'I could look it up on the computer. But why don't you ask her herself? She's on her way up to see me, as it happens. I'll tell my secretary to show her in as soon as she arrives.'

THIRTY-ONE

Kirsty tapped on Nick's door and walked straight in. She found a man and a woman sitting across the desk from her boss, who introduced them as police detectives. She was surprised to find Rachel with them. In fact she was surprised to see any of them. She thought she was here to discuss what had happened in theatre a couple of days ago. She'd no idea what had gone wrong, but the theatre staff clearly thought it was her fault. That was bollocks. She would never mix up patients. She was far too obsessional, particularly these days, to do that.

The only reason the police and Rachel could be here was because of Gilly.

The policeman stood up. He was tall, well built, and dressed in a dark suit, the tops of his white socks peeping out from the cuffs of his trousers. His thick black hair needed a trim and his pockmarked face and rubbery mouth should have made him unattractive, but Kirsty found his features oddly appealing. The other police officer was in her late twenties, with sparkling eyes.

The male officer held out his hand. 'I'm Inspector Du Toit

and this is Detective Constable MacDonald. I believe you've met Miss McKenzie.'

'Yes. Hello, Rachel.'

'Thank you for sparing us a few minutes of your time. I know how busy you doctors are,' Du Toit continued. 'Yes, there have been developments.'

Nick was tapping away at his computer keyboard.

'Please, sit down, Dr Burns.' Du Toit waited until Kirsty sat before continuing. 'I can tell you there is an active investigation into Mrs Robertson's death. I can't tell you much more than that at the moment. But we do have a couple of questions for you.'

Kirsty felt the blood drain from her body. They had to have reason to believe that Gillian had been murdered. What had they found out?

'I gather you saw Caroline Telford at your clinic a few weeks before you left for Africa,' Du Toit's question cut through the fog in her brain.

'The name doesn't sound familiar.'

Nick looked up from his computer. 'I've logged into her records. She saw you, a month before you left for Africa.'

'I see hundreds of patients. What about her? Is she in some kind of trouble?' Kirsty asked.

'I'm afraid she's dead,' Du Toit said softly, giving her a searching look.

Kirsty's pulse skipped a beat. What did that have to do with Gillian? 'What happened?' she asked.

'We're not sure,' Du Toit replied. 'That's why we're here. If you could answer our questions that would be helpful. What can you tell us about her?'

Kirsty looked to Nick for support. Catching her eye, he nodded. 'Tell them what you know, Dr Burns. Patient confidentiality goes out the window in cases like this.'

Nick swivelled his computer screen so that Kirsty could see

it. No one spoke in the few minutes it took Kirsty to read Mrs Telford's records.

Now she recalled the impish-looking woman with an infectious smile. Nevertheless, she took a moment to scan what she had recorded about the consultation.

'As you say, I saw her about nineteen months ago. Caroline had had two normal live births, followed by a long gap. She and her husband decided they wanted another child, but despite trying for over twelve months, she didn't get pregnant. I explained that I could refer her for investigations but not on the NHS. If IVF was required, it would have to be done privately as she had two living children.' She glanced at Du Toit, who was listening intently. 'Apparently money wasn't an issue, so I referred her to Nick.'

Nick pivoted the screen back towards him.

'Apart from my NHS work, I see patients privately at the hospital up the road,' he explained. 'But I don't remember seeing this lady. It's possible that she made an appointment and someone else saw her. Or she could have changed her mind.' He shrugged. 'It happens.'

'Once I referred her to Nick, my contact with her ended,' Kirsty added. 'But what does this have to do with her death? Or Gillian's, for that matter? She was in good health as far as I could determine. Not on any medication or seeing her GP.'

'How many times did you see her?'

'Only the once. Why?'

'Who else would have come into contact with her?'

'I don't know. The nurses. Clerical staff. Why do you ask?' Kirsty was becoming increasingly puzzled. What had this to do with Gilly?

'Could we have a copy of her records?' Du Toit asked Dr Ballantyne, without answering Kirsty's question.

'You need to go through the right channels,' Nick replied.

'You have to have a legitimate reason to obtain a copy of patients' records. Perhaps if you explained?'

The policeman's eyes were no longer smiling.

'Are you familiar with the use of ketamine as an anaesthetic agent?' he asked Kirsty.

'Well, yes.'

'Do you still have access to ketamine?' Du Toit pressed.

'Absolutely not. Why would I? I have no need to anaesthetise anyone here. Anyway, it's only used as an anaesthetic in this country in particular situations.' Her heart gave a sickening jolt. 'Why are you asking me this?'

'We think there is a reasonable chance Mrs Telford and Mrs Robertson were killed by someone who works in a clinical setting. Possibly at this hospital.'

Nick blanched. 'Are you suggesting they were murdered by a clinician? What nonsense!'

'Why?' Du Toit responded mildly. He stood. 'Doctors and nurses are as likely as anyone to be murderers. Have even been known to murder their patients. I'd still like a copy of Caroline Telford's medical records, as well as Gillian Robertson's and Ashley Carmichael's. As soon as possible. Whoever did this is out there, and the sooner we catch him' – Du Toit turned his gaze on Kirsty – 'or her, the better for us all.'

THIRTY-TWO

Bleary-eyed from lack of sleep, Rachel stumbled out of bed to answer whoever was thumping on her door. She glanced at her watch – it wasn't six yet. Her pulse skipped a beat. She hoped to hell it wasn't Du Toit or Selena bringing news of more murdered women.

But when she opened the door it was to find Angus looking down at her. He was wearing loose trousers and his Gore-Tex climbing jacket. 'Get dressed and pack a rucksack. We're going climbing.'

'Good morning to you too,' she said, stepping aside to allow him to enter. Why did men think it was acceptable to pitch up at a woman's doorstep without warning? Her hair was like a furball, she was wearing old tracksuit bottoms, a T-shirt that had more holes than fabric and yes, there was a pimple on her chin. 'And I'm having coffee before I agree to anything.' She headed for the kitchen, leaving him to follow. 'You want some?' When he nodded, she pointed to a chair. 'Sit down.'

Her cottage could have been tidier too, Rachel thought, taking in the sink full of dishes, the basket of laundry waiting to be shoved in the machine and the open can of cat food on the kitchen counter. But crap, she hadn't asked him to come and certainly not before dawn. She should have left him kicking his heels on the doorstep.

He ignored her and moved to the window instead. 'Nice view, by the way. You forgot to text me your address when you moved. Have you any idea how long it took me to track you down?'

'Why are you really here?' she asked. 'You haven't tried to follow me up a mountain in years.' It was a reference to the competitive nature of their climbs.

As children they'd go hillwalking with their fathers, but soon they were outpacing them. When she was ten, she and Angus had started going on their own and quickly their walks had turned into steeper and more difficult climbs. Angus learned to belay at the climbing centre in Inverness and had taught her, soon allowing her to take the lead rope. Although Rachel was three years younger, she'd been the one demanding they took the more challenging and technical routes. Angus might have been stronger, but she was more flexible, her long limbs giving her a reach that almost matched his.

Back then he'd treated her like a slightly irritating little sister. He'd teased her, ignored her and patronised her, but there was no one she trusted more to get her up a mountain in one piece and she was pretty sure he felt the same about her.

Over the years most of their climbing had been done in near silence, which had suited them both. She'd always been on the quiet side, but Angus took silence to a whole new level. The climbs had stopped when he'd gone off to university and Rachel had gone off the rails.

They'd met again, a few months before her mother's body was found, when he'd turned up at her university's halls of residence, climbing gear in hand. He'd been clearly taken aback. His eyes had widened and he'd given her a slow smile of appreciation. She'd been equally gobsmacked. The skinny lad with bumfluff on his chin had metamorphosed into six foot three of lean muscle. His dark hair was fashionably cut, still longer at the front than at the back, emphasising his beautiful face.

The relationship between them, although charged, had stayed essentially the same. He'd never asked why she ran away, what she'd got up to in Glasgow, or why she'd come back. And she'd never offered to tell him.

They'd gone climbing together over the summer holiday and it had been on the last occasion when, trapped on the mountain by thick mist, they'd been forced to spend the night in a bothy. As her mind immediately went there again, heat flooded her cheeks. She'd been the instigator, him an enthusiastic participant.

He'd called her several times after that, but she'd made excuses not to see him. Until her father had been charged with murder and he'd appointed the firm Angus worked for to represent him. As Angus had been devilling at the time, shadowing the advocate defending her father, he'd only had a junior, investigatory role.

That was when she'd pitched up at his flat in Edinburgh, tanked up with vodka, looking for an update on her father's case, beginning to realise her father was probably guilty after all.

Every excruciating detail was seared into her memory. How she'd come on to him, pressed herself against him like a bloody piece of sticking plaster, and he'd pushed her away, steered her out of the door, telling her he couldn't sleep with her while working on her father's case. Whether he'd believed that or not, the humiliation had never quite left her. Between that rejection and her parents' marriage, no wonder she had a problem with relationships.

She handed him his cup of coffee. 'It's Sunday. Did it occur to you I might have plans?'

'Do you?'

'As it happens, no. But I haven't been climbing for a couple of years. I'm not sure my muscles are up to it.'

Cool blue eyes swept over her. 'You look in pretty good shape to me.' Once more she caught a ghost of a smile. 'One way to find out. We could do Ben Wyvis. That shouldn't be too taxing.'

Rachel capitulated. The forecast promised sunshine. And she missed climbing. It would be good to go climbing with Angus again. Furthermore, there was something she wanted to discuss with him.

'OK. Make yourself at home while I have a shower.'

'I'll give the village a quick recce while you do.'

Twenty minutes later she was opening the door to Angus's Porsche.

'Business going well then,' Rachel remarked as she lowered herself into the passenger seat.

Angus said nothing. He tossed her rucksack next to his in the narrow back seat. The car sprang into life with a roar.

The sun had fully risen while Rachel was getting ready and as they roared along the A9 it spread its rays across the fields on either side of the dual carriageway. Rachel loved this part of the world with its mountains, valleys and glens.

'What made you ask about your mother the other morning?' Angus asked as they swept along, overtaking tractors and slower-moving vehicles with exhilarating ease.

'Mum told Gran that she was worried about something or someone and that it had to do with work. I want to know what it was.' She took a long shaky breath. 'I was a terrible daughter when Mum was alive. There is so much I regret, not least that I never really got to know her. I want to find out what worried her. I know she's gone, but I feel that is something I can do for her. Maybe put it right if it's still a problem. Maybe feel better somehow if it's not...' She tailed off. This wasn't the sort of conversation they usually had, but if she couldn't have it with

Angus, who knew this horrible secret in her life, who could she have it with? Besides, she needed his help. She wanted a copy, or access to, the trial files of the human-trafficking ring that Mrs Goodall had mentioned her mother was due to give evidence in.

'She was a social worker, right? I imagine there was a lot in that job to worry her.'

'That's what I thought.' She told him about her trip to Nora Goodall and the case her mother had been due to testify in. 'Did Dad ever mention anything like this to you?'

Angus was quiet for a long time. 'You know I can't discuss your father's case with you. At least not anything said in private conversations. Everything that came out at the trial is fair game, of course. But I don't remember this case coming up.'

'But don't you think it's a bit of a coincidence Mum went missing shortly before she was due to testify in court.'

He pulled into a car park at the foot of Ben Wyvis and turned to look at her. 'Let me do some digging. But Rachel, people-trafficking usually involves pretty serious criminals, so promise me you won't go looking into this alone. In the meantime, let's get up this mountain.'

She gave him side-eye. She'd promise nothing. He should know her better than that. As he'd said when they went fishing, she was all grown up. She'd been looking after herself since she was fifteen and had no intention of stopping now.

An hour later they were leaning, shoulder to shoulder, against the cairn at the summit of Ben Wyvis. Rachel's heart was racing and it wasn't entirely due to the breakneck speed with which they'd climbed the hill.

If she were honest, it was more to do with the weird, complicated sensations flooding her body. She felt flustered, hot, anxious, uncertain; almost exactly the same way she'd felt around him when she was nineteen.

Back then he was the person in whose company she could most be herself, the person who in many ways knew her best, even if he hardly knew her at all.

Could they be friends again? Was that what she wanted?

He reached into his rucksack and offered her a choice between a Morrison's egg mayonnaise and cress, and a chicken salad. She chose the egg mayo.

He unscrewed the top from the flask of coffee he'd brought. She was touched that he'd remembered she took it black. They ate their sandwiches in companionable silence, while taking in the view that stretched from one mountain to another. The tension and turmoil in her body seeped away.

'What are you working on at the moment?' she asked.

'You wouldn't believe it,' he said. 'A case where a group of people in Morningside have been accused of ritual murder and witchcraft.'

She laughed. Morningside was an affluent suburb of Edinburgh.

'I'm serious,' he said, giving her a smile. 'The coven includes a doctor, two teachers and a judge.'

'And the victim?'

'Alleged victim, you mean? A French woman who was working for one of the families as an au pair.'

'Don't you get fed up defending the worst of people?' she asked

'The trial isn't finished so we don't know they are the worst of people yet. It beats playing whack-a-mole with the usual bad guys though.'

'You know I'll never agree. How do you do it? Why do you do it? You defend murderers, drug dealers, rapists – all sorts of scum. Look, I know the argument about everyone having the right to a defence, but...' She tried to sort out her thoughts. Life wasn't black and white, she knew that. Better ten guilty men go free than one good one goes to jail. But could she ever be part of the system that freed the guilty, when they were likely to go on and commit even more heinous crimes?

'Had things not turned out the way they did, you might have ended up defending the man who tried to kill me.' She turned to face him. 'What would you have done then?'

'I would have pointed him in the direction of another advocate.'

'But say he'd insisted on you? What then?'

'Where are you going with this, Rachel? Is this to do with your father?'

'Maybe. I don't know. Do you believe your firm looked into every possible angle in my father's defence? Can you be sure?'

'I have no reason to doubt it. Enough about the past though, tell me about your job.' He scrunched up their empty sandwich cartons and put them in his backpack. He passed her an apple.

She told him about the dead women. Her increasing suspicion that they were linked in some way. But soon her thoughts returned to her mother. 'I forgot to mention earlier that the social worker I saw, Nora Goodall, mentioned that the police and the social work department believed that the traffickers were being warned in advance when the police were about to raid. Do you think that might have been a policeman? The Met in London is full of bad apples.' She'd even identified one in Uist. 'Couldn't there be one here?'

Angus frowned, tossed his apple core into the grass and stood. 'It's always possible.' He held out his hand and, when she took it, tugged her to her feet. 'All the more reason for you to leave the snooping to me.' He touched her lightly on the nose. 'Don't you think you've had enough crap in your life?' For a moment they stood there, inches from one another, as a wee fantasy involving clan chiefs as in the Highlander series vied with the potential repercussions of having sex in public buzzed around Rachel's head, making her dizzy. God knew what was going on his. Judging by the look in his eyes, something similar.

Equally thrilled and terrified where things might go, Rachel stepped away.

'I need to know, so I'm going to find out,' she told him. She shrugged into her rucksack and headed down the hill, leaving him to follow.

THIRTY-THREE

Feeling exposed and embarrassed, Annie perched on the side of her hospital bed waiting to be taken to theatre. She had been made to put on the ridiculous paper gown she remembered well from her nursing days. For some reason she had never fully understood, the gown was worn back to front with the opening revealing a naked bottom if the wearer were unlucky enough to forget to hold it closed. Since this meant walking with one hand twisted behind in an awkward position, she wasn't surprised that most patients simply gave up and let their naked buttocks flash those unfortunate enough to be walking in their wake.

The pre-med she had been given was beginning to work, making her feel woozy. She had been told not to eat or drink since midnight the previous night and her tongue was sticking to the roof of her mouth.

The children were staying with David for a couple of nights so that she could rest when she left the hospital. They had seemed pleased to be spending time with their father, although her daughter had worried.

'I'll stay and look after you, Mum,' Susan had said. 'I don't think you should be on your own.'

It was at times like these that Annie was acutely reminded how responsible for her mother her fifteen-year-old had become. When most other young adolescents were out having fun and enjoying a first taste of independence and freedom, Susan was more concerned about looking after her. But all that was going to change. It would take time to repair her relationship with Susan, but once her daughter realised Annie was off the booze for good, maybe she'd begin to trust her mum again.

She wondered if Rachel had looked into Caroline's death. Or got round to telling the police what Jody had said.

A couple of porters and a nurse arrived to take her down to theatre, interrupting her musing.

'Ready?' the nurse asked with practised reassurance. Although she smiled, her eyes were blank. Annie could tell her thoughts were elsewhere. Perhaps she too had problems at home, or more likely she was simply thinking about her tea break. Strong arms slid her onto the trolley and Annie watched the overhead lights rush by as she was wheeled through swing doors and into the operating room.

'Annie. How are you feeling?' Kirsty asked. Already gowned, gloved and wearing her mask she looked reassuringly capable and at home in the theatre suite. 'This won't take long,' Kirsty continued, her eyes, visible above her mask, creasing at the corners. 'You'll be back in your room before you know it.'

Apart from Kirsty, there were a number of people in the operating room all dressed in scrubs of various hues. Annie knew some of them would be nursing staff, the man who had come to see her earlier on the ward was an anaesthetist and the nondescript-looking man with the bland expression was one of the porters who had come to fetch her from the ward. The anaesthetist introduced himself again, stuck a needle into her arm, and asked her to count back from 100. At 96, Annie let sleep claim her.

When she came to, she was back on the ward. There was a

stabbing pain low in her abdomen where she guessed the incision had been made. The pain was on par with that of painful contraction and Annie moaned as her abdomen spasmed. A nurse Annie hadn't met before stood by the bed, fiddling with the drip. Kirsty was next to her, still wearing her theatre greens, her mask pushed down around her throat.

'I'm going to add antibiotics to your drip and give you morphine to help your pain. It'll probably make you a little sleepy, but that's good. Everything went well and you should be able to go home tomorrow.'

Annie had wanted to go home that day, but Kirsty had advised against it on the grounds that there would be no one there to keep an eye on her.

All the same, Annie planned to leave as soon as she had fully recovered from the anaesthetic. Feeling nauseous and groggy, she closed her eyes once more.

The next time she opened them, a new member of staff was at her bedside. This person was wearing green scrubs and a theatre hat and mask and, even in her befuddlement, Annie thought it a little strange. She was still sick and disoriented from the anaesthetic, but some sixth sense left over from her nursing days was firing away. The figure was injecting something into the bag of saline that fed antibiotics into Annie's system. Kirsty had explained earlier that the antibiotics were a preventative measure and would be discontinued after the bag ran through.

Annie struggled to prop herself on an elbow. Squinting at the empty vial that had been placed on the bedside table beside her bed she could read the writing on the label: *Potassium Chloride*.

Christ. What was the nurse doing? It had been a long time since Annie worked in a hospital, but she knew that potassium given incorrectly could be fatal. The nurse was about to make an error that would kill Annie.

'Hey.' She tried to shout but the sound came out as a whisper. 'Stop.'

Her voice was firmer now, but the figure paid no attention. In a blur of green, he, or she, left the room. Annie began to feel the effects of the drug almost immediately. Her heart started to race and there was a burning sensation in her chest.

She lunged for the cord to call for help, but it was out of reach. She slipped sideways, almost falling out of bed. *Someone was trying to kill her! What the hell!* As she felt herself slip under she thought of one last thing she could do to save herself. She didn't know whether she had enough strength left but she had to try.

THIRTY-FOUR

Kirsty raced along the corridor, her heart in her throat. She'd been paged by the ward to let her know that one of her patients, Annie Colston, had arrested. The operation had gone smoothly. What the hell had happened?

By the time she pushed through the ward doors and skidded into Annie's room, the crash team was already there working on Annie. The bed cover was crimson with blood. The band across her chest tightened. Exactly like Gilly. Where had it come from? Not her wound. The surgery had been done through the umbilicus and there had hardly been any bleeding.

'What happened?' Kirsty asked as she gloved up.

'We heard a thump and when we came in to investigate we found her on the floor. Her drip's out, but whether that happened as a result of the fall or whether she pulled it out, we don't know. But that's what's caused the blood everywhere.'

'We found an empty vial of potassium chloride. We're working on the assumption that she's had some in error. We've given her a stat dose of calcium,' one of the medical staff working on Annie told Kirsty.

The doctor was doing chest compressions as he spoke.

Kirsty felt Annie's wrist for a pulse, found one and checked the monitor to be certain.

'She's got a pulse,' she called out. 'Stop compressions.'

The doctor backed off and Kirsty held her breath as they waited to see whether Annie's heart would continue beating unaided. Within seconds the monitor started emitting the regular beats of a heart in sinus rhythm.

'Looks like you might have been right about the potassium. Have you given her IV insulin and glucose?'

The doctor shook his head. 'Haven't had time.'

Nurse Boyle, who Kirsty knew from theatre, handed Kirsty a syringe. 'It's 5 units insulin plus 10 mils of 50 per cent glucose. Don't worry, I've double-checked.'

Kirsty slipped the needle into a vein in Annie's forearm. 'Any idea how she got the potassium?' she asked. *Bloody stupid mistake*, she was thinking, but now wasn't the time for recriminations.

'We think she must have got it with her antibiotic,' Nurse Boyle said with one of her sucked-on-a-lemon looks, turning away quickly when Kirsty tried to hold her gaze. There was something about the intensity with which the nurse was examining the chart that chilled Kirsty. None of the other staff in the room would look at her either.

'But I gave her the antibiotic,' Kirsty said. Then, as realisation hit her: 'You think it was me who slipped up? No way. I would have never made a mistake like that.'

Nobody said anything. Kirsty opened her mouth to protest again but changed her mind. There would be time later to get to the bottom of it. First, she had to make sure Annie would survive the potentially lethal mistake. Annie remained unconscious but she was breathing on her own and her heartbeat was regular and strong.

'Any idea how long she was out for?'

'It couldn't have been long,' the nurse replied. 'We came as

soon as we heard her fall and started cardiac massage immediately.'

'With a bit of luck, she'll get through this without having
mince for brains,' Kirsty muttered.

Once Annie had been stabilised she was transferred to
ITU. The nurses continued to avert their gazes and Kirsty
guessed that Jessie Boyle, who had worked with her before she
left for Zambia, had made sure everyone knew about Kirsty and
her history. No doubt she had also told them about the mix-up
with the patients in theatre last week too. Bloody woman.
Without the confidence of the nurses, her job would be impossible. The sooner all of this was cleared up, the better.

THIRTY-FIVE

A bleeping sound like the noise a van made to warn it was reversing pierced Annie's dream. Her throat ached as if the same lorry had driven down it, reversed and then driven all the way back up. In between the bleeps she heard whispers and moans of pain. She struggled to open her eyes. They felt heavy as if they were taped shut. Perhaps she was blind? Panic-stricken, she tried to claw at her eyes, but her arms were too heavy and no matter how much she tried, they wouldn't obey her commands. She gave up. It was easier to leave her eyes closed and lie quietly and wait. She tried to swallow, but her mouth was as dry as an elephant's hide.

'She's breathing on her own,' said a female voice. Who? Who was breathing on her own? Was it her they were talking about? Her heart started to pound. She vaguely remembered coming round after the anaesthetic, but after that, only fragments filtered through her mind like the remnants of a half-remembered dream. She shook her head in frustration. There was something she needed to remember. Something she needed to tell these people.

'Hey, hey,' the disembodied voice soothed. 'Take it easy, relax if you can. I won't be a sec.'

There was a gentle tugging at her eyelids and then at last she was able to open her eyes. Her vision was blurry at first, her lids caked with the remnants of a deep sleep, but gradually shapes came into focus. A nurse, dressed in the crisp white top and slacks of Inverness General, was bending over her, appraising her with coolly professional eyes.

'Welcome back. How are you feeling? Sorry about the eyes, we taped them while you were asleep. We didn't expect you to come around so soon. I bet you could do with a drink.'

At that moment there was nothing that Annie desired more in the world. If necessary, she would sell her soul for a sip of water. Unable to speak, she nodded her assent. The movement made her head ache.

The nurse slid an arm behind her head, raising her gently while holding the glass to Annie's lips. Annie drank greedily, the water spilling from her mouth and dripping down her front. God, it tasted good.

'Hey, slow down,' the nurse chided, still in that same soft voice. 'Only a few sips at a time or you'll make yourself sick.' She removed the glass and set it beside the bed. 'I'm going to call a doctor to give you a look over. You had us all worried for a while.'

As she turned to leave, Annie grabbed her hand. Fragments were coming back. The figure injecting the potassium chloride. Her heart catapulting within her chest. Her last thoughts as she tried to call for help. The belief that she was about to die. As she remembered, she panicked again, perhaps the person was still here.

'Don't go,' she croaked. 'Please, you mustn't leave me on my own.'

'It's OK, I'll be back in a moment. The doctor is by the desk over there. You won't be out of my sight for a second.'

When she next came to, she was back in the gynae ward and Kirsty and a dark-haired man with pale blue eyes were standing next to her bed.

'I'm Dr Nick Ballantyne,' the blue-eyed man introduced himself. 'We haven't met, but I'm the consultant in charge of your case. How are you feeling?'

'I'm all right.' Annie could only manage a croak through her painful throat. Actually she felt like shit.

'I'd like to look in your eyes, if that's OK,' Dr Ballantyne said, bending over Annie with an ophthalmoscope. She could smell the faint tang of mint on his breath as his examination brought his face uncomfortably close to hers. She resisted the impulse to press her head into the pillows.

'You're back in the ward now but we had to admit you temporarily to ITU, Annie. Do you know why?' Kirsty asked.

'Is that where I was? I remember feeling really ill – then nothing till I woke up here.' She frowned, trying to remember. She could recall feeling terrified, but not why.

Kirsty looked at Dr Ballantyne, who had straightened after completing his examination. He wrapped Annie's wrist in cool fingers.

'Pulse and pupils normal,' he said to Kirsty, before turning back to Annie. 'You are going to be fine. But I have to tell you, Mrs Colston, you've had a very lucky escape.'

Annie managed a feeble laugh. 'I fail to see what's fortunate about landing up in ITU after a simple procedure. What happened?' It was difficult to get the words past her aching throat.

'We believe you were given a drug in error. We think your antibiotics were mixed with potassium chloride instead of normal saline. The potassium sent your heart into arrhythmia. Luckily your drip came out and the alarm was raised and although your heart stopped, we managed to bring you back.'

Annie struggled to grasp hold of the images that darted through her mind.

'Oh, my God, I remember the empty vial on my bedside table. I knew that whoever was injecting that into my drip was making a terrible mistake. I tried to tell them, but they didn't listen. I called for help.' Suffocating fear returned as she remembered. 'No one came, so I pulled the cannula out of my hand. I knew I had to stop the drug getting into my system – I used to be a nurse.'

'Good thinking,' Dr Ballantyne said. 'You probably saved your life by doing that. Did you see who it was? Had you seen them before? Did you recognise him? Was it one of the nurses? A doctor?'

'I didn't see his face. He had his back to me. He was doing something to the drip.'

'Are you sure it was a man?' Dr Ballantyne asked.

Annie thought about it for a moment. 'No. The person was quite tall, but I couldn't tell if it was a man or woman. Their hair was hidden by a theatre hat.'

'Was the person about Dr Burns's height?' he asked, indicating Kirsty with a nod of his head.

Annie looked at Kirsty, puzzled. 'Yes. I would say so. But it wasn't Kirsty.'

'Are you sure?' Ballantyne persisted. 'You said you couldn't see the face.'

Annie struggled to recreate the scene in her head. The person fiddling with the drip, adjusting the flow. There was something about the hands. But the memory flitted away, refusing to be captured.

'It wasn't Kirsty. I would have recognised her. She would have spoken to me when I called out. It wasn't you, was it?' Annie looked at Kirsty, uncertain where the conversation was going.

'It wasn't me,' Kirsty said flatly. 'But we have to find out who it was. Whoever made the mistake needs to understand that they very nearly killed you.'

'Mrs Colston,' Dr Ballantyne interrupted with a sharp glance at Kirsty. 'We intend to get to the bottom of this. I can't tell you how sorry I am about what happened. If you remember anything more, please let us know at once. In the meantime, try to get as much rest as possible while we keep an eye on you.'

'No. I want to leave the hospital. Please let me go home. I'll be safe there.'

Dr Ballantyne drew his brows together. 'Hey, it's OK,' he said gently. 'You're perfectly safe now. Whoever made the mistake is unlikely to do the same thing twice. Besides, we've taken your drip out.'

Despite his reassuring tone, Annie wasn't convinced. 'You can't keep me here against my will. I never wanted to stay overnight in the first place and as soon as I can get out of bed I'm discharging myself. Please' – she held up a palm – 'Look, nothing you can do or say will convince me to stay. At the moment, I have no intention of filing a complaint about what happened, but I will if you try to stop me from leaving.'

Dr Ballantyne frowned and looked at Kirsty, who shrugged. Annie could tell he thought she was overreacting. How would he bloody well feel if someone had given him a drug that had almost killed him?

'Very well, Mrs Colston. You'll have to sign some forms absolving the hospital from any responsibility if anything goes wrong while you are at home, but you are right, we can't hold you against your wishes.'

As Annie slumped back exhausted, Dr Ballantyne took Kirsty to one side. They spoke for a couple of minutes in heated whispers before Dr Ballantyne strode off.

Once Dr Ballantyne had left, Kirsty returned to Annie's bedside.

'I am so sorry this happened to you,' she said, 'but I wish you'd reconsider discharging yourself.'

'Would you stay if you were me?' Annie demanded. 'This hospital scares the shit out of me. Before I passed out I was terrified and I still feel scared. It might be because I nearly died, but I don't think it's just that.' She sat up. 'Please, get me out of here, Kirsty. As soon as possible.'

Kirsty sighed. 'Very well. I'll do my best. In the meantime, nothing can happen here. See,' Kirsty indicated the ward with a sweep of her hand. 'There are three other patients in the bay with you. You're in full view of all the nurses. And I've got a patient two beds along that I need to check up on every couple of hours, so when I look in on her, I'll check up on you. OK?'

'Fine. But only until I can manage to walk, then I'm out of here. In fact' – Annie pushed aside the bedclothes – 'I think I can manage to get up now, if you'll help me?'

'The only help I am going to give you right now is to keep you in bed.' Kirsty pressed Annie gently back onto the pillows before tucking her in. 'And don't worry, I'm going to make it my business to find out exactly what happened to you, and make sure it can't happen to you – or anyone else – again.'

Annie was unconvinced. But her efforts had exhausted her, and she stopped struggling.

'Hurry back,' she mumbled. 'I'm not spending the night here, whatever you say.'

Annie meant it; as soon as Kirsty left, she sent a quick text to Peggy, and was relieved beyond words when an hour later she woke up from her nap to see two familiar figures approaching her bed.

Mags was clearly enjoying the startled looks of the nursing staff as she teetered her way down the ward in tower-block shoes, short skirt slung low on her hips. She wore full make-up and a wolfish grin, apparently delighted with the effect she was having.

Jody, on the other hand, slunk alongside Mags as if she wished she was anywhere else but there. Her face was bloodless and from time to time she would look over her shoulder nervously as if expecting someone to grab her and turf her out.

Mags, still enjoying herself, pulled a chair up to Annie's bedside and plonked herself down.

'How are you, hen? We wis down the centre when Peggy got your message and I said Jody and me would spring you. Jody here was all for it, until we arrived. Now she's acting like I'm forcing her at gunpoint.'

Jody looked at Annie for the first time. 'This place freaks me out. Look can we get out of here already?'

Jody sat down sullenly while Annie exchanged a puzzled glance with Mags and then set about collecting her things. She didn't know what was up with Jody, but she totally agreed she didn't want to be here for a second longer.

THIRTY-SIX

Rachel was in her front garden, coffee in hand, watching the houseboats go by. Sometimes, depending on the date and time, she'd have her coffee in the back garden and watch the *Flying Scotsman* trundle its way North.

Her phone rang. She felt a thrill of anticipation when she recognised Angus's number.

'Hello you,' she said.

'Hello you back.' It was their greeting when they were children. His voice was deep, rich, melodic.

'I have something for you,' he continued. 'I've a client to see in Perth prison this afternoon. Could I swing by on the way home?'

'What time?'

'Sixish. If it isn't too short notice. You might have plans.'

'As it happens, I don't.' She rarely had plans but wasn't going to tell him that. 'Aren't you going to tell me what you have for me?' Oh for God's sake, she sounded breathless. Worse, she sounded flirty. 'This evening is fine.'

'Great. I'll see you later.'

. . .

Rachel had taken out the chilli she'd frozen, agonised over what music to play on her Sonos, eventually settling on Adele (everyone liked Adele, didn't they?) and chilled a bottle of white wine when she heard the crunch of tyres.

She went outside to meet Angus, her heart giving a series of little blips when he got out of the car. He was in a dark suit and white shirt and, as he stretched, his shirt rode up, giving Rachel a glimpse of his washboard stomach. No man should be that good-looking.

'So,' she said with a smile. 'Are you going to tell me what you've got for me?'

In reply, he opened the tiny boot of his Porsche, revealing several cardboard boxes.

'Copies of the court documents for the trial your mother was supposed to testify in.'

Really? That was his gift? The thing he'd appeared so pleased about. Not that she didn't want to see it. It was just that she'd hoped... She didn't try to articulate what she'd hoped, even to herself.

'I had to lean on one of the clerks, but happily they came through,' Angus said as he stashed the boxes on top of each other. 'There's nearly a thousand pages between all of the files. You take these and I'll get the rest from the back seat.'

The clerk was probably a woman, Rachel thought bitterly. Who else would stand at a photocopier for all that time for something that wasn't court business, at least not currently?

She carried the boxes into her kitchen. Angus came in behind her and added his three boxes to hers.

'It's going to take me weeks, if not months to go through them.'

'I'll come over when I get a chance and help you.'

She wasn't sure what to make of his offer. Was he being helpful, or did he want to spend time with her? And why was she thinking like this?

'Do you think there's something in all that' – she tipped her head at the boxes – 'that will tell me what Mum was frightened of?'

'I hope so. But if there isn't, then at least you'll know.' He sniffed the air. 'Something smells good.'

'Are you staying for dinner?'

'I'm sorry, Rae, I can't.' He grinned. 'I'm meeting someone hot for dinner in Edinburgh. I think it might be serious this time.' He glanced at his watch. 'I'd better shoot.'

THIRTY-SEVEN

The day of Gillian's memorial service dawned wet and miserable. When the family had been told it might be months before Gillian's body was returned to them, they'd organised a celebration of Gillian's life on the day they'd earmarked for the funeral. It had been raining heavily overnight and the ground was sodden.

Rachel had taken time off work to attend. She wanted to pay her respects to a woman she'd admired and respected. Coincidentally she and Kirsty met at the gate to the church. The doctor was pale, her eyes rimmed with red.

Kirsty tucked her arm under Rachel's elbow. 'I'm glad you're here. It's going to be a tough couple of hours.'

They walked along the path to the church doors, where a man flanked by two children, a boy and a girl, was shaking hands with people as they offered their condolences. 'That's Steve, with Gillian's stepkids,' Kirsty whispered. 'They adored Gilly. As did Beth. I left her with my mum. I felt she was too young to understand what was going on. And I didn't want her to see me upset.'

Gillian's ex-husband was wearing a dark suit over a red

shirt. The children wore red too. 'Gilly's favourite colour,' Kirsty whispered. Only then did Rachel notice that Kirsty was wearing a red blouse.

'He called me last night,' Kirsty continued. 'To ask me to wear red. He was very upset that your office hasn't given authority to have the body released, horrified that it seems Gilly was murdered.'

Although his expression was stoic, his face was ravaged with grief.

The small church was packed to the rafters with friends and colleagues of Gillian's. Rachel saw Nick Ballantyne with the woman she recognised from the photo as his wife. Suzi was there with a number of staff from the Accident and Emergency department and, in the back row, Jamie De Banzie stood slightly apart. Kirsty pointed out Gillian's parents as they entered the church. Gillian had to have inherited her auburn hair from her mother, who took a seat next to her husband in the front pew. Steve and his children joined them a few minutes before the service started.

Steve said a few words about Gillian before breaking down. Then Kirsty stood and gave a moving eulogy to her friend. Outside, the rain continued fall, muting Gillian's mother's sobs of anguish.

The service over, before the mourners dispersed, they shook hands with the bereaved family and offered their condolences. Rachel and Kirsty waited in line with the rest of the mourners to offer theirs.

Kirsty, after holding the grieving woman in her arms for a few minutes as they cried together, stepped back and introduced Rachel as the lawyer responsible for ensuring her daughter's death was properly investigated.

'I still don't understand,' Gillian's mother said. 'Who would want to kill my beautiful daughter?'

'That's what we're going to find out,' Rachel promised. She leaned closer and spoke in a hushed voice.

'I wanted to say how much I admired your daughter. I knew her from school, and she was someone you must have been proud of even then. I was a bit of a brat at school but Gillian never ratted me out.' She swallowed hard. 'I met her again at a low point in my life. Your daughter saved my friend's life and helped turn mine around. To be frank, if it hadn't been for Gillian I probably wouldn't be where I am.' She took a deep breath. 'I might not even be alive. I owe her and I'm going to make it my business to catch whoever killed her. You have my promise.'

'Thank you,' Mrs Robertson replied. 'That means a lot.'

On the way out of the churchyard, Rachel and Kirsty almost collided with Dr Ballantyne and his wife in the crush of people waiting to approach the family.

'Oh hello, Nick,' Kirsty said. 'I didn't expect to see you here.'

'I came into contact with Gillian on a regular basis.' He looked around. 'I see a good number of our colleagues here. We've lost an excellent nurse.' He touched her awkwardly on the shoulder. 'And I know you've lost a friend.'

Kirsty bowed her head in acknowledgement.

Jennifer Ballantyne's eyes were downcast, and there were deep shadows in the area beneath the sockets. Rachel wondered if she'd been ill. Or was she simply painfully shy? Kirsty held out her hand.

'Mrs Ballantyne? I'm Dr Kirsty Burns. I work with your husband. And this is Rachel McKenzie.'

Nick's wife took first Kirsty's and then Rachel's hands almost reluctantly, the fingers cool and limp in Rachel's palm.

'I'm so sorry about your friend,' Jennifer said to Kirsty. Her voice was low, almost a whisper.

'Thank you. I gather you knew her?'

The woman slithered a sideways look at her husband. 'Not really. I met her once or twice at hospital functions. We talked a little, she seemed nice.'

At that moment a man tapped Nick on the shoulder and indicated he wanted a word. With a murmured *Would you excuse me*, the two men stepped away.

'I heard you saw Gillian at the hospital the day before she died?' Rachel said.

A look of alarm crossed Jennifer's face. 'At the hospital? Oh...' It took her a moment to recover and continue: 'Yes, yes I did. I fell off a horse. Stupid really. I sprained my wrist, but I was worried I might have done something more serious.' She gave a thin smile. 'I really couldn't be bothered waiting in a queue to have it X-rayed, so I asked Gillian if she could have a quick look. There's no point in being the wife of a consultant if you can't take advantage every now and again is there?'

'No, I guess not,' Kirsty said.

'Is he a good doctor?' Jennifer asked Kirsty, looking over at her husband.

The change in tack and the question surprised Rachel. It wasn't really the sort of thing a wife asked, especially in the current circumstances.

'Very good,' Kirsty said. If she were as taken aback as Rachel, she didn't show it. 'Put it this way: if ever I needed surgery, I'd choose him. He's both technically excellent and has a lovely manner with the patients. Most of them seem to adore him.'

Jennifer acknowledged Kirsty's summation with a twist of her lips. 'Yes I can see why his patients would adore him, as you say.'

Before either of the women had a chance to reply, Nick returned and ushered his wife away.

'That was strange,' Kirsty said when they were out of earshot. 'Knowing Gillian, she would have insisted on getting the wrist X-rayed, to be on the safe side. She wouldn't have wanted to take any chances with the wife of a consultant.' She thought for a moment. 'On the other hand, if Mrs Ballantyne refused, then there wouldn't have been much Gillian could do about it. Still, she should have made a note somewhere to cover herself.'

'Can you find out?' Rachel asked.

Kirsty shot Rachel a look. 'I already have. After Suzi didn't get back to me. To be honest, I shouldn't have accessed her records, but I did. I needed to know what Gilly wanted to speak to me about. I can't help but think it was important. There was no note of Jennifer's visit in the A&E records. Which is very odd. Everyone who comes into A&E is clerked in and out and a note made of time from admission to disposal. It's part of the data that every casualty department in the country has to collect for government statistics.'

The two women started trudging through the soggy ground towards her car. 'Unless something happened to distract Gillian?' Kirsty continued, almost to herself. 'No. I can't see it. She was professional to her core. If she'd examined Mrs Ballantyne's wrist and found nothing wrong, she'd still have made a note. Patients have become very litigious in recent years, so staff are told to make sure their notes are contemporaneous.'

'Perhaps she intended to go back and write up her notes and simply forgot?' Rachel suggested, thinking about the medical mishaps that had crossed her desk. It was always better for clinical staff to write up their notes as soon as possible after they saw patients. That way they couldn't be accused of changing events to suit themselves.

'It's possible I suppose,' Kirsty said. 'I'll speak to Suzi again. She mentioned there had been a couple of emergencies that day.' She unlocked her car with a press of her key. 'Perhaps something happened while Mrs Ballantyne was there and I can jog Suzi's memory. Maybe Gillian mentioned it to her. The more I think about it, the more it makes sense. And perhaps someone should go and see Mrs Ballantyne. One of your friendly cops, maybe,' she added with a sarcastic lilt.

Selena popped into Rachel's head. It wasn't a bad idea. She didn't buy it that Jennifer had still been shaken from the fall. Distressed was the word Suzi had used. However, there wasn't enough to warrant an official visit by the police. The hospital, like any community, was rife with secrets, gossip, love affairs, innuendo. If Jennifer's visit had any bearing on Gillian's death, even tangentially, Rachel wanted to know.

'Look,' Kirsty said, 'There's something you need to know. I admitted Caroline Telford's sister for surgery on Monday. While she was recovering in the ward someone injected Potassium Chloride into her drip. It damn near killed her. I told Nick we should inform the police and he said he'd handle it.' She sighed. 'But I'm not sure he has. I think he, as well as the other staff, think I'm to blame. I'm not. But drug errors are frighteningly common. What I told Jennifer is true; he's a good doctor, adored by staff and patients, but he'd also do anything to protect the hospital's reputation.'

Rachel made a mental note to make sure Du Toit knew. In the meantime, there was another avenue she wanted to explore.

'You don't happen to have an address for the Ballantynes?' she asked Kirsty.

THIRTY-EIGHT

He waited until he saw Dr Burns and her daughter leave their flat. The little girl skipped along, a toy monkey under one arm, the other hand firmly held by her mother.

Rage bubbled inside him. The doctor took the love of her child for granted. Assumed she would grow up, have a successful life filled with joy, get everything her little heart desired.

Except she wouldn't. Not if it were up to him. And assuming it all went to plan. So far it had – bar a minor hiccup or two.

He pulled his hat down lower on his head and waited until the external door swung open again. He pushed his way through with a murmured thanks. What was the point of a security door if people just let anyone in? He supposed it helped that he looked like a man who had a right to be there.

He climbed the three flights to the flat, not too slowly, but not too quickly either. He'd learned rapid movement attracted attention.

Before he entered the flat he paused to slip on a pair of latex gloves and a disposable surgical hat.

Then he took the card from his pocket and slid it between the snib and the lock. The door opened easily.

Unlike the times he'd been here before, he went inside.

The layout was as he'd expected. A hall with laminated flooring ran the length of the apartment, with five doors opening off: two on one side and three on the other. He slipped off his shoes and placed them in the plastic bag he'd brought with him.

He opened the door on the left. Kirsty's bedroom. It smelled faintly of perfume. The double bed was neatly made, the chest of drawers clutter-free, the walk-in wardrobe doors closed.

He opened the drawers, repelled by the silky underwear in the top one. He felt nothing. He rarely felt desire for other women.

The bedroom opposite was the child's. The bed was also made, a Barbie duvet on top, partly covered with soft toys and dolls all lovingly dressed and, a smile crossed his lips, several were bandaged as if they'd recently visited A&E. Cutouts of stars, and moons in their various stages, were pasted on one wall. Tiny slippers had been placed next to the bed, a pair of pink pyjamas on the end. He picked up a doll with dark curls, warm bronze-coloured skin and rosebud lips that looked unnervingly similar to its owner. A strip of cloth had been tied around the doll's head, covering one of the eyes. He studied it for a moment before carefully unwrapping the bandage. He took the scalpel from his pocket, removed the protective sheath from the tip and very carefully gouged the eye out. Then he replaced the bandage exactly as he'd found it. Pleased, he continued to explore.

The sitting room was sparsely furnished, as if Kirsty hadn't moved in properly or was undecided whether to stay. It had a burnt orange sofa, an armchair and a dining table with two chairs. A small TV was perched on a side table.

The kitchen was the brightest room in the flat and overlooked the golf course. The child's drawings were plastered on the fridge door, unwashed breakfast dishes filled the sink. A half-finished bowl of cereal lay on a circular table in the centre of the room. As he approached the window, something crunched underfoot. He examined the bottom of his sock and smiled. A Rice Krispie. The little girl was cute, he had to admit. Perfect even. The thought flooded him with rage again.

He retraced his steps, committing every detail of the layout to his memory until he knew he could find his way around in pitch darkness if necessary.

He glanced at his watch. He needed to go. He was due in theatre.

He put his shoes back on, stuffed the hat into the plastic bag, shoved it in his pocket and glanced around to ensure everything was exactly as it had been when he entered. Satisfied, he opened the front door a crack, made sure there was no one on the landing, no footsteps on the stairs, before stepping out and closing the door softly behind him.

THIRTY-NINE

Rachel's breath thrummed in her chest as she jogged along Castle Street. She turned into the broad street that would take her in a loop towards the botanic gardens and into Cameron Drive where Dr Ballantyne lived. The street was lined with oak trees and large detached houses. Stopping to catch her breath, she took in the imposing facade of number 4, his house. She was crossing a line coming here, but there was no official route for her to question Jennifer. Naturally she'd neglected to mention this unofficial visit to any of her colleagues although she'd passed on what Kirsty had told her about Annie's brush with death to Du Toit.

She walked up the driveway and knocked on the double storm doors, wondering if she was making a mistake. But she was here now and there was nothing left to lose.

Jennifer Ballantyne opened the door. She was wearing Levi's, a primly buttoned white blouse and heels that had Rachel wanting to ask where she'd bought them. Her face was heavily made up, but no amount of make-up was ever going to disguise the dark circles under her eyes.

'Miss McKenzie! To what do I owe the pleasure?' She took

in Rachel's running gear with a flick of her light green eyes. 'Is everything all right?'

'I'm sorry to bother you at home,' Rachel said, wondering how she was going to explain herself. 'But might I come in for a minute?'

Jennifer hesitated. It was obvious that the last thing she wanted was to talk to Rachel.

'Please,' Rachel said. 'I promise I won't take up much of your time.'

'Of course, come in.' Jennifer stepped back to let Rachel enter and gestured to an open door on her right. 'We're in here,' she said.

Rachel was shown into a room that could have appeared in the pages of a weekend supplement. Modern white sofas squatted on a snow-coloured carpet, framing a coffee table that looked like an expensive one-off. A number of original watercolours hung from picture rails and Rachel stepped forward to study an oil of a West Coast beach with tipsy red-roofed cottages. Rachel thought she recognised the painter – a prolific artist of Scottish landscapes who was all the rage in Scotland and whose pieces cost a small fortune. Rachel found his work too ubiquitous for her taste, which was fortunate as she was a long way off being able to afford any of his paintings.

An oversized vase of long-stemmed lilies by the side of the fireplace leaked a nauseating scent in the overly warm room. All in all, it was exactly the sort of house she expected a hospital consultant with a private practice to live in.

Sitting cross-legged, small hand under his chin, was a boy of around six or seven. With perfectly symmetrical features and thick black hair, he was simply the most beautiful child Rachel had ever seen. But it was his large vacant dark eyes that really caught her attention. Although he had looked up when they entered the room, his focus moved quickly to a point above

Rachel's head where it remained fixed. All the while he rocked himself gently, keening quietly under his breath.

Jennifer bent to pick him up, but he twisted his head from side to side and she was forced to let him go. He sat back down in the same position and continued his rocking motions.

'This is Luke,' Jennifer said, the anguish in her eyes plain to see. 'My – our – son. Poor Nick, he so wanted a perfect family – and he got us.'

'I'm sorry,' Rachel said uncomfortably. It was another odd thing for Jennifer to say. Especially to someone she barely knew.

Jennifer shook her head, dismissing Rachel's sympathy, and reached over and for a tumbler resting on the coffee table.

'Luke's autistic,' Jennifer continued. 'I always knew something wasn't quite right, but it wasn't until last year that he was formally diagnosed. Not that a diagnosis helps particularly, but at least we have some contact with the health services now. Speech therapy in particular. Who knows, we might yet see an improvement. In fact, we've just returned from there.'

Rachel's heart went out to the woman in front of her. She wondered how she would cope if she were in her shoes. No wonder she looked so tired.

'I'd offer you a coffee, but I need to prepare supper.' She made a show of looking at her watch. 'Please, take a seat for a moment.'

Rachel sat down feeling a fraud. She had no real right to walk into this woman's life. On the other hand she wanted to know why she had been to see Gillian. It was probably nothing, but she had to be sure.

'It must be hard for you,' she said. 'I imagine your husband is kept very busy at the hospital.'

'It's part of the deal when you marry a doctor – especially one as ambitious as Nick.' Jennifer fiddled with her wedding ring. 'I hardly saw him in the first years we were married.

Hardly see him these days, for that matter. Apart from his NHS work he has his private practice, papers to research, committees to chair. No end of important work.'

Rachel couldn't tell from the flat tone or the hooded eyes whether Jennifer was proud or resentful of her husband's professional success.

'Oh yes, he's ambitious,' she murmured almost to herself. 'I suppose it's to do with his childhood—' She broke off and took another swig from her glass.

'His childhood...?' Rachel prompted.

Jennifer stood and, swaying slightly, crossed over to the fire-place, licking a finger to rub an imaginary mark off her cheek.

'He was adopted,' Jennifer continued. 'When he was seven. It took that long for social services to persuade his mother to sign the papers.'

Why was Jennifer telling Rachel all this personal stuff?

'His birth mother had... not to put too fine a point on it, a bit of a drug problem.' Jennifer turned away from the mirror. She was beginning to slur her words and Rachel suspected the glass she was drinking from contained more than water. Jennifer drew a breath as if aware that she had said more than she wanted to. 'Now, what can I do for you?'

Rachel welcomed the change of subject. She would have liked to continue the conversation, but she needed to get the answers before Nick came home. 'It was Gillian Robertson I wanted to talk to you about.'

Across the room, Luke continued to rock.

'I was so sorry when I heard about her. Do the police know what happened yet?'

'No, not yet.'

'What is it you want to ask me?'

'Did you know Gillian well? I gather you met her once or twice at hospital functions.'

'Yes. She was charming. Easy to talk to.'

'And how's your wrist?'

Jennifer frowned down at her forearm as if it didn't belong to her.

'It's fine. A little bruised perhaps, but on the mend.' She pulled the sleeve of her blouse down to cover her hand.

'I'm surprised Gillian didn't keep a note of your visit.'

'Why would she? I wasn't there for very long and I didn't need any treatment. She strapped it herself, and that was it.'

'I understand from Dr Burns that Mrs Robertson was meticulous when it came to making notes. I don't think that you being the wife of a consultant would have prevented her – quite the opposite, in fact.'

Jennifer shrugged. 'I'm afraid I can't help you. I went to A&E, asked to see the charge nurse, was seen by Gillian, declined an X-ray, had it strapped, then came home. Why are you asking me this? How is it any of your business?'

She bent down to pick up a new, apparently untouched toy tractor from the immaculate floor. As she stood she winced, rested her hand on her ribs and took shallow breaths with her eyes closed, as she waited for the pain to pass.

'Are you all right?' Rachel asked. She stepped closer to Jennifer. 'Can I get you something?'

Jennifer shook her head. 'You should go,' she said. She looked frightened now.

'Are you sure there isn't something I can help you with? Someone I can call for you?' 'Look,' Jennifer said through gritted teeth. 'I don't wish to be rude, but I think I've said enough. My life, my marriage, my family' – she gestured to the sitting room with a sweep of her hand that took in Luke – 'are none of your business. Nick gets stressed sometimes, that's all. Understandable for a man in his position. Now, please, I'd like you to leave.'

Rachel stood, uncertain of what to do next. There was something wrong here. Something Jennifer was determined to keep to herself. She was more certain than ever that Gillian had known what it was.

Reluctantly, she turned to go. 'Does Nick know you saw Gillian in A&E?' she asked.

Jennifer smiled, but it was grim, without humour.

'Oh yes,' she said. 'He does now. You could say that Nick knows everything.'

As Rachel emerged from the gate of No. 1 Crown Crescent he turned his back to her, pretending to examine the bric-a-brac in the window of the antique shop opposite. Christ, they'd nearly bumped into each other.

Not that that would have made her suspicious, he told himself. She wouldn't have been surprised to find him in the area.

But why had she gone to see Jennifer? What was the lawyer up to now? What did she know? Did she have any idea what she was getting involved in?

He had to find out. If she carried on poking around, she was going to ruin everything.

As she started running down the hill towards the town centre, his eyes followed her.

FORTY

Jogging home, Rachel switched the playlist on her phone to Zach Bryan. The singer's morose voice and angst-filled songs suited her mood perfectly. The sun was shining for the first time in days although the air was still cool. Perfect running conditions. She let the mindless rhythm of putting one foot in front of another ease the tension from her muscles.

She thought about everything that Jennifer had told her. Her marriage didn't seem very happy. Jennifer clearly felt unsupported and not a little resentful.

Maybe it was disinhibition bought on by gin or vodka or whatever had been in the glass?

Even so, why tell her that Nick was adopted and that he'd spent his early years in the care of his drug-abusing birth mother? Unless she was implying that Nick had something against drug addicts. To the extent he might murder them. That was crazy, surely?

Jennifer had been in pain – not just mental pain, although there was that – real physical pain. The way she'd winced and clutched her midriff could mean an injury to her ribs. Was domestic abuse the reason she'd gone to see Gillian, the story about falling off a horse a lie to hide it. Maybe she'd sworn Gillian to secrecy so she wouldn't record the visit in her records? To make sure her husband wouldn't find out?

It was a possible scenario. In which case, Rachel wouldn't be surprised if Gillian had been worried and planned to talk it over with her friend. On the other hand, wouldn't it be an unforgivable breach of confidentiality?

She felt slightly sick. If Nick was abusing Jennifer, he needed to be stopped. Physical abuse only ever got worse. Every year, across the UK, a woman was murdered by her partner every fourth day on average. Rachel knew every chilling damn statistic. She decided to have a word with Selena. Ask her if she could look into it.

If he was abusing his wife, maybe Nick had found out she'd confided in Gillian and had killed her to prevent her from blabbing.

But why would he have murdered Caroline? He could have seen her as a patient, despite what he'd told them. He knew Gillian, more importantly she knew him. She would have opened the door to him without a second thought. No, wife-abuser or not, she couldn't see it.

She took her usual shortcut through the park to get to the towpath. There were a few people walking their dogs and another runner going the opposite way to Rachel. Largely regarded as safe in daylight hours, most people avoided the path after dark. The unlit park and clumps of woodland acted as a spillover from the harbour for sex workers plying their trade, which made it a no-go area. In one of Scotland's mercurial changes of weather, the clouds had thickened, draining light from the sky. It began to pour, the rain dripping down her neck. Rachel had almost reached Witches Coffin Pool, a tidal pond on the edge of the park, when her arm was grabbed from behind.

She whipped around to find a perspiring Dr De Banzie, doubled over and taking deep lungfuls of air.

'What the fuck are you doing, creeping up on me like that!' she yelled.

Jamie pointed to her ears. Rachel removed her earbuds. 'Have you been following me?' Rachel demanded.

'No! Christ, no! I saw you go into the park. I was on my way home and thought I'd catch you up. I called out your name. Several times, in fact. Then I realised you couldn't hear me. I didn't mean to give you a fright. I'm sorry,' he wheezed.

'What do you want?' A quick glance around told Rachel they were alone in the park. The dog walkers and runner were no longer anywhere to be seen.

'I need to speak to you. I know I didn't create a great impression when we met. I want to put the record straight.'

'OK,' Rachel said, starting to walk in the direction of the canal. The towpath was a few hundred yards away and she wanted to reach it before darkness fell. She didn't feel comfortable alone in the park with Jamie.

'I've heard the rumours that Gillian was murdered. I don't know what to do,' Jamie said, falling into step beside her.

'What do you mean?' Rachel asked, quickening her pace.

'I was there. In her flat. The day she died. I lied to the police. About that and not knowing she was pregnant. I did know. I went to see her that morning. I'd found out from one of the nurses that she was pregnant. She hadn't told me, that bit was true.' He was sweating more profusely than ever. 'I asked her if it was mine. She wouldn't say either way. We argued and I left. But she was alive, I promise you.'

'Have you told the police this?'

'No, I wasn't sure what to do. I know it doesn't look good that I didn't tell the truth. When I saw you, I thought I'd run it by you. You're a lawyer. You have to keep what I've told you to yourself, don't you?

They emerged onto the towpath almost opposite where the houseboats were moored.

'I'm not *your* lawyer,' Rachel snapped. 'So, no, I'm not bound by client confidentiality. Of course you have to tell them. If they find out, which they will eventually, it will only look worse for you. And if you don't tell them I most certainly will. I'll give you till I get home to tell the police what you've told me.'

'OK, OK, I will. I'll do it now. God!' He pulled his hand through his thick hair. 'It feels like I'm in a nightmare.' He looked like a wee boy caught with his hand in a cookie jar. She reminded herself that psychopaths – and he must be one if he'd done what he had to Gillian – were good at pulling the wool over people's eyes. Charming and self-assured, they were often the last person friends and colleagues suspected.

Jamie stepped onto the gangway leading to the dozen or so residential boats and Rachel ran the rest of the way home.

When she let herself in and picked up her phone to call Du Toit, it pinged in her hand. The text was from an unknown number.

Stop looking or you will go the same way as the others.

FORTY-ONE

TUESDAY

Rachel forced herself to concentrate on the notes she was making for a trial she had to prosecute in the summary court. It wasn't easy, especially since it appeared that their killer had her on his radar.

When she'd got home late yesterday afternoon, she'd called Du Toit. She'd repeated her conversation with Dr De Banzie, omitting the visit to Dr Ballantyne's home.

'He's already been in touch,' the DI said. 'He's coming in later to give a statement.'

That had to be something in Dr De Banzie's favour.

Rachel told Du Toit about the text she'd received shortly after parting ways with Jamie. 'I have to be honest, it freaked me out.'

'Did you recognise the number?'

'No.'

'Bring your phone into the station tomorrow and I'll get someone to look at it.'

'Do you think it might be our killer?'

There was a long pause at the other end of the phone. 'That's the most obvious explanation, I'm afraid.'

'How does he know what I'm doing?'

'That's what we need to find out.' Once more there was silence on the other end of the phone.

'Look, why don't you take some time off?' Du Toit said eventually, 'Go away for a few days. Come back when we've caught our killer.'

'You must be kidding! Now, when we're so close? I'll be fine. I've locked my door. Besides' – she attempted a laugh – 'I have the toughest sex worker in Scotland as a neighbour.'

'Promise me you'll take care,' Du Toit said, 'Don't do anything without checking with me. And if you see or hear anything suspicious, call me or nine-nine-nine straight away.'

For God's sake. Bloody men! Treating her as if she were made of porcelain. All the same, she locked her door and made sure the chain was fastened. She might not be made of china, but neither did she have a death wish.

Rachel pushed the conversation to the back of her mind, stifled a yawn behind her hand and took a gulp of her black coffee, needing a shot of caffeine to wake her brain. Despite her bravado the previous evening, she'd spent a sleepless night, tossing and turning, trying to put all the pieces of the puzzle together and failing. She'd given in and got up, gone for a run along the canal – resisting the impulse to constantly look over her shoulder – and then headed into work.

The phone on her desk rang.

It was a male pathologist who phoned Rachel with Ashley's PM results.

'I know you wanted Miss Carmichael's results as soon as, so I thought I'd ring you direct, prior to emailing them.'

'Thank you, I appreciate that. What can you tell me?'

'She was an otherwise healthy female of around seventeen, with an intact pregnancy of around twelve weeks gestation. Toxicology found ketamine in her blood. Not unusual in a drug addict, but Dr Halliday said you were asking about anaesthetic agents so I requested they look. They didn't find anything. But the syringe found with her contained propofol as well as ketamine.'

'What's that?' Rachel asked.

'An anaesthetic agent. Normally used when light, short sedation is needed.'

'A bit like ketamine then?'

'Yes. You could say that.'

'And how would someone like Miss Carmichael get hold of it?' Rachel asked.

'She couldn't. It's not available on the streets, just in hospitals, wholesale pharmacies perhaps. Only someone working in theatres such as an anaesthetist would have access.'

'How is it administered?'

'IV, via a syringe.'

'Was that the cause of death?'

'Can't say for certain. But it certainly contributed. It would have rendered her pretty much incapable of defending herself.'

'Does that mean you found evidence of a struggle?'

'Yes. Some bruising around her mouth. And contusions on her heels as if she'd been dragged along the ground. Maybe to where her body was found. Out of sight of casual passers-by.'

'She was definitely murdered?'

'It's possible. Not for me to say.'

'Why would she have both ketamine and propofol in her system? I understand they are very similar.'

'I have no idea. Propofol wears off very quickly. Maybe she was trying to prolong the effect of the ketamine. Drug addicts often take whatever they can get their hands on.' Rachel felt a spurt of anger as she visualised an unconscious Ashley being dragged across the ground as well as the undertone of contempt in the pathologist's voice. She was pretty sure Ashley hadn't taken the drugs voluntarily. But could she prove it? Her gut was telling her that Caroline, Gillian and Ashley had all been sedated then murdered. *If* they had been unconscious when he'd killed them. The thought of Ashley being aware but unable to defend herself made Rachel feel sick.

'Did anyone look for propofol in Caroline Telford's PM toxicology?' she asked.

'Not as far as I'm aware. That is not to say there might have been. Unfortunately, propofol is a drug that disappears from the blood within days.'

And Gillian and Caroline – had they too been aware of what was happening to them when they'd been killed?

He wasn't going to get away with it. Each of the women would get the same promise from her. They would catch him. Prosecute him. Put him in jail and throw away the key. Hopefully before he murdered someone else. She shivered as she recalled the text she'd been sent. *Stop looking or you will go the same way as the others.* Well, she hadn't stopped looking and she'd no intention of doing so.

'Any evidence Ms Carmichael was raped?' she asked the pathologist.

'No. She'd had sex recently. That's not surprising. But there was no evidence of trauma to the genital area or elsewhere. There was no semen recovered from her body. Of course her killer might have used a condom or not ejaculated, or not managed to have sex in the first place. I took swabs from her to try and recover DNA, but there's likely to be multiple DNA, given her line of work. So that's a long shot at best.'

'Anything else?'

'That's it for the time being, I'm afraid.'

After ending the call, Rachel re-ran the conversation in her head.

Had the man who followed Ashley behind the building given her the drug? How had he got hold of it? Her mind went back to Jamie. He lived close to the harbour where Ashley's body was found – only a short walk through the park. He was very likely the father of Gillian's baby. Could roam the hospital without anyone batting an eye and, as an anaesthetist, he would have access to propofol and would know better than most about ketamine. Could he also have been the man Caroline Telford met up with? She needed to know. She punched in Selena's number. Time to access Jamie's internet searches.

FORTY-TWO

'Right, what do we know about the murder victims?' Du Toit asked his sergeant. He'd convened the meeting as soon as he'd received Ashley's PM results.

Ten of them were squashed in the incident room at the police station. Apart from Selena and Du Toit there were a number of detective constables. Although they had been kidding around only moments before, the laughter stopped as soon as Du Toit had entered the room.

The detective sergeant, who'd been introduced to Rachel as Audrey Liversage, picked up a marker pen and crossed over to the whiteboard. Audrey had sandy hair and an expression that looked as if she'd come face to face with everything that was wrong with the world, and despaired.

'Let's start with Caroline Telford, who we suspect was the first victim,' Audrey said, addressing the team. When there were no protests, she took the cap off her marker pen and started to write on the board.

'Caroline Telford. Married mother of two. Her body was found in an alley close to the town centre eighteen months ago.' She stuck a photo of the dead woman beside her name. Rachel winced. Caroline Telford was propped against a wall, her head lolling to one side, her legs spread, her knickers caught on an ankle. It was one thing reading about death but another thing entirely seeing it blown up and in vivid colour, particularly when you'd learned about the victim from someone who loved them. That made it personal.

'According to her husband, who was away on a golfing trip with friends that weekend looking, she was supposed to be out with friends the night she died, their children having gone to stay with the grandparents overnight. His alibi checked out. Mrs Telford's friends denied ever having an arrangement but couldn't tell us what she was up to. However, Caroline told her sister, Annie Colston, that she was hooking up with someone. She refused to say where or how she'd met him.

'Contrary to what her sister believes, Caroline's death was investigated as clearly suspicious. She was a married teacher with small children and had no history of recreational drug use. When her body was found she had a fresh graze on her cheek and SOCO found flakes of paint in her hair that matched the paint on the wall in the alley. Unfortunately there were no clues on her phone or laptop to the identity of the man she was with, no CCTV images apart from a single blurry one of her leaving the White Lion with an unknown individual.

'Toxicology found ketamine in Mrs Telford's blood,' DS Liversage continued. 'At the time, it was thought she might have overdosed by accident and the man she was with scarpered in panic. The cause of Mrs Telford's death was ruled as unascertained but possibly due to a ketamine overdose. Due to lack of leads at the time, her case was put on ice.

'Now, because of certain similarities between her death and that of Mrs Robertson's and Ashley Carmichael's – similar MOs – we have reason to believe she was murdered and have re-opened her case.

'Footage from the pub Mrs Telford visited that evening,

shows her entering about ten forty-five and leaving again at five past eleven, accompanied by a man – or a tall woman. The footage is too blurry to make out their features. However, we believe this individual might be responsible for all three deaths.'

'We need to track down every person who was there that night,' Du Toit addressed the room. 'Find out if they spoke to her or saw her speaking to someone.'

'We've already started. So far we've been only able to track down about a quarter of the clients. None of them remember recall seeing her,' Audrey said. 'We are talking about a night over eighteen months ago now.'

'Find the rest,' Du Toit ordered. 'Someone must have seen something. Now let's move on to Gillian Robertson.'

Audrey pinned the photo of Gillian's body lying in the pool of blood to the whiteboard. Selena gave an audible gasp.

'Twenty-eight at the time of death,' Audrey said. 'Had been a nurse for ten years. Did her nursing degree in Glasgow, worked in the Royal Infirmary there, before meeting her husband and relocating to Inverness where she'd been to school. She divorced her husband Steve a couple of years ago, apparently it was amicable. She wanted children, he didn't – he already had two children from a previous relationship. His alibi for the time of her death checked out. He was at home with his children and his new partner from late afternoon when Mrs Robertson was still at work until the afternoon her body was found. Toxicology found ketamine in her system too. Like Mrs Telford, Mrs Robertson had no history of recreational drug use.'

'As a single woman Gillian used dating apps,' the DS continued. 'Looking at the dates they were last accessed though, it appears she hadn't accessed them for six months – well before she got pregnant. She was thirteen weeks at the time of her death.'

'It doesn't mean that she couldn't have met her killer on one before she died, does it?' Selena offered.

'That is why it's important you continue to search the dating sites she used. Find out who she met and interview them. Cross-reference them against the people who attended the pub the night Caroline Telford died,' Du Toit said.

'And the father of *her* baby? Do we know who it was?' one of the constables asked.

'Apparently Mrs Robertson refused to say,' Audrey said. 'But the gossip around the hospital is that the baby was fathered by Dr James De Banzie. Who happens to be an anaesthetist.'

Du Toit hooked his arms behind his back and stretched. 'We've spoken to Dr De Banzie. When we first interviewed him, he claimed he didn't know Gillian was pregnant, but this was a lie. Later he admitted the baby could be his. When we first interviewed him he said he hadn't seen Mrs Robertson outside work in weeks, but last night he confessed to Miss McKenzie that he had been at Mrs Robertson's home the day she died. Said he'd found out she was pregnant and wanted to know if the baby was his. In other words, he lied to us again. However, we don't have enough to hold him. In the meantime, I want us to keep a close eye on him.'

'Moving on to the latest victim, Ashley Carmichael.' Audrey turned back to the whiteboard and added Ashley's name and scene-of-crime photo. 'Seventeen at time of her death, and five months pregnant. Cause of death probably due to a combination of IV propofol and ketamine taken intravenously, although the pathologist also found some suspicious bruising around her mouth and a pinprick directly into a vein in her neck as well as the contusions on her heels.'

'Propofol is a short, fast-acting anaesthetic which has similar effects to ketamine,' Du Toit explained. 'There might have been traces of propofol in the other two women, but it disappears from the blood quickly – usually within a few hours. While it is possible Ms Carmichael managed to get hold of ketamine, only someone working in theatres – a doctor, for example, or a wholesale supplier – would have access to propofol. Which is why we are treating her death as murder.'

'So someone with medical knowledge probably gave it to her?' A young constable with closely cropped hair interrupted.

'It all fits!' Rachel said, more loudly than she'd intended. 'One of the sex workers who knew Ashley well, saw a man follow her into the lane the night she died. She thought he was wearing pyjamas – but what if it was hospital scrubs?'

There was a collective murmur from the room. The thought their murderer might be a doctor didn't sit well with anyone.

'DC Souter and DC Wright,' Du Toit continued, 'I want you to get a list of all hospital employees at Inverness General Hospital and to interview all the male staff between eighteen and fifty. DS Liversage and DC Stuart will continue to track down the names of all those in the pub. DC MacDonald, you will cross-reference those names with the dating sites. The rest of you will assist them.'

There was a collective groan, quickly silenced by a glance from Du Toit.

'None of the female staff then?' Audrey asked. 'Isn't it possible we could be looking for a woman? Take Dr Burns, for example. She's tall. And looks to be pretty strong. And all the dead women were her patients. They would have trusted her, making it easy for her to overcome them. I know it's unlikely, but we shouldn't rule her out at this stage, surely?'

'I have no intention of ruling Dr Burns out,' Du Toit said. 'Whether she knows it or not, she's involved, and we need to find out how.' He shoved his hands in his pocket.

'Who was the father of Ashley's baby?' Selena asked.

'Unknown,' Audrey replied. 'Very likely her boyfriend and pimp, Taffy. However, he can be ruled out. He was locked up the night Ashley was murdered.'

'Both Ashley Carmichael and Caroline Telford were

patients of Dr Burns. As was the second victim, Gillian Robertson,' Selena added.

'Returning to Dr Burns,' Du Toit said, rocking back in his chair. 'What do we know about her?'

'Not a whole lot,' Audrey replied. 'She's twenty-nine. A widow. Her husband was killed in a road traffic accident in Africa. After his death, Dr Burns returned to Scotland with their daughter. She was given a job as a locum and has been offered a chance to re-join the obstetric training scheme by her old boss, Dr Nick Ballantyne. Doctors Burns and Ballantyne had worked together until Dr Burns accompanied her husband to Africa. He was also a doctor.'

'Boyfriends?'

'Not according to the staff. Apparently all she does is work, run, and look after her child.' Audrey looked rueful. 'Perhaps if I jogged I'd be as slim as she is.'

One of the constables screwed up a piece of paper and threw it at her. 'We love you the way you are, darling.'

Audrey threw it back. 'Only because I'm almost old enough to be your mother.'

Everyone, including Du Toit, laughed.

'If you think Dr De Banzie could be in the frame for Mrs Robertson's death, does that mean you think he might also be responsible for Caroline Telford and Ashley Carmichael?' Rachel asked when the room had settled down again. She'd been following the discussion with interest. 'But why? As far as we know, he never met either of them. And Caroline was murdered eighteen months ago. If the same person killed all the women, why the long gap?'

'A long gap like that is unusual,' Du Toit admitted, 'especially when followed by two murders in close succession. Nevertheless, he's the closest thing we have to a suspect at the moment. I want to know if his name turns up on the pub list. He could have met Caroline Telford there. Or on one of the thousands of dating apps in existence. As for Ashley, there's no reason to suppose he wouldn't visit prostitutes.'

'But he's gorgeous,' Selena protested. She'd accompanied Audrey when she'd gone to interview De Banzie. 'He could have anyone he wanted.' Realising what she'd said, she blushed furiously. 'I mean...'

But it was too late. From now on, Selena would be the butt of her fellow officer's jokes. Thank God she was tough. Rachel hoped she'd give as good as she got.

'Good-looking men have been known to visit prostitutes,' Du Toit said mildly. 'What links the three women? All three met men for sex, but it is important to note that there is no evidence any of them had sex before being murdered. All three had a sedating agent in their blood, most likely given to them without their permission. All three were patients at the hospital and were patients of Dr Burns. As was Annie Colston, Caroline Telford's sister. As you know she almost died while an inpatient at Inverness General.'

'What differentiates them?' Audrey asked.

'Caroline and Ashley were killed outside, Gillian in her home. Meaning Gillian trusted whoever killed her enough to let him in, to allow him to get close enough to her that she had no time to struggle. Mrs Colston is older, mid-forties, and isn't pregnant or planning to get pregnant. It's also entirely possible, although too co-incidental for my liking, that she was given the drug in error.'

Du Toit wrote Jamie De Banzie's name on the whiteboard and circled it in red. 'For the time being he's our chief – only – suspect. He knew Gillian Robertson, and he has medical expertise. Perhaps, despite his protestations to the contrary, he wasn't happy when he found out Gillian was pregnant.'

'What about his ex-wife? Rachel asked. 'Has she been interviewed? What if she found out Gillian was pregnant and went round to her flat to confront her? Perhaps she wasn't over Jamie after all. Maybe she thought a separation would jolt him into line.'

'Good point. She's a theatre nurse at the hospital and did cross our radar. However, she's been interviewed and eliminated from our enquiries. She too has a cast-iron alibi. She has a new partner and was out hillwalking in Skye with him the day Gillian was killed, and stayed the night with him afterwards.

'So I'm sticking with Dr De Banzie as our chief suspect for now, although everyone' – his gaze swept the room – 'must keep an open mind. I haven't ruled out that there could be two murderers, given the long interval between the first murder and the next two. So let's not stop looking.

'Dr De Banzie has given us permission to search his phone records and computers, although that does not include the one he uses at the hospital. We need a court warrant to access that, due to patient confidentiality.'

Sensing the meeting was coming to a close, the troops started to shuffle in their seats.

'Right, get going, everyone. We need to catch this devil before he kills anyone else.'

FORTY-THREE

After the meeting Rachel returned to her office and brought Alastair up to speed. He had little to say, only grunted, but she could tell he was relieved she was on top of things.

She spent what was left of the day writing up her notes, thinking about what had been said. Even if Jamie De Banzie had murdered Gillian, she still couldn't see him being responsible for the other murders. However, like Du Toit, she'd keep an open mind.

It was after seven when she left the office and was putting her cycle helmet on when a shadow detached itself from the wall. Her heart missed several beats.

'Can I have a word, Rachel?'

It took a moment or two for Rachel to recognise the broad-shouldered man with a full beard and hair that reached the neckline of his T-shirt as Eric Hunter. The last time she'd seen him had been at university when they'd both been members of the climbing club. She'd heard he was part of the Lochaber Search and Rescue team. She hadn't been surprised. He'd been a talented and fearless climber.

'Will you men never learn that creeping up on women is not a good thing.' First Jamie and now Eric.

'I'm sorry.' His grin belied his words. 'I didn't mean to frighten you.'

'You didn't frighten me,' Rachel bit back but with a smile. 'Startled is the word I'd use.' She frowned. 'Why do you want to speak to me?'

'You might not know but I'm a freelance journalist now.'

Rachel felt her hackles rise. Her experience of the press hadn't been good. 'I'm always on the lookout for stories,' Eric continued. 'And I think I might have found one in you.'

'I've no idea what you mean.' Rachel swung her leg over the crossbar of her bike.

'Come on! You're an interesting person. A lawyer whose father murdered her mother. But you haven't let what happened stop you. I heard you played a part – a significant part – in taking down a drug ring recently. Almost got murdered yourself. I'm thinking of doing a profile piece on you. Local girl overcomes the odds to wage war on criminals. Something like that.'

'You can't be serious,' Rachel said, horrified. She couldn't imagine anything worse.

'I am. Deadly serious. Particularly when I gather you are looking into the deaths of' – he checked his notebook – 'Caroline Telford, Gillian Robertson and Ashley Carmichael?'

Rachel said nothing and kept her expression neutral. He knew that already? He clearly had a source somewhere. She hoped it wasn't someone in Du Toit's team.

'I heard that these murders are linked to the hospital,' Eric continued. 'To one of the doctors there. Is that correct?'

'Where did you hear that?'

He tapped his nose. 'Can't say, I'm afraid.'

Most likely one of the hospital staff. As a journalist he'd spend a fair amount of time in A&E chasing stories and would know the A&E staff well. As Rachel had been told several times, hospitals might be tight-lipped when it came to their patients, but they were hotbeds of gossip where everything else was concerned.

'Are these cases linked?' Eric asked. He caught her gaze and held it. 'Does Inverness have a serial killer?'

A very good question. Not one she was going to answer.

'If you want any information you have to ask Police Scotland,' she said, looking away.

'Don't you think that the public has a right to know?' Eric continued. 'Before someone else gets killed. Shouldn't women be warned to stay away from the hospital until the murderer is caught.'

To be fair, it was what she'd been thinking. Maybe she needed to get over her inbuilt aversion to the press, use Eric to put the word out. If the same person was responsible for the deaths of the three women Eric had read out like an ominous roll call, who was next on the list? But where would women go instead? Perth or Dundee, perhaps. Assuming they could get there. Not seeking medical attention could be fatal for some women. All the more reason the killer needed to be caught.

However, briefing the press was up to Du Toit. Not her. Eric Hunter would need to find another source.

FORTY-FOUR

The next day Rachel was finishing her notes for the summary trial she was due to prosecute when her mobile rang.

'There's been another murder,' Selena's breathless voice came over the phone. 'Another sex worker. Jody Tamsworth. No doubt this time. She was suffocated and left on a piece of waste ground.'

Rachel's heart dropped to her boots. She slumped back in her chair as she recalled the young, anxious woman who'd come to her house with Mags to tell her about the man she'd seen follow Ashley behind the warehouse. Had she been killed because of what she'd seen?

'Where?'

'You know the empty buildings behind the main road, on the left immediately before you come to Clachnaharry Inn?'

Rachel did. It was near her house. 'Give me twenty minutes.'

She grabbed her bag and cycle helmet. There were three police vehicles at the scene, blue lights flashing, as well as an ambulance and a couple of unmarked vehicles when Rachel arrived at the crime scene. Du Toit was talking to DS Liversage and Selena, while uniformed police officers kept curious bystanders from getting too close. A white-suited scene-of-crime officer was examining the ground behind fluttering yellow tape. A white tent had been erected around the body.

Rachel's gaze landed on Mags, who was sitting on a bench by the side of the road, staring at her feet.

Rachel locked her bike to a railing and went over to the older woman. She knelt by Mags's side, ignoring the damp seeping through her trousers.

'Mags,' she said, laying a tentative hand on the older woman's knee. 'Are you OK?'

Mags looked at Rachel as if unsure of who she was. Her hair was pasted to her head and Rachel could see glimpses of scalp through the bands of red. She'd clearly been caught in the same rain shower Rachel had passed through and her painted brows had smeared, giving her a clownish air. For the first time since Rachel had met her she appeared beaten. Instead of her usual boob tube and short skirt she was wearing a shapeless dress that came below her knees. She looked more like a grandmother than a prostitute.

'O'course ahm no fuckin all right,' she said. 'Another one of my girls – wee Jody – has been done away with by some friggin' mad bastard. And you ask if ahm OK. What fuckin' planet do you live on?'

Rachel reeled from the unexpected onslaught. Then recovered. Mags was right. It was a bloody stupid question. If Rachel was upset by Jody's death, how must Mags be feeling?

'I'm so sorry, Mags,' she said. 'Is there anything I can do?'

The fire went out of the older woman. She seemed to fold in on herself before taking a deep breath and puffing out her cheeks.

'I want you to see that they do right by her,' she said. 'Don't let them treat her as if she doesn't matter. As if she's a nobody.' She looked up, her eyes tracking something in the distance.

Rachel followed her gaze. They were lifting a black, zipped bag into the back of an ambulance.

'I'll do what I can for her,' Rachel said. 'In the meantime, let me take you home.'

'They say I've to stay here. Till they're finished with me. Fuckin' polis.'

Rachel stood. They couldn't keep Mags here, soaking wet. The woman needed to get indoors, have a hot bath, a strong drink and then bed.

'Stay here,' Rachel said, before striding towards Du Toit and his team.

'What are you doing here? How did you get here so fast?' he said. Selena shuffled her feet and looked away.

'Selena called me. Mags, the woman on the bench' – she indicated Mags with a tilt of her head – 'asked for me. She's my neighbour and a friend of the victim – the young woman who told me she saw someone follow Ashley to the back of the warehouse.'

Du Toit shot a look at Selena and gave a small shake of his head.

'Who found Jody?' Rachel asked.

'A man walking his dog. He's pretty shaken. The dog ran off and wouldn't come back when called. He went after him, found him pawing at the ground up there' – Selena jerked her thumb in the direction of the tent – 'and whining. Jody had been dumped there, like a piece of rubbish. He's getting bolder. Didn't try to hide the body, or even cover her up.'

'Not just getting bolder, he's out of control,' Audrey added. 'He suffocated her by ramming her underwear down her throat. I hope to God he sedated her first.'

'You do know this almost certainly means we are looking for a serial killer.' The words were out before Rachel could help herself.

Du Toit gave her a look of exaggerated astonishment. 'I think I have worked that out, Rachel.'

Rachel flushed. Of course he had. 'Don't you think we should tell the press? Get word out to women – particularly the sex workers.'

'I intend to call a press conference later for exactly that reason. Now, if you'd let me get on with doing my job, I'd be grateful.'

Rachel bit back the retort that came to her lips. As much as she liked Du Toit, Police Scotland should have alerted the public sooner. Maybe Rachel should have briefed the journalist. Put women on their guard. Would that have prevented Jody's death?

Rain that had been falling as a fine drizzle began to fall in earnest.

'While you get on with that, can I take Mags home?' She indicated the huddled woman on the bench with a brief tip of her head.

'She has to come down to the station.' It was Selena who answered. 'We need her to go over her statement. Apparently Jody texted her last night to say she'd seen the person in scrubs again. Mags told her she had to tell you. We think she was on her way to see you when she was murdered.'

'Did she say who she thought it was?'

'Apparently she wanted to tell you. No one else.'

Rachel's heart ached for the young woman. If it was the last thing she did, she would make sure the bastard was caught.

She looked over at Mags, who was huddled on the bench, the picture of misery.

'Can't Mags's statement wait? She needs to get some dry clothes on. If you let her go now, I promise I'll bring her down later. Or, better still, you can interview her in her own home.'

Du Toit's expression softened.

'Very well. But take Selena with you,' he capitulated.

'Thank you,' Rachel said.

She and Selena left Du Toit and DS Liversage to it and walked over to Mags.

'Come on, Mags. The inspector says you can go home. DC MacDonald here will give us a lift.'

Mags let Rachel lead her to the police car and settled her in the passenger seat as a WPC held the door open. The WPC took in Mags with her garish hair and her dress and coat that had seen better days and sniffed. Rachel was tempted to take her to task but managed to resist. Selena started the car, looking pissed off to have been taken away from the murder scene.

A few minutes later they were in Clachnaharry. Rachel and Selena accompanied Mags inside her house. 'Why don't you sit down and I'll make us a cup of tea?' Selena said.

Mags sat down at her kitchen table with a sigh. 'Top cupboard for the cups – use the ones with the saucers. The tea's on the shelf below.'

Rachel waited until the tea was made and she had fetched a towel from the bathroom for Mags before sitting down herself.

Mags pulled a pack of Regal King Size from her bag and offered the pack to Selena, who shook her head.

The women sat in silence until Mags finished her cigarette. 'She wisnae my daughter, Jody, you know,' Mags said eventually. 'My daughter lives in Birmingham. It was the furthest she could get away from me. She's a secretary – executive assistant she calls it, married to a bloke with a good job. I think she told him I'm deid.'

'I'm sorry,' Rachel said, her heart cracking a little more.

'I don't blame her. What sort of man would marry a woman who has a hoor for a mother?'

Rachel said nothing.

'I look after the girls – the ones on the street – as best as I can,' Mags went on. 'In my day it was different. You only did it for a bit extra on the side. Shoes for the weans, a night out at bingo, that sort of thing. It never did anyone ony harm.' She glared at Rachel, defying her to contradict. 'It's different noo-a-days. The girls, they do it for the smack. They take it so they can bear to hov sex with the punters, then the drugs take a hold, so they hov sex to get the drugs. And that's it.'

She took a swig of her tea and swallowed loudly.

'That's what happened to Jody. She came from a decent home. Had a family who didn't have much but loved her tae bits. She loved her parents too, that's why she left home. She was stealing what little they had to pay for her habit. Couldna stop. So she left. She called them noo and again when she could find a phone box that worked. To let them know she was all right. She didnae want them to have her mobile number and try and trace her. Well, she's not all right noo. Someone will have to tell her folks. It will break their bloody hearts.' Selena placed her hand over Mags's. They were silent as they waited until Mags was ready to continue.

'She texted me the night afore to say she saw the man again and thought she recognised him. I told her to go to the polis but she said she'd only speak to you, Rachel.'

'What time was this?'

'About nine. She said she'd go to your house. I thought she'd chap me up but I wasn't too worried when she didn't.'

Mags poured herself another cup of tea from the pot Rachel had set next to her elbow.

'I went to get her this morning – we were going to go to the centre together – but when I got to her hoose she wasn't there. Her bed hadn't been slept in and the others said they hadn't seen her since the night afore. Like with Ashley, I knew in ma bones there was something wrong. When one of the lassies came to tell me they had found a body, and I knew it'd be her.'

'Do you think it's the same person who killed Ashley?' Selena asked.

'Of course I fuckin' do. Are you thick as mince, or what? Jesus Christ, woman.'

'I'm sorry,' Selena said, clearly miffed but trying not to show it.

'Did she tell you anything more about the man who followed Ashley into the alley?' Rachel asked, with a warning glance at Selena. No need. Selena would have dealt with far worse in her time as a police officer. 'Did she tell you who she thought the person was she recognised?'

Mags stood up and crossed to the window. 'She telt me she didnae know if she was getting mixed up, but she thought she recognised him. From the hospital. When we went to see Mrs C.'

'You visited Annie?' Rachel said. 'Yeah. Peggy, the woman who runs No. 79, asked us to. Mrs C was in a right funk. Insisted we call her a taxi to take her home. She said she didn't feel safe there.'

Rachel felt a kick of adrenaline. 'Inverness General Hospital? Who was he? A doctor, a nurse, a technician?'

'She said she couldn't tell. He was wearing one of those green outfits – you know the ones I mean. The ones they all seem to wear in those hospital programmes. As soon as she saw him she knew it wasn't pyjamas he'd been wearing when she'd seen him afore. It was hospital clothes. The type doctors wear. I told her it couldn't be a doctor she'd seen following Ashley. What would one of them be doing with the likes of us? Someone like that would go for the more high-class girls, not want to do it in the street.'

So Rachel had been right when she guessed the 'pyjamas' were scrubs.

'Did you tell the inspector this?' Rachel asked.

'Course I did. I knew it had to be important.'

'He's on it,' Selena said quietly. 'He plans to get our suspect in for questioning again.'

'Why did Mrs Colston not feel safe in the hospital?' Selena asked Mags.

'Cos some idiot gave her the wrong drug. They very nearly kilt her. They think Dr Burns, her doctor, did it. Mrs C reckons they're wrong.'

Rachel's pulse quickened. So Nick hadn't reported the incident to the police.

'Was this reported to the police?' Selena asked. 'It wasn't in your statement.'

Mags shrugged and looked at Selena. 'You're the polis, aren't you? So you're more likely to know than I am.'

Mags pushed away from the table. 'If you don't mind, I'd like to be by myself for a bit. I'll come to the station later and sign whatever you want.' She glared at Selena and Rachel. 'What are you two standing around for? Get that man before he kills another of ma girls.'

FORTY-FIVE

Kirsty was towelling a wriggling Beth after giving her an early bath when the doorbell rang. She glanced at the clock wondering who it could be. It was nearly five. Almost no one knew her address. She had deliberately kept it that way. Apart from Gillian and Steve, she hadn't time to foster friendships. Thinking of Gillian brought a fresh wave of grief and guilt. She'd meant to phone Steve to find out how he was coping, but with everything that had happened she simply hadn't had the time or the energy.

She opened the door to Inspector Du Toit and DC Selena MacDonald.

'I'm sorry to disturb you, Dr Burns,' Inspector Du Toit apologised. 'But there have been new developments that we need to speak to you about. May we come in for a moment?'

Kirsty stood back to let them in. 'Please make yourself at home. Let me sort Beth out, then I'll be with you. Five minutes?'

Kirsty took Beth to her bedroom, finished drying her, popped her pyjamas on and allowed her to select a cartoon on Kirsty's iPad.

'Why is that policeman here?' Beth asked. 'And the lady? I don't like them here, 'sbetter when it's just you and me.'

'They won't be here for long. As soon as they've gone, I'll make some sandwiches and we can eat them while I read you a story. OK?'

Beth nodded and with Mr Monkey tucked in beside her, turned her attention to the cartoon.

In the sitting room, the two police officers had remained standing. The inspector was looking out of her sitting-room window.

'Nice view you have here, Doctor,' he said.

'Yes, there are advantages to being on the top floor. As long as the lift doesn't break down. Please, sit down. Coffee?'

'No thank you. We won't keep you.' He settled himself on the sofa facing the window while the constable took the armchair. She took out her tablet. 'Progress, Doctor,' she said in response to Kirsty's enquiring look. 'We take our notes this way these days. Saves us going back to the office and typing them up.'

'What can I do for you?' Kirsty asked. 'Have you found out more about Gillian?'

'We have a number of leads, but I'm afraid I have to tell you the body of another prostitute was found early this morning. There is no doubt she was murdered.'

'That's horrible,' Kirsty said and waited for him to go on.

'We tried to contact you at the hospital. When we couldn't get you, we spoke to Dr Ballantyne. I gather there have been some problems with patients of yours and that you've been suspended?'

'You interviewed Nick again?'

'We're interviewing a lot of the staff at the hospital. Dr Ballantyne was only one of them.'

'I wonder why he felt it was necessary to bring my professional life into this?' Kirsty felt unreasonably disappointed with Nick.

'I assume he thought it was relevant for us to know why we couldn't meet with you at the hospital. He said you'd been told to stay away from Inverness General for the time being and the reason why. He told us someone had confused two patients, almost resulting in them getting the wrong blood – which I understand can be fatal. And then there was the near-miss with Mrs Colston, who nearly died after someone – and I understand some staff think it was you – gave her the wrong drug.'

'I wasn't me.' Kirsty folded her arms. And then, becoming aware how defensive it made her look, unfolded them again. It was so humiliating. Nick had called her a couple of days ago to tell her that he wanted her to take some time off – work from home – until he had a chance to investigate the complaints against her. He'd suggested she edit some papers he was working on if she wanted to keep herself occupied.

'I didn't mix up the bloods and I didn't give Mrs Colston potassium chloride. That's a mistake even a baby doctor wouldn't make.'

'Why don't you take us through what happened? Tell us about the bloods first.'

'When you think a patient might need to be transfused at any point you arrange to have blood taken and sent to the lab for cross-matching. That means the lab will ensure blood with the appropriate group will be available should the patient need to go to theatre, which was the case for the two patients I saw in A&E around the same time on the same day. I took their blood, stuck on a label for each patient with all their details, and left the vials in a tray to go to the lab. One of the patients had to go to theatre urgently, but, luckily for her, the lab picked up that the blood had been cross-matched incorrectly. They checked the vial and realised that the label on her vial should have been on the other I sent. If they hadn't, and she'd been given the wrong blood type, she might have died. It was a frightening near-miss. But I know I labelled those vials correctly.' Du Toit was listening carefully. 'I thought the CCTV recordings of that day would show me who had taken them to the labs, because whoever it was must have switched round the labels, but all I could see was the ward clerkess handing them over to someone. I asked if she could remember who she gave them to, but she couldn't. People are always picking up and dropping off stuff in that tray. It's usually the porter's job, but if anyone is heading to the lab they will take whatever is in the tray too.'

'And the incident with Mrs Colston?' His expression was unreadable.

'I most definitely did not give her the wrong drug. I know damn well how dangerous potassium chloride can be. Anyway, it's usually the nurses that administer the drugs, the doctors who prescribe it. Although, on this occasion, I was the one who injected Mrs Coston's antibiotics into her drip. The nurses were all busy so I thought it was easier, and quicker to do it myself. But that was before the potassium was added – at least an hour before. Look, I don't know what's going on but you can't lay it at my door.' Once more she was aware of how defensive she sounded.

'Mrs Colston is the sister of Caroline Telford,' Du Toit stated.

Kirsty noticed the constable had stopped taking notes and was watching Kirsty intently.

'What does that have to do with anything?' As realisation dawned, a knot of anger formed in her stomach. 'Oh my God. Are you suggesting I tried to kill Mrs Colston because she's the sister of another dead woman who was also my patient, however briefly? Why on earth would I do that?' Kirsty felt chilled all over.

'Don't you think it's odd that the only person linked to each of these women is you? We know their killer probably has medical training, access to a range of anaesthetic drugs. Did you ever come across Jody Tamsworth?'

Kirsty spluttered coffee all over the beige sofa. Shit. She'd have to get it cleaned. More crap to add to her growing list. She forced herself to concentrate. The policeman couldn't possibly be suggesting she was implicated in any of these deaths, particularly Gillian's.

'I loved Gilly. She was my best friend. Why on earth would I want to harm her?' she demanded with rising fury. 'You're forgetting I was the one that wanted her death investigated! And as for other women, why on earth would I want to hurt them? Anyway, surely you should be looking for a man.'

'Not necessarily. You're quite tall for a woman and it seems to me you work out quite a bit. Am I right?'

Kirsty nodded, still in shock.

'The victims were all sedated. Someone who had their trust could have got close enough to administer the drug. Once they were sedated, it would be easy enough for the killer to do whatever he, or she, pleased.'

Kirsty thought back to the pool of blood under Gillian and felt sick. Had the miscarriage caused the blood loss, or had her murderer given her ketamine to sedate her so he could do what he pleased to her? Something to make her miscarry.

'Gillian. Was she...' she managed through dry lips.

'I can't tell you any more right now, not while you may be involved. But I can tell you we're not looking at a simple overdose and a spontaneous miscarriage here.'

It was too much. Kirsty's stomach gave one last heave and she narrowly made it to the bathroom in time to spew into the toilet. She sat hunched over the bowl, waiting for the nausea to pass. God, what had the killer done to Gilly? Whatever had actually happened couldn't be any worse than what she was imagining.

There was a soft tap at the door and DC MacDonald came in with a glass of water.

'Here, drink this,' she said, holding the glass out to Kirsty. 'Take your time.'

Kirsty twisted so that the cool china of the toilet bowl was behind her. She took the glass gratefully.

'Is the Inspector out of his mind suggesting I might have harmed Gillian? Harmed anyone!' she said. 'I'm a doctor, for God's sake. We do our best not to kill people.'

'He's only doing his job,' Selena replied. 'It seems likely that whoever is doing this is coming into contact with the victims through, or at, the hospital.'

'But you're no nearer to finding out who is doing this, are you? Otherwise you wouldn't be here questioning me.' Kirsty stood up and rinsed her mouth.

'Come on,' the police officer said, not unkindly. 'Let's hear what else the inspector has to say.'

'Are you OK to continue?' Du Toit asked when they returned. He appeared genuinely concerned.

'Yes... Actually, no.'

She'd had enough. Her best friend had been murdered. She'd been suspended and she had vomited her guts into the toilet pan in the hearing of the two officers. Her daughter was in her bedroom waiting for a mother who never seemed to have enough time for her, and now it seemed as if she was being accused of multiple murders. She shook her head in disbelief.

'Have you come here to arrest me?' she asked. 'Because if you have, I need to call someone to look after Beth.'

The inspector shook his head sorrowfully. 'Ach, Doctor,' he said, 'I don't really think you killed these women. I'm not convinced you aren't involved in some way, but at the moment I'm inclined to believe you. But if you didn't kill them, then it seems likely that someone is targeting women who were your patients and that Jody Tamsworth was murdered because she realised who it was. In the meantime, until we find whoever is responsible, if I were you, I'd be very careful. Maybe it's a good thing you're no longer working at the hospital in the short term.'

'This is hardly going to help patient confidence. The newspapers are full of the murders and, from what I've been hearing, patients have already started cancelling appointments. Apparently they're too scared to attend. Next, it'll be the staff who refuse to come to work. It'll be chaos. I suggest you leave me alone, do your job and find out who is at the bottom of this.'

Kirsty stalked to the door and held it open. 'I want you to leave now.' She watched impatiently until they were outside her flat. 'And in case you want to speak to me again, be assured I'll have a lawyer standing by. Good evening, Inspector Du Toit, DC MacDonald. You will let me know when you find out who really killed my friend?'

Du Toit looked unimpressed. 'Lock the door behind you, Doctor, and don't let anybody in. The last thing I want is another dead woman.'

Kirsty checked that Beth was OK and started folding clean laundry in preparation for putting it away. Her thoughts kept spinning between Gillian and the other murdered women. Was a doctor, or nurse, responsible for their deaths? Someone Kirsty knew, worked beside? The thought freaked her out. She hoped to hell the police would catch whoever it was soon. If they spent less time investigating her, maybe they would.

She went into her bedroom to put her underwear away. As she opened the top drawer something caught her eye. She froze. One of Beth's dolls was sitting on top of her dresser, propped up against the wall.

How had it got there? Kirsty tried to remember when she'd last seen Beth playing with it. Last night? Or the night before? She couldn't be sure. So much had happened. In any case, Beth couldn't reach the top of the tall dresser, even with a chair. Kirsty's skin prickled from head to toe. Noticing that the bandage her daughter had carefully wrapped around the doll's head to cover her 'bad' eye was loose, she reached for the doll, lifting it gingerly. As she did, the bit of cloth came loose and fell to the floor.

The doll's moving eyelids flicked open and Kirsty's breath caught in her throat. One of the eyes was missing. It had definitely been there the last time she'd played nurse to Beth's doctor. She peered closer, and every nerve ending zinged. The doll's glass eye had been removed very skilfully with something pinpoint sharp, like a needle or a scalpel. And she was damn sure her child had access to neither.

FORTY-SIX

Kirsty turned up at Rachel's door, eyes blazing, holding the hand of a bewildered Beth. She plonked her child on Rachel's sofa, covered her with a duvet she retrieved from Rachel's bed and cued up a cartoon on an iPad that she placed gently into her daughter's hands. She kissed the top of her head and signalled to Rachel that they go into the kitchen.

She sat at Rachel's kitchen table, head in hands. 'Christ, on top of everything, I'm a terrible mother. My daughter should be home in bed. Not babysat by an iPad.'

Rachel poured a glass of wine and thrust it into the doctor's hands. 'You can leave your car here and Uber home.'

'I'm not going home. Not tonight. Maybe not ever.' She took the glass of wine as if it were a life raft, a dazed look on her face. 'Someone has been in my flat. In. My. Flat. In my daughter's bedroom.'

'Jesus! Did you call the police?'

'Bugger the police. They were round at the flat just before I found the doll, implying all sorts of crap. Practically suggesting I was involved in these murders in some way. Instead of searching for the real killer.'

Rachel was about to protest she was sure this wasn't the case, but clearly now wasn't the time.

'How did they get in?'

'No idea. They must have a key.' She buried her head in her hands. 'Oh crap. What did they want? Apart from scaring me to death.' She straightened and sucked in a deep breath. 'They chose the wrong person to fuck with. Especially now they've involved my daughter.'

That was more like the Kirsty Rachel remembered.

Kirsty took a swig of wine.

'I was finally starting to find my feet again after Tembo's death, but now it's like my life has gone off a cliff. Our daughter, who he would want me to protect with my life, is in danger because of me.'

'You don't know that,' Rachel said, although she suspected Kirsty was right.

Kirsty took another gulp of wine.

'I find my dearest friend dead, I think I'm going to get a promotion but instead I'm suspended, accused of making basic, life-threatening mistakes. Which I didn't do, by the way.'

Rachel listened in silence while Kirsty told her how two patients had their blood samples mixed up with potentially catastrophic results, and reminded her how Annie, one of her patients had been given a lethal drug in error, *for which she was being blamed.*

'Neither error was down to me, despite the suggestions that my mind isn't on my work – that I've become careless, if not downright negligent. Someone is screwing with my life. Whoever it is needs to be stopped. I'm not going to stand back and let some psycho put my daughter in danger – ruin everything I've worked so hard for.'

Rachel heard her out in silence, but something Kirsty said had struck a chord. Before she could formulate her thoughts, there was a knock on the door. She groaned inwardly. What now? She flung open the door to find Red Mags, Annie Colston and a teenager she hadn't seen before.

'You going to let us in?' Mags said, brushing past Rachel. Anne smiled weakly and followed her.

'This is cool,' the teen said, thrusting out her hand to be shaken. 'I'm Susan, Annie's daughter, by the way.'

Rachel surveyed her cramped sitting room with dismay. Mags was in the chair next to the patio doors, legs spread, the tops of her stockings plainly visible. Kirsty and Annie were side by side on the small sofa with Annie's daughter, Susan, and Kirsty's daughter, Beth, at their feet. This gathering couldn't be legal. At best Rachel was sailing close to the wind professionally. When Beth had cast her iPad aside in favour of sizing the up the visitors, Rachel had given in to the inevitable and supplied glasses of wine to the grown-ups and orange juice and Diet Cokes to the children.

Apparently, Annie and her daughter had gone to see Mags to commiserate with her over Jody, after which they'd decided to knock on Rachel's door to ask if she had any updates.

'Susan, why don't you take Beth into the kitchen? You can take your drinks with you,' Annie suggested.

'But—' Susan started.

'Now please,' Annie said firmly. Rachel was surprised. Annie hadn't appeared to have much gumption when she'd met her before. Perhaps her unlikely alliance with Mags had stiffened her backbone? She immediately regretted the thought. Annie had lost someone she loved to murder and had almost died herself. No one remained unaffected by those kinds of events.

Now they had another dead woman. And there wasn't any doubt she'd been murdered.

No one spoke until the children were out of earshot.

'What's going on, Rachel?' Kirsty broke the silence. 'Why are the police questioning me? Why are the police so sure a medic is responsible for these murders?'

'Jody, the latest victim, saw someone follow Ashley into the alley. She saw him again in or near the hospital. He – or she – was wearing scrubs,' Rachel replied.

'Oh, for God's sake! They can't possibly think it was me. She could have seen this person, whoever it was, anywhere in the hospital. And it doesn't have to have been a doctor. It could have been a nurse – or anyone who works in a hospital, for that matter. In fact, it doesn't even have to be a member of staff. Anyone can get hold of scrubs these days – after Covid, tons disappeared. And if someone were to put scrubs on and walk around the hospital as if they knew what they're doing, it's unlikely anyone would question them.'

'Aren't hospitals more security-conscious now?' Annie said. 'I thought all staff had to wear ID badges?'

'Yes. But people don't always look at them closely. Staff come and go, particularly locum doctors and agency nurses. Security isn't foolproof.'

Kirsty took a sip of wine before continuing. 'Leaving that aside for the time being, if the same person did kill Gillian and Ashley, and now Jody, why? As far as I know, I never saw Jody.'

'Don't forget someone injected potassium chloride in my drip and it nearly killed me,' Annie said. 'I'm certain it wasn't you, Kirsty, but it was a clinician. Or at least someone who was comfortable in a clinical setting.'

The hospital had to be key. According to Selena, the police were still making their way through the male members of staff at the hospital.

'Something ties the murdered women together. If the link isn't you, Kirsty, maybe it *is* Jamie De Banzie,' Rachel said. 'Or Dr Ballantyne?'

Kirsty blanched. 'No, the idea that he's a murderer is preposterous.'

But then Kirsty didn't know about Rachel's visit to Jennifer Ballantyne and Rachel's suspicion that all wasn't right with her marriage, that it was possible Jennifer Ballantyne was being physically abused by her husband. Some things had to remain confidential. Rachel had, however, passed her suspicions on to Du Toit. Furthermore, Dr Ballantyne was also linked to Gillian and Caroline Telford, and had also, notionally, been Ashley's consultant. As Kirsty's boss, didn't that link him to Annie too? He was as linked to the women as Kirsty was. And if Rachel was correct about the domestic abuse, then he was a misogynist with violent tendencies.

'As much as I'm not a fan of Jamie De Banzie, I can't see it being him either,' Kirsty added.

Rachel tended to agree. He had the easiest access to drugs, would know exactly the right cocktail to give to keep the women compliant. On the flip side, as far as she was aware, Jamie had no connection with any of the women apart from Gillian. She found it impossible to believe there were two different murderers.

'Can you check the hospital records?' Rachel asked. 'Find out who else might have seen Ashley and Jody? Particularly a member of staff who saw the both of them.'

Everyone turned to look at Kirsty.

'I've been suspended.' Her mouth twisted into a wry smile. 'Nick says I have to stay away from the hospital until they've finished investigating what happened when you were in hospital, Annie.'

'Suspended?' Annie echoed. 'God, I'm sorry, Kirsty. I thought they couldn't prove it was you who gave me the wrong drug. I told them it wasn't.'

'But can you really be sure, Annie? After all, you were pretty out of it. And anyway, it's not the only thing.' Kirsty looked at Rachel with imploring eyes. Rachel realised Kirsty couldn't bring herself to tell the women in front of her that she was being held responsible for another error.

'What if it wasn't a mistake?' Mags said to Annie. 'What if someone wanted you dead?'

Rachel had been wondering the same thing. It was looking increasingly like the potassium hadn't been a mistake. But what part did Annie play in all this? Apart from being Caroline Telford's sister, and Kirsty's patient – and therefore notionally Nick's. She'd known Jody too. Quite a number of connections, now Rachel thought about it.

'Did you know Gillian?' she asked Annie.

'We never met as far as I know,' Annie replied. 'Why? Do you think the same person who killed her tried to kill me?'

'I don't know. I wouldn't rule it out.' Of course, the murderer couldn't be Annie. Unless she'd tried to kill herself with the potassium chloride. That line of thinking was nuts.

Everything kept coming back to Kirsty Burns. With the exception of Jody, all the women had been her patients.

'Was Jody ever your patient?' Rachel asked Kirsty, realising she hadn't actually posed the question.

'I don't remember the name. I'd have to access her records.'

'Who has access to patients' records?' Rachel asked, her theory beginning to coalesce in her mind.

'Anyone who has a legitimate reason. Nurses, doctors, secretarial staff. Almost everyone who works at the hospital really.'

Rachel straightened, electrified. 'When you access notes, what information can you see about patients?'

'Anything. Everything. Medical history, social history – when they've been seen in hospital, which department and what for. Dates of birth, addresses, occupation, name of their GP. What drugs they're on, blood results, test results, diagnoses – a whole bunch of things.'

Was this the link? Did the killer find his victims through

their hospital records? Rachel ran the different scenarios through her head. The more she thought about it, the more it made sense. It was a terrifying thought.

'Can you tell when the records have been accessed and who by?'

'In theory. Every time a staff member logs in, it's recorded. But people don't always log out, which means the next person on the computer won't be logged in under their own name.'

'Can you access the patient information remotely, Kirsty?'

'No. I don't have remote login access.'

'Then can we go to the hospital. Tonight? Access the patient information system? Establish if Jody was seen at the hospital and, if so, by whom. Maybe that way we can find something that will link our killer to Jody and Ashley.'

'I'm suspended! I'm not supposed to go anywhere near the hospital.'

'Do you still have your ID though? Your access codes?'

The police would need to get a warrant to look at the records, and that would take time. And time wasn't on their side.

'I know it's putting you in a spot,' Rachel continued. 'But what if our killer is planning to strike again. Maybe even tonight.'

'I suppose I could sneak in,' Kirsty said after a while. 'Although if I'm caught in the hospital when I've been told to stay away, my career is well and truly f—' She glanced at her daughter, who'd come into the sitting room holding Susan's hand. 'In trouble. But I want to get to the bottom of what's going on more than anyone.'

She smiled as her daughter climbed onto the sofa next to Mags and sat quietly sucking her thumb. Mags flicked the channel across to a cartoon and the two sat staring intently at the television screen.

'What about Beth? I don't want to let her out of my sight. I should have taken her to my mother's in Wester Ross. It's too late now. Thank goodness, Mum's coming to Inverness tomorrow. She can take Beth back with her then.'

'I'll look after her,' Mags offered. 'In ma hoose.'

'Susan can help keep an eye on her,' Annie said. 'Won't you, darling?'

'Yeh, I'll watch her if you like,' Susan answered. 'But it will cost you a tenner.'

'No way,' Annie sputtered.

'I'm assuming you don't want Dad to know whatever it is you're up to?' Susan said, looking pleased with herself.

'That's blackmail!'

'Yes or no? Remember, I'll have to keep George from gassing to Dad. So, I think it's fair.'

'All right,' Annie conceded, taking a ten-pound note from her bag and handing it to Susan.

Rachel thought for a minute. If someone was going around killing people – and someone was – it wasn't a good idea to leave two children and an ageing prostitute alone. There was always the possibility that whoever had murdered Jody would come after Mags. Especially as it seemed likely Jody had been killed because the murderer thought she could identify him. On the other hand, the five of them couldn't traipse around the hospital. They'd stick out like horses in a race without riders.

In the kitchen, out of hearing of the children, she shared her concern with the others.

'Perhaps it's better I go alone?' Kirsty said.

Mags hadn't said anything. She didn't even appear to be listening to what they were saying. She had picked up a toothpick and seemed intent on excavating something from the back of her mouth. As Rachel, Kirsty and Annie watched her, she appeared to find something and, removing the toothpick, examined it triumphantly. 'Got the bugger! Thing's been bothering me a' day.'

She sat down at the kitchen table resting her ample breasts on the surface. 'I've got an idea. Why don't we all go to the hospital and me, Mrs C and the kids could hang about in the waiting room of A&E? There's likely to be plenty buggers around at this time, so I doubt anybody will notice a few more.'

'There's usually a surge in patients coming to A&E around this time,' Kirsty agreed. 'No one would dare try anything when there's lots of people around.'

It was a good idea, along the lines of hiding a tree in a forest, Rachel thought.

It took another half an hour to convince a reluctant Susan to come with them. Beth wasn't very happy either to have her cartoon-watching interrupted, but Kirsty promised they'd stop for ice cream on the way home if she came quietly. The promise was enough for Beth to pick up Mr Monkey and stand at the door. Annie, Mags and the two children piled into Annie's car, while Kirsty went with Rachel.

Rachel and Kirsty were silent as they drove towards the city, passing the place where Jody's body had been found. Rachel saw that a couple of bouquets of flowers still in cellophane had been left by the side of the road.

'Why do you care so much?' Kirsty asked suddenly.

'It's my job to care.'

'No, it's more than that. You're putting your job on the line, even I know that. And your job is as important to you as mine is to me. Anyone can see that. I'm prepared to take the risk because Gilly was my best friend. You barely knew her.'

The light from the street lamps lit up the interior of the car in rhythmic flashes. It felt a little like a confessional. Kirsty was entitled to know what Gillian had done for Rachel. But it would mean Rachel opening up about one of the darkest periods of her life.

Kirsty didn't need to hear Rachel's story to know what her friend was like.

'Gillian was an amazing person. She didn't deserve to die. None of them did. If I can help get her – their – killer put away, then perhaps I've earned my place on this earth.' She gave Kirsty a quick smile. 'I'm afraid that's the best explanation I can give.'

FORTY-SEVEN

It was after seven by the time Kirsty and Rachel walked into the department of obstetrics and gynaecology. They'd left the others in A&E, which was mobbed with the usual evening crowd, unlike the department of Obs and Gyn which, as Kirsty had predicted, was deserted. At this time of night women in labour would be directed straight to the labour ward while other emergencies would come via A&E. Picking up the phone on the counter, Kirsty rang switchboard and asked them to page Dr Ballantyne.

'What are you doing?' Rachel asked. 'We don't want anyone to know we're here. That's the whole point, isn't it?'

'If he answers, then we'll know he's still at work and probably in his office. He often hangs about until this time. And if he does answer, I'll ring off.'

But as Kirsty had hoped, switchboard came back saying that Dr Ballantyne had left for the day and would she like to be connected to him at home? Kirsty told the voice at the other end that it didn't matter, she would catch him later, and rang off.

'C'mon,' she said to Rachel, and ignoring the lift they ran upstairs to the consultants' offices, which were located in a corridor next to the labour suite. Happily, there were no staff around, only a delighted-looking man carrying balloons emblazoned with *It's a boy!* waiting to be buzzed into the labour suite. Rachel and Kirsty slipped past, hoping to make it inside the office suite, as someone came to let him in him.

Kirsty punched the code into the security pad by the side of the door leading to the doctors' offices. As they gained entry to the corridor, Kirsty told Rachel there was always the possibility that one of the other consultants would be around, either finishing off paperwork or hanging about in case one of their juniors got into trouble with a difficult case. Sure enough, there was a sliver of light under the door of one of the other consultants.

She held her finger to her lips and beckoned Rachel to follow her. Dr Ballantyne, as befitting his stature, had the largest office with the best view at the end of the corridor. Holding their breath, they crept past the office with the light on and into Nick's. Kirsty opened the door and they slipped inside.

'None of the consultants bother to lock their doors, even though they're supposed to. Most of them consider the keypad at the end of the corridor security enough. Besides, they know that a junior or someone from medical records might need to look for case notes during the night.'

It was still daylight outside so they didn't have to switch on a light.

Nick's office was as tidy as Rachel remembered. Rachel could smell the distinctive whiff of his aftershave – something not too obtrusive but obviously expensive. Precisely the image he liked to present, she thought. On the left-hand side of his desk was a neat pile of paperwork. To the right was his penholder, the photo of his wife, Jennifer, and his in tray. His computer monitor was in the middle of the desk.

'I'll boot up the computer,' Kirsty said. While she waited, she picked up a letter from Nick's in tray and read it quickly.

'Oh, wow. Dr Ballantyne is in line for the chair of obstetrics and gynaecology. I'd not heard. I'm stunned, to be honest. Nick isn't an academic and these positions usually go to those working in research who have the greatest chance of attracting funding to the university departments. Then again, he is on a large number of committees, spending at least 50 per cent of his time in London. That in itself could be enough to make him a suitable candidate. The dean certainly seems to think so. Maybe whatever Gillian wanted to tell me was about this. Maybe she'd discovered something that put appointing him to the chair in jeopardy?'

Rachel took it from her. Was it relevant? If Nick was abusing his wife and it got out, the offer of the chair would vanish. But was that a good enough reason to murder? It didn't seem likely. Nevertheless, it was something to consider later. When they got out of here.

Then something else caught her attention. When Kirsty had picked up the letter, it had exposed a buff-coloured folder lying on top of Dr Ballantyne's in tray. The logo emblazoned on the front was one Rachel knew only too well. It was from her office. Curious, she picked it up and flicked it open to the front page. Pinned to the cover was a letter to Dr Ballantyne from the hospital's legal department, thanking him for his contribution to the case of Fiona Mitchell versus Highlands and Islands Health Board, and advising him the case had been settled. She flicked through the pages. As the doctor who had carried out the procedure in question, Kirsty's report had been central to the case.

OK,' Kirsty said, pulling Rachel's attention back to the room. 'I'm in. I have Jody's records.' Her mouse clicked as she moved through them. 'Oh my God,' she said. 'I've found something.'

'What?' Rachel asked, peering over Kirsty's shoulder.

'Jody Tamsworth. It's the right date of birth and the correct address – was admitted here for surgery six weeks ago for an abscess in her groin. The surgery was performed under general anaesthetic. And guess who the anaesthetist was?'

'Dr Jamie De Banzie?'

'Got it in one.'

Had everyone been right about Dr De Banzie? Did he select his victims from the patients attending the hospital? If so, he was one sick bastard. Perhaps Gillian had found out? Confronted him? And he'd murdered her. It didn't seem so far-fetched now.

Kirsty was still stabbing away at the keyboard. 'This is weird.'

'What is?'

'I thought, seeing as I was already breaking the rules, I would look up Jennifer on the system.'

'And?'

'There *was* a record created the day she saw Gillian, but someone has deleted it. However they didn't do a very good job. The system doesn't allow you to delete a record completely. I can see there was an entry, but not what it was. And Nick's name is beside it.'

'Why would someone delete an entry?'

'Because they had something to hide. Maybe because they'd cocked up in some way. For no legal reason, at any rate.'

It looked like Nick was back in the frame.

'What can you tell me about this?' Rachel passed the folder to Kirsty. Kirsty rifled through the pages, sinking back in her chair when she came to the final one. Her face was almost completely devoid of colour. 'Why didn't he tell me?'

FORTY-EIGHT

Before Rachel could ask Kirsty what she meant, she heard voices coming from outside in the corridor. Shit. Someone was heading their way. The voices stopped outside the door and Rachel watched in dismay as the handle turned. Without thinking, Rachel shoved the file into her rucksack.

At the same time Kirsty returned the paper she'd been reading to the in tray before the door swung open and light flooded the room.

'What the hell is going on here?' said a voice Rachel recognised. *Fuckity fuck.* Dr Ballantyne. How the hell was she going to get out of this? She couldn't imagine her being found in Dr Ballantyne's office at night would go down well with her boss, and definitely not with acting-boss Alastair. Rachel might well end up suspended too.

'Oh hello, Nick,' Kirsty said, sounding guilty. Nick wasn't alone. Beside him stood the porter Rachel recognised from the recording of A&E they'd watched in the porter's office. He'd been the one helping Johnny evict King and his partner from the department.

'I asked you a question, Dr Burns. Could you please tell me what you are doing in my office at this time of night with Miss McKenzie? Did I not tell you, I didn't want you in the hospital until I'd looked into matters?'

'I tried to page you,' Kirsty said – truthfully, as it happened. 'But switchboard said you were at home. You know how I've been working on that paper for you? I thought since I couldn't do any clinical work, this would be a good time to finish it. I needed a reference and thought it might find it in your office. I assumed being suspended meant I was prohibited from treating patients, not from doing research.'

Nick narrowed his eyes at her. 'And is Miss McKenzie helping with you with this paper?'

'Hello, Dr Ballantyne,' Rachel said evenly, holding out her hand. Inside she was cringing. The shit was going to hit the proverbial fan over this. 'I'm pleased to see you again.'

Nick reached for his chair and sank into it. 'Will someone please tell me what the hell is going on? What were you looking for on my computer?'

'Why have you left your kid in A&E?' the porter inter- jected, addressing Kirsty. 'I was there to collect a patient for theatre when I saw her. Without you. I thought it was strange, so I asked her where you were. She said you were here, at work, and you had told her to wait there.'

If possible, Kirsty looked paler.

'Billy went to the room where they have the CCTV moni- tors and saw you and another woman heading this way. He thought it best to let me know.'

At that moment Rachel's mobile pinged with a text: Selena. Apparently Jamie De Banzie had been arrested. His DNA had been found all over Gillian's body. *Got him!* Selena finished, adding a smiley face. It appeared she had indeed been wrong about Jamie De Banzie.

'That was the police,' Rachel said, after she'd read the message 'They've arrested Jamie De Banzie this afternoon on suspicion of murder.'

'Dr De Banzie? Jamie De Banzie, the anaesthetist? Arrested. For murder?' Dr Ballantyne echoed. He shook his head. He turned to the porter. 'Billy, could you leave us alone, please.'

Billy, his eyes flitting from Rachel to Kirsty, then back to Nick, hesitated.

'I'll make sure they are escorted off the premises,' Nick reassured him, 'Thanks for letting me know they were here.'

'I'll be downstairs if you need me,' Billy said, closing the door behind him.

'For Christ's sake, Kirsty. What the hell are you doing here?' Nick demanded. 'Can't you see that creeping around the hospital with people not authorised to be here' – he looked pointedly at Rachel – 'is not going to improve your current circumstances.'

'I didn't know you were in line for a chair,' Kirsty stalled.

'I didn't want anyone to know until it had been confirmed,' Nick said. 'That's not the issue here. What the fuck is going on? You'd better talk fast, Dr Burns.'

'I wanted to look up a patient's record.'

'Please tell me, not my wife's?'

'I asked Dr Burns to look,' Rachel lied. 'I was curious to know what she wanted to see Sister Robertson about.'

'Why was her record deleted?' Kirsty asked.

'You had no right to look up the records of patients who are not yours,' Nick snapped. 'That's another disciplinary offence to add to the others.'

'And a disciplinary offence to delete one,' Kirsty said quietly.

'Why did she ask to see Gillian?' Rachel said. 'What reason

did you have to delete the record of her visit? Why was it so important no one knew why she'd attended A&E?'

Even if Nick wasn't the killer, he could still be a wife abuser.

'I don't know why you think any of this excuses you being in my office. But, yes, she had been to see Gillian at the hospital and wanted it kept secret. My wife had persuaded herself that she had acute myeloid leukaemia. You know those bruises you saw?' He swivelled his furious gaze to Rachel. 'She told me you subtly suggested I was the one inflicting them on her.'

Rachel would have put it the other way around. It had seemed to her that Jennifer had been the one who'd implied abuse.

'She thought they were the first signs of the disease,' Dr Ballantyne continued. 'She looked it up on the internet. She asked Gillian to take some blood for testing and made her promise not to tell me.'

Rachel supposed it made sense. Gillian wouldn't have wanted to break Jennifer's confidence. On the other hand, Gillian must have wanted her to see a doctor to have the full battery of tests. Maybe Jennifer's refusal had been what was worrying Gillian. The matter she wanted to discuss with Kirsty.

But why not share her concerns with her husband? Nick's position in the hospital would have meant she would have had the quickest and most expert attention.

'Why didn't she tell you?' Kirsty asked, clearly thinking the same thing.

'She knew I had been approached about the professorship and she said she didn't want to worry me when I was already under pressure. She also worried that the university might not be keen to offer the chair to a man with a sick wife. In that respect, she was right. I couldn't have taken the job if Jennifer had been seriously ill.'

Kirsty furrowed her brow. She looked unconvinced.

'Enough about that. You still haven't explained why you were in my office. And don't even try that ridiculous excuse about papers and research. I don't believe it for a minute. You could have asked to be put through to my home and I would have arranged for one of the porters to accompany you.'

Realisation dawned behind blue eyes. Looking incredulous, he leaned forward and focused on Rachel. 'I see now. You thought I was hitting my wife, ergo you thought I might be a murderer.' He turned back to Kirsty. 'And you were in on this. Good God, woman! Have you some kind of death wish as far as your career is concerned?' He laughed but there was no humour in the sound. 'I think we can say you've blown your chances this time.'

'Can't you at least try and understand, Nick?' Kirsty said, sounding desperate. 'I needed the killer to be found. He was screwing with my life – he's even been in my flat, for God's sake. He must have been watching me and my daughter. Do you have any idea how that feels? I had to find out what was going on. I thought my child wasn't safe, my career at stake. I didn't mix up those damn bloods and I didn't give Annie the potassium. I can't be struck off. I accept that I've lost any chance of getting a consultant job here, but if I can clear my name at least I have a chance somewhere else. I can't see how Jamie was involved or why, but if he killed those women, he must have been involved in the errors.'

Dr Ballantyne shook his head. 'I don't see how the clinical errors and the murders could be related. I don't know why Dr De Banzie killed Gillian and those women, but I guess we'll find out soon enough.' He drew a hand across his eyes. 'Look, I appreciate you've been under a great deal of stress. You are still suspended from clinical work but you can use my office and my computer to help me finish the paper I'm presenting next week. In the meantime, I will have someone undertake an independent review of the errors you are accused of.'

Kirsty stumbled to her feet. 'Thank you.'

Rachel indicated to Kirsty with a tip of her head that it was time for them to make themselves scarce. She headed for the door, Kirsty following close behind. At the doorway Kirsty turned back to Dr Ballantyne. 'You might have told me the Mitchell case was settled. I've been worrying myself sick about it.'

FORTY-NINE

Rachel sank into a chair with a glass of wine. She eased her shoes off with her toes. It had been some night and she wasn't looking forward to the bollocking she'd no doubt receive in the morning. It would be a minor miracle if she wasn't suspended or even chucked out of the fiscals' office.

She ran the night's events through her head. She'd called Du Toit to tell him that Jody had been a patient of Jamie's too. She'd been partly right. Dr De Banzie used his position in the hospital to pick his victims.

He knew Gillian, she was carrying his baby, he saw her that night. His DNA was found all over her and her flat. It was pretty damning evidence. She could get her head around him murdering Gillian, but the others? It bothered her that they didn't know why he'd killed them. Perhaps Gillian had found out somehow that he'd killed Caroline Telford and challenged him? But why had he killed Caroline? There was no evidence they'd met. Unless he'd bumped into her when she'd come to the hospital for her outpatient appointment with Kirsty.

Why then go on and kill Ashley? And Jody shortly after? Maybe the thought that Ashley was going to have a baby when

Gillian wouldn't let him be part of her baby's life pushed him over the edge. And he'd killed Jody because she recognised him as the man who followed Ashley into the alley.

Whatever the police were thinking, it didn't really add up for Rachel. If they were to make a charge of murder stick they'd need more – much more.

Was he also responsible for the missing drugs in A&E?

She leaned forward and stared into the flames of her gas fire. Why then did she feel this sense of something not quite right? There was also the mix-up with the bloods Kirsty had been blamed for. There was nothing to indicate that Jamie had anything to do with that. Why would Jamie want to damage Kirsty's professional reputation? As for Annie, why would he want to hurt her? Unless he thought Annie knew something too. Perhaps he had found out that she worked at No. 79 and was worried the prostitutes would tell Annie something that would point to him. It all did seem to tie in. But the uneasy feeling wouldn't go away. There were still too many holes. Her gut still told her Jamie De Banzie wasn't their killer.

Rachel sighed and closed her eyes. Her brain was in over-drive and she was exhausted. Maybe a good night's sleep would make everything clearer.

It was only the next morning while she was making coffee that she remembered the file she had taken from Nick's office. She took her mug over to the kitchen table and opened it. There were several statements from staff, around forty pages of them. She read them with growing dismay and turned to the summary report.

Two years ago Fiona Mitchell, an insulin-dependent diabetic, had been under the care of Dr Nick Ballantyne and the diabetic antenatal team. She had attended regularly and there were no concerns about her or the baby's wellbeing during that period. An elective caesarean section was recommended, as was often the case with diabetic mothers.

The day prior to her planned delivery Ms Mitchell was admitted to Inverness General maternity unit in early labour. Dr Kirsty Burns was the duty registrar in the labour ward that day. Ms Mitchell was very anxious that her partner be present for the birth. He was in Edinburgh attending a pharmaceutical conference, so was several hours' drive away. Following discussion with Ms Mitchell and Dr Ballantyne, it was agreed that Ms Mitchell be allowed to labour and deliver naturally. She would be continuously monitored throughout.

Unfortunately as labour established there were concerns about the baby's heartbeat and the need for caesarean section was suggested. However Ms Mitchell's partner was still en route to the hospital. At the patient's request, Dr Burns agreed to review Ms Mitchell in thirty minutes but was kept busy dealing with another emergency and there was a delay in contacting Dr Burns to ask for a further review as concern mounted. When Dr Burns subsequently returned, later than intended, to the labour ward there were signs of a much more serious problem needing immediate delivery.

In theatre Dr Burns performed a rapid caesarean section but tragically found that the uterus had ruptured and Ms Mitchell's baby son was born in very poor condition. Despite lengthy attempts at resuscitation by the full paediatric team, no heartbeat was ever established and he was pronounced stillborn.

There was ongoing massive blood loss which persisted despite closure of the uterine rupture, multiple drugs to assist uterine contraction, a 10-unit blood transfusion as well as other blood products. Help was requested from both Dr Ballantyne and the anaesthetic and ITU consultants. As Ms Mitchell was about to exsanguinate – bleed out – and in consultation with the rest of the theatre team, there being no relative to give consent, Dr Burns felt compelled to perform an urgent caesarean hysterectomy, after which the mother's condition stabilised. Dr Ballantyne arrived as surgery was being completed. However Ms Mitchell had suffered prolonged periods of low blood pressure and had required chest compressions during the surgery when no pulse could be felt. She was taken to intensive care for ongoing life support. Dr Ballantyne had debriefed Fiona's partner and explained that, while there was a delay in delivering the baby, this was, in his opinion, an unavoidable tragedy.

The case had been settled out of court two weeks ago.

Rachel breathed out and read the summary report again. In short, this was exactly the kind of case that got reported to her office. A succession of delays that couldn't really be laid at anyone's door but had led to the avoidable death of a baby and a catastrophic outcome for the mother. Dr Kirsty Burns had been one of the key players in the tragedy. Dr Ballantyne had a part to play too.

Everything made more sense now – why everyone was so quick to doubt Kirsty's competence.

That the case had been settled didn't necessarily mean that Kirsty had done something wrong. Sometimes it was cheaper for a health board to settle out of court than rack up legal bills. She thought back to the scene last night. It appeared no one had told Kirsty the case had been settled.

Several things hit Rachel at once.

Fiona's partner – William Strain, according to the file – had been attending a pharmaceutical conference. He had sued the hospital over what had happened. Perhaps he still bore a grudge? Where was he now? What if he worked in the hospital pharmacy? He would have unlimited access to drugs, as well as access to the hospital patient system. He had every reason to want to make Kirsty's life a misery and could move around the hospital unnoticed. There was a lot that didn't tie in, but at the very least, someone should speak to him.

She grabbed her phone from the kitchen counter. She needed to tell Du Toit and his team. Get them to find out where he was now. Track him down. After she'd spoken to Du Toit, she'd call Kirsty. Find out more. See if she knew where Strain was now. If he worked in the hospital, Kirsty might know. There was no time to waste. If Strain was in the hospital and had access to hospital records, no one was safe.

FIFTY

The unmistakable odour of urine hit him as soon as he walked into the room.

She lay on the bed curled up like a wounded bird, her stick-like arms outside the covers, her face barely visible in the dim morning light. She was in exactly the same position as he'd left her the night before. And why wouldn't she be? He had long ago given up expecting a miracle. She couldn't move, feed herself, go to the toilet or any of the other hundred things other people took for granted. She couldn't even speak, except for the meaningless grunts or the small mews which escaped her slack mouth whenever she was in pain. Which was far too often.

Today was one of the days Nurse Turkey Neck and Nurse Curly Top normally came to wash and dress his wife. There were always two carers, unless they were short-staffed, when there would be one or sometimes no one at all. If they hadn't insisted on coming, he wouldn't have let them touch her. But it was either that or his wife would have to go to a nursing home. And he couldn't allow that. Fiona should be at home. With him. Where she belonged.

But they wouldn't be coming this morning. He'd taken the day off work. Cancelled the nurses this evening too.

He pulled the covers back gently so as not to wake her, wincing as the warm smell of faeces wafted up from under the covers. It was a double day. Every second day was a double day. But he didn't mind. He liked doing things for her and if Fiona had been aware she would be mortified to have strangers see her in a state. That's why he got up at six every morning, so she'd be ready for the morning nurses. Fresh. They told him to leave her, it was their job after all, but he couldn't. It was *his* job. His duty. As a husband.

God he'd loved her. She'd been his world, still was. Always had been. They'd met at university. He'd been doing a degree in pharmacology, she was studying geography. He'd fallen almost immediately for the dark-eyed woman with the shy, warm smile. He couldn't believe his luck when she seemed to like him too, laughing at his weak jokes and looking at him as if he were a god instead of a skinny man with a poor attempt at a goatee.

All that had been taken away. By the hospital. By Dr Burns and Ballantyne in particular.

Fiona's eyes fluttered open and she looked at him with blank eyes. Did she know him? Still recognise him? Sometimes he thought so. Sometimes he saw something move in her eyes and her lips would purse as if she was about to say something. His name perhaps? But she never did. A sound would escape, a little pah, or bah, a puff of air, then she would retreat back inside herself to that place where he couldn't go, no matter how much he wanted to.

He left her long enough to fill a plastic basin with warm water and to collect a clean face cloth and towel from the bathroom down the hall. When he returned, she had closed her eyes again. He had no way of knowing whether she was asleep.

He rolled the soiled sheet into a pipe behind her back and used the edge to wipe away the worst of the faeces. Then he dampened the face cloth and began to wash, starting from above her buttocks and working his way down between her legs. He had to change the water four times before all traces of the brown sludge had been removed. He took his time, knowing that too much pressure on her papery skin could cause it to tear and the resulting wound would take months to heal. She hadn't had a bedsore in the two years since he had brought her home, and he was damned if she was going to get one now.

When he had finished washing her, he replaced the soiled sheet with a clean one and rolled her over using her rigid legs for leverage. Now she was facing him he could wash her other side.

He'd been the happiest man in the world when she'd discovered she was pregnant.

When it had happened, when he'd first taken her home, he'd spent hours flexing her legs, doing the passive exercises just as the physiotherapist at the hospital had shown him, but it hadn't stopped her developing the contractures that pulled her knees towards her chest. Day by day her legs had contracted into her preferred fetal position. Now the only way her legs could be straightened was if someone snapped them in two.

Once Fiona was clean and dry, he reached into the chest of drawers for a clean nightgown. It was much too big, the right size for someone twice her size, the right size for Turkey Neck, but it was the only way he could get her into something without hurting her. Like her legs, her arms had contracted until they resembled little bird wings. The nurses had suggested he use backless hospital gowns; they would bring him some from the hospital and that way he could slip her arms in without the twisting and pulling and manoeuvring which left him giddy and sweaty with the sheer effort of it all. But he couldn't do that to her. It was the apparel of a geriatric, not a twenty-nine-year-old woman, for Christ's sake! Didn't she deserve some dignity? Not that there was much left to preserve.

He compromised with the voluminous nightdress and, once he had her in it, brushed her hair and added a bow, she looked quite pretty again. Especially if he hid her misshapen arms under the sheets. When she was like this he could almost believe she was his Fiona again and that any minute she would open her eyes and call out his name and he would pull her into his arms and cover her face with kisses and it would all be all right, and he would tell her that he would *never, ever* let anything bad happen to her.

But he couldn't. It wasn't all right. He had let something bad happen to her. Now all he could do was seek out those responsible and punish them, make them suffer the way his wife was suffering. Only then could he lay down his burden and release Fiona. Go with her to a place where nothing and no one could ever hurt her again.

He'd done the first one when they'd told him Fiona would never get better, that she would stay the way she was for what remained of her life. When he'd killed Caroline, it was like all the anger had flowed out of him and into the woman. It had helped. For a while. Particularly when the bitch doctor resigned. But then she'd returned, child in tow, and started working at the hospital again. His rage had started to build again the moment he'd seen her. That's when he promised himself he'd destroy her, take everything she cared about bit by bit, until she wished she were dead.

He tucked the duvet around Fiona, careful to leave her arms free and rubbed moisturising cream into her hands. She liked that. Time was running out. He'd avoided being interviewed by the police until now, but they had finally pinned him down by arranging a time with the head porter. It wouldn't be long before they put two and two together. If he wanted to make Burns and Ballantyne pay, it had to be today.

As he massaged Fiona's hands, William ran through his plan in his head. It was fraught with difficulties, but it was the best he could come up with at short notice. Kirsty would be in Nick's office working on the paper for him, so she would be out of the flat. Somehow he had to get hold of her daughter. That was an essential part of the plan. Dr Burns had to be made to know what it was like to lose a child. But how would he manage to get her away from the nursery? Those places were fortresses these days.

He checked his watch. Ten o'clock. He had spent hours following Kirsty and knew the routine off by heart. On Thursdays when Kirsty was working, her mother collected Beth from the nursery at half past twelve. They would then take the bus back to the flat. That would be his opportunity. He would grab her then.

He had to get Dr Burns and Ballantyne to where he needed them to be. That was the tricky part.

He thought he knew how. It wasn't a perfect plan, but it would have to do. He put everything he needed, syringes, sterilising wipes, a scalpel, a couple of Fiona's scarves, and a roll of duct tape into a large carpet bag, along with vials of all the drugs he could possibly need.

But first he had something else to do. He filled a syringe with sux and another with propofol. The sux would paralyse her muscles in seconds, stopping her breath. Which is why he needed to give her propofol first. That would knock her out so she wouldn't be aware of what was happening.

He leaned over Fiona and pressed his lips to hers. 'I'll see you soon, my love.' And then he inserted the first needle into her vein.

FIFTY-ONE

After Strain had done what he needed to at Kirsty Burns' flat, he went to the hospital. He made sure no one saw him entering by waiting, hidden, outside one of the fire doors that were regularly propped open by staff sneaking out for an illicit cigarette. Finally, as he'd hoped, Johnny came out, fumbling in his pocket for his cigarettes. Strain waited until he turned his back to him to light his cigarette and slid inside.

Making sure the porters' office was empty, he checked the CCTV screens until he found the one he wanted. There she was. As he'd anticipated, Dr Kirsty Burns was making her way up to Nick's office. Nick had done as he asked. He'd turned out to be easier to manipulate than he'd hoped. His reputation meant everything. When Strain had threatened to go to the newspapers if Nick didn't pay him off, he'd done so with barely a murmur. He hadn't realised he was buying time, not his life.

Once he reached the basement, he called Nick. 'I need to see you,' he said. 'Could you meet me in theatre 11 in fifteen minutes?'

Theatre 11 was never used but kept equipped in case of a major incident when extra theatres might be needed.

'What, today?' Nick said. 'Can't it wait?'

'No, it bloody well can't,' Strain said. He softened his tone. 'I have something important to tell you. After this I'm going away and you'll never have to see me again.'

After Nick reluctantly agreed to meet him, Strain composed the message and attached the video he had taken. He had to send it at precisely the right time.

He breathed deeply, forcing himself to relax. He had reached the end game. The torment would soon be over.

FIFTY-TWO

Dr Kirsty Burns let herself into her boss's office. Nick had emailed her earlier with the details of the paper on perinatal deaths he wanted her to work on. He was due to submit it in a few days so had suggested she use the computer in his office while he was seeing patients. He'd also suggested she present the data at the upcoming conference. She was grateful for the gesture. It would be a step towards salvaging her career in obstetrics and gynaecology, and God knew she needed all the help she could get. Thankfully, it was her mother's day to come to Inverness and collect Beth from the nursery. Now that Jamie was in custody, everyone was safe. Even so, it would take time before she absorbed everything that had happened.

Rachel had texted this morning too, asking for an urgent meeting. She'd arranged to meet her in reception in thirty minutes, which gave her enough time to make a start on it.

The computer flickered into life, and Kirsty, with a few strokes of the keyboard, logged in.

Her phone buzzed with a message. On automatic pilot she glanced at it. It was a WhatsApp. From Gillian. But that was impossible. Dead women didn't WhatsApp. She clicked on it.

Maybe it had been lost in the ether. Taking a breath, she opened it.

At first Kirsty wasn't sure what she was seeing except that it was an image from a webcam or phone. The camera was focused on something that looked like a table. Slowly the camera zoomed out until it focused on a packet of Rice Krispies with a half-empty bowl beside it. Bewildered, Kirsty recognised the bowl with its depiction of Disney characters around the rim. It was the one Beth insisted on eating her breakfast from every morning. As the camera continued to zoom out, Kirsty saw the cabinets from her kitchen, the plate with a half-eaten slice of toast on the worktop, and the carton of juice she hadn't had time to put back in the fridge that morning. It was her kitchen, there was no doubt about it. Her kitchen this morning. She felt a jolt of nausea. The camera swept around to the right, focusing on the large picture windows that overlooked the golf course at the back of her flat. Then the camera dipped. Kirsty swallowed a mouthful of vomit. On the sofa, in front of the window, was her mother. She was lying on her side, her ankles and wrists bound together behind her. Her eyes were closed and Kirsty couldn't tell from the picture whether she was unconscious or dead. But where was Beth?

She reached for the phone, her heart in her throat. She had to get help. But as she picked up the receiver, a voice she knew slid into the room. The webcam remained fixed on the still figure of her mother.

'With a bit of luck – the first you've had in a while, you'll have opened this video before my deadline. If you haven't, well – too bad. You'll have missed the opportunity to save the lives of your mother and daughter. If you have opened it then you still have a chance to save them, but only if you do not call the police or anyone else for help. Unless you do exactly what I say, I will kill them both. Come immediately to theatre 11. Do not speak to anyone on the way. I promise I will know if you do. You have four minutes to get to the theatre. Click on reply and we will start the clock.'

Kirsty's stomach clenched. She bent over and vomited into Nick's wastepaper basket, wiped her mouth and started running.

FIFTY-THREE

Kirsty paused outside theatre 11 and listened. She couldn't hear any sound coming from inside. Slowly she pressed the doors with her fingers and slipped in. The theatre was brightly lit and set up as if an operation was about to start, the operating table in the centre, a stainless-steel instrument trolley fully set up with a number of syringes in a row beside it.

At first Kirsty thought the room was empty. A groan from the other side of the room attracted her attention. Propped up against the far wall of the theatre was Nick. His shirt was soaked in blood and he appeared to be barely conscious. Kirsty hurried across to him and, dropping to her knees, felt for a pulse. It flickered beneath her fingertips. Nick's eyes were open, his pupils constricted. But apart from a tiny movement of his eyes, Kirsty realised he was heavily sedated.

His eyes swivelled and stretched. In the tiny movement Kirsty could see fear and regret. 'What have you done with her?' she hissed. 'Where is my child?'

She bent over him, felt a stinging pain in her neck, then it all went dark.

. . .

Slowly Kirsty became aware of the beeping of a cardiac monitor. The beat was steady, describing the pattern of a heart in normal rhythm. Next, she realised that she was lying on something hard, but that she couldn't move. She prised open her eyes. Now she could see and hear, but even the slightest movement was impossible. All she could see was the roof of the theatre. Then into her line of vision stepped a figure she recognised as Billy, the porter who had been with Nick the previous night.

'You're awake are you?' he said softly. He shone a torch in her eyes. 'Pupils reacting, that's good. Now I know you can hear me.' The beats of the monitor increased, mirroring her racing heart. 'And this beauty here will tell me how close to dying you are before I need to pull back. Because believe me, Dr Burns, I want you to know exactly what is happening to you.'

The killer wasn't Jamie. And it wasn't Nick. It was Billy.

His face swam in and out of focus. Although she couldn't move, Kirsty was able to breathe. That was something. She had to hang onto anything, no matter how small. Forcing the panic away, she tried to concentrate. He must have Beth, and unless she survived, her daughter might die. The pitch of the monitor rose and she pushed the thought away. She'd no chance of saving her child if she panicked.

'You didn't even take the time to come and see me. If you had... if you'd said sorry, it might have helped,' Billy said.

Bewildered, Kirsty frantically tried to think what he was talking about. She hardly knew this man. She'd seen him in theatre, in A&E, and once or twice about the hospital. Why was he doing this to her?

He lowered his face until it was inches above hers. She could smell garlic on his breath. 'Fiona Mitchell. My fiancée?' he said. 'Did she mean so little to you?'

Finally the truth slammed into her. Billy the porter was

William Strain, Fiona's partner and the man Rachel had said she wanted to talk about when they met.

It was all beginning to fall into place. The night she had never been able to forget came rushing back. Fiona Mitchell had bled profusely after delivery. Kirsty had called Nick, telling him she needed his help, but he had been slow to respond. She had tried to stop the bleeding, and when she couldn't, had pumped litres of blood into the patient while she waited for Nick to arrive. But still, the bleeding wouldn't stop. Everyone had been looking at her. She remembered the panic – the realisation they were going to lose their patient unless she did something. So she'd performed an emergency hysterectomy, standard procedure in cases like this, knowing that she was condemning her patient to a childless future. But the hysterectomy had been too late. Although it had stopped the bleeding, Fiona had already lost too much blood. She'd been left with a severe brain injury and Kirsty heard she'd been transferred to intensive care before being discharged home to the care of her partner. She didn't remember William Strain, because he hadn't been there.

Fiona's partner had been a pharmacist. She remembered that now. The conference he'd been away on was a pharmaceutical. Normally she would have gone to speak to him, but seeing how distraught she'd been, Nick had told her that he would speak to the family. He had made her go home. It was better, Nick had said, that a consultant explained everything to them. But what had Nick told the family? That it was her fault?

It would have been the truth. She'd been the responsible doctor, had let things get out of hand, waited too long before she'd acted. She'd caught the sly disapproving glances of the theatre staff, known they'd blamed her too.

She'd felt so bad about what had happened she'd given up her training post and encouraged Tembo to take the post in Africa. It was Tembo who eventually convinced her she'd only been partly responsible, that Nick had been slow to respond when she'd asked for help. Was that why he'd brought Nick here too?

'All these women,' Strain continued. 'All these women having children they don't want or deserve. When all my Fiona wanted was what you have. A normal, healthy baby. Now she has nothing. Knows nothing. Feels nothing – except pain. She can't even feed herself and needs someone to clean her when she messes the bed. Because of you.'

Kirsty tried to shake her head, but her body wouldn't obey her commands. But was that the slightest feeling beginning to return to her fingers? Using every piece of willpower she could summon, she concentrated on trying to move her little finger. It twitched. Whatever he had injected into her system – some sort of paralysing agent – was beginning to wear off. Perhaps he'd underestimated the dose. She was taller than average and although she was lean, she was strong. If he'd keep talking long enough for the drug to wear off, she might have a chance.

He leaned over and she could hear the sound of a switch being flicked. A faint smell of burning trickled into her nostrils.

'I did the first when Fiona was still in hospital. It felt unbelievably good. It was as if all the sadness and anger flowed out of me and into her. I might have stopped there' – he shook his head – 'but then you dared to return here with a child. Got your job back with the hospital – and he' – he jerked his thumb in Nick's direction – 'helped you. Don't believe any of the crap he told you. His wife does not have myeloid leukaemia. Her bruising is caused by a vitamin deficiency associated with alcoholism. She drinks because she's fucking miserable. He cares as much about his wife and child as he cared about mine.'

Strain disappeared from her line of vision.

'I'm not a bad man,' he said from somewhere off to her right. 'I want you to know that. I chose the women I killed carefully, from those you saw in your clinic. I was unsure about Sister Robertson at first, but she was your best friend – someone you loved. I started to follow her. I wanted to make sure she deserved to die. I watched her go into nightclubs and pubs and come out with random men. I saw everything the slut did. Then I discovered from her medical records she was pregnant, For Christ's sake, she didn't care who fathered her child. I knew then I had made the right decision. It was perfect you were the one to find her.'

'I could have killed you straight away, I had plenty of opportunity, but that would have been too easy. In case you're wondering, it was me who switched the names on the blood samples. Sister Matthews gave them to me to take down to the labs. It was an opportunity too good to miss. I wasn't sure what would happen, but I knew whatever the outcome, you'd be blamed. I hoped they'd fire you then.'

Kirsty concentrated on her fingers, careful lest William read anything in her face. This time she could move all the fingers of both hands. What about Nick? It was clear he had also been drugged. He was still alive – or had been earlier – although Kirsty had no way of knowing whether this was still the case. She shouldn't count on help coming from that direction. She was on her own.

'Then there was that prostitute, Ashley Carmichael. What made her think she was fit to be a mother? She should have done the right thing and terminated the pregnancy. Oh yes,' he said conversationally. 'It was all in the hospital records. Their medical history as well as addresses, next of kin – that's how I knew Gillian lived on her own. And of course the notes you added to their records after you saw them. I wouldn't want you to think there was anything random in the way I selected them. The prostitute was easy. She told you she'd stopped taking drugs, and maybe if she hadn't accepted them when I offered her, I would have let her live. But then again, probably not. Once a user, always a user. All our yesterdays have lighted fools.'

He turned away from her again and she could hear him fiddling with something. It sounded like a sterile pack being opened. When his face came back into view, he had covered his mouth with a mask and his hair with a theatre cap. 'Mustn't let you get an infection,' he said almost cheerfully. 'I've watched you guys often enough to know the score.'

Kirsty felt a small frisson of hope. Did that mean he wasn't planning to kill her?

He seemed to read her mind. 'I don't want you dead, Dr Burns – or at least not straight away, that would be too easy. No, I've got something else in mind which I think you'll find much more unpleasant. Believe you me, by the time I'm finished, you are going to wish for death. But as I don't expect to be around much longer, let me finish telling you what I did. Now where was I? Oh yes. The one that got away. Annie Colston was a drunk, according to her medical record. Her husband left her because of it. Left their two children with an unstable mother. And if that wasn't bad enough, she socialised with prostitutes. What sort of mother does that? You could say I was putting her out of her misery. But she outsmarted me. It was a delicious irony that the first one I killed was her sister.'

William Strain was crazy, Kirsty realised.

'The other one, what was her name? Julie? No, Jody, that was it. She wasn't in the plan. I had no beef with her, but I slipped up when I let her see me. I knew eventually she'd point me out and I couldn't let that happen. Not until I had finished what I needed to do.'

He held up a syringe and a vial of clear liquid. He pulled back on the plunger until the syringe was full. Then he placed the syringe somewhere out of Kirsty's sight.

Where was Beth? Had he killed her? Kirsty felt a primal surge of anger overriding her fear. If the bastard had so much as touched a hair on her daughter's head, she would see him burn in hell.

He leaned over her until his pale eyes were a couple of centimetres above hers. 'You want to know about your wee girl. I can see it in your eyes. Is she dead? Or tied up somewhere, screaming for her mummy? And Mummy isn't coming. Is she hidden somewhere, waiting for you to come and get her and wondering why Mummy hasn't come? Today or tomorrow, tomorrow, and tomorrow. How does that feel, Dr Burns? To know that there is nothing you can do to help the person you love the most? How does it feel to have all that power stripped away?'

Kirsty wriggled her toes. There was definitely movement coming back. What had he given her? A muscle relaxant. Propofol? That's what he'd given the others. What was the half-life? How quickly did it wear off? Was the syringe he'd held up a moment ago filled with more of the same? If so, she didn't have much time left.

He turned away from her and picked up a scalpel.

'When I take out your uterus, the way you took out my Fiona's, I want you to feel everything. But I don't want the shock to kill you, so I'm going to give you a local anaesthetic. It won't take all the pain away, but it'll help. And I don't want you to bleed out, so I have the diathermy machine ready.'

So that was the faint burning smell. He was preparing the machine they used to cauterise blood vessels to stop them bleeding. *Please God, no.* He was going to operate on her when she was awake.

'I can't promise I'll be able to keep you alive – I'm not a surgeon, after all. But that's a risk you'll have to take. Put it this way, you have no option.'

Kirsty felt a movement behind her shoulders.

'I'm going to raise you slightly so you can see what I'm doing. You won't be able to tell me what I'm doing wrong, unfortunately, but that's a gamble we'll have to take.'

As the back of the operating trolley was lifted, more of the

theatre came into view. Careful not to make the slightest movement to alert Strain, Kirsty concentrated on keeping her
muscles still. She had to do something before he started cutting
into her, and she'd only have one shot.

'First, before we start your hysterectomy, I have something
to do.'

He picked up her right hand and traced the tendons on the
front of her wrist.

'I'm going to make a tiny incision right here. It's so small we
won't need a local, so I'm afraid you're going to feel it.' He
swabbed the skin. 'You may remember from your anatomy
lessons that there is a nerve that runs under the skin where I'm
going to make the cut. It will be a practice run for both of us.
Me practising my technique, you practising taking the pain.'

It took everything Kirsty had not to show the slightest
movement.

Images of basic anatomy flashed into her head. Exactly
where he was going to cut, underneath the skin, was the median
nerve. Once that was severed, it would never heal. She would
never be able to hold a scalpel, never be able to operate. But the
loss of the use of her hand was the least of her worries
right now.

FIFTY-FOUR

Selena was in the back seat of the police car, DS Audrey Liversage in the front passenger seat, with Du Toit driving. Selena braced her feet against the back of his seat as the car careened around a corner before skidding to a halt in front of a run-down block of flats. Rachel had insisted that they track down William Strain, laying out exactly why she thought he might be the killer and not De Banzie. They'd found his name on their list of male staff at the hospital. Ironically he'd been due to be interviewed there today but had called in sick. It had been enough for Du Toit to decide to visit him at home.

Strain lived in the north of Inverness, close to the harbour area. Most of the windows in the block were boarded with aluminium. Selena knew it was to keep the drug addicts out. But there were several windows that remained intact. Not everyone had left.

'Stay by the car,' Du Toit ordered her. 'In case Strain appears. If he does, do not approach him, but call us.'

He and Audrey climbed out of the car and Selena watched as they hurried inside the tenement. Heavy clouds scudded across the sky. Selena distracted herself by watching as a mother pushed a stroller along the pavement. She was loaded with plastic bags of shopping from the cut-price grocery store they passed on the way. A couple of children cycled past on new bikes. Cars rushed by, towards the more salubrious parts of Inverness.

Eventually, just as it began to rain in earnest, Kirk and Audrey emerged from the flats. Alone. Audrey was talking into her police radio while Kirk issued instructions on his in a low voice. From the expressions on their faces, she knew whatever they had found inside the flat had not been good.

'We found Fiona, his partner,' Du Toit said heavily. 'She's dead. We won't know if he killed her, or whether she died from natural causes, until the pathologist gets here. But it looks like Rachel was right and Strain is our man.'

'And Strain?'

'There's no sign of him. I've called for backup and scenes-of-crime officers. They might be able to find something that will tell us where he is.' Kirk looked towards the sound of approaching sirens. 'In the meantime, we need to warn Kirsty Burns. She's not answering her mobile. No one has seen her at the hospital. Given she's been suspended, I'm going to gamble on finding her at home.'

'Unless Strain has got to her already?' Audrey said.

'Let's hope not. That's why we have no time to waste in finding them.'

Two police cars screeched to a halt and four uniformed policemen hurried towards them. Du Toit ordered them to secure the scene.

'Let's get going,' Du Toit said.

Audrey switched on the blues and twos.

'I'll keep trying to get Dr Burns on the phone,' Selena said as they pulled away, tyres spinning.

FIFTY-FIVE

Rachel kicked her heels for fifteen minutes in the foyer of the obstetrics and gynaecology department but, despite calling Kirsty on her mobile several times, the doctor hadn't picked up. Nor answered when switchboard had paged her. Rachel's gut was screaming something was wrong.

What if her suspicions were right and Kirsty had been the target all along? What if Strain had her in his sights. Worse, had already got to her?

Making up her mind, she hurried along the corridor to the porters' office. Johnny was pretty much in the same position as he'd been when she'd last seen him.

'Have you seen Dr Burns?' she asked. 'I was supposed to meet her in reception fifteen minutes ago but she's not answering her page.'

'Maybe she's busy,' Johnny replied.

'Could you check to see if she came into the hospital?' she asked.

'If you insist,' Johnny said. 'Do you know what car she drives? I can check the car parks.' Rachel shook her head in frustration. 'Didn't you say there's a camera covering the entrance to the obstetric department?'

'I did.'

Rachel didn't know when Beth's nursery opened its doors but didn't imagine it would be much before seven thirty, so she asked Johnny to run the CCTV from then.

At five to twelve, half an hour before she was supposed to meet Rachel, Kirsty entered the building.

'That's strange,' Johnny said. He was looking at one of the other screens. 'What's Billy doing here when he called in sick?'

Rachel peered at the camera. The camera caught the porter who had been with Nick last night, looking over his shoulder before pushing open double doors.

'And what is he doing down there?' Johnny continued.

It took a moment for it to register. The porter's name was Billy.

Billy was short for William.

'What's Billy's surname?'

'Strain. Why?'

'How long has Billy worked here?' she asked.

'I dunno. Not that long. He had to give up his business when his partner took ill. Apparently she was in hospital for near enough six months and he hardly left her side. Said he took the porter's job so he could earn some money and be near her at the same time.'

'What business was that?'

'He owned a pharmacy, I believe. It went under when he was never there. Couldn't afford to keep paying locums.'

The last piece clicked into place. She'd been right.

Billy the porter was William Strain.

'And what's Dr Burns doing down in the basement too?' Johnny murmured.

They both leaned into the screen.

Fuckity fuck. It was Kirsty, running full pelt down a corridor.

'Can you tell where in the hospital she is?' Rachel asked Johnny.

'It's the underground passage that leads to a disused theatre suite. Theatre 11,' the porter said. 'It's used for storage mainly, but it could be made operational pretty quickly if ever there was a major alert. Most hospitals have one.'

'How do I get to it?'

'Take the stairs on the left where you came in. Turn right at the bottom and follow the corridor to the end. But wait a minute. I can't let you go down there.'

'Johnny, I need you to phone the police, right now. Ask them to get an urgent message to Detective Inspector Du Toit or one of his team. Tell him that he needs to come to theatre 11. That Strain is there and so is Dr Burns. Tell him that I think he means to hurt her. Wait for them at the entrance and bring them straight to the theatre.'

Johnny was looking at her in disbelief. 'Do it,' Rachel ground out. She spun on her heel and began racing towards the stairs. Strain was the killer, Kirsty his ultimate target.

She skidded around a corner, the soles of her shoes slipping on the worn hospital linoleum. Strain's guilt was clear now, as was his motive. He blamed Kirsty for the death of his child, the brain injury to his wife.

She hadn't put it all together yet – except that it was all about Kirsty and all about babies. And that Kirsty was his final target. She raced through patients and staff, flattening herself against the wall to allow a trolley to pass, before taking the stairs to the basement two at a time.

He'd selected his victims through their records, choosing them because they were patients of Kirsty's. Probably trying to discredit Kirsty and ruin her career. But why go so far as to kill them?

The underground corridor was eerily deserted, the fluorescent strip light muted.

She slid to a halt outside theatre 11, took a moment to get her breathing under control and reached for the door.

FIFTY-SIX

Selena ran after Du Toit and Audrey up the three flights of stairs to Kirsty's flat. They'd rung Kirsty's phone continuously since they'd found Strain's partner, a tray of empty syringes beside her, but there had been no reply.

Rachel had been correct when she'd begged them not to stop looking for the murderer – to go after Strain.

Du Toit was a lot fitter than Selena and Audrey, and by the time they huffed their way to the third floor, the DI was banging on the door. Getting no response, he put his shoulder to the door, but it resisted his weight. 'Get a key from the supervisor,' he instructed Audrey, who turned on her heel and sped back down the stairs.

Kirk lifted the letterbox. 'Police! Is anyone in?' he called through the door.

'Let me,' Selena suggested. 'I've met Beth. Kirsty, Beth, Mrs Burns! Can you hear me?'

Despite their continued knocking and shouting, there was no reply. Du Toit's phone rang as Audrey emerged at the top of the stairs brandishing a key. Kirk listened while Audrey fitted the key in the lock.

'Apparently Strain is at the hospital. As are Dr Burns and Rachel. Rachel told the porter to call us and tell us to get our arses over there. Not sure if that was her words or his,' Kirk said as the door opened.

Audrey ran into the sitting room while Selena and Du Toit searched the rest of the small flat, finding each room empty.

'Gran's OK,' Audrey yelled from the sitting room. 'But I'll call the paramedics to look her over.'

Kirsty's mother was lying on the sofa, her hands and feet tied with duct tape, her mouth gagged with the same.

'What about Beth?' Selena asked.

'I don't know. Maybe she's with her mother at the hospital?' Audrey suggested, gently moving the duct tape from Kirsty's mother's mouth.

'No,' the older woman mumbled. 'He took her. Gave her something to knock her out – put her in a holdall. Please, for God's sake, you have to find her!'

'Audrey, you stay here until the ambulance and help arrives. Make sure the scene is cordoned off. As soon as you've done that, come to the hospital. In fact, radio for backup and ask them to meet me there.'

'Yes, sir.'

'Come on, Selena. Let's go.'

FIFTY-SEVEN

As Strain turned away from her, Kirsty saw that Nick had raised his head. The propofol, or whatever Strain had used, must have worn off. For a second Kirsty's eyes locked with her boss. Then Strain was bending over her again holding a scalpel. He pressed the blade against her skin.

When he sliced into her, the pain was excruciating and Kirsty had to clench her jaw to stop herself screaming from the awfulness of it. William was concentrating hard, his attention focused on what he was doing. Using the sickening pain as an antidote to the heaviness of her limbs, she inched her left hand along the table until she found the diathermy machine. She might have only this one chance. Her daughter's life depended on it. Thinking of Beth gave her the strength she needed. Her fingers latched onto the grip and she swung the metal rod, and using every ounce of strength she could muster thrust the heated implement towards his eye. But, before she could connect, her sudden movement alerted him and he jumped back, the diathermy catching him under his eye socket. Despairing, Kirsty knew it wasn't enough, but this moment was all she had. Fighting against the paralysis, she rolled off the table and onto the floor. She hit her head and felt a sickening crunch as her wounded hand folded underneath her.

Strain crouched down beside her and shook his head. 'Good try, Dr Burns,' he said. 'But not good enough. I see I'll have to give you some more propofol. We don't want you trying that again.'

As he bent to pick up the syringe, the theatre door flew open and, to Kirsty's astonishment, Rachel burst through. She launched herself on top of Strain. It wasn't enough to knock him to the ground, but the impact spun the syringe out of Strain's hand and it skittered across the floor, coming to rest close to Kirsty. Strain stood and, with Rachel clinging to his back like a limpet, tried to knock her off by repeatedly bashing her against the wall. Kirsty knew it was her only chance. Forcing herself to her feet, she grabbed the antiseptic from the trolley and threw it into Strain's face.

Strain screeched with pain, spinning around and clutching at his eyes. As he stumbled across the room, Rachel was flung to the floor, where she lay unmoving.

Kirsty scooped up the syringe from where it had fallen and plunged it into William's neck. He stared at her for one never-ending moment before sinking to the floor.

Breathing hard, Kirsty tried to ignore the pain in her hand and the pounding of her heart against her ribs. She bent over Rachel to feel for a pulse and found it beating strongly and steadily. The fall had knocked her out but she should come around soon. Leaving her where she was, she knelt beside Nick, frantically looking for something to stem the blood pumping from the hole in his neck. It was no use. The wound was too severe. Nick would bleed out in a couple of minutes and there was bugger all she could do about it.

Nick looked at her through hazy eyes.

'Help me,' he said. His lips turned white as his blood pooled on the floor.

Kirsty pulled her T-shirt off over her head and, folding it, pressed hard on the wound on his neck. Within seconds, the cloth had become saturated with blood. She felt the tears rolling down her cheeks, dribbling into her mouth.

If she released the pressure on the wound to call for help, Nick would exsanguinate within seconds. If she didn't – he was going to die anyway.

Kirsty looked around frantically. On the trolley that William had laid out was a line with a bag of saline attached. If Nick was to stand any chance at all, she needed to replace the blood he had lost. If she could insert the line into his vein, the saline might keep Nick alive long enough for her to get help. It was almost certainly hopeless, but she had to try. Still pressing down on Nick's neck, she stretched her legs out as far as she could reach, just managing to touch the leg of the trolley with her foot. Concentrating, she squeezed another inch from her elongated body. The extra length was enough for her to be able to hook her toes under the leg and pull the trolley towards her inch by painful inch.

Finally it was beside her. She had to stop compressing the gaping hole in Nick's neck to reach for the bag of fluid, get a line into a vein, and then squeeze as much into him as possible. The saline might buy her enough time to call for help. It would be difficult enough if she could use both her hands, but her right hand was almost useless. There was nothing else for it. She released her hold on Nick's neck and struggled to her feet. As she stood, the room cartwheeled around her. A wave of nausea rolled through her and she swallowed a mouthful of vomit.

Don't pass out, she told herself, gritting her teeth. *Hang on a little longer.*

She reached for a cannula and held it in her shaking left hand. Strain had partly opened the sterile wrapping, so it was ready for use and she managed to fumble the needle out of its package. Dropping to her knees, she located a vein in Nick's hand. He had lost so much blood that his blood vessels were beginning to collapse. Kirsty knew that she'd have one shot to get the needle in. Taking a breath, she pressed down above the vein with her shattered hand, the pain almost causing her to pass out. The pressure was enough to raise the vein slightly and Kirsty slipped the needle in as accurately as she could with her left hand. A flashback of blood told her she had made it. Now she needed to attach the tube of the bag of saline to the cannula. But she had left the bag of saline on the trolley. Kirsty wanted to cry. To get to her feet again needed more than she had left to give. But she forced herself up once more. The room spun as she got to her feet and she grasped at the trolley almost pulling it down on top of her, barely managing to maintain her balance.

She dropped back down on her knees. Out of the corner of her eye she could see that Strain's eyes were fluttering and he was mumbling something she couldn't make out. She was terrified he would come around fully before she'd finished with Nick. But she had no choice. And Beth? Was her daughter even alive? Or was she tied up somewhere crying for a mother who wasn't coming? She pushed the thoughts from her mind. If she worried about Beth now, panic would paralyse her and she wouldn't be able to do what she had to.

Attaching the two tubes together was the hardest part and she was sobbing with frustration when at last she succeeded. She squeezed the bag with her good hand, forcing the fluid into Nick as quickly as she could. It wasn't enough. He needed at least five times the amount. What she had given him would buy him only a few more minutes at the most. She needed to get help.

Struggling to her feet once again, she staggered over to the phone on the wall, praying it hadn't been disconnected. She used her blood-soaked left hand to punch in 2222, the number all hospitals used for medical emergencies. Thankfully the operator answered immediately.

'Arrest team, theatre 11,' Kirsty gasped, as a hand grabbed her ankle. She fell to the ground as Strain pulled her down, the phone falling from her grip and onto the floor. Kirsty had no idea whether anyone would respond to her call. She hadn't identified herself, and switchboard must know that theatre 11 wasn't in use. She gave a howl of frustration.

As Strain rolled on top of her, Kirsty knew it was out of her hands. To her left, Rachel was still unconscious, but next to her Kirsty saw the glint of the scalpel he had dropped earlier. Although he was using the weight of his body to keep her pinned down, he was still weak from the drug she had given him and Kirsty managed to shift her body far enough to reach the scalpel. Clenching it in her fist, she rolled away from him and, pushing him down, sat on his chest. She pressed the scalpel against Strain's carotid artery.

'Tell me where my daughter is,' she hissed. 'Or so help me God, I will take your balls off.' Staggered by the rage she felt, but knowing she had to use it, Kirsty flicked the scalpel away from his neck and cut into his top lip. It wouldn't be fatal, she needed him alive, but it would hurt like buggery. 'Where is she, you bastard – you worthless mound of shit?' she shouted and cut again.

Strain smiled up at her, blood streaming from his mouth, his teeth washed with crimson.

'Go on, bitch. If you have it in you. Do you think I'm scared of dying? The only reason I've stayed alive is to see you pay. You'd be doing me a favour.'

Kirsty believed him. It was hopeless. If she killed him, she would have no chance of finding out what he had done with Beth and her mother. She couldn't waste any more time. She had to find her daughter.

'Why?' she asked Strain. 'Why my daughter? She's an innocent child.' She held out her hand. 'I won't be able to operate again, you've seen to that. You've killed my friend because of me and I'm going to have to live with that for the rest of my life. Nick's dying. You've had your revenge. Please let my daughter go. At least tell me you haven't hurt her.'

'She's alive,' Strain whispered. 'For the time being. But time and tide waits for no man. So, tell me, Dr Burns, are you prepared to give your life for hers? Because if you are, you still have a chance to save your daughter. If you really want to save her, I'll trade her life for yours.'

'How can I trust you?' Kirsty asked. 'If I do what you ask, how do I know you won't let Beth die anyway?'

'You can't be sure. It's a chance you'll have to take. Her fate is in the lap of the gods now – unless you can work out where she is.'

'What do you mean? Tell me!'

'For God's sake,' Strain said tiredly, as if he'd lost interest. 'I've given you enough hints. You can still save her if you put your mind to it.'

She hadn't a clue what he was talking about. *What hints? Think!* she told herself But her brain felt like porridge.

'What about Fiona?' she asked. 'If you're not there to help her, what will happen to her?'

'Don't you think I know that?' Strain said. 'Fiona won't be needing anyone anymore. I did what I had to.'

'She's dead, isn't she?' Kirsty said flatly. 'You killed her.'

'I loved her. I couldn't leave her. Without me, they'd put her in a home. I've seen those places. There's no way I could do that to her.'

'If you loved her, then you must have some feelings. You can't think that killing me will solve anything.'

'It will make me feel better,' he said with a smirk. 'Fair is foul and foul is fair: Hover through the filthy air. You'll know what it was like for me to lose everything. Before you, I had it all. A woman who was pregnant with my child, who was going to marry me. I had a successful business, my own pharmacy. Life couldn't have got much better.'

'I'm sorry about what happened to Fiona,' Kirsty said. 'If there had been any other way...'

She glanced across at Nick. He was unconscious. From the corner of her eye, she saw Rachel move slightly.

'Her brain was stuffed. I had to give up everything to look after her. The pharmacy. My life. Then the money started to run out. I pinned my hopes on a big settlement from the hospital. They offered me an out of court settlement of fifty thousand! Christ,' he spat. 'Barely enough to pay her care for six months.'

Rachel had opened her eyes and was watching them.

'Enough of this,' Strain said. 'What's done is done. Time's running out.' If Kirsty didn't know better, she'd think she saw pity in his eyes. 'You have to decide. Take the drug and save your daughter's life. Or don't take it, and she dies. Double, double toil and trouble. Which is it to be?'

Kirsty picked up the syringe from the trolley. It had been neatly labelled suxamethonium. It was an anaesthetic agent. In many ways she admired how organised Strain had been, but this time he had made a fatal error.

She crossed over to him and held the syringe under his nose.

'You think you know me,' she hissed. 'Well you don't. I don't know as much about drugs as you, but I do know that if I inject you with this it will paralyse you. You won't be able to move a muscle. You won't even be able to breathe. It will feel as if you are going to suffocate to death and maybe you will. It all depends whether I get the dosage correct. Whatever, you'll have enough time to realise that I can, and will, kill you if I have to. Now, will you tell me what you've done with my daughter?'

Strain smiled up at her through swollen, red-veined eyes. 'You wouldn't dare,' he said. 'You don't have it in you.'

Kirsty plunged the syringe into his thigh and squeezed a

few mils out of the syringe. 'I think you'll find I do. You asked me if I would trade my life for my daughter's? I would. But I'd far rather trade yours.'

She watched the panic in his eyes as the anaesthetic agent began to take hold.

'I'm going to give you the whole dose. Time things carefully. I'll wait two and half minutes. Then if you're not able to breathe on your own, I'll bag you until you can. Then, once the paralysis wears off, you can decide whether you want to tell me where my daughter is. If you don't, we'll do it all over again. And maybe I won't be able to keep bringing you round.'

'You're fucked, whatever,' Strain said, his words slurring. 'Your career is over, especially when people learn you were responsible for my death. No one will want a killer for a doctor, whatever the provocation might have been.'

'Kirsty, no. You have to stop,' Rachel called out from across the room. She looked dazed. She tried to stand but only managed to get to her hands and knees.

Kirsty became aware Rachel was crouching beside her. The lawyer placed a restraining hand on her arm. 'You have to stop. You're going to kill him. You will go to jail. Probably for a long time. Is that what you want for Beth?'

Kirsty paid no attention, her focus on Strain. 'You know exactly how this will go. Once I inject you, you'll stop breathing, but you'll remain conscious. It will feel as if you are drowning.' She should be appalled at what she was doing, but she wasn't. She would do whatever it took, even the death of this poor, damaged, deranged man to save her daughter.

'That's what you did to Gillian. And to Ashley and Jody. None of them were responsible for what happened to Fiona, but you killed them anyway. You think I have any sympathy for you? I don't. I couldn't care less whether you live or die. All I care about is my daughter. Where is she, you bastard?'

But Kirsty's brain was working too slowly. Strain reached

up, and before she could react, he placed his hand over hers and squeezed the rest of the contents of the syringe into his thigh.

She watched as he slid into unconsciousness.

'Oh no, you don't,' she screamed at him, throwing the empty syringe aside. He wasn't going to do this to her. He had to live. Had to tell her what he'd done with Beth. Where the hell was the resus team? It was at least five minutes since she had called them.

FIFTY-EIGHT

Rachel could scarcely believe what was seeing. Nick and Kirsty were splattered in blood, the theatre looked as if it had been hit by a mini typhoon. And if she didn't do something, William Strain was going to die, and Kirsty would be blamed.

She shook the last of the fog from her head.

'Kirsty, listen to me. We can't let him die.' Kirsty looked as if she wasn't really present. Her eyes were glazed. Rachel remembered what she'd learned about ketamine. If Strain had given some to Kirsty she'd be disassociating.

Rachel placed her hands on either side of Kirsty's face and turned it so the doctor was forced to look at her. 'The police are on their way. They were going to check on you at your flat first. They will find Beth. You cannot kill Strain. Not if you want your child to grow up with a mother in prison.'

She held Kirsty's gaze until her eyes lost their glazed look. Thank God it seemed she'd returned from whatever dark place she'd been.

'I can't use my hands properly,' Kirsty said calmly. 'You'll have to help me get oxygen into him until the drug wears off and he can breathe for himself. Switch on that oxygen dial on the machine, the one that says O, then get that trolley over.'

When Rachel did what Kirsty asked, Kirsty attached the oxygen tubing to the ventilation bag with Rachel's help. She held it over his face with his chin lifted.

'Can you squeeze the bag for me, Rachel, while I try to hold the mask on.'

Rachel gave the bag a couple of big squeezes but even she could tell that gas was coming straight out of the side of the mask.

'It's no good,' Kirsty said in despair. 'I can't get enough in.'

'Surely there something else we can do,' Rachel urged, more for Kirsty's sake than Strain's. His lips were turning bluer by the second.

'There's one thing. See the second drawer in the trolley with a B on it. That's for breathing. There should be a laryngeal mask in there. It's a fat tube with a cuff on one end.'

Rachel rummaged in the drawer. 'This?' she asked holding up a piece of bendy plastic.

'That's it. But you'll need to stick it down his throat – I simply can't manage – the end with the cuff first.'

'OK, tell me what to do.'

Kirsty took off the ill-fitting mask and supported Strain's chin while Rachel slid the tube down his throat.

'Now twist it around 180,' Kirsty ordered as Rachel felt the tube hit the back of Strain's throat. 'And give it an extra shove.'

Rachel nodded to Kirsty when she was done.

'Brilliant. Now swap the tubing over from the bag attached to the side of the mask you gave me, to your airway. I'll fill the cuff with the air from his syringe and let's hope we can keep him going.'

Rachel started squeezing the bag again regularly and gradually the blue tinge disappeared from Strain's lips. He was still alive. She looked at Kirsty. She didn't look so good.

The doors crashed open. Du Toit stood in the doorway taking in the scene. 'Godverdomme,' he said as police officers rushed in from behind him. 'What the hell is going on here? Are you both OK?'

'Did you find Beth?' Kirsty shouted as the officers rushed to the injured men's side, the crash team following closely behind. They started working on Nick.

'We found your mother, but not Beth,' Du Toit said gently. 'He sedated her and took her away in a holdall, according to your mother.'

'We have to find her! He said time was running out. That must mean she's still alive!'

'He didn't say anything else?'

A nurse knelt by Kirsty's side and tried to examine her hand. Kirsty shoved her away. 'Not now,' she snapped. 'He said I should be able to work it out. Kept spouting lines of poetry or proverbs. Like Time and Tide waits for no man.'

The radio on Du Toit's chest came alive. Rachel recognised Selena's disembodied voice. The hope in Kirsty's eyes was hard to see, but worse was the despair when du Toit shook his head.

'Double, double toil and trouble,' Rachel murmured, remembering. It had been a strange thing to say. 'Can you remember what else?'

'Oh I don't know. What does it matter? We have to find Beth.'

'Indulge me for a minute,' Rachel said.

'Something about tomorrow, tomorrow, tomorrow. And what else? "Fair is foul and foul is fair; Hover through the fog and filthy air."'

'Did you do *Macbeth* at school?' Rachel asked.

'Yeah. Why?' Kirsty said.

'Those lines are from the witches scene, aren't they?'

Kirsty looked at Rachel in furious disbelief. 'What? You seriously want to talk plays now?'

Time and tide, witches. Maybe Rachel was crazy but it had to be worth a punt. The Witches Coffin Pool next to the canal end of the path was tidal. When the tide was in, it was flooded, when it went out, it became sand again. She thought back to that morning. When she'd looked out of her window at 7, the tide had been fully out, which meant it was currently on its way back in. It was a long shot but surely, in the absence of a better idea, worth a try.

'Have you got cars out looking for Beth?'

'Four of them. I've ordered a heat-seeking helicopter too. It's already airborne,'

'Tell it to fly over the Witches Coffin Pool in Merkinch Nature Reserve and send one of the cars there,' Rachel said, sending a silent prayer upwards.

Thankfully, Du Toit wasted no time arguing. He spoke into his radio and instructed his officers and the pilot of the heli- copter to search the park, paying particular attention to the pond. He instructed another car to pick him up at the hospital entrance.

Rachel checked the time on her phone. If she was correct, the pond would soon be flooded again.

As the trollies bearing Nick and Strain were wheeled away, Kirsty grabbed Rachel's arm. 'You really think she might be there?'

'I don't know,' Rachel said honestly. 'But it fits.'

'I need to go there!' Kirsty whirled on Du Toit who was moving towards the door. 'Take me with you!'

Once again, Du Toit didn't hesitate. 'Come on then. You too Rachel.' A smile crossed his face. 'I know you'll never agree to being left behind.'

. . .

Their patrol car had barely come to a halt in the street closest to the Witches Coffin Pool, when Rachel and Kirsty spilled out and started running. There were already three other patrol cars there.

Rachel's heart was in her throat as she sprinted towards the pond, Kirsty at her heels. Was Beth there? Was she alive? Was she conscious? If so, how terrified the little girl would be to feel the water lapping around her, getting higher and higher. Judging by the wild look in Kirsty's eyes in the five minutes it had taken the patrol car, blue lights flashing, siren blaring, to travel the 7k, the same thoughts had passed through her head.

The beat of helicopter blades came from above as it circled and as she approached the park she became aware a number of police officers, Audrey amongst them, were lining the part of the path that overlooked the pond. Their silence chilled her soul. Judging by the anguished cry from behind her, it seemed Kirsty had come to the same conclusion.

Rachel ran towards Audrey 'Have they found Beth?' she asked.

Audrey pointed to the flat stone in the centre of the pond, on top of which, surrounded by rising water was a red holdall.

Kirsty and Du Toit came to a panting stop beside her.

'Oh Jesus,' Kirsty cried. 'That's my bag.' She started ran down the slope to the water's edge followed by Rachel and Du Toit. As she was about to plunge into the water, Du Toit stopped her. He pointed to a uniformed police officer accompanied by a smaller figure, Rachel immediately recognised, wading towards the bag.

The 'copter picked up heat coming from the bag,' he told Kirsty. 'There's a good chance your daughter, if she's in it, is alive.'

'I need to go to her!' Kirsty shouted, trying to push past Du Toit. 'She'll be so terrified.'

Clearly Du Toit realised that there was no way he was keeping this mother from her child as he stepped aside.

Rachel and Du Toit stood side by side as the police officers approached the bag. 'Selena insisted she go,' Du Toit said. 'She thought it might be less frightening for her to see a familiar face.'

Rachel held her breath as the police officers reached the bag. The sound of Selena's soft, gentle voice came over Du Toit's radio. 'Beth! Can you hear me? Now, mo ghráigh, everything is going to be all right.' She bent over and it looked as if she were unzipping the bag. 'I've come to take you back to your Mammy.' Her voice faltered as she pulled the sides of the bag apart. The uniformed police officer next to her reached in and lifted a small, limp body with thick curly hair and handed the child to Selena who cradled her in her arms before turning towards Kirsty. 'Don't worry. Your Mammy is here,' Selena said, 'Come to take you home.'

Rachel held her breath as the little girl stirred and turned her head towards Kirsty.

'Mummy?' the tentative whisper came over the police radio. 'Mummy!' Her voice was louder now. Excited, Beth reached out to Kirsty who was wading towards her as fast as the rising tide would allow, 'Mummy. Where were you? Take me home, Now!'

FIFTY-NINE

Rachel pulled into the car park of Peterhead prison where her father was incarcerated. In the distance the imposing building surrounded by a high fence topped with barbed wire appeared to glow in the late afternoon sunshine. She still wasn't sure why she'd come. It was years since she'd seen him and she wasn't sure how she felt about seeing him now.

What did she owe him after all? On one side, once-a-month fishing trips and the occasional hike up a hill, on the other, an abused, murdered mother. The scales were tipped so far in one direction they were practically vertical. It wasn't as if she had more than a sliver of doubt about his guilt. But there was the crux. She did have doubt, no matter how minuscule, and if she believed everyone deserved justice she owed him this one last hearing. At the very least she needed to ask him what he knew about the trafficking case her mother had been involved with.

It took an hour, preceded by searches, form filling and searches, before she got to sit on the opposite side of a table from her father.

He'd aged badly in the decade since she'd seen him. He'd

lost most of his hair, one of his incisors and there were deep lines creasing his once handsome face. Despite herself, Rachel felt a pang of sympathy for him.

'Rachel,' he said, his voice gruff. 'It's so very good to see you.'

'I'm not going to stay long.'

The smile left her father's face. 'I best make the most of every minute, hadn't I.'

'I want to talk about Mum. Or rather a case involving Mum.'

He waited her to go on.

'It involves a human-trafficking ring.'

Still, he said nothing.

'She was due to be a witness when the lead players stood trial about a week after you...' She faltered to a halt and took a breath. 'Murdered her. What do you know about that?'

Rachel's father was silent for a long time. 'Don't go looking into any of that,' he said eventually. 'It could be dangerous for you.'

'So, you know about it?'

Her father jumped to his feet, his eyes fixed on her face. She wasn't sure what she saw there. Regret, desperation, love?

'I've taken every measure to protect you. Even allowed myself to be sent down for the murder of your mother to protect you. Don't make the last six years of my life mean nothing.'

He looked behind him to the guard standing at the door he'd come through. 'I want to go back to my cell.'

'Hey wait. What are you saying?' Rachel demanded.

Her father looked in her eyes. 'Please, Rachel, promise me. Stop asking your questions. I couldn't bear it if anything happened to you.'

Rachel stood as the guard took him by the arm.

'What do you mean? You have to tell me!' she cried.

'Let sleeping dogs lie, Rachel,' he said as the guard led him away. 'Get on with your life. Be happy. And don't come back to see me.'

EPILOGUE

Clachnaharry Inn was packed to the gills. To Rachel's astonishment a number of its customers had come to her local pub to hang out with her.

Selena was playing darts with Clive and Suruthi. Du Toit and Kirsty, whose hand was still bandaged but healing well, were at a table in the corner chatting easily. Du Toit had a pint in front of him, Kirsty a glass of red. Beth was being babysat by Kirsty's mother who had moved to Inverness to be closer to her daughter and granddaughter. Beth could easily have died. Fortunately though, she was recovering well with no side-effects from the day's events.

Despite Kirsty and the crash team's desperate attempts to save him, Nick had died. Strain, however, had survived and was in prison awaiting trial.

Kirsty had been reinstated and returned to medical duties, despite not being able to operate because of the damaged nerve in her hand. However, she was adamant sensation was returning to her fingers.

Mags, dressed reasonably conservatively in a low-cut top and loose trousers, was next to Annie, who seemed to grow more cheerful every time Rachel saw her. Rachel placed a diet tonic and a pint in front of Annie and Mags respectively. Annie was still off the booze and had vowed to stay dry.

It was strange that working for the dead had brought these people into her life and somehow, along the way, they had become *her* people. Whether she liked it or not.

Rachel was meeting Angus for dinner next week. She was going to ask him to revisit her father's case. And if he couldn't help, she planned to ask Du Toit. She hadn't told anyone yet about the visit to her father in prison, or what he'd said. She wouldn't be surprised if it were more lies. Her father was good at that.

Selena came to stand next to Rachel. 'Did your boss give you a hard time?' she asked.

'Not at all.' To her astonishment, Alastair hadn't said anything about her going way out on a limb. Quite the opposite, in fact. He'd said, 'Good work, McKenzie,' and given her a metaphorical pat on the head. What Mainwaring would have to say when he found out was another matter.

When Douglas was well enough to return, Alastair would be transferring to Homicide. She had no doubt that Alastair had taken full credit for helping to put Inverness's first serial killer behind bars. That was OK by her.

She was tired. It had been a long day and she fancied an early night. She wished everyone a good night, stepped into the darkness and sucked in a lungful of air.

Her skin prickled and she whirled around, expecting to find someone behind her. The street was empty, her imagination in overdrive. She was like a cat on a hot tin roof these days. Maybe a challenging climb would help get rid of the nest of wasps that seemed to have taken up residence behind her ribs? She might even invite Angus.

She crossed the bridge. It was far darker here than on the other side. Her phone pinged. She smiled to herself. Probably

Suruthi or Clive trying to persuade her to continue the evening round at hers.

She looked back towards the pub. Maybe she should go back. Join the celebration?

Then she thought of the thousand sheets of paper that made up the dozens of files that Angus had dropped off.

If there was any truth in what her father had said, that he'd taken the fall for her mother's murder to protect Rachel, she had to know.

If he was innocent, and she had her doubts, every minute he stayed in prison was one less minute he had to enjoy what remained of his life in freedom.

She gave the pub a last regretful look and walked on.

A LETTER FROM THE AUTHOR

Huge thanks for reading *The Highland Dead*. I hope you were hooked on the second book in Rachel's story. If you want to join other readers in hearing all about my new releases and bonus content, you can sign up for my newsletter.

www.stormpublishing.co/morag-pringle

If you enjoyed this book and could spare a few moments to leave a review that would be hugely appreciated. Even a short review can make all the difference in encouraging a reader to discover my books for the first time. Thank you so much.

Some years ago, as a hospital manager, I was responsible for the medical records department; back then, everything about a patient was kept in a paper file that could be transferred anywhere in the hospital at any time. I got to thinking: who had access to these records that included the most intimate details of a person's life? (More people than most of us would like to imagine.) What if someone used that information for their own purpose – to get revenge, perhaps? Or to pick their victims? *The Highland Dead* is the result of this. I hope you enjoy and that – relatively assured that nowadays your medical information is securely stored on a computer – you sleep easy at night.

Thanks again for being part of this amazing journey with me and I hope you'll stay in touch – I have so many more stories and ideas to entertain you with!

ACKNOWLEDGEMENTS

Thanks to everyone who helped me write this book: Fiona for letting me stay in 'Rachel's' house in Clachnaharry, Duncan Maclauchlan for so patiently answering all my questions, Hells Belles for reading chunks and giving feedback and to all the others who so generously allowed me to pick their brains.

A big shout out to the whole team at Storm, in particular the amazing Emily Gowers and the eagle-eyed Anne O'Brien. Couldn't have done it without you all!

Printed in Great Britain
by Amazon